KU-481-333

cecelia
ahern

The Year
I Met You

HarperCollins*Publishers*

HarperCollins*Publishers*
77–85 Fulham Palace Road,
Hammersmith, London W6 8JB

www.harpercollins.co.uk

Published by HarperCollins*Publishers* 2014
1

Copyright © Cecelia Ahern 2014

Cecelia Ahern asserts the moral right to
be identified as the author of this work

A catalogue record for this book
is available from the British Library

ISBN: 978-0-00-750177-9

This novel is entirely a work of fiction.
The names, characters and incidents portrayed in it are
the work of the author's imagination. Any resemblance to
actual persons, living or dead, events or localities is
entirely coincidental.

Typeset in Sabon by Palimpsest Book Production Ltd,
Falkirk, Stirlingshire

Printed and bound in Great Britain by
Clays Ltd, St Ives plc

All rights reserved. No part of this publication may be
reproduced, stored in a retrieval system, or transmitted,
in any form or by any means, electronic, mechanical,
photocopying, recording or otherwise, without the prior
permission of the publishers.

MIX
Paper from
responsible sources
FSC
www.fsc.org   FSC™ C007454

FSC™ is a non-profit international organisation established to promote
the responsible management of the world's forests. Products carrying the
FSC label are independently certified to assure consumers that they come
from forests that are managed to meet the social, economic and
ecological needs of present and future generations,
and other controlled sources.

Find out more about HarperCollins and the environment at
www.harpercollins.co.uk/green

The Year
I Met You

Cecelia Ahern is an international bestseller. She was cata-
pulted into the spotlight with her hit debut novel, *P.S. I
Love You*, which was adapted into a major movie.

Her subsequent novels have captured the hearts of readers
in 46 countries – her themes strike a chord with people in
every continent, with over 15 million copies of her books
sold. As well as writing novels, Cecelia has also created
several TV series including the ABC comedy, *Samantha
Who?*, in the USA. She lives in Dublin with her family.

For exclusive updates on her tours and events, her new books
and projects, follow her on Twitter @Cecelia_Ahern, join
her on Facebook www.facebook.com/CeceliaAhernofficial
and visit her website www.cecelia-ahern.com. She would
love to hear from you.

By the same author

P.S. I Love You
Where Rainbows End
If You Could See Me Now
A Place Called Here
Thanks for the Memories
The Gift
The Book of Tomorrow
The Time of My Life
One Hundred Names
How to Fall in Love

Short stories
Girl in the Mirror

For my friend Lucy Stack.
Just when the caterpillar thought the world was over,
it became a butterfly . . .

Our greatest glory is not in never falling,
but in rising every time we fall.

Confucius

Winter

*The season between autumn and spring,
comprising in the Northern Hemisphere the
coldest months of the year: December, January
and February.*

A period of inactivity or decay.

1

I was five years old when I learned that I was going to die.

It hadn't occurred to me that I would not live for ever; why would it? The topic of my death hadn't been mentioned in passing.

My knowledge of death was not tenuous; goldfish died, I'd learned that first-hand. They died if you didn't feed them, and then they also died if you fed them too much. Dogs died when they ran in front of moving cars, mice died when they were tempted by chocolate HobNobs in the mousetrap in our cloakroom under the stairs, rabbits died when they escaped their hutches and fell prey to evil foxes. Discovering their deaths was not cause for any personal alarm; even as a five-year-old I knew that these were all furry animals who did foolish things, things that I had no intention of doing.

So it was a great disturbance to learn that death would find me too.

According to my source, if I was 'lucky' my death would occur in the very same way as my grandfather's had. Old. Smelling of pipe smoke and farts, with balls of tissue stuck to the stubble over his top lip from blowing his nose. Black lines of dirt beneath the tips of his fingernails from gardening; eyes yellowing at the corners, reminding me of the marble from my uncle's collection that my sister used to suck on and swallow, causing Dad to come running to wrap his arms around her stomach and squeeze till the marble popped back out again. Old. With brown trousers hiked up past his waist, stopping only for his flabby boob-like chest, revealing a soft paunch and balls that had been squished to one side of the seam of his trousers. Old. No, I did not want to die how my granddad had, but dying old, my source revealed, was the best-case scenario.

I learned of my impending death from my older cousin Kevin on the day of my granddad's funeral as we sat on the grass at the end of his long garden with plastic cups of red lemonade in our hands and as far away as possible from our mourning parents, who looked like dung beetles on what was the hottest day of the year. The grass was covered in dandelions and daisies and was much longer than usual, Granddad's illness having prevented him from perfecting the garden in his final weeks. I remember feeling sad for him, defensive, that of all the days to showcase his beautiful back garden to neighbours and friends, it was on a day when it wasn't the perfection he aspired to. He wouldn't have minded not being there – he didn't like to talk much – but he would have at least cared about the grand presentation, and then vanished to listen to the praise somewhere, away from everyone, maybe upstairs with the window open. He would pretend he didn't care, but he would, a contented smile on his face, to go with his grass-stained knees and black fingernails. Someone, an old lady with rosary beads tied tightly around her knuckles, said she felt his presence in the garden, but I didn't. I was sure he wasn't there. He would be so annoyed by the look of the place, he wouldn't be able to bear it.

Grandma would puncture silences with things like, 'His sunflowers are thriving, God rest his soul,' and 'He never got to see the petunias bloom.' To which my smart-arsed cousin Kevin muttered, 'Yeah, his dead body is fertiliser now.'

Everyone sniggered; everyone always laughed at what Kevin said because Kevin was cool, because Kevin was the eldest, five years older than me and at the grand old age of ten said mean and cruel things that none of the rest of us would dare say. Even if we didn't think it was funny we knew to laugh because if we didn't, he would quickly make us the object of his cruelty, which is what he did to me on that day. On that rare occasion, I didn't think it was funny that Granddad's dead body beneath the earth was helping his petunias grow, nor did I think it was cruel. I saw a kind of beauty in it. A lovely fullness and fairness to it. That is *exactly* what my granddad would have loved, now that his big thick sausage fingers could no longer contribute to the bloom in his long beautiful garden that was the centre of his universe.

It was my granddad's love of gardening that led me to be named Jasmine. It was what he had brought my mother when he had visited her in hospital on my birth: a clutch of flowers he'd plucked from the wooden frame he'd nailed together and painted red that climbed the shaded back wall, wrapped in newspaper and brown string, the ink on the half-finished *Irish Times* cryptic crossword running from the rainwater left on the stems. It wasn't the summer jasmine that we all know from expensive scented candles and fancy room vaporisers; I was a winter baby, and so winter jasmine with its small yellow star-like blooms was in abundance in his garden to help brighten up the dull grey winter. I don't think Granddad had thought about the significance of it, and I don't know if he'd been particularly honoured by the tribute my mother made by naming me after the flower he brought. I think he felt it was an odd name for a child, a name meant only for the natural things in his garden and never for a person. With a name like Adalbert, after a saint who was a missionary in Ireland, and with a middle name Mary, he wasn't used to names that didn't come from the Bible. The previous winter, he'd brought purple heather to my mother when my winter sister was born and Heather she had become. A simple gift when my sister was born, but it makes me wonder about his intentions on my naming. When I looked into it, I discovered the winter jasmine is a direct relative of winter-flowering heather, another provider of colour to winter gardens. I don't know if it's because of him and the way he was, but I've always hoped generally that silent people hold a magic and a knowledge that less contained people lack; that their *not* saying something means that more important thoughts are going on inside their head. Perhaps their seeming simplicity belies a hidden mosaic of fanciful thoughts, among them, Granddad Adalbert wanting me to be named Jasmine.

Back in the garden, Kevin misinterpreted my lack of laughter at his death joke as disapproval and there was nothing he disliked or feared more, so he turned his wild look in my direction and said, 'You're going to die too, Jasmine.'

Sitting in a circle of six, me the youngest in the group, with my sister a few feet away twirling by herself and enjoying getting dizzy and falling down, a daisy chain wrapped around my ankle, a lump so enormous at the back of my throat I wasn't sure whether I had swallowed one of the giant bumble bees swarming around the flower buffet beside us, I tried to let the fact of my future demise sink in. The others had been shocked that he'd said it, but instead of jumping to my defence and denying this awful premonition-like announcement, they had fixed me with sad gazes and nodded. *Yes, it's true*, they'd concurred in that one look. *You are going to die, Jasmine.*

In my long silence, Kevin elaborated for me, twisting the knife in further. I would not only die, but before that I would get a thing called a period every month for the rest of my life that would cause excruciating pain and agony. I then learned how babies were made, in quite an in-depth description that I found so vile I could barely look my parents in the eye for a week, and then to add salt to my already open wounds, I was told there was no Santa Claus.

You try to forget such things, but such things I couldn't.

Why do I bring up that episode in my life? Well, it's where *I* began. Where me, as I know me, as everybody else knows me, was formed. My life began at five years old. Knowing that I would die instilled something in me that I carry to this day: the awareness that, despite time being infinite, *my* time was limited, *my* time was running out. I realised that my hour and someone else's hour are not equal. We cannot spend it the same way, we cannot think of it in the same way. Do with yours what you may, but don't drag me into it; I have none to waste. If you want to do something, you have to do it now. If you want to say something, you have to say it now. And more importantly, you have to do it yourself. It's *your* life, you're the one who dies, you're the one who loses it. It became my practice to move, to make things happen. I worked at a rhythm that often left me so breathless I could barely catch a moment to become at one with myself. I chased myself a lot, perhaps I rarely caught up; I was fast.

I took a lot home with me from our meeting on the grass

that evening, and not just the daisies that dangled from my wrists and ankles and that were weaved into my hair as we followed the dispersing sunburnt grievers back into the house. I held a lot of fear in my heart then, but not long after that, in the only way a five-year-old could process it, the fear left me. I always thought of death as Granddad Adalbert Mary beneath the ground, still growing his garden even though he wasn't here, and I felt hope.

You reap what you sow, even in death. And so I got about sowing.

2

I was terminated from employment, *I was fired,* six weeks before Christmas – which in my opinion is a highly undignified time to let somebody go. They'd hired a woman to fire me for them, one of these outside agencies trained in letting unwanted employees go properly, to avoid a scene, a lawsuit or their own embarrassment. She'd taken me out for lunch, somewhere quiet, let me order a Caesar salad and then just had a black coffee herself, and sat there watching me practically choke on my crouton while she informed me of my new employment situation. I suppose Larry knew that I wouldn't take the news from him or anyone else, that I'd try to convince him to change his mind, that I'd slap him with a lawsuit or simply slap him. He'd tried to let me die with honour, only I didn't feel much honour when I left. Being fired is public, I would have to *tell* people. And if I didn't have to tell people it's because they already knew. I felt embarrassed. I feel embarrassed.

I began my working life as an accountant. From the ripe young age of twenty-four I worked at Trent & Bogle, a large corporation where I stayed for a year, then had a sudden shift to Start It Up, where I provided financial advice and guidance to individuals wishing to start their own businesses.

I've learned with most that there are always two stories to one event: the public story and the truth. The story I tell is that after eighteen months I left to start up my own business after becoming so inspired by those passing through my office I was overcome with the desire to turn my own ideas into a reality. The truth is that I became irritated by seeing people not doing it properly, my quest for efficiency always my driver, and so started my own business. It became so successful someone offered to buy it. So I sold it. Then I set up another business and again, I sold it. I quickly developed the next idea. The third time I didn't even have long enough to develop the idea because somebody loved the concept, or hated that it would be a strong rival to theirs, and bought it straight away. This led me to a working relationship with Larry, the most recent start-up and the only job that I have ever been fired from. The business concept was not my initial idea but Larry's, we developed the idea together, I was a co-founder and nurtured that baby like it had come from my own womb. I helped it grow. I watched it mature, develop beyond our wildest dreams, and then prepared for the moment when we would sell it. That didn't happen. I got fired.

The business was called the Idea Factory; we helped organisations with their own big ideas. We were *not* a consultancy firm. We'd either take their ideas and make them better or create our own, develop them, implement them, see them through completely. The big idea might go from being *Daily Fix*, a newspaper for a local coffee shop with local stories, a publication that would support local businesses, writers, artists; or it might be a sex shop's decision to sell ice cream – which, as my idea, was an enormous success, both personally and professionally. We didn't struggle during the recession, we soared. Because if there was one thing that companies needed in order to keep going in the current climate, it was imagination. We sold our imagination, and I loved it.

As I analyse it now in my idle days I can see that my relationship with Larry had begun to break down some time ago. I was heading, perhaps blindly, towards the 'sell the company' route, as I had done three times already, while he was still planning on keeping it. A big problem, with hindsight. I think I pushed it too much, finding interested parties when I knew deep down that he wasn't interested, and that put him under too much pressure. He believed 'seeing it through' meant continuing to grow it, whereas I believed seeing something through meant selling it and starting again with something else. I nurtured with a view to eventually saying goodbye, he nurtured to hold on. If you see the way he is with his teenage daughter and his wife, you'd know it's his philosophy for pretty much everything. Hold on, don't let go, it's *mine*. Control must not be relinquished. Anyway.

I'm thirty-three years old and worked there for four years. I never had a sick day, a complaint, an accusation, never received a warning, never an inappropriate affair – at least none that resulted in a negative outcome for the company. I gave my job everything, notably all for my own benefit because I wanted to, but I expected the machine I was working for to give something back, to honour my honour. My previous belief that being fired wasn't personal was based on never having been fired but having had to let go others. Now I understand that it is personal, because my job was my life. Friends and colleagues have been incredibly supportive in a way, which makes me think that if I ever get cancer, I want to treat it alone without anyone knowing. They make me feel like a victim. They look at me as if I'll be the next person to hop on the plane to Australia to become the next overqualified person to work on a watermelon farm. Barely two months have passed, and already I'm questioning my validity. I have no purpose, nothing to contribute on a day-to-day basis. I feel as though I am just taking from the world. I know that this is short-term, that I can fulfil that role again, but this is currently how I feel. Mostly, it has been almost two months and I am bored. I'm a doer and I haven't been doing much.

All of the things I dreamed of doing during my busy stressful days have been done. I completed most of them in the first month. I booked a holiday in the sun shortly before Christmas and now I am tanned and cold. I met with my friends, who are all new mothers on maternity leave and extended maternity leave and I-don't-know-if-I-ever-want-to-go-back leave, for coffee at a time of day that I have never had coffee before out in public. It felt like bunking off school for the day, it was wonderful – the first few times. Then it became not so wonderful, and I focused my attention on those serving the coffee, cleaning the tables, stocking the paninis. Workers. All working. I have bonded with all my friends' cute babies, though most of them lie on their colourful mats that squeak and rustle if you step on them by mistake, while the babies don't do anything but lift their lardy legs up, grab their toes and roll over on to their sides and struggle to get back over again. It's funny to watch the first ten times.

I have been asked to be godmother twice in seven weeks, as if that will help occupy the mind of the friend who's not busy. Both requests were thoughtful and kind, and I was touched, but if I had been working I would not have been asked because I wouldn't have visited them as much, or met their children, and everything eventually relates back to the fact that I have no work. I'm now the girl that friends call when they are at their wits' end, with their hair like an oil slick on their head, reeking of body odour and baby vomit, when they say down the phone in a low hushed voice that gives me goosebumps that they are afraid of what they will do, so that I run to hold the baby while they have their ten-minute shower. I've learned that a ten-minute shower and the gift of going to the toilet without a ticking clock restores much more in new parents than personal hygiene.

I spontaneously call my sister, which I was never able to do before. This has confused her immensely and when I'm with her she constantly asks what time it is, as if I've upset her body clock. I Christmas-shopped with time to spare. I bought actual Christmas cards and posted them on time – all two hundred of them. I even took over my dad's shopping list. I am ultra-efficient, always have been. Of course I can be idle – I love a two-week holiday, I love to lie on the beach and do nothing – but only when I say so, on my terms, when I know I have something waiting for me afterwards. When the holiday is over, I need a goal. I need an objective. I need a challenge. I need a purpose. I need to contribute. I need to do something.

I loved my job, but to make myself feel better about not being able to work there any more, I try to focus on what I won't miss.

I worked mainly with men. Most of the men were cocks, some were amusing, a few were pleasant. I did not like to spend any hours outside of work with any of them, which might mean my next sentence doesn't make sense, but it does. Of the team of ten, I slept with three. Of the three, I regret sleeping with two; the one I don't regret sleeping with strongly regrets sleeping with me. This is unfortunate.

I will not miss people at work. People are what bother me most in life. It bothers me that so many lack common sense, that their opinions can be so biased and backward, so utterly frustrating, misguided, misinformed and dangerous that I can't stand to listen to them. I'm not pointlessly prickly. I like non-PC jokes in controlled environments where it is appropriate and when it is obvious that the joke is at the expense of the ignorant who say such things. When a non-PC punchline is delivered by someone who genuinely believes it to be true, it is not funny, it is offensive. I don't enjoy a good debate about what's supposedly right and wrong; I would rather everyone just knew it, from the moment they're born. A heel-prick test and a jab of cop-on.

Not having my job has made me face what I dislike most about the world, and about myself. In my job I could hide, I could be distracted. Without a job, I have to face things, think about things, question things, find a way to actually deal with things that I have been avoiding for a long time. This includes the neighbourhood that I moved into four years ago and had nothing to do with until now.

It also includes what happens at night: I'm not sure whether I somehow managed to ignore it before, whether it has escalated, or whether my idleness has led to me become fascinated, almost obsessed by it. But it is ten p.m. and it is a few hours away from my nightly distraction.

It is New Year's Eve. For the first time ever, I am alone. I have chosen to do this for a few reasons: firstly, the weather is so awful I couldn't bring myself to go out in it after almost being decapitated by the door when I'd opened it to collect my Thai takeaway from the brave man who had battled the elements to deliver my food. The prawn crackers had practically dissolved and he'd spilled my dumpling sauce in the bottom of the bag, but I didn't have it in my heart to complain. His long forlorn look past my front door and into the safety and warmth of my house stopped me from mentioning the state of the delivery.

The wind outside howls with such force I wonder if it will

lift the roof off. My next-door neighbour's garden gate is banging constantly and I debate whether to go out and close it, but that would mean I'll get blown around like the wheelie bins that are battering each other in the side passage. It is the stormiest weather this country – Ireland – has seen since whenever. It's the same for the UK, and the US is being pounded too. It's minus forty in Kansas, Niagara Falls has frozen, New York has been attacked by a frigid, dense air known as a polar vortex, there are mobile homes landing on clifftops in Kerry, previously sure-footed sheep on steep cliff faces are being challenged and defeated, lying beside washed-up seals on the shoreline. There are flood warnings, residents in coastal areas have been advised to stay indoors by miserable saturated news reporters with blue lips reporting live from beside the sea. The road that takes me most places that I need to go has been flooded for two days. At a time when I've wanted, *needed* to keep busy, Mother Nature is slowing me to a standstill. I know what she's doing: she's trying to make me think, and she's winning. Hence all thoughts about myself now begin with *Perhaps* . . . because I'm having to think about myself in ways I never did before and I'm not sure if I'm right in my thinking about those things.

The bark of the dog across the road is barely audible above the wind, I think Dr Jameson has forgotten to take him in again. He's getting a bit scatty, or else he's had a falling out with the dog. I don't know its name but it's a Jack Russell. I find it running around my garden, sometimes it shits, it has on a few occasions run into my house and I've had to chase it around and deliver it back across the road to the right honourable gentleman. I call him the right honourable gentleman because he is a rather grand man in his seventies, retired GP, and for kicks and giggles was the president of every club going: chess, bridge, golf, cricket, and now our neighbourhood management company, which handles leaf-blowing, street-lamp bulb replacement, neighbourhood watch and the like. He is always well turned out, perfectly ironed trousers and shirts with little V-neck sweaters, polished shoes and tidy hair. He talks at me as if he's directing his sentences over my head, lifted chin and head-on nostrils, like an amateur theatre actor, yet is never blatantly rude so gives me no reason to be rude back, but just distant. Distance is all I can give someone I can't truly fathom. I didn't know until one month ago that Dr Jameson even had a dog, but these days I seem to know too much about my neighbours. The more the dog barks over the wind, the more I worry if Dr Jameson has fallen over, or been blown away into somebody's back garden like the trampolines that have been garden-hopping during the storms. I heard about a little girl waking up to find a swing set and slide in her back garden; she thought Santa had come again, but it turned out it had come from five houses down the road.

I can't hear the party down the street, though I can see it. Mr and Mrs Murphy are having their usual family New Year shindig. It always begins and ends with traditional Irish songs and Mr Murphy plays the bodhrán and Mrs Murphy sings with such sadness it's as though she's sitting right in a field of dead rotten black potatoes. The rest of their guests join in as though they're all rocking from side to side on a famine ship on stormy seas to the Americas. I'm not sad that the wind is lifting their sounds away in another direction, I can however hear a party that I can't see, probably from a few streets away; a few words from those crazy enough to smoke outside are blown down my chimney, along with a distant rhythm of party music before it gets swiped away again; sounds and leaves circling in a violent frenzy on my doorstep.

I was invited to three parties, but couldn't think of anything worse than party-hopping from one to the other, finding taxis on New Year's Eve in this weather, feeling like this. Also the TV shows are supposed to be great on New Year's Eve and, for the first time ever, I want to watch them. I wrap the cashmere blanket tighter around my body, take a sip of my red wine, feeling content with my decision to be alone, thinking that anybody out there, in that, is crazy. The wind roars again and I reach for the remote control to turn the volume up, but as soon as I do, every light in my house, including the television, goes off. I'm plunged into darkness and the house alarm beeps angrily.

A quick look outside my window shows me the entire street has lost electricity too. Unlike the others, I don't bother with candles. It is further reason for me to feel my way to the stairs and climb into bed at barely ten o'clock. The irony that I am powerless is not lost on me. I watch the New Year's Eve show on my iPad until the battery dies, then I listen to my iPod, which displays a threateningly low red battery that diminishes so quickly I can barely enjoy the songs. I turn then to my laptop, and when that dies I feel like crying.

I hear a car on the road and I know it's action time.

I climb out of bed and pull open the curtains. The lights are out on the entire street, I see the flicker of candles from a few houses but mostly it is black, most of my neighbours are over seventy and are in bed. I'm confident that I can't be seen because my house, too, is black; I can stand at the window with the curtains open and freely watch the spectacle that I know is about to take place.

I look outside. And I see you.

3

I am not a stalker but you make it difficult for me not to watch you. You are a circus act all of your own and I cannot help but be your audience. We live directly across the road from one another on this suburban cul de sac in Sutton, North Dublin, which was built in the seventies and was modelled on an American suburb. We have large front gardens, no hedging or shrubs to separate the pathway from our gardens, no gates, nothing to stop a person from walking straight up to our front windows. Our front gardens are larger than our back gardens and so the entire street has taken pride in maintaining the front, each one pruned, groomed, fed and watered within an inch of its natural life. Everybody on our street, bar the occupants of your house and mine, is retired. They spend endless hours in their gardens and, because they are outside, in the front, every-body knows about who comes and goes and at what time. Not me though. Or you. We are not gardeners and we are not retired. You are probably ten years older than me but we have lowered the age of the street by thirty years. You have three children, I'm not sure what ages they are but I guess one is a teenager and the other two are under ten.

You are not a good father; I never see you with them.

You have always lived opposite me, ever since I moved in, and you have always bothered me beyond belief, but going to work every day and all that came with that for me – distraction and knowing that there are more important things in the world – took me away from caring, from complaining and marching over there and punching your lights out.

I feel now like I'm living in a goldfish bowl and all I can see and hear from every window in my home is you. You, you, you. So at two thirty in the morning, which is a rather respectable time for you to return home, I find myself, elbows on the windowsill, chin resting on my hand, awaiting your next screw-up. I know this will be a good one because it's New Year's Eve and you are Matt Marshall, DJ on Ireland's biggest radio station and, despite not wanting to, I heard your show tonight on my phone before that too died. It was as intrusive, disgusting, repulsive, unpalatable, foul, nasty and vomitous as the others have been. Your talk show *Matt Marshall's Mouthpiece* which airs from eleven p.m. to one a.m. receives the highest number of listeners of any show on Irish radio. You have been at the helm of late-night talk shows for ten years. I didn't know you lived on this street when I moved in, but when I heard your voice travel to me across the road one day, I knew instantly it was you. Everybody does when they hear you, and mostly they get excited but I was repulsed.

You are everything I do not like about people. Your views, your opinions, your discussions that do nothing to fix the problem you pretend you want to fix and instead stir up angry frenzies and mob-like behaviour. You provide a hub for hatred and racism and anger to be vented, but you present it as free speech. For those reasons I dislike you; for personal reasons, I despise you. I'll go into them later.

19

You have driven home, as usual, going sixty kilometres per hour down our quiet retirement-home-like street. You bought your home from an aged couple who were downsizing, I bought mine from a widow who'd died – or at least from her children, cashing in. I did well, buying when houses were at their lowest, when people were taking what they could, before anything had risen again, and I am aiming to be mortgage free, an ambition I've had since I was five, wanting everything that's mine to actually be mine and not at the mercy of others and their mistakes. Both of our homes looked like an episode of *The Good Life* and both of us had extensive work to do and had to fight with the management company who accused us of ruining the look of the place. We managed to compromise. Our houses look like *The Good Life* from the front; inside, we have extensively renovated. I, however, broke a rule with my front garden that I am still paying for. More on that later.

You drive dangerously close to your garage door as usual and you climb out of the car, leaving the keys in the ignition, the radio blaring and the engine running. I'm not sure if you have forgotten or if you are not planning on staying. The car lights are on and are the only light on the street; it adds to the drama, almost as if the spotlight is on you. Despite the wind, which has died somewhat, every word of the Guns N' Roses song is audible from the car. It's 'Paradise City'; 1988 must have been a good year for you. I was eight years old, you would have been eighteen, I bet you wore their T-shirts and had them on your school bag, I bet you engraved their names into school journals and went to The Grove and smoked and danced all night and shouted every word of their songs to the night sky. You must have felt free and happy then, because you play it a lot and always when you're driving home.

I see a light go on in Dr Jameson's bedroom; it must be a torch because it is moving around, as though the person holding it is disorientated. The dog is barking like mad now and I wonder if he'll let him in before some little girl wakes up in the morning to find Santa has left a dizzy Jack Russell in her back garden. I watch the torch moving around the rooms upstairs. Dr Jameson likes to be at the helm of things, apparently. I learned this from my next-door neighbour Mr Malone, who called to my door to let me know that the bin truck was coming and he'd noticed I'd forgotten to put out my bins. I sense Mr Malone and Dr Jameson are at loggerheads over who should be in charge of the management company. I had forgotten to put my bins out because not being at work means I often confuse my days, but him calling to my home to tell me annoyed me. Seven weeks on, it wouldn't bother me. I find it helpful. Everything neighbourly and anything helpful bothered me then. I had no community spirit. It wasn't because I turned my back on it, it was because I was too busy. I didn't know it existed and I didn't require it.

You try the handle of the front door and appear full of shock and dismay that it isn't unlocked for you or some masked gunman to freely enter your home. You ring the doorbell. It never begins politely, it is always rude, offensive. The amount of times you ring, the length of time you ring it for, like the burst of a machine gun. Your wife never answers straight away. Neither do the children; I wonder if they sleep through it now because they're so used to it, or if she's in there with them, all huddled in one room while the children sob, telling them to ignore the scary sounds at the door. Either way, nobody comes. Then you bang on the door. You like the banging, you spend most nights doing this, relieving your tension and anger. You work your way around the entire house, knocking and banging on every window you can reach. You taunt your wife in a sing-song voice, 'I know you're in there,' as if she is pretending that she isn't. I don't think she is pretending, I think she is making it quite clear. I wonder if she is asleep or wide awake and hoping you will go away. I guess the latter.

Then you pick up your yelling. I know she hates the yelling because that above all embarrasses her, perhaps because your voice is so distinctive – though we couldn't ever think it was any other couple on the road behaving like this. I don't know why you haven't figured this out by now and just cut straight to the yelling. She remains resolute for the first time I've witnessed. You do a new thing. You go back to your car and start blowing the horn.

I see Dr Jameson's torch moving from upstairs to a downstairs room and I hope he isn't going to go outside to try to calm you down. You will no doubt do something drastic. Dr Jameson's front door opens and I hold my hands to my face, wondering if I should run out and stop him, but I don't want to get involved. I will watch and when it turns violent I will step in, though I have no idea what I will do. Dr Jameson doesn't appear. The dog comes running around the house at top speed, almost falls over himself on the flooded soggy grass in the race to get inside. The dog runs inside and the door is slammed. I laugh in surprise.

You must hear the door slam and think that it's your wife, because you stop honking the horn and Guns N' Roses is all that can be heard again. I'm thankful for that. The honking was above all the most annoying thing you've done. Almost as if she was waiting for you to calm down before letting you in, the front door opens and your wife steps out in her dressing gown, looking frantic. I see the dark shadow of someone behind her. At first I think she has met somebody else and I seriously worry about what will happen, but then I realise it's your eldest son. He looks older, protective, the man of the house. She tells him to stay inside and he does. I am glad. You don't need to make this any worse than it already is. As soon as you see her you jump out of the car and start shouting at her for locking you out of the house. You always shout this at her. She tries to calm you as she makes her way to your still-open jeep door, then she takes the keys out, which kills the music, the engine and the lights. She shakes the keys in front of you, telling you that you have the house key on your set. She told you that. You knew that.

But I know, as does she, that your practicality belongs with your sobriety, and in its place is this desperate, wild man. You always believe that you're locked out, that you have been *deliberately* locked out. That it is you against the world, or more that it is you against the house, and that you must get inside using any means necessary.

You go quiet for a moment as you take in the keys dangling in front of your face and then you stagger as you reach for her, pull her close and smother her with hugs and kisses. I can't see your face, but I see hers. It is the picture of complication, inner silent torture. You laugh and ruffle your son's head as you pass, as if the whole thing was a joke, and I detest you even more because you can't say sorry. You never say sorry – not that I've witnessed, anyway. Just as you step into the house the electricity goes back on. You twist around and you see me, at the window, my bedroom lights on full, revealing me in all my sneaky glory.

You glare at me, then you bang the door closed, and with all that you've done tonight, you make me feel like the weird one.

4

One of the things I liked about the Christmas break just gone was that nobody was working, it put us all on the same level. Everyone was in holiday mode, I didn't have to compare and contrast me from them, them from me. But now everybody is back at work, so I am back to feeling how I felt before the break.

Initially I felt shocked, my whole system felt shocked, and then I believe I went through a grieving process as I mourned for a life that I'd lost. I was angry, of course I was angry; I had considered Larry, my colleague, my firer, to be my friend. We went skiing together every New Year, I stayed in his Marbella holiday home with him and his family for a week every June. I was one of the few invited to the house for his daughter's over-the-top debs gathering. I was one of the small inner circle. I had never considered that he could take this course of action; that, despite the often heated arguments, our relationship would come to this, that he would very simply have the balls to *do this to me*.

After the anger, I was in denial about it being a bad thing that had happened. I didn't want losing my job to own me, to define me. I didn't need my job, my job needed me – and

24

too bad, it had lost me. And then Christmas came and I got lost in social events; dinners and parties and drunken festivities that made me feel warm and fuzzy and forgetful. Now it is January and I feel as bleak as the day outside, for I am overcome by a new feeling.

I feel worthless, as though a very important part of my self-esteem has been utterly diminished. I have been robbed of my routine, my schedule which once determined my every single waking and sleeping hour. Routine of any kind has been difficult to establish; there don't seem to be any rules for me, while everybody else marches to the beat of their own important drum. I constantly feel hungry, metaphorically and literally. I am hungry for something to do, somewhere to go, but I'm also hungry for everything in my kitchen because it's there, right beside me, every day and I have nothing better to do than eat it. I am bored. And as much as it pains me to say it, I am lonely. I can go an entire day without any socialisation, without a conversation with anyone. I wonder sometimes if I'm invisible. I feel like the old men and women who used to bother me by engaging in unnecessary chit-chat with the cashiers while I was stuck behind them, in a hurry, wanting to get on to the next place. When you don't have a next place to go to, time slows down enormously. I feel myself noticing other people more, catching more eyes, or seeking out eye contact. I'm now ripe and ready for a conversation about anything with anyone; it would make my day if somebody would meet my eye, or if there was someone to talk to. But everyone is too busy, and that makes me feel invisible; and invisibility, contrary to what I believed before, lacks any sense of lightness and liberty. Instead it makes me feel heavy. And so I drag myself around, trying to convince myself that I don't feel heavy, invisible, bored and worthless, and that I am free. I do not convince myself well.

Another of the bad things about being fired is that my father calls by, uninvited.

He is in the front garden with my half-sister Zara when I arrive home. Zara is three years old, my dad is sixty-three. He retired from his printing business three years ago after selling it for a very good price that allows him to live comfortably. As soon as Zara was born he became a hands-on husband and father while his new wife, Leilah, works as a yoga instructor in her own practice. It is lovely that Dad has had a second chance at love, and also lovely that he has been able to fully embrace fatherhood, properly, for the first time in his life. He fully embraced the nappy-changing, night feeds, weaning and anything else that raising a child threw at him. He glows every day with the pride he has for her, this remarkable little girl who has managed to do such incredible things all by herself. Grow, walk, talk. He marvels at her genius, tells long stories about what she has done that day, the funny things she has said, the clever picture she drew for one so young. As I said, it is lovely. Lovely. But he views it with a first-time joy, a beginner, someone who has never seen it happen before.

In the last few weeks it has made me think, because I've had time to, and I wonder where was his wonderment, his absolute shock and awe, when Heather and I were growing up? If it was ever there at all, it was hidden by the mask of inconvenience and complete bafflement. Sometimes when he points out something wonderful that Zara has done I want to scream at him that other children do that too, you know, children like Heather and I, and how incredible we must have been to have gotten there first over thirty years ago. But I don't. That would make me bitter and twisted,

26

and I am not, and it would create an energy around something where there is nothing. I tell myself it's the idleness that leads to these frustrating thoughts.

I often wonder, if Mum was alive, how would she feel seeing Dad as the man he is now – loyal, retired, a dedicated father and husband. Sometimes I hear her on her forgiving, wise days being all philosophical and understanding about it and other days I hear the tired voice of an exhausted single mother that I grew up with, spitting venom over him and his insensitivities. Which of her voices I hear may depend on what mood I am in myself. Mum died from breast cancer when she was forty-four. Too young to die. I was nineteen. Too young to lose a mother. It was most difficult for her, of course, having to leave this world when she didn't want to. She had things she wanted to see, things she wanted to do, things she had been putting off until I was finished school, an adult, so that she could begin her life. She wasn't finished yet; in many ways, she hadn't even started. She'd had her first baby at twenty-four, then me the accident at twenty-five, and she had raised her babies and done absolutely everything for us and it should have been time for her.

After she died, I lived on campus and Heather stayed in the care home she had moved into while Mum was undergoing treatment. Sometimes I wonder why I was so selfish and didn't decide to care for Heather myself. I don't think I even offered. I understand that it was necessary for me to begin my own life, but I don't believe I even thought about it for a moment. It's not selfish not to want to, but it was selfish not to think about it. I look back and realise I could have been more helpful to my mother at the time too. I feel like I let her go through it all alone. I could have been there more, accompanied her more, instead of asking her about things afterwards. But I was a teenager, my world was about me then, and I saw my aunt being there for my mum.

Heather is my Irish twin: older by one year. She treats me as though I am the baby sister by many more years. I love her for this. I know that I was an accident, because my mum had no intention of planning another child so soon after the birth of Heather. Mum was shocked, Dad was appalled; he could barely cope with a baby in the first place, let alone one with Down syndrome, and now there was a second child on the way. Heather scared him; he didn't know how to deal with her. When I came along, he moved further away from the family, seeking out other women who had more time on their hands to adore him and agree with him.

Meanwhile my mum dealt with reality with such strength and assurance, though she would admit later that she did it with what she called 'Bambi legs'. I never saw that in her, never saw a shake or tremble or wrong-step, she always made it seem as if she had it all under control. She joked, and apologised, that I raised myself. I always knew that Heather was more important, that Heather needed more attention; I never felt unloved, it was just the way it was. I loved Heather too, but I know that, when Mum left this world, the one person she did not want to leave behind was Heather. Heather needed Mum, Mum had plans for Heather, and so she left the world with a broken heart for the daughter she was leaving behind. I'm okay with that, I understand. My heart broke not just for me but for the two of them too.

Heather is not happy-go-lucky, as people with Down syndrome are stereotypically thought to be. She is an individual who has good days and bad, like us all, but her personality – which has nothing to do with Down syndrome – is upbeat. Her life is tied up in routine, she appreciates it as a way of feeling in control of her life, which is why when I show up at her home or when she's at work, she gets confused and almost agitated. Heather needs routine, which is something that makes us even more similar and not at all different.

Zara is hopping from one cobblestone to the other and trying not to step on the cracks. She insists Dad does the same. He does. I know this about him now and yet, seeing him, his Christmas belly hanging over his trousers and bouncing up and down as he hops from stone to stone, I still can't help but not know who this man is. He looks up as I pull in.

'I didn't know you'd be here,' I say, lightly. Translation: You didn't tell me, you must always tell me.

'We were taking a drive along the coast, watching the waves – weren't we, Zara?' He scoops her up in his arms. 'Tell Jasmine about the waves.'

He always gets Zara to say things for us; I'm sure most parents do, but it infuriates me. I would rather have a conversation with Zara that isn't dictated by Dad. Hearing her tell me things is hearing it twice.

'They were huge waves, weren't they? Tell Jasmine how huge they were.'

She nods. Big eyes. Holds her arms out to show what would be a disappointingly small wave, but an enormous stretch for her.

'And weren't they crashing up against the rocks? Tell Jasmine.'

She nods again. 'They were crashing against the rocks.'

'And the waves were splashing over on to the coast road

in Malahide,' he says, again in his childish voice, and I wish he would just tell me the story directly instead of relaying it like this.

'Wow,' I say, smiling at Zara and reaching out to her. She immediately comes to me and wraps her skinny long legs around my body and clings to me tightly. I do not have anything against Zara. Zara is lovely. No – Zara is beautiful. She is perfect in every way and I adore her. It is not Zara's fault. It is not anybody's fault, because nothing has happened and it is merely the annoyance of my dad making a habit of dropping by since I've been at home that is beginning to create something that is not there. I know this. I tell my rational self this.

'How's my spaghetti legs?' I ask her, letting us into the house. 'I haven't seen you for an entire year!' While I'm talking, I glance at your house. I do that a lot lately, I can't seem to help it. It's become a habit now, some ridiculous OCD thing where I can't get into my car without looking across the road, or I can't close my front door without looking, or sometimes when I pass a front window, I stop and watch. I know I need to stop. Nothing ever happens during the day time, not with you, at least; you barely surface, it's just your wife coming and going with the kids all day. Occasionally I might see you pull a curtain open and go out to your car, but that's it. I don't know what I'm expecting to see.

'Did you tell your dad that we made cupcakes together last week?' I ask Zara.

She nods again and I realise that I'm doing exactly what Dad does. It must be frustrating for her, but I can't seem to stop.

Dad and I talk to each other through Zara. We say things to her that we should be saying to one another, so I tell her that my electricity went off on New Year's Eve, that I met Billy Gallagher in the supermarket and he has retired, and various other things that she doesn't need to know. Zara pays attention for a while, but then we confuse her, and she runs off.

'Your friend is in trouble again,' Dad says when we're sitting at the table with a cup of tea and biscuits left over from my enormous drawer of Christmas goodies that I'm consistently working my way through, and we watch Zara tip over the box of toys that I keep for her. The noise of Lego hitting floorboards takes away his next sentence.

'What friend?' I ask, worried.

Dad nods in the direction of the front window that faces your house. 'Your man – what's his name?'

'Matt Marshall? He's not a friend of mine,' I say, disgusted. All talk always turns to you.

'Well, your neighbour then,' Dad says, and we both watch Zara again.

It's only the silence dragging on for too long that causes me to ask, because I don't know what else to say: 'Why, what did he do?'

'Who?' Dad says, snapping out of his trance.

'Matt Marshall,' I say through gritted teeth, hating having to ask about you once, never mind twice.

'Oh, him.' As if it was an hour ago that he first raised it. 'His New Year's Eve show got complaints.'

'He always gets complaints.'

'Well, more than usual, I suppose. It's all over the papers.'

We are silent again as I think about your show. I hate your show, I never listen. Or rather, I never used to listen but lately I've been listening to see if what you talk about has any direct link to the state you return home in, because you're not trashed every single night of the week. About

31

three or four nights a week. Anyway, so far there seems to be no direct correlation.

'Well, he tried to ring in the New Year by getting a woman to—'

'I know, I know,' I say, interrupting him, not wanting to hear my dad say the word *orgasm*.

'Well, I thought you said you hadn't heard it,' he says, all defensive.

'I heard *about* it,' I mumble, and I climb down on all fours to help Zara with her Lego. I pretend our tower is a dinosaur. I use it to eat her fingers, her toes, then I crash it into the second tower with a great big roar. She's happy with that for a moment and goes back to playing by herself.

To recap on your New Year's Eve show, you and your team felt it would be hilarious to ring in the New Year with the sound of a woman's orgasm. A charming treat for your listeners, a thank you in fact, for their support. Then you had a quiz to guess the sound of a fake orgasm from a real orgasm, and then a full discussion about men who fake orgasms during sex. It wasn't offensive, not to me, not in comparison to the filth you've spoken about in other shows, and I hadn't been aware of men who faked orgasms so it was slightly informative, if not disturbing, maybe even personally enlightening – with regard to the man I didn't regret in the office, who regretted me, *possibly* – though the douche-bags you had on the show to tell their side of their story did little to educate. I sound as if I'm defending you. I'm not. It just wasn't the worst show. For once the issue is not you and your lack of charm but the right to hear the sound of a woman climax without it being considered offensive.

'How is he in trouble?' I ask moments later.

'Who's that?' Dad asks and I count to three in my head.

'Matt Marshall.'

'Oh. They've fired him. Or suspended him. I'm not sure which. I'd say he's out of there. Been there long enough anyway. Let somebody younger have a chance.'

'He's only forty-two,' I say. It sounds like a defence of you, but I don't mean it personally. I'm thirty-three and I need to find a new job, I'm concerned about age right now, particularly the attitude towards age in the workplace, that's all. I think of you suspended and I immediately feel delight. I've always disliked you, have always wanted your show off the air, but then I feel bad and I'm not sure why. Maybe it's because of your children and your nice wife, who I've taken to waving at in the morning.

'Turns out it was a real woman in the studio,' Dad says, looking a bit uncomfortable.

'Well, it hardly sounded like a man.'

'No, she was really . . . you know,' he looks at me and I've no idea what he is implying.

We are quiet.

'She was really pleasuring herself. Live in the studio,' Dad says.

My stomach turns, both because I've just had that conversation with my dad and also because I can see you orchestrating that in your studio, the countdown to twelve o'clock, the team all guffawing over a woman, like idiots.

I once again loathe you.

I lift Zara into her car seat and plant a kiss on her button nose.

'So I could talk to Ted, if you like,' Dad says suddenly, as though continuing a conversation that I don't remember having.

I frown. 'Who's Ted?'

'Ted Clifford,' he shrugs like it's no big deal.

Anger rises within me so quickly I have to fight the urge to lose it right there. And I'd come so close. Dad sold his company to Ted Clifford. He could have sold it for three times the amount in the good times, he likes to tell everybody, but it is not the good times now and so he settled on a reasonably good sum of money that will ensure month-long holidays in the summer with Leilah and Zara, dinners out four times a week. I don't know if he paid off his mortgage, and this annoys me. It would have been the first thing I'd have done. I'm not sure how me and Heather have come out of this, but I'm not bothered, though I might sound it. I'm financially okay right now, I'm more concerned about Heather. She needs security. As soon as I made enough money, I bought the apartment she was renting. She moved out of residential care five years ago, a big deal for her, a big deal for anybody. She lives with a friend, under the caring eye of her support assistant, and they are getting along perfectly well together, though it doesn't stop me from worrying about her every second of every day. I got the apartment at a good price; most people were trying to get rid of their negative equity, that second property where it was suddenly a struggle to meet the payments. It was something I expected Dad to do when he retired, instead of buying the apartment in Spain. He thought she was fine in the care home, but I knew that it was a dream for her to have her own place so I took control. Again, I'm not angry, it's just that things like this come to me now and I can't help but ponder them . . . I need distraction.

'No,' I say abruptly. 'Thanks.' End of.

He looks at me as if he wants to say more. To stop him, I continue: 'I don't need you to get me a job.'

My pride. Easily damaged. I hate help. I need to do things

all by myself, all of the time. His offer makes me feel weak, makes me think that he thinks I'm weak. It has too many connotations.

'Just saying. It'd be an easy foot in the door. Ted would help you out any day.'

'I don't need help.'

'You need a job.' He chuckles. He looks at me as though he is amused, but I know that this is the precursor to his anger. That laugh is what happens when he's annoyed; I'm not sure whether it is supposed to wind up the person he is annoyed at – which is what happens now and has always happened to me – or if it is his way of covering up his anger. Either way, I recognise the sign.

'Okay, Jasmine, do it your way, as usual.' He holds his hands up dramatically in the air, in defence, keys dangling from his fingers. He gets into the car and drives off.

He says it like it's a bad thing: *do it your way*. Isn't that a good thing for anyone to do? When would I ever, have I ever, wanted to do it *his* way? If I wanted help, he would be the last person I would go to. And then it occurs to me again that there seems to be an issue, when there really never has been an issue, and it startles me. I realise I'm standing out in the cold, glaring down the street at where the car has long since disappeared. I quickly look across the street to your house and I think I've seen a slight movement in an upstairs curtain, but I've probably imagined it.

Later, in bed, I'm unable to sleep. I feel as though my head is overheating from thinking too much, like my laptop when it's been used for too many hours. I am angry. I am having half-finished conversations with my dad, with my job, with the man who stole my space in the car park that morning, with the watermelon that I dropped carrying from the car to the house which burst all over the ground and stained my suede boots. I am ranting to them all, I am setting everything right, I am cursing at them, I am informing them all of their shortfalls. Only it doesn't help, it is just making me feel worse.

I sit up, frustrated and dehydrated.

Rita the Reiki woman I'd seen earlier that day told me this would happen. She'd told me to drink lots of water after our unusual session that I feel didn't alter me at all, and instead I had a bottle of wine before bed. I'd never been to Reiki before and I probably won't go again but my aunt had given me a voucher for Christmas. My aunt is into all kinds of alternative therapy; she and my mum used to do that kind of thing when Mum was sick. Maybe that's why I don't believe in it now, because it didn't work, Mum died. But then the medicine didn't work for her either, and I still take that. Maybe I will go back. I made the appointment when everybody went back to work, something to do, something to keep myself busy, something to put in my new yellow Smythson diary with my initials in gold on the bottom right corner which would usually be filled already with appointments and meetings and now is a sad depiction of my current life: christening times, coffee meetings and birthday celebrations. At the Reiki session I'd sat in a small white room that was filled with incense and made me feel so sleepy I wondered if I was being drugged. Rita was a tiny woman, bird-like, in her sixties, but she twisted her legs into a position on the armchair that showed her agility. She was soft-faced, almost out of focus, and I'm not sure if it was the incense smoke that blurred her, but I couldn't quite see her edges. Her eyes were sharp though, the way they took me in and held on to every word that I said so that it made me take note of my own voice and

I could hear how clipped and contained I sounded. Anyway, apart from a nice chat with a supportive woman, and a relaxing twenty-minute lie-down in a nicely scented womb-like room, I didn't feel in any way altered.

She'd given me one piece of advice though for my busy head. I'd immediately disregarded it as soon as I'd left, but now I am barely able to formulate a single thought for long enough to be able to see it through, to process it, to get rid of it, so I take her advice. I remove my socks and pad around the carpet for a while, hoping I'll feel 'rooted' to stop my head from drifting again into ranty angry territory. I step on something sharp – the end of a clothes hanger – and curse as I inspect my foot. I cradle my foot in my hands. I'm not sure how rooted is supposed to feel, but this can't be it.

She'd suggested walking barefoot, preferably on grass, but if not, generally barefoot as much as possible as soon as I returned to the house, The scientific theory behind the health benefits to walking barefoot, is that the Earth is negatively charged, so when you ground, you're connecting your body to a negatively charged supply of energy. And since the Earth has a greater negative charge than your body, you end up absorbing electrons from it. The grounding effect has an anti-inflammatory effect on your body. I don't know about all that but I need to clear my head and as I'm trying to cut down on the headache tablets, I may as well try barefoot.

I look outside. There is no grass in my garden. That was the terrible, unspeakable thing I did when I moved in four years ago. I wasn't a fan of gardens, I was twenty-nine years old, I was busy, I was barely at home, I was never home long enough to notice my garden. To avoid the effort involved in its upkeep, I had the relatively nice garden that was there when I bought the place dug up and replaced it with maintainable cobble-locking. It looked impressive, it cost a fortune, it horrified the neighbours. I put some nice black pots outside my front door with plants that stayed green all year round, pruned into clever modern twisted shapes. I cared a little bit about how it affected my new neighbours, but I was never home to discuss it with them at length, and I reasoned with myself that it would save me paying a gardener – because I wasn't about to do it myself; I wouldn't know where to start. There is still grass on the pathway outside of my house, which is maintained by my neighbour, Mr Malone, who did this without asking me. I think he sees it as his because he was here first, and anyway, what do I know about grass? I am a grass-defector.

I'd thought that buying my own house at the age of twenty-nine – a semi-detached, four-bedroom family home – was quite a mature and grounding thing to do. Who knew that when I dug up the garden I was losing the very thing that could have kept me grounded.

I check your house and your jeep isn't there and all the lights are out. I never need to worry about anybody else's house. I never seem to care. I put on a tracksuit and go downstairs barefoot. Feeling like a sleuth, I run on tiptoe across the cold paving down my driveway and straight to the grass that lines the path. I check the grass for dog poo. I check for slugs and snails. Then I pull up the ends of my tracksuit bottoms and I allow my feet to squelch into the wet grass. It is cold but it's soft. I chuckle to myself as I walk up and down, surveying the street at midnight.

For the first time since I've moved in, I feel guilty for what I've done to my garden. I look at the houses and see how mine is dark and grey amidst the colour. Not that there is much colour in the gardens in January, but at least the bushes, the trees, the grass, break the grey concrete of the paths, the brown and grey of my paving.

I'm not sure if going barefoot in the grass is helping anything other than the onslaught of pneumonia, but at least the cool air has soothed my hot, over-wired head and freed up some space. This is unusual behaviour for me. Not the walking on grass at midnight, but the lack of control. Sure, I've had stressful days at the office where I've needed to regroup, but this is different. I feel different. I'm thinking too much, focusing on areas that didn't require thinking about before.

Often, when I'm searching for something, the only way I can find anything is to acknowledge out loud what it is, because I can't see it unless I fully register and envision in my mind what it is I'm looking for. For example, rooting around in my oversized handbags for my keys, I say either in my head or aloud, 'Keys, keys, keys.' I do the same in my house: I wander from room to room, saying or muttering, 'Red lipstick, pen, phone bill . . .' or whatever it is I'm looking for. As soon as I do that, I find the thing quicker. I don't know the reason for this, but I know that it makes sense, that it's true, that Deepak Chopra would be able to explain in a more sophisticated, informed, philosophical manner, but I feel that when I tell myself what it is I'm looking for, then I fully know what it is that I must find. Order given: dutiful body and mind respond.

Sometimes the very thing I am looking for is staring me straight in the face, but I can't see it. This happens to me a lot. It happened this morning when I was looking for my coat in my wardrobe. It was right in front of me, but because I didn't say, 'Black coat with the leather sleeves,' it didn't appear to me. I was just idly searching, eyes running over clothes and not finding anything.

I think – in fact, I have come to know – that I have applied this thinking on a larger scale, I've applied it to my life. I tell myself what I want, what I am looking for, I envision it so that it's easier to find, and then I find it. It has worked for me all my life.

So now I find myself in a place where all that I've envisioned and worked hard for has been taken away, it is not mine any more. First thing I do is try to get it all back again, make it mine again, straight away, immediately; and if that's not possible – which it usually isn't, because I'm a realist, not a voodoo practitioner – then I must find something else to look for, something else to achieve. I'm obviously talking about my job here. I know I will get back to work eventually, but I have been put on hold. I have been stalled, and there is nothing I can do about it.

I'm on what is called 'gardening leave'. It has nothing to do with gardening, thankfully, or I'd have a very long year power-hosing and weeding between the cracks of my cobble-locked garden. Gardening leave is the practice whereby an employee who has left their job or who has been terminated is instructed to stay away from work during the notice period, while still remaining on the payroll. It's often used to prevent employees from taking with them up-to-date and perhaps sensitive information when they leave their current employer, especially when they are leaving to join a competitor. I wasn't leaving to join a competitor, as I've already explained, however Larry felt certain that I would work with a company we were in relative competition with, a company I had tried to schmooze to buy ours. He was right. I would have worked with them. They called me the day after I was fired to offer me a job. When I told them about the gardening leave they said they couldn't possibly wait that long – *twelve months gardening leave!!* – and so they went off to find somebody else. Not only has the length of my gardening leave chased away other employers, I have absolutely nothing to do while I wait. It feels like a prison sentence. Twelve months gardening leave. It *is* a sentence. I feel as if I'm gathering dust on some shelf while the world is moving on around me and I can't do anything to stop it or join in. I don't want my mind to start growing moss; I'll need to continuously power-hose it, to keep it fresh.

Blades of wet grass stick to my feet, working their way up my ankles as I walk back and forth on the patch of grass. So what happens when I'm put on hold for an entire year and there's nothing I can do about it? What do I do?

I pad up and down on the wet grass, my feet starting to feel cold but my mind buzzing with a new idea. A new project. A goal. An objective. Something to do. I must right a wrong. I will uproot the very ground I walk on, which will be easy because I feel as if I have been uprooted already.

I will give the neighbourhood a gift. I will bring back the garden.

5

'He's beautiful,' I whisper, looking at the tiny baby in my friend Bianca's arms.

'I know,' she smiles, gazing at him adoringly.

'Is it amazing?' I ask.

'Yeah, it's . . . amazing.' She looks away, her smile a bit wobbly, her eyes sunken into the back of her head from two nights' lack of sleep. 'Hey, have you started a new job yet?'

'No, I can't – you know, the gardening leave thing.'

'Oh yeah,' she says, then winces and goes quiet for a moment. I don't dare interrupt her thoughts. 'You'll find something,' she says, giving me a sympathetic smile.

I have grown to hate that smile on people. I am in the Rotunda Hospital, once again finding myself visiting somebody as they do something else. It has occurred to me lately that most of my visits have been this way. Calling into a friend at work, dropping by one of my sister's classes to watch, seeing my dad while he is busy with Zara, chatting to friends while they are watching their children swimming or dancing, or at a playground. Every time I see people lately it is me interrupting their life, them busy with something – distracted heads that have one eye on me and another on their job – while beside them or across from

42

them I am still, patiently waiting for them to finish what they're doing to answer me. I am the still person in every scene of my life and I have started to see myself from afar each time it happens, like I'm outside of myself, watching myself be still and silent while the others move around, tend to their work, their children. Since realising this, I have tried not to meet anyone during the day when they are in the middle of something and I am not. I have tried to make appointments for nights out, dinners, drinks – times when I know we can be on even ground, face to face, one on one. But it is difficult, everybody is so busy, some can't get a babysitter, we can't seem to synchronise a night out that suits everybody, and so we struggle to arrange anything. It took me weeks to organise a dinner party in my house this weekend. Then I will be busy, and they can be still. In the meantime, here I am in the hospital, sitting at the bedside of one of my dearest friends who has just had her first baby, and while I am happy for her, of course I am, and was secretly delighted about the nine months maternity leave so that I could have company for the remainder of the year, I know the reality is that I will not see her very much, or if I do, she will be busy and I will be still, I will sit opposite her or beside her and wait for her to be ready, holding half her attention.

'We were thinking, me and Tristan . . .' Bianca breaks into my thoughts.

My body turns rigid as I sense what's coming.

'He's not here, but I'm sure he wouldn't mind me asking you . . .'

I feel dread but I fix my face into what I hope is the perfect look of interest.

'Would you be his godmother?'

Ta-da. Third one in two months, it has to be a world

record. 'Oh, Bianca. I'd love to,' I smile. 'Thank you, that's such an honour . . .'

She smiles back at me, delighted by her request, one of the most special moments in her life, while inside I feel like a charity case. It's as if they've all made a pact to ask me to be godmother in order to give me something to do. And what will I do? Go to the church and stand by their side while they hold the baby, while the priest pours water, while everybody does something and I stand idly by.

'Did you hear about your friend's son?'

'What friend?'

'Matt Marshall,' Bianca says.

'He is *not* my friend,' I say, annoyed. Then, deciding it's best not to argue with a woman who has just given birth, I ask, 'What did his son do?'

'He put a video up on YouTube telling the world how much he hates his dad. Mortifying, isn't it? Imagine talking about a family member like that.'

The baby in Bianca's arms lets out a scream.

'This little fucker keeps biting my nipple,' she hisses, and I'm immediately silenced as her mood swings again and darkness descends in the hospital room.

She moves her three-day-old son into a different position, holding him like a rugby ball, her enormous breast bigger than his head and looking like it's smothering him. The baby sucks and is silenced again.

It is almost a beautiful moment, apart from the fact that when I look at her she has tears streaming down her face.

The door opens and her pale husband Tristan ducks his head in. He sees his firstborn and his face softens, then he looks up and sees his wife and his face tightens. He swallows.

'Hi, Jasmine,' he steps inside and greets me.

'Congratulations, Daddy,' I say gently. 'He's beautiful.'

'He's got a mouthful of fangs, is what he has,' Bianca says, wincing again.

The baby screams as he's pulled away from her chapped red raw nipple.

'Seriously, Tristan, this is . . . I can't . . .' Her face crumples.

I leave them to it.

I tell myself while driving that I am not interested in watching your son on YouTube. I tell myself I won't stoop to your level, that I have far more important things to do than think about you and absorb myself in your world, but all I actually have to do that day is shop for dinner. Shopping for one person doesn't depress me as it does some of my other single friends; I am happy to be alone and everybody needs to eat, but it has come to this. Eating. Eating was something I had to squeeze into my busy day because I had to, to stay alive. Now it is something to string out, make an afternoon of. The last few days I have made elaborate meals for myself. Yesterday I spent fifty-five minutes in Eason's browsing the shelves for recipe books, spent sixty minutes buying the ingredients, which took me two and a half hours to prepare and cook, and then I ate it in twenty minutes. That was my entire day yesterday. It was enjoyable but the novelty has worn off many of the things I was looking forward to doing in my 'time off'.

When I pull into the supermarket car park, the day surprisingly bright and sunny for the first time in weeks though it is still cold, I take my phone out of my bag and go straight to YouTube. I type in Matt Marshall and immediately 'Matt Marshall's son' pops up as an option. I select it. Posted late last night, it already has thirty thousand views – which is impressive.

Though I have never seen your son close up, the image

of him is immediately familiar to me. It is what I see most days as he leaves for school, head hidden under a hood, his face downward, earphones on his head, red hair peeking out from under his hood as he walks from the house to the bus stop. I have been his neighbour for four years and it occurs to me I don't even know his name, but the comments beneath the video tell me that it is Fionn.

Way to go, Fionn!

My dad is a loser 2, know how u feel!

Your dad shud be locked up 4 da shit dat he says.

I am a registered psychologist and I am concerned by your outburst, please contact me, I can help.

I'm a big fan of your dad, he helped my son when he was being bullied in school, he helped shed light on bullying laws in Ireland.

May the angels heal your inner anger.

Your dad's a loser and you're a fag.

A small slice of the supportive comments the viewing public have made.

Fionn is fifteen years old and from his uniform each morning I can tell he attends Belvedere, a costly private school in Dublin. Though I haven't watched it yet, I already know that they will not like this. Here on the screen I can see he has brown eyes, his cheeks and nose are lightly freckled. He is looking down at the webcam, his laptop at an angle to take him all in so that the lights on the ceiling are blaring in the camera. His nostrils are wide and flaring with anger. There is music in the background, I guess he is at a party, I'm guessing he is drunk. His pupils are dilated, though perhaps the anger is causing that. What ensues is a four-minute rant about how he would officially like to separate himself from his loser dad, you, who he believes is not a real dad. He says that you are an embarrassment, a waster, his mum is the only person who keeps things going, you have no talent. And on it goes, a well-spoken boy, attempting to be harder than he is in a badly constructed attack on you, outlining why he believes you should be fired and never rehired. It is a rather embarrassing rant that makes me cringe and watch from behind my hands. The music in the background gets louder, as do male voices. He takes a quick look behind him and then the video is over.

Despite the way I feel about you, this does not fill me with any kind of happiness or entertainment. I feel bad for watching it, I feel bad for you, for all of you.

I do a quick shop, feeling glum as I hurry down the aisles. Sometimes I forget why I feel that way, I just have this feeling that something bad has happened to me and affected my life. Then I remember why I feel down and I try to shake it off, because it has nothing to do with me. Trouble is, even though I know it's silly of me, I can't help feeling connected to what happened.

I keep the dinner simple – aubergine parmigiana – and I finish the last glass of the bottle of red wine from the night before. I settle down to ponder your problem as if it is mine. What should we do about Fionn, Matt? There is no action in your house. Your wife's car is gone, and you are all out. Nothing.

Dr Jameson's bedroom light goes out. I have no solutions, Matt.

I have fallen asleep on the couch for the first time in my life and at some hour I wake up, very confused as to where I am; the only light in the room is the flickering, muted TV. I jump up and kick my plate and cutlery to the floor, smashing my wine glass. I'm fully alert now, heart pounding, and I realise what has woken me. It is the familiar sound of your jeep speeding down the street. Avoiding the broken glass at my feet, I go to the window to see you driving erratically, swerving into your driveway coming dangerously close to your garage door as usual. However this time you don't brake and you crash directly into the white door. The garage door shudders and vibrates, the noise echoing loudly off the sleeping houses. I can picture Dr Jameson waking with a start, fumbling to remove his eye mask. On cue, Dr Jameson's bedroom light goes on.

The garage door stays standing, the house doesn't topple on to your car. Unfortunate really. Nothing happens for a while. 'Paradise City' is still playing, blaring. I can see you, unmoving in the driver's seat. I wonder if you're okay, if the airbag has exploded and knocked you out. I think of calling an ambulance for you, but I don't know if it's needed and it could be seen as wasting emergency services' time. Though I very much do not want to leave the safe haven of my home, I know I can't just leave you there.

You slept in the car last night, not even bothering with your usual routine of banging at the doors and windows of the house, but somewhere between me falling asleep and waking up, you'd managed to get inside the house. I wonder if your son let you in. I wonder if it had become too much for him and he'd disobeyed his mum's orders to ignore you and instead answered the door and confronted you. Already fired up from the video he'd made, he told you what he thought of you. I'd like to have seen that. I know that's weird.

Tonight you are worse than usual. I suspected this would be the case. I'm sure you know about the YouTube posting. I listened to the radio to see if was true about your suspension and there was another DJ filling in for you and the team. You and the team have all been suspended for your naughty New Year's Eve antics and I see you have used your time not to spend a rare midweek evening at home with your family or to ponder your actions, but by drinking the night away. It was odd not to hear your voice on air; you've become synonymous with that time of night in most people's homes, cars, workplaces, vans and lorries on long overnight drives. Learning of your suspension makes me surprisingly not as happy as I'd imagined, but then I come to the conclusion that it might be a good thing. It might make you think about all the lowly things you have said and discussed on your show, and how that has affected people and how you can improve yourself and thereby improve the lives of so many that you have such influence over. It makes me think of the one that makes me hate you, the entire reason for this anger I feel towards you.

Sixteen years ago, on another station at another hour, you hosted a discussion about Down syndrome. It was about many aspects of Down syndrome, and some of it was informative, thanks to the angry but firm woman who called in from Down Syndrome Ireland to explain the realities. Unfortunately she was deemed too calm and patient for your show and you quickly hung up on her. The others were uneducated, obnoxious ignoramuses who were given far too much airtime. Much of the discussion was about CVS, Chorionic Villus Sampling, and amniocentesis, also referred to as amniotic fluid test or AFT, which is a medical procedure used in prenatal diagnosis of chromosomal abnormalities and foetal infections. The most common reason to carry out such a test is to determine whether a baby has certain genetic disorders or a chromosomal abnormality such as Down syndrome. Women who choose to have this test are primarily those at increased risk for genetic and chromosomal problems, in part because the test is invasive and carries a small risk of miscarriage. I can see why you wanted to have this conversation; it is worth having the conversation, it could help women make the decision, if dealt with in a mature and honest way – but not in your way, not in the way your show handles things, trying to stir up controversy and drama. Instead of handling it in a mature, honest way you invited lunatics on to show the worst side and voice their uninformed opinions of Down syndrome. For example, an eejit anonymous man who had just discovered his girlfriend was having a baby with Down syndrome and what rights did he have about stopping this?

I was seventeen years old, at a party with a guy I had fancied for ages. Everyone was drunk, someone's parents had gone away, and instead of listening to music it had been cool to listen to Matt Marshall. I didn't mind you then; in fact I thought you were cool, because it was cool to hear the kinds of things you were discussing back when we were still trying to find our own voice. But the conversation made me feel ill, the conversation drifted from the speakers and continued into our room at the party and I had to listen to my friends, who should have known better, and to people I didn't know, and the guy that I fancied, giving their opinions on the matter. Nobody wanted a child with Down syndrome. One person said they'd prefer one to a baby with AIDS. I was sickened by what I heard. I had a beautiful sister asleep at home, with a mother who was undergoing treatment for cancer who was more distraught about leaving my sister than leaving anything else in her life, and I couldn't quite take what I was hearing.

I just got up and walked out. The guards picked me up along the coast road. I wasn't falling around the place, but I was quite emotional and the alcohol only made me worse so they brought me to the station for my own safety, and a warning.

Mum was sick, she needed her rest. I couldn't call my

aunt after what had happened over the past few weeks in her house between me and her son Kevin, nor could I go back to stay in her house after the event, so they called Dad. He'd been out on a date with a new girlfriend, and they collected me in a taxi, him in his tuxedo and her in her ballgown, and they brought me back to his apartment. They'd both been throwing eyes at each other and giggling in the cab; I could tell they were finding the entire thing so much fun. As soon as we got to the apartment they went straight out again, which was a blessing.

So I stand at the window now and watch your unmoving body in your jeep, not caring whether you see me watching or not because I'm worried. Just as I'm thinking about going outside to assist you, the jeep door opens and you fall out. Head first, your back facing out as if you've been leaning it against the door. You slide down slowly and your head hits the ground. Your foot is tangled in the seat belt on the leather seat. You don't move. I look around for my coat and then I hear you laughing. You struggle to untangle your foot from the seat belt, your laugh dying down as you become irritated and need to concentrate on freeing yourself as the blood rushes to your head.

You finally free yourself to begin your shouting/doorbell-ringing/banging act, but there is no response from the house. You honk the horn a few times. I'm surprised none of the neighbours tell you to be quiet; perhaps they're asleep and they can't hear. Perhaps they're afraid, perhaps they watch you as I do, though I don't think so. The Murphys go to bed early, the Malones never seem to be disturbed by you and the Lennons beside me are so timid I think they would be afraid to confront you. It is only Dr Jameson and I who seem to be disturbed by you. Your house is completely still and I only notice now that your wife's car is not parked on the street as it usually is. The curtains are not drawn on any of the windows. The house appears empty.

You disappear around the back of the house and then I hear you before I see you. You reappear pulling a six-seater wooden table across the grass. The legs of the table destroy the grass, digging up the soil, leaving deep tracks as though you've been ploughing. You heave the table from the grass and on to the concrete. The wood drags across the ground, across the driveway behind the car, making an awful screeching sound which goes on for almost a minute. Sixty seconds of screeching and I see the Murphys' lights go on down the street. Once you have dragged the wooden table on to the grass in the front garden, you disappear into the back garden again and take three trips to carry the six matching chairs. On the last trip you return with the sun umbrella and struggle to position it in the centre hole. You fire it across the garden with frustration and as it flies through the air, it opens like a parachute, takes flight and then lands, open, in a tree. Out of breath, you retrieve a carrier bag from the jeep. I recognise it as being from the local off-licence. You empty the bag, line up the cans on the table and then you sit down. You put your boots up on the wooden table, making yourself at home, and settle down as though you couldn't be more comfortable and you couldn't be more at home. You invade my head with your voice and now you are an eyesore, right in front of my house.

I watch you for a while but I eventually lose interest because you're not doing anything other than drinking and blowing smoke rings into the still night sky.

I watch you watching the stars, which are so clear tonight that Jupiter can be seen next to the moon, and I wonder what you're thinking about. What to do about Fionn. What to do about your job. Are we not so different after all?

6

It is 8.30 a.m. and I am standing in the garden with a builder named Johnny, a large red-cheeked man who acts like he detests me. Nobody is saying anything; he and his colleague, Eddie, leaning on the jackhammer, are just looking at me. Johnny peers over at you in the front garden, asleep in your garden chair with your boots up on the table, and then back at me.

'So what do you want us to do? Wait until he wakes up?'

'No! I—'

'Well, that's what you said.'

It is exactly what I said.

'That's not what I said,' I say, firmly. 'Isn't eight thirty too early to start making so much noise? I thought the official start time for building works was nine a.m.'

He looks around. 'Most people are at work.'

'Not on this street,' I reply. 'No one works on this street.' Not any more.

It is an unusual thing to say, but it is entirely true. He looks at me, confused, then back at the guy with the jackhammer like I'm crazy.

'Look, love, you said you needed this done immediately.

53

I have two days to finish this job and then I'm on to something else, so I either start now or—'

'Fine, fine. Start now.'

'I'll be back at six to take a look.'

'Where are you going?'

'Another job. Eddie can handle it.'

Without a word, Eddie, who looks about seventeen, puts
on his headphones. I hurry inside. I stand at the window
in the TV room that faces your garden and I watch you at
the table, head back, in a peaceful sleep after your drunken
stupor. You have a blanket draped over you. I wonder if
your wife did this or if you got it from the car during the
night after you woke up, freezing. Common sense ought
to have told you to stay in the car and put the heater on,
but you're not one for listening to sense.

Something most definitely seems off this morning. Aside
from the fact you are sleeping in the middle of your
destroyed garden on lopsided, badly placed garden furniture
for everybody to see, your house would usually be busy at
this hour. The kids are back at school, your wife should
be coming and going as she drops them off and goes about
her errands, but there's nothing happening this morning.
There have been no signs of life from the house, the curtains
are exactly as they were yesterday morning. Your wife's car
is gone. The umbrella is still stuck in the tree. There are
no visible signs of your family at home.

Suddenly the jackhammer starts up and even from inside
the house the noise is so loud that I feel the vibrations in
my chest. I think for the first time that I should have alerted
the neighbours to the disruption that will be occurring over
the next few days as they dig up my perfectly fine paving
to make way for some grass. They would have done that
for me, I'm sure.

You leap up from the chair, arms and legs flying everywhere, and look around as if you've come under attack. It takes you a moment to assess where you are, what's happening, what you have done. And then you take in the builder in my garden. You immediately charge over to my house. My heart pounds and I don't know exactly why. We have never spoken before, not so much as a hello or a wave in passing. Apart from when you caught me watching you from my bedroom window on New Year's Eve, you have never even acknowledged my existence, nor I yours, because I detest you and everything you stand for, because you couldn't understand how any mother, even a dying mother, could be sad about leaving her child with Down syndrome in the world without her. I relive the comments I heard you and your callers say on that night that I fell in hate with you and by the time you reach my garden I am ready for the fight.

I can see you shouting at Eddie. Eddie cannot possibly hear you over the noise and the headphones, but he can see the man standing in front of him, mouth opening and closing angrily, hand on one hip, the other arm pointing to a house, demanding to be heard. Eddie ignores you and continues digging up my expensive paving. I make my way to the hall and I pace before the door, waiting for you to call. I jump when the doorbell rings. Just once. Nothing rude about it at all. A single push, a bright briiing, nothing at all like the routine with your wife.

I open the door and you and I are face to face for the first time ever. This is for my sister, this is for you, Heather, this is for my mother, for the unfairness in her having to leave the daughter she never wanted to leave. I say this to myself over and over, opening and closing my hands, ready to fight.

'Yes?' I say, and already it's confrontational.

You seem taken aback by my tone.

'Good morning,' you say patronisingly, as if to tell me, that's how to begin a conversation, as if you know the tiniest, minutest thing about polite conversation. You hold out your hand. 'I'm Matt, I live across the road.'

This is very difficult for me. I am not a rude person, but I look at your hand and back at your unshaven face, your bloodshot eyes, the smell of alcohol emanating from every pore, your mouth that I dislike so much because of the words that come out of it, and I move my hands to the back pockets of my jeans. My heart drums maniacally as I do this. For you, Heather, for you, Mum.

You look at me, incredulous. You take your hand back, shove it into your coat pocket.

'Have I missed something? It's eight thirty a.m. and you're digging up the ground! Is there something we should all know about? Some oil reserves, perhaps, that we can all share?'

You are still drunk, I can tell. Despite your feet being planted firmly on the ground, your body is moving in a circular motion like Michael Jackson's leaning dance move.

'If it's disturbing you so much, maybe you'd find it easier to camp in your *back* garden for the next few days.'

You look at me like I'm the biggest, craziest bitch and then you walk away.

There are many things that I could have said. Many many ways I could have conveyed my disappointment in the way you discussed Down syndrome. A letter. An invitation to coffee, perhaps. An adult conversation. Instead I said that, on our first meeting. I am immediately sorry, not because I may have hurt you, but because I think I may have wasted an opportunity to actually do something important in the right way. And then it occurs to me for the first time that you probably don't even remember that particular show. You have done so many, they probably mean nothing to you. I'm just an obnoxious neighbour who didn't tell you about her building works.

I watch you cross the road to your house. Eddie is still ignoring the world and digging up the ground, the sound of it drumming in my head. You walk up and down the front and back of your house, staring in the windows, trying to figure out how to get in. You stagger a little, still drunk. Then you go to the table and I think you're going to sit down but instead you pick up a garden chair and carry it to the front door. You swing it back with all your might and then slam it once, twice, three times against the window beside your front door, smashing the glass. None of this can be heard over the sound of the drill. You turn your body sideways, your stocky build making it difficult for you to slide in through the narrow space you've created, but eventually you gain entry to your house.

Despite the fact I have witnessed you do this, you once again have made me feel like the irrational one.

7

Eddie works solidly for two hours, then disappears for three hours. During this time the machine is sitting in my front garden, which now resembles the scene of an earthquake. He has wreaked mayhem and I hate looking at it, but I can't help it because I am watching out the window, not for you – I know you won't surface for hours – but for Eddie who wandered off down the road still wearing his hard hat and never came back. I call Johnny, who doesn't answer and his phone has no messaging service. This is not a good sign. He was recommended to me by the landscaper I've hired for my garden, which is also not a good sign.

My mobile rings and it's a private number so I don't answer. My aunt Jennifer has told me, drunkenly on Christmas Day, that my cousin Kevin is coming home in the New Year and wants to get in touch. This is the New Year and I have been fielding my calls like the CIA. Kevin left Ireland when he was twenty-two, at first travelling the world, and then eventually settling in Australia, though I don't think Kevin ever *settled*. He went off to find himself after a flurry of family drama and never came back, not even for Christmas, birthdays or my mum's funeral. This is the same Kevin who told me I'd die when I was five – and who told me he was in love with me when I was seventeen.

My aunt was away with my mum for the weekend on one of their retreats to help Mum and, as I always did then, I was sleeping over in their house. My uncle Billy was watching TV and Kevin and I were sitting in the back garden on the swing set, spilling our hearts out to one another. I was telling him about Mum being sick, and he was listening. He was doing a really good job of listening. And then he told me his secret: that he'd just discovered he was adopted. He said he felt betrayed, after all this time, but it suddenly made sense to him, all the feelings he'd been having. About me. He was in love with me. Next thing I knew, he was on me, hands everywhere, hot breath and slippery tongue in my mouth. Whenever I thought about him after that I'd wash my mouth out for as long as I could. He may not have been my cousin in blood, but he was my *cousin*. We'd played Lord of the Flies in the trees at the back of his garden, we'd tied his brother Michael up and roasted him on the spit, we'd played dress-up and put on shows standing on windowsills. We'd done *family* things together. Every memory of him I had was tied up in him being my *cousin*. I felt disgusted by him.

We didn't speak after that. I never told my aunt, but I knew that she knew. I assumed my mum had told her, but she never discussed it with me. After that first year she went from being nervously apologetic about what had happened to being irritated by me. I think she felt that my forgiving him would be the one thing that would bring him back to her. He hadn't left the country at that stage, but Kevin had never wanted to be a part of anything or anyone, not least his family, he'd always been troubled, he'd always been unsure of himself and everyone around him. I'd had enough to deal with at that time; his issues were too much for me. Maybe that's cruel, but at seventeen there was no understanding of his problems; he was my gross adopted cousin with problems who'd kissed me, and I wanted him the hell away from me. But now he is back and one of these days I will have to face him. I don't have an issue with him any more, I no longer have the need to wash my mouth out when I think of him. Nevertheless, even though I have nothing of importance to do, I can think of better ways to spend my days than engaging in an awkward conversation with a cousin who tried to French kiss me on a garden swing sixteen years ago.

It is while I'm watching out the window and waiting for Eddie to return that the house phone rings. Nobody has the number apart from Dad and Heather, and it is usually only Heather who calls, so I answer it.

'Could I speak with Jasmine Butler, please?'

I pause, trying to place the voice. I don't think it's Kevin. I'm imagining he would have an Australian accent now, but maybe not. Either way, I don't think it's him. Aunt Jennifer would have to be incredibly cruel to give him the number. There's an accent that I can't quite place hiding behind a Dublin accent, somewhere outside of Dublin but inside Ireland. A gentle country lilt.

'Who is speaking?'

'Am I speaking to Jasmine Butler?' he asks.

I smile and try to hide my amusement. 'Could you tell me who's speaking, please? I'm Ms Butler's housekeeper.'

'Ah, I'm sorry,' he says, perfectly happy and charming. 'And what is your name?'

Who is this? *He* called *me* and now he is trying to take control, but not in a rude way, he is utterly polite and has a lovely tone. I can't place the accent. Not Dublin. Not Northern. Not Southern either. Midlands? No. Charming, though. Probably a salesman. And now I have to think of a name and get him off the phone. I look at the hall table beside me and see the pen beside the charging base for the phone.

'Pen,' I say, and try not to laugh. 'Pen-ny. Penelope, but people call me Penny.'

'And sometimes Pen?' he asks.

'Yes.' I smile.

'Can I get your surname?'

'Is this for a survey or something?'

'Oh no, just in case I call you again and Ms Butler isn't home. On the off chance that that happens.'

I laugh again at his sarcasm. 'Ah.' I look down at the table and see the notepad beside the pen. I roll my eyes. 'Pad.' I cough to conceal my laugh. 'Paddington.'

'Okay, Penelope Paddington,' he repeats, and I'm sure he knows. If he has any sense, he knows. 'Do you know when Ms Butler will be home?'

'I couldn't say.' I sit down on the arm of the couch, still looking outside, and I see Dr Jameson at the front door of your house. 'She comes and goes. With work.' Dr Jameson is looking in through the broken glass. 'What's this about?'

'It's a private matter,' he says politely, warmly. 'I'd prefer to discuss it with her herself.'

'Does she know you?' I ask.

'Not yet,' he says, 'But maybe you could tell her I called.'

'Of course.' I pick up the pen and paper to take his details.

'I'll try her on her mobile,' he says.

'You have her mobile?'

'And her work number, but I called the office and she's unavailable.'

That stops me. Somebody who knows me well enough to have all three numbers yet has no idea that I was fired. I am flummoxed.

'Thanks, Penelope, you've been a great help. Have a good day.' He hangs up and I'm left listening to the dial tone, confused.

'Jasmine,' I call to myself in a sing-song tone. 'An absolute weirdo just called looking for you.'

Dr Jameson is walking across the road to me.

'Hello, Dr Jameson,' I greet him, seeing the white envelope in his hand and wondering what on earth the street is planning now and how much I need to contribute.

'Hello, Jasmine.'

He is dressed perfectly as usual in a shirt and V-neck sweater, trousers with the perfect crease down the middle, polished shoes. He is smaller than me, and at five foot eight I feel like an exotic, unnatural creature beside him. My hair is bright red, fire-engine red, or *booster scarlet power* as L'Oréal calls it. Naturally I'm brown-haired, but neither me nor the rest of the world has seen that since I was fifteen, the only traces of it now are my eyebrows, as my scalp is increasingly sprouting grey hairs rather than brown. The red, I'm told, makes my eye colour stand out even more than usual; they're a shade of turquoise that I'm used to most people commenting on. My eyes and my hair are the first things anybody ever sees of me. Whether I'm at work or at a party, I always, absolutely always go out with my ultra-jet-black eyeliner. I'm all eyes and hair. And boobs. They too are rather large, but I do nothing unnatural to accentuate them, they stick out and up all by themselves, clever things.

'I'm sorry about the noise this morning,' I say, genuinely meaning it. 'I should have warned you in advance.'

'Not at all . . .' He waves his hand dismissively, as though in a rush to say something else. 'I was across the way, looking for our friend, but it seems he's otherwise detained,' he says, as if our friend – meaning you – is out in the back garden making animal balloons for a group of kids and not passed out on the bathroom floor in a pool of his own vomit. Just guessing.

'Amy gave this to me for Mr Marshall – we can call him Matt, can't we?' The way he looks at me conspiratorially makes me think that he knows I've been watching, a lot. But he can't know that, unless he's watching me, and I know that's not true because I watch him.

'Who's Amy?'

'Matt's wife.'

'Ah. Yes. Of course.' Like I'd known but had forgotten. I had not known.

'I think it's rather urgent that he receives this' – he waves the white envelope – 'but he's not responding. I would leave it in the, er . . . open window, but I couldn't be sure that he'd get it. Besides there's a copy which I'd like to give to you.' He holds out an envelope to me.

'A copy of what?'

'The house key. Amy cut two extra keys for the neighbours – she thought it might come in handy,' he says, in a surprised way, when we both know it is the most obvious and sensible thing we've ever heard. 'I don't think she's there, or that she'll be there for a while,' he says, his eyes piercing into mine.

Ah. Understood.

I move my hands away from the key and envelope that he's thrusting at me.

'I think it's best if you keep these, Dr Jameson. I'm not the right person to mind them.'

'Why so?'

'You know my life, I'm coming and going all the time. I'm so busy. Work and . . . you know, *things*. I think it would be better to leave them with somebody who is here more.'

'Ah. I was under the impression that you . . . well, that you are home more often these days.'

Stung. 'Well, yes, but I still think it's better that you keep them.' I am standing my ground.

'I have a key already, but I'm going away for a fortnight. My nephew has asked me to go on holiday with his family. This is the first time,' his face lights up. 'Rather polite of them, though I'm sure he had to be convinced of it by Stella. Lovely lady. And I do appreciate it. Spain,' he says, eyes twinkling. 'Anyway . . .' his face darkens, 'I'll have to find a home for these.' He looks extremely bothered by this.

As guilty as it makes me feel, I can't do this. I can't take somebody's key into my home. A perfect stranger. It's weird. I don't want to be involved. I want to keep to myself. I know I watch you, but . . . I can't do this. I won't be moved, despite his worried, befuddled face. If I had a job, I wouldn't be in this suburban mess right now, having to care about other people's issues that they ought to be keeping to themselves.

'Maybe you could give them to Mr and Mrs Malone.' I have no idea of their names. I've lived next door to them for four years and I still don't know, even though they send me a Christmas card every year with both their names on.

'Well, that's an idea,' he says uncertainly, and I know why he is uncertain. He doesn't want to bring them trouble. When you are locked out of your house in your angry drunken state it should not fall upon Mr and Mr Malone, who are in their seventies, to deal with your problems. The same can be said of the Murphys and the Lennons. He's right, I know this, but I just can't. 'Are you sure you won't?' he asks one more time.

'Positive,' I say firmly, shaking my head. I will not get drawn into this.

'I understand.' He nods, lips pursed, and takes the envelope back into his two hands. He fixes me with a look and I know that he has witnessed the same nightly scene that I have. 'I *do* understand.'

He bids me farewell and I have to break into a run to prevent him stepping into the road as an ambulance comes racing along at full speed. We both automatically look across to your house, thinking something must have happened, but the ambulance stops outside the Malones' house and the paramedics rush to the door.

'Oh, goodness,' he says. I have never known anyone to say as many crikeys, fiddlesticks, goodnesses, goshes, and okey-dokeys as Dr Jameson.

Standing beside him, I watch as Mrs Malone is carried out on a stretcher, an oxygen mask over her face, and loaded into the back of the ambulance. A grey-faced Mr Malone follows behind them. He looks shell-shocked. It breaks my heart right there and then. I hope it wasn't my fault. I hope it wasn't the drill in my garden that gave her a heart attack as it had almost given you one.

'Vincent,' he says, seeing Dr Jameson. 'Marjorie.' I assume this is his wife and feel terrible for never knowing her name. Poor Marjorie. I hope that she is okay.

'I'll take care of her, Jimmy,' Dr Jameson says. 'Twice a day? Food in the cupboard?'

'Yes,' Mr Malone says breathlessly as he is helped into the back of the ambulance.

No. Not the wife.

The doors close and the ambulance speeds off, leaving the street as empty as it was, as if nothing has happened at all, the siren quietening as it drives further away.

'Dear, dear,' my neighbour says, seeming shaken too. 'Goodness gracious.'

'Are you okay, Dr Jameson?'

'Vincent, please – I haven't practised for ten years now,' he says absent-mindedly. 'I'd better go feed the cat. Who will feed it while I'm gone? Perhaps I shouldn't go. First this' – he looks at the envelope and key in his hand – 'now the Malones. Yes, perhaps I'm needed here.'

I feel nothing but guilt and dread, and a slight grudge that the universe has conspired against me. It would be rude of me to suggest another neighbour at this point, though it is what I want to do. Two no's in one day would not make me look good.

'I'll feed the cat while you're away,' I say. 'As long as you show me where everything is.'

'Rightso.' He nods, still shaken.

'How do we get in?' I look at their empty house, perfect with its garden gnomes, its little signs for leprechauns crossing, and fairy doors stuck on to a tree for their grand-children, slab stones leading all around the garden to explore behind trees and under weeping willows. The blinds are from the eighties, beiges and salmon pinks, all scrunched up like puffballs at the top of the windows, chintzy china on the windowsills and a table near the window filled with photographs. It is like a dollhouse stuck in a time warp, lovingly decorated and cared for.

'I have their key,' he says.

Of course he does. It seems everybody has everybody's keys on this street apart from mine. He looks down at the envelope in his hands, your single key inside it, as though it's the first time he's seen it. I notice his hands are shaking.

'Vincent, I'll take that,' I say gently, placing a hand over his as I take it from him.

And so that is how I end up with the letter from your wife to you and a spare key to your house.

Just so you know, I never wanted them from the start.

8

Eddie returns and does another two hours' work. I know this because I am in the middle of forking cat food into Marjorie's bowl when she leaps out of her skin with fright at the sound of the drill and she disappears. I think about searching for her but I don't want to wander around the rooms and intrude, and she's a cat, she'll be fine. Eddie is hard at work when Johnny returns to inspect the job and it's as if he never left at all. He listens to my complaint about Eddie without blinking, or without commenting, inspects the work, declares that they're on schedule and they leave in a battered red van half an hour early because they have another job. They don't go far, they reverse directly into your driveway and hop out. I'm aware that I've turned into a curtain twitcher but I can't help it, I'm intrigued. Johnny measures the broken window panel beside the front door, then they take a wooden board from the back of the van, and I can't see them but I can hear them sawing from behind the open doors. It's only five thirty and it's pitch-black outside. They are working in relative darkness, lit only by the porch light, and there is a faint glow coming from the back of the house, the kitchen. You must be awake now.

They spend ten minutes securing the wooden board to your window, then they hop into the red van and drive off. My garden is nowhere close to being complete.

I have your letter in my hand. Dr Jameson has made me promise that I will hand it to you directly. He and I must know that you've received it so he can tell Amy. I've left the key to your house on my kitchen counter, it looks alien there but I can't think of where to put it. The key seems to stick out, almost throbbing on the table; wherever I sit or stand my eye is drawn to it. It feels wrong, having something of yours in my home. I look down and turn over the letter. I guess your wife, Amy, has left you, finally, and has entrusted her neighbours to make certain her words, her reasoning – I'm sure she would have taken a long time, painstakingly labouring over the letter – will reach you. I feel that I owe it to her to see that you get this letter. I should enjoy giving it to you, but I don't and I'm glad about that. I'm not numb to human emotions the way you are.

I put on my coat and pick up the envelope. My mobile rings, a number I don't recognise. Thinking it is the peculiar salesman, I answer it.

'Hi, Jasmine, it's Kevin.'

As my heart sinks into my stomach I watch as you leave the house, get into your car and drive away while I listen to the cousin who tried to kiss me tell me he's home.

I can't sleep. Not just because I've arranged to meet with my cousin Kevin in a few days – out, not in my home so I can leave him when I want to – but because I'm trying to run through all the possible scenarios that could happen later when you return. Me giving you your key, your letter, me opening your door, you attacking me in your drunken state, throwing a chair at me, shouting at me, who knows.

I did not want to take this on, but neighbourly duty made me feel obliged.

I'm wide awake when you drive home. 'Paradise City' is blaring again. You brake before you hit the garage door, you take the keys from the ignition, you stumble to the door, trip over your feet a few times while you concentrate on the keys jingling in your hands. It takes you a while, but you get the key in the door. You stumble inside and close the door. The hall light goes on. The landing light goes on. The hall light goes off. Your bedroom light goes on. Five minutes later your bedroom light goes off.

Suddenly my bedroom is eerily quiet and I realise I've been holding my breath. I lie down, feeling confused.

I am disappointed.

At the weekend I have my dinner party. There are eight of us. These are close friends of mine. Bianca is not here, she is at home with her newborn son, but Tristan has come out. He is asleep in the armchair by the fire before we even sit down to our starters. We leave him there and begin without him.

Most of the conversation revolves around their new children. I like this, it's a distraction. I learn a lot about colic and I put on a concerned face when they discuss sleep deprivation; then they move on to weaning, discussing appropriate vegetables and fruits. A daddy has to google whether kiwi fruit is an acceptable first fruit. I get a thirty-minute earful from Caroline about her sex life with her new boyfriend since separating from her dirt-bag husband. I also like this, it's a distraction. It's real life, it's things that I want to hear about. Then attention turns to me and my job, and though they are my friends and I adore them and they are gentle, I can't bring myself to talk about it honestly. I tell them I am enjoying the break and join in with them about how great it is to be paid to kick around at home. They laugh as I try to make them jealous with exaggerated stories of lie-ins and book-reading and the mere luxury of *time* that I have to myself to do whatever I please. However it feels unnatural and I'm uncomfortable, like I'm playing a part, because I don't believe a word of what I'm saying. I am never more grateful to hear the sound of your jeep. I hope that you are more trashed than usual.

I haven't told my friends about your recent drunken late-night antics. I don't know why this is. It is perfect fodder. They would love to hear all about it, and what makes it juicier is that you're famous. But I can't bring myself to tell anyone. It's as if it's my secret. I've chosen to protect you and I don't know why. Perhaps I take your behaviour and your situation too seriously to make a joke about it at a dinner party. You have children, a wife who has just left you. I loathe you, everybody who knows me properly knows that, and nothing about you makes me want to laugh at you. I pull the curtains so that they can't see you.

I hear you banging, but everybody continues talking, this time a debate about who should get their tubes tied and who should get the snip, and they don't notice your noise. They think I'm joking when I say that I would like the snip, but I haven't been concentrating.

Suddenly everything is quiet outside. I can't concentrate and start to feel agitated, nervous that they will hear you, that the boys will want to go outside and see you, jeer at you or help you, and ruin my private thing that I have with you. I know this is odd. This is all that I have and only I can truly understand what goes on with you at night. I don't want to have to explain.

I clear away the dessert plates; my friends are talking and laughing, the atmosphere is great and Tristan is still asleep in the armchair, baking by the open fire. Caroline helps me and we spend another few minutes in the kitchen while she fills me in on the things she and her new boyfriend have been doing. I should be shocked by what I hear, she wants me to be shocked, but I can't concentrate, I keep thinking of you outside. And the key is beside me on the counter, still throbbing. When Caroline nips out to go to the toilet, I make my escape; grabbing the letter and your key, I pull on my coat and slip outside without anybody noticing.

As I cross the road I can see you sitting at the table. It is 11 p.m. Early for you to return home. You are eating from a McDonald's bag. You watch me cross the road and I feel self-conscious. I wrap my arms around my body, pretending to feel colder than I do with the alcohol keeping me warm. I stop at the table.

'Hi,' I say.

You look at me, bleary-eyed. I've never seen you sober, up close. I've never seen you drunk up close either; you were in between when we met the other morning so I'm not sure exactly what state you're in, but you're sitting outside eating a McDonald's at eleven o'clock at night in three-degree weather, the smell of alcohol heavy in the air, so you can't be fully compos mentis.

'Hi,' you say.

It's a positive start.

'Dr Jameson asked me to give this to you.' I hold out the envelope.

You take it, look at it and put it down on the table.

'Dr J's away?'

'He said his nephew invited him to Spain.'

'Did he?' You light up. 'About time.'

This surprises me. I didn't know that you and Dr Jameson were close. Not that your response hints at closeness, but it hints at some kind of relationship.

'You know Dr J's wife died fifteen years ago, they had no kids, his brother and his wife both passed away, the only family he has is that nephew and he never visits or invites Dr J to anything,' you say, clearly annoyed about this. Then you burp. 'Excuse me.'

'Oh,' is all I know to say.

You look at me.

'You live across the road?'

I'm confused. I can't tell whether you are pretending we have never met or if you genuinely don't remember. I try to figure you out.

'You do. In number three, don't you?'

'Yes,' I finally say.

'I'm Matt.' You hold out your hand.

I'm not sure if it's a new beginning; it could be staged, in which case you will pull your hand away and stick out your tongue as soon as I reach out to you. Whatever your motive, if you've forgotten my rudeness from a few days ago, this is a fresh chance for me to do what I should have done.

'Jasmine,' I say, and reach out to take your hand.

It's not so much like shaking hands with the devil as I thought. Your hand is ice-cold, your skin rough like it's chapped from the winter chill.

'He also gave me a copy of the key to your house. Your wife made copies for him and me.' I hold it out to you.

You look at it warily.

'I don't have to keep the key if you don't want me to.'

'Why wouldn't I want you to?'

'I don't know. You don't know me. Anyway, here. You can let yourself in and keep the key if you want.'

You look at the key. 'It's probably better if you keep it.'

You carry on looking at me and I start to feel uncomfortable. I'm not sure what to do; you clearly have no intention of moving, so I go to your front door and open it.

'Are you having a party?' you ask, looking across at the parked cars.

'Just dinner.'

I feel bad then. You're eating from a McDonald's bag; am I supposed to invite you in? No, we're strangers, and you have been the enemy since I was a teenager, I can't invite you in.

'What are you doing to your garden?'

'Putting down grass.'

'Why?'

I laugh lightly. 'Good question.'

You pick up the envelope. 'Will you read this to me?'

'No.'

'Why not?'

'Why don't *you* read it?'

'I can barely see straight.'

But you don't seem that drunk and your speech is fine.

'And I've left my glasses inside,' you add.

'No.' I fold my arms and back away. 'It's private.'

'How do you know it's private?'

'It's for you.'

'It could be a neighbourhood thing. Dr J's always organising something. A barbecue.'

'In January?'

'A drinks reception about recycling then.' You like that and you chuckle. I can hear the cigarettes in your chest, a wheezy, dirty laugh.

'He said it's from your wife.'

Silence.

At certain angles I see your handsomeness. It's the way you tilt your head when you're thinking, or maybe it's the moonlight, but whatever it is you have moments when you transform. Blue eyes, strawberry-blond hair, button nose. Or maybe that's how you always look and my dislike for you taints you.

You put the envelope down on the table and push it with one finger towards me. 'Read it.'

I pick it up and look at it. Turn it over a few times.

'I can't. I'm sorry.' I place it down on the table. You stare at the envelope and say nothing. 'Goodnight.'

I walk back to the house, straight into the sound of the raucous laughter of my friends. I take my coat off. Tristan is still asleep on the chair. I don't think anyone has noticed I'd even left. I rejoin the table with another bottle of wine and sit down for a moment, before getting up to open the curtains a little. You're still at the table. You look up and see me and then you stand and go into the house, close the door behind you. I can still see the white envelope on the table, glowing under the moonlight.

A light rain starts.

I watch the envelope as the rain gets heavier. I can't concentrate. Rachel is talking about something now, everybody is listening, her eyes are filled, I know that it's important, it's about her dad who's sick, they've just learned he has cancer, but I can't concentrate. I keep looking out the window at the envelope as the rain gets heavier. Rachel's husband reaches for her hand to help her continue. I mumble something about getting her a tissue, then go outside without my coat, run across the road and retrieve the envelope.

I don't know you, and I don't owe you, but I do know that we all have a self-destruct button and I can't let you do that. Not on my watch.

9

Johnny and Eddie finally finish digging up my paving one week later than promised, citing so many excuses and technical reasons that I don't know where to begin arguing with them, but at least one hundred square metres has been cleared for laying turf and the remainder of my garden is still my lovely paving. My dad tells me to hang on to the broken stones that they have dug up from the ground because he believes they have value, so I keep them in a small skip on my driveway. His beliefs are vindicated by Johnny's sudden eagerness to help 'get rid' of them for me. I try to think of ways that I can use them, but really I have no idea and suspect that I will probably throw them out.

Dad and Leilah invite me and Heather to lunch on Thursday. On Mondays Heather works in a restaurant, clearing tables and stacking the dishwasher; on Wednesdays she works at the cinema, escorting people to their seats and cleaning up the popcorn and mess afterwards, and on Fridays she works at a local solicitor's office, doing the post, shredding papers and photocopying. She loves all of her jobs. On Saturday mornings she attends her drama and music class and on Tuesdays she goes to a day service where she hangs out with friends. It only leaves Thursdays and Sundays for us, and my work hours used to mean that Sunday was our day. It's been that way for the past ten years. I would go to the ends of the earth to avoid missing that day with her. Our activities vary; sometimes she has very specific aims in her head, other times she is quiet and will let me make the decision. We go to the cinema a lot: she loves animation and knows every single word to *The Little Mermaid*. Sometimes all she wants to do is sit on the floor in front of the television and watch it on repeat. My Christmas gift to her was a trip to see Disney on Ice. They dedicated the entire first act to *The Little Mermaid* and I have never seen Heather so quiet, so completely lost in anything in all of my life. It was beautiful, and being with her is always beautiful. When Ursula the Sea Witch came on stage, an enormous blow-up Octopus slid across the ice and there was evil witch music and loud cackling. Lots of children started crying and I was worried that Heather would be afraid, but she held my hand and gave it a squeeze, and whispered to me, 'It will be okay, Jasmine,' so I knew that she was minding me, she was worried about me being afraid. She is my older sister and is constantly protecting me, even when I think it's me that is protecting her. When the show was over and the lights went up and the mess of spilled popcorn and slush puppies was revealed and all the magic was gone, she looked at me, her hands on her chest where her heart is, her tear-filled eyes enormous behind her thick glasses, and she said, 'I am moved, Jasmine. I am so moved.'

I love her, I love everything about her. The only thing I would change about her is the discomfort she often feels due to her hypothyroidism which manifests sometimes for her as fatigue, sluggishness and irritability. I would watch her like a hawk, but she won't let me. After years of trying to teach her in ways that she could understand, what I finally learned about my sister is that Heather always has been and always will be the teacher and that I am her student. Her speech is often unclear, though I can generally understand her, and she has difficulty with her motor skills and her hearing, but Heather can tell you the name of every single Disney character in every single Disney movie, and the writers and singers of every song. She loves music. She has quite a collection of vinyl – despite me introducing her to iPods and iPads, she's an old-school girl at heart and prefers her records. She can tell you the musicians playing the instruments and who has produced and arranged every song. She reads the small print on every album and offers the information at the drop of the hat. When I saw that she had an appetite for this, I fed it and continue to feed it, buying her music, bringing her to live performances. When I was fourteen, I took Heather on a playdate with a little boy called Eddie, with Down syndrome. Eddie loved music too, especially the song 'Blue Suede Shoes' by Elvis. While speaking with his sister I learned that, because he likes the song, they let him play it on repeat all day, which annoyed everybody in the household. But none of them could have been as annoyed as I was; it made me furious that they failed to recognise that this boy had a love for music, not just that one song. They weren't helping to bring out the best in him. When Heather shares her knowledge, people are always surprised and impressed. And what happens when she sees that they're impressed by her? Like all of us, she flourishes.

The most admirable, almost magical thing about Heather is her insight into people, more specifically her insight into their insight into *her*. I see their views of her reflected in her own behaviour. She can read strangers like no one else I've encountered in my life. When speaking with someone who views her with pity or who wants to get away from her, she shrinks, she almost disappears, she becomes a person with Down syndrome because she knows that that is all they see of her. When she is in the company of someone who doesn't care about Down syndrome, like children before they learn to tease, or someone who has experience with the condition, she absolutely glows, she blossoms, she becomes Heather, the person. She often senses these things before I do, and I have learned to understand strangers or at least their opinions of her through Heather. She has the ability to get straight to the truth. This is something that many children possess, but perhaps we lose it as we get older. Heather, on the other hand, has honed this with age and as a result, her sense of right and wrong are so finely tuned.

I drive Heather to where Dad, Leilah and Zara live in a three-bedroom apartment in Sutton Castle. Built in 1880 by the Jameson family – no relation to Dr Jameson that I know of – it is in a prestigious location on seven acres of landscaped gardens overlooking Dublin Bay. The castle was a hotel where we often ate Sunday lunches as a family; it was refurbished during the boom time and the main house was broken up into seven apartments. It's an impressive home, kept beautifully by Leilah in her bohemian style. At thirty-five, Leilah is around the same age as Heather and I, yet she seems so far away from becoming any kind of a friend of mine. She is a young woman who married my dad and for that I will always wonder what is wrong with her. I have no actual problem with Leilah, but distance is my friend and that's where I keep her. Heather on the other hand warmed to her immediately, holding her hand on the first meeting, which made Leilah blush. It was an act that neither Leilah nor Dad knew was the greatest compliment ever given. Heather has correctly sensed my feelings toward Leilah and, though we've never discussed it, she tries to find things that Leilah and I have in common, like a mother trying to help two little girls become friends at a party. It is endearing and sweet, and I love this about her. Even though we both go along with it purely for Heather's sake, it does oddly enough help us to communicate.

Zara pulls the door open dressed as a pirate. She punches the air before us with a plastic hook on the end of her hand and yells 'Arrrrrrgh, mateys!'

I feel Heather flex beside me. Heather is fond of Zara, though a little unsure. Zara, at three, can be temperamental. Her loud protests, or sudden explosive tears, or even extreme hyperness can make Heather very unsettled.

'Well, arrrrrgh yourself.' I go down on my knees to hug her, battling her pirate protestations and walk-the-plank threats, and I end up lying on the floor with her straddling me, the tip of her hook held to my neck. Heather swiftly sidesteps us and softly makes her way down the hall and into the living area.

Zara presses the plastic hook against my skin, and pushes her face near mine. 'If you see that Peter Pan, you tell him I'm lookin' for him – him and that little fairy he's with.' She glares at me meanly then jumps up and runs down the hall.

I'm left lying on the ground alone, laughing.

On this occasion I've brought a bracelet-making set for Heather and she settles down at the table to focus on sliding the beads on to the string. Zara is keen to play with it too and though we tell her calmly that it is not a toy, that it is Heather's, that Zara must play with her own toys – and the new vet set that I brought her – she has a meltdown, which makes Heather extremely tense. I can see her shoulders bunch up as she focuses threading the beads, her cheeks getting hotter as Zara's wails get louder. Leilah's voice is calm and firm and she removes Zara from the room. I stay beside Heather, my elbow on the table to keep my head propped up, and I watch her intently.

'What are you doing, Jasmine?' she asks.

'Watching you.'

She smiles. 'Why are you watching me, Jasmine?'

'Because you're beautiful,' I say, and she smiles shyly and shakes her head.

'Jasmine!'

I laugh and continue watching her. She giggles, but then eventually disappears into bracelet-making concentration zone. Zara returns into the room quietly, her eyepatch discarded to reveal two sad red eyes. Lollipop in hand, she settles in her corner of the room and plays with the new vet game I bought for her, talking to herself in badly constructed sentences with random words thrown in that she has overheard from us. Heather gives her a quick look and concentrates on her beading. It is easy company for twenty minutes while the two girls concentrate, while Leilah prepares the lunch. I'm not being lazy, we both know it's best that I stay in the room with Zara and Heather in case any further conflict arises.

The smell of garlic drifts from the kitchen as Leilah massages butter and garlic into the lamb. She snips rosemary from the herb garden on the balcony and, after rinsing it off, makes quick little nips into the flesh and inserts the rosemary. My dad isn't home; he's playing golf and will be back in time for lunch, so I put on *Tangled*, the only movie that Zara will concede to watching, and I settle down on the couch for a lazy hour. I wake to feel little butterfly kisses on my face. Heather is smiling down at me, and just seeing her is the most beautiful way to wake up.

'Dad is here, Jasmine,' she says.

I'm groggy, with my shoes off, and my dress up around

81

my waist, and who follows Dad into the living room but Ted Clifford. Ted is over six feet tall and very broad. He fills the doorframe and I feel Heather freeze beside me, her body tensing. In fact everybody tenses, including Leilah, whose look of composure drops for a moment to show that she had no idea Ted was coming to visit.

'Ted,' she says, not hiding her surprise. 'Welcome.'

'Hello, Leilah,' he says, giving her a wet kiss and an overly familiar hug. 'I hope you don't mind me invading your lunch, but Peter lost the golf which meant he had to invite me!' He guffaws loudly.

Leilah smiles, but I can see the true meaning beneath, the tightness around the mouth, the warning signals in her eyes. It ruffles Dad's feathers a bit.

'This must be little Zara,' Ted says, looking down at Zara. From her position on the floor she is looking up at him as if he is the giant from *Jack and the Beanstalk*. She looks at Leilah uncertainly, a wobbly smile-cry expression on her face, but Ted ignores the signs and scoops her up in his arms to plant a big smacker on her face. Leilah diplomatically lifts Zara from his arms and Zara wraps her legs tightly around Leilah's waist and buries her head into her neck to hide from the giant. All the while Dad is beaming, all the while I am seething because this is no coincidence: me and Ted in the same room barely two weeks after Dad raised the issue of asking him to find a job for me. Leilah works two half-days a week so that she can spend afternoons with Zara, Dad is retired, I am unemployed, Heather has a day off: it makes sense for all of us to be eating lunch on a Thursday, but it makes no sense that Ted would be here. He should be working. Instead he is here to talk to me. I feel the anger rising within me and can barely look Dad in the eye.

'You know my daughter, Jasmine,' he says, holding out his hand to display me.

Ted gives me the once-over and comments on how I've grown since we met last. Ted is sixty-five years old, no excuse to treat a woman half his age as though she has just reached puberty and it was all for his benefit. It is clear that he is not surprised that I am here. I'm either paranoid or right about this. We shake hands, and I intend to keep it at that, but he pulls me in for a wet kiss that I find myself wiping off my cheek immediately. Leilah looks at me, empathetic.

'And this is Heather,' Dad says.

As an aside. Not, this is my *daughter* Heather, no display of the arm, no grand gesture. I am sensitive when it comes to Heather – very; I think that is clear from my treatment of you – so I don't always know if what I feel about other people's treatment of her is real or heightened or simply a case of me projecting my fears. Everyone will probably always make mistakes when it comes to her, in my eyes. I do, however, feel that in thirty-four years Dad has done very little to overcome the awkwardness he feels when introducing Heather to strangers, particularly those that he looks up to, people like Ted that he has always had an embarrassing schoolboy crush on, constantly trying to please him, sell his company to and then ultimately under-sell it because *it's Ted* and he wouldn't want Ted to think that he's uncool. It is not necessarily that he is ashamed of Heather, because he is not so cold-hearted, but he is conscious of the fact that some feel uncomfortable around Heather. He deals with this by paying as little attention to her as possible, making as little a deal of her as possible, playing everything down, as if that will make everyone feel more comfortable. Of course his apparent lack of affection for his daughter has the opposite effect. I have on many occasions raised this with him, but he thinks I'm overly emotional and irrational about the whole thing.

'Ah,' Ted says, looking at Heather in a way that I don't like. 'Hallo!' he says in an unusual voice. 'Well, I can't leave you out, can I?' he says and reaches out to shake her hand.

This is a risky move.

As a student of Heather I have learned that all individuals, regardless of disability, are sexual beings. Ensuring that Heather, whose physical development outstrips her emotional development, understands the physical and more particularly the psychological aspects of sexuality has always been of concern to me. It is a continuing lesson, more than ever now, when she yearns for a boyfriend. The last thing I want is for her to be rejected or ridiculed, never mind abused.

To deal with this, from a young age we learned the Circles concept, a system that helps categorise the various levels of personal relationship and physical intimacy. The reason why someone like Ted concerns me is because he has a misguided take on intimacy, seeing as he has kissed and picked up a three-year-old, squeezed a wife, checked me out, and now doesn't want Heather to feel left out. I think this is one time that Heather would be more than happy to be left out.

The Purple Private Circle represents the individual; in this case Heather. The Blue Hug Circle comes next. This represents people who are closest to the person in the purple circle, both physically and emotionally, and it's where close-body hugs are the norm; this circle includes me, Dad, Zara and Leilah. Next comes the Green Faraway Hug Circle. Close friends and extended family members are assigned to this circle. Sometimes friends may want to be closer than this, but Heather must tell them exactly where they stand. Then comes the Yellow Handshake Circle, for friends and acquaintances whose names are known, followed by the

Orange Wave Circle for other, more distant acquaintances, such as children who may want to hug and kiss Heather but she knows she must not, that she must wave at them instead. No physical or emotional contact is involved at this level of intimacy. Finally there is the Red Stranger Circle. No physical contact or conversation is exchanged with people in this category, unless the person is identified by a recognisable badge or uniform. If somebody tries to touch Heather when she doesn't want to be touched, Heather should say 'Stop.' Some people remain strangers forever.

Heather and I are firm in keeping to this, no matter how uncomfortable it makes people feel. While Dad knows the circles code exists, it was Mum who taught it to us. Dad never involved himself in these kinds of things.

I watch Heather looking at his outstretched hand in confusion. I know that she knows what to do, but she looks at me for support.

'Orange, Heather.' Though personally I'd rather keep him in the red zone.

Heather nods then turns to him and waves.

'Only a wave for me?' he asks, like he's speaking to a child and not a thirty-four-year-old woman.

He moves closer and I am about to step in front of him and tell him to stop when Heather holds out her hand. 'Stop. You are not in my Blue Hug Circle.'

But Ted doesn't take her seriously. He chuckles at what she has said, not giving it any consideration, and wraps his arms around her in a bear hug. Heather immediately starts screaming and I pull at his arms to get him away from her.

'Jasmine!' Dad says, as he watches me trying to wrench Ted's arms off her. Leilah gives out to Dad. Zara starts crying and Heather is screaming, manically.

Ted backs off, hands in the air as if he's the victim of a

hold-up, saying, 'All right, all right, I'm only being friendly,' over all the noise.

Dad is apologising to Ted, trying to get him to sit down at the table, barking at Leilah to get him a drink and make him comfortable, but Leilah isn't listening.

'Are you okay, Heather?' Leilah is by my side.

Heather is still screaming, huddled in my arms, and I know that the best thing is for us to leave. She will not want to settle at the table for dinner with him here, after he broke a rather serious rule of hers.

'There's no need to overreact,' Dad says, following us out into the hall. Heather is hiding her head in my chest, cuddling into me, and I wish Dad would shut up. He is talking to me, but she might think it's her he's saying it to.

'Dad, she told him no.'

'It was only a hug, for feck's sake.'

I bite my tongue. I don't even know where to start with telling him off, but before I can get a word out, he erupts.

'That is the last time this happens. We're not doing this any more. I've had enough,' he says, anger rising in him in a way I haven't seen in years. 'No more of this!' He points at me and Heather and then the dinner table, as if this entire episode has happened before and it is our fault.

'Any excuse,' I snap back at him, and I leave the apartment.

I offer to bring Heather home with me, to stay overnight at my place, but she declines, giving my face a maternal pat before she gets out of the car, as if she's sorry that this has all been too much for me. She is happier when she is in her own home, surrounded by her things.

I, on the other hand, return home alone.

10

I am disappointed Heather doesn't stay overnight with me for a number of reasons: one, because I like her company; two, because I want to make sure she is okay after the incident at Dad's; and three, because it would have been a great way for me to cancel the dreaded meeting with my cousin Kevin, which is to take place tomorrow. Or maybe even bring her to see Kevin with me, but Heather is too busy with her Friday job in the solicitor's office.

Our meeting is planned for noon in Starbucks on Dame Street beside the Wax Museum. Lots of tourists, nothing intimate. I will be able to leave when I want to.

Deep down I know that it will be fine. He will apologise for his twenty-two-year-old self, tell me how he always felt lost and alone, an outcast who used force and fear as a way of maintaining control over a life that he felt was out of control. He will tell me that he has done some soul-searching on his travels – kept a journal, started a novel, or maybe he'll have gone all 'hairy feet and sandals' and become a poet. Then again, maybe he ended up working in a bank. He probably met a woman – or maybe a man, who knows – and now that he is content with who he is, he is able to face who he was and apologise for the incident all those years ago. I know that the ice will quickly melt and we can forge on, laughing about how we tied his brother Michael to a tree, danced around him dressed as Indians and accidentally fired an arrow into his leg; or how we stole Fiona's clothes while she was skinny-dipping and put them on the rocks so that she was forced to climb up to get them, barefoot and butt-naked. I might mention the whole 'You are going to die, Jasmine' talk that changed the course of my thinking for ever, and maybe I will go as far as mentioning Santa Claus.

When I see him, I am surprised by his appearance. I don't know what I'm expecting, but it's not what I see. He is thirty-eight and so I should have prepared myself for that. Seeing him makes me feel old; we're grown up now. Suddenly everything disappears and I just feel a fondness towards him. My cousin. So many memories come flooding at me, so many with my mother in them, and I am dumb-founded by how overcome I feel. It has been a long time since I've felt that longing for my mum; it leaves me feeling winded and lost and childlike again, as if I'm reaching for something that is beyond my grasp. For a while her smell lingered at home and I would wrap myself up in her bed in an effort to be close to her; other times I would get a whiff of her perfume from somebody else and I would stop midstride, almost hypnotised as I was transported and locked in the vivid memory of her. But it happened less and less as the years passed by. Everything that used to remind me of her, everything that I saw and heard – restau-rants, shops, roads we'd driven down, buses we'd sat on, parks, songs on the radio, phrases overheard in passing conversations – absolutely everything linked back to her in some way. But of course it did, she died when I was young, when she was still the centre of my world, before I'd had a chance to start making a life for myself. As I'd stayed in the same city that all of those memories were made in, I thought that I would never lose them. Whenever I needed her – my mum fix – I'd go back to those places, hoping to bring her back, summon her energy. Instead, the act of going back made new memories, and every time I went I would add another layer on top of her memory, until eventually I'd buried them completely and all of those places stopped being about my past with her and became my present. It is rare, twelve years on, that I am struck like this, and I know it is because of him, because I haven't seen him since she passed away, so everything I can tie him to is connected with her. He looks up and sees me, and he beams. I feel okay. This is going to be nice, nostalgic. I immediately feel guilty for the Starbucks venue and wonder if I should move our meeting to a restaurant nearby.

He has found a small table, with two chairs where we will have to sit diagonally to avoid our knees meeting. I was hoping to get there first to grab two sinking armchairs well away from each other. He gives me a big hug, a long warm embrace. His hair is thinning, he has wrinkles around his eyes, I think he is the only person I have gone so long without seeing. It's a big leap for the brain and it's oddly disconcerting.

'Wow,' I say when I sit down and stare at a familiar face peeking out at me from behind an unusual mask of time. I don't know where to start.

'You haven't changed,' he beams. 'Still have the red hair.'

'I do,' I laugh.

'And those eyes.' He looks at me intently, then shakes his head and laughs.

'Eh. Yes. Decided to keep the eyes.' I laugh. Nervously.

'So . . .' Long silence while we stare at one another. He is

89

beaming and keeps shaking his head as if he can't believe it. I get it, but enough now, let's move on. I'm once again happy we didn't choose an actual lunch date.

'Coffee?' I say, and he jumps up.

I take a look at him as he orders at the counter. Brown cords, V-neck jumper, shirt, quite conservative, not exactly the latest trend but respectable, responsible, a far cry from the ripped-jeans, long-haired troublemaker.

When he sits down, the routine questions begin. Jobs, life, how long are you here, are you still in touch with Sandy, do you still see Liam, do you remember Elizabeth? Who married who, who's having babies with who, who left who. How Aunt Jennifer is so happy he's returned. I knew I shouldn't have said it as soon as I did. It was a simple enough thing to say, but I should have kept it lighter, more vague, devoid of anything issue-related. Mentioning his 'adoptive' mother who he hadn't travelled home to see in over ten years – though she had visited him – was not safe territory. I kick myself. His posture changes.

'She's happy to have me back here, of course, but she's finding the circumstances difficult. I'm back to find my birth parents,' he says, his hands cupped around the enormous mug of coffee. He is looking down, all I can see are long black eyelashes, and when he looks up I recognise those lost, confused, tortured puppy eyes. He is still searching, though he seems less angry, the spiteful look is gone. We talk about seeking his biological mother some more, about his long-lost sense of identity, his inability to settle down and have his own children without understanding his own lineage, about not being able to settle in relationships, about feeling tied to someone else, elsewhere all this time. I hope I am reassuring him. And then we get to the awkward moment.

'What I said on the swing . . .' he begins, as if it was five minutes ago and not sixteen years, 'It was wrong of me to do what I did. I was young, I was so confused, I scared you, I know that, and I'm sorry. I went away and tried to figure it out, tried to figure everything out really, I told myself that I must have got our friendship confused. We always had so much in common, I always felt you understood me. The whole thing with you and your dad . . .' Which confuses me again, because there was nothing between me and dad, but never mind. 'I went away and tried to forget you, but when I was gone, all the other women . . .' And it gets uncomfortable for a while as I hear about his long list of conquests with whom he does not feel at peace, and then, BAM! 'I couldn't stop thinking of you. All the time, my mind kept coming back to you. But I knew how you felt about me. How the whole family felt about me. It's why I couldn't come back. But now . . . Jasmine, I haven't changed my mind at all from that moment on the swing. I am utterly in love with you.'

I am usually an emotionally stable person. I feel that I cope with things well. I am not dramatic, I am rational, I reason things relatively well. But this . . . I can't. Not now, in the middle of my own stuff. I apologise, then stand up and take my leave.

When I get home later, I find the landscaper packing up his van. Though the days are slowly stretching longer, the sky is again black. The new grass is still in rolls, piled up in my driveway in the streetlight.

'What are you doing?' I ask him.

He can hear the edge in my voice; he looks a little taken aback.

'You said the grass would be finished today,' I say.

'The ground took me longer to prepare than I thought. I'll have to come back on Monday.'

'Monday? You told me you work weekends. Why can't you come tomorrow?'

'Another job, I'm afraid.'

'Another job,' I say in a disturbing hiss of a voice. 'Why don't people finish one job before starting another?' He doesn't respond to this so I sigh. 'I thought the turf was supposed to be laid within a day of delivery.'

'They're stored in a shaded area, no frost expected this weekend. It's perfect conditions.' He looks at the turf in a long silence as if waiting for it to speak on its own behalf. He shrugs. 'If you really need to, open the rolls and water them.'

'Water them? It hasn't stopped raining in a week.'

'Well then.' He shrugs again. 'Should be fine.'

'And if they're not, you're paying for them.'

I watch him drive away. I stand in my garden, hands on my hips, staring him off as if my look alone is going to make him stop the van and finish the job. It doesn't. I survey the pile of grass beside me. The first day of February tomorrow. Almost three weeks of waiting for this garden when I could have used the money to go on a holiday, to sit on someone else's green grass.

You leave your house, wave at me. I ignore you because I'm mad at you again, I'm mad at everyone and you are always first on my list, you will always feel my wrath. You get in your jeep and drive away. Dr Jameson is away, Mrs Malone is still in hospital, as is Mr Malone who is keeping vigil. I no longer have to feed the cat full-time but only when Mr Malone asks, which doesn't bother me so much any more as Marjorie has turned out to be quite the conversationalist. I look around. I can't tell whether anyone's home in the other houses, but it feels like an empty street. There is nothing I can do about the garden, only pray that a deep frost doesn't suddenly descend on my new grass.

That night I can't sleep. I am tossing and turning with anger over my father: his treatment of Heather, his attempt to line me up for a job in his old company – for I'm almost convinced that's what he's doing. I am further distressed by Kevin's declaration of love for me yet again and my messy garden bothers me. Everything feels unfinished – worse than unfinished: torn, as if everything's been ripped and left ragged at the ends. It is a peculiar way to explain it, but that's how I feel. I can't settle with all of these thoughts, these angry thoughts that can't be contained or filed away somewhere else while I sleep. I have nothing to distract me. Ordinarily I would have a meeting to plan for, an aim, an objective, a new idea, a presentation – something, *anything* to take my mind off the useless thoughts that circulate in my head. Getting up, I go downstairs and turn the security lights in the front garden on full. They are so bright they are like floodlights. What I see angers me. Inefficiency. My blood boils.

I put my coat on over my pyjamas and go outside. I look at the stacked rolls of grass and I look at the cleared patch of soil to my right. If you want something done properly, you should do it yourself: always my philosophy. It shouldn't be too hard.

I pick up the first roll of grass and it is heavier than I thought it would be. I drop it, curse and hope I haven't broken it. I stare at the space and try to figure out how to do this. Then I roll. Two hours later I am dirty and sweating. I've lost the coat, which restricted my movements, and instead layered up with an old fleece. I'm covered in muck, grass, sweat and at one stage there are even tears of frustration: for the grass, for the job, for Kevin and for Heather and my mum and the fingernail that I chipped when I bumped it against the skip. I am so lost in myself, in my chore, that I almost jump out of my skin when I hear a cough breaking the silence.

'Sorry,' I hear you say suddenly.

It is three a.m. I look across the road to your garden and I can't see a thing. I see the shape of the garden furniture, but the rest is blackness, all lights are out on the house. My heart is pounding while my eyes furiously search the dark. Then I see the glow of a cigarette, brightening as it's inhaled. It's you. How long have you been there? I didn't hear or see your jeep arrive, and I still don't see it now, which means you have been there the entire time. I want to cry. I mean, I have been crying, quite loudly, thinking nobody could hear me.

'Got locked out,' you say, breaking the silence.

'How long have you been there?' I repeat. Now that I know that you're there I can start to see the outline of you, sitting in the chair at the head of the table, the same chair as usual.

'Few hours.'

'You should have said something.'

I go inside the house to get the spare key and when I walk outside you're standing at your door.

'Why is it so dark over here?'

'Streetlight is broken.'

I look up and realise that's why I couldn't see you. Dr Jameson will be annoyed about this when he returns. On the ground underneath is smashed glass which has fallen and one of my bricks from the skip is in the middle of the road. I wonder why I didn't hear that happening, I was so sure I hadn't slept. I look at you accusingly.

'It was too bright. I couldn't get any sleep,' you say softly. You don't seem that drunk, you are composed, you've had time to sober up – in my company, when I didn't even know you were there – but I can smell the alcohol.

'Where's your jeep?'

'Clamped in town.'

I hand you the key. You open the front door and gives it back to me.

'You should have said something,' I say again, finally looking you in the eye, then glancing away, feeling so vulnerable.

'I didn't want to disturb you. You seemed busy. Sad.'

'I'm not sad,' I snap.

'Sure you're not. Four a.m., you're gardening, I'm smashing lights, we're both fine.' You do the chesty chuckle that I hate. 'Besides, it was nice not to be alone out here for once.'

You give me a small smile before gently closing the door.

When I return to the house I realise my hands are shaking, my throat is dry and closed, my chest feels tight. I can't stop moving. I haven't quite realised what a frenzy I am in until I see that I have walked muck everywhere in confusing circles on the floor, the stop-start trail of a madwoman.

It's the middle of the night, but I can't help it: I pick up the phone.

Larry answers groggily, he always answers. He leaves his phone on all night, constantly expecting to hear the worst news about his daughter every time she leaves the house to go to a disco or stay over in a friend's house in a skirt that's too short, wobbling with Bambi legs on heels that she can't balance on. The stress of her will kill him.

'Larry, it's me.'

'Jasmine,' he says groggily. 'Jesus. What time is it?' I hear him fumbling around. 'Are you okay?'

'Not really, you fired me.'

He sighs. He has the decency to sound embarrassed in the stuttering, half-asleep, respectful response he gives me, but I interrupt him.

'Yeah, yeah, you said that before, but listen, I need to talk about something else. This gardening leave. It's not working for me. We need to cancel it. Stop it.'

He hesitates. 'Jasmine, it was part of the contract. We agreed—'

'Yeah, we agreed, four years ago when I didn't think you were going to fire me and then force me to sit on my arse for an entire year. I need you to stop it.' I sound wired, strung up, like I need a fix. I do. I need work. I need work like a heroin addict needs a fix. I am desperate. 'It's killing me, I swear, Larry. You don't know what this shit does to your head.'

'Jasmine,' he is alert now, his voice steady. 'Are you okay? Are you with—'

'I'm fucking fine, Larry, okay? Listen to me . . .' I tear off the chipped nail with my teeth and realise I've pulled away too much; the air hits the exposed nail bed and it stings and causes me to suck in air loudly. 'I'm not asking for my job back, I'm asking you to reconsider. Actually, not reconsider, just stop this gardening leave thing. It's unnecessary. It's—'

'It's not unnecessary.'

'It is. Or else it's too long. Shorten it. Please? It's been over two months already. That's okay. Two months is fine. Lots of companies leave it at two months. I need to be busy – you know me. I don't want to turn into him across the road, some nocturnal crazy owl man that—'

'Who's across the road?'

'It doesn't matter. What I'm saying is, I need to work, Larry. I need—'

'No one's expecting you not to do anything, Jasmine. You can take on projects.'

'Fucking projects. Like what? Build a volcano of baked beans? This isn't school, Larry, I'm thirty-fucking-three. *I can't NOT work for a year.* Do you know how hard it will be for me to get back to it next year? After a whole year? Who wants someone who *hasn't worked for a year?*'

'Fine. So where will you work?' He is getting feistier, fully awake now. 'Exactly what line of business do you have in mind? Tomorrow, if you were able to go back out there and get a job – tell me where you'd go. Or would you like me to help you out with that answer?'

'I . . .' I falter, because he's intimating something, which is confusing me. 'I don't know what you're—'

'In that case I'll tell you. You'd go to Simon—'

I freeze. 'I wouldn't go to Simon—'

'Yes, you would, Jasmine – you would. Because I know that you met with him. I know that you two had coffee. Straight after you walked out of here, you walked into a restaurant with him. Grafton Tea Rooms, wasn't it?' He's angry now and I can hear the sense of betrayal in his voice. 'The same place where you both used to meet when you were trying to sell the company that you weren't supposed to be selling – isn't that right?'

I'm not expecting him to stop talking so suddenly and my silence is like an admission. By the time I'm ready to speak for myself again, he has resumed:

'See, Jasmine, you have to be careful, don't you? Never know who's watching you. Did you think I wasn't going to hear about that one? Because I did, and I was really fucking pissed, to be honest with you. I also know that he offered you a job and that you said yes, but he wouldn't work with you under the gardening leave terms. I know that because his legal people got in touch with our legal person to enquire about the exact details. Seems a year is too long for him. You're not worth waiting that long for. So don't call me up now, begging me to go easy on you, not when you were going to betray me—'

'Excuse me, who are you to talk about betrayal? We started that company together, Larry, *together* . . .'

We continue talking over one another, the same conversation we had eleven weeks ago when I was fired. In fact, the same conversation we had before I was fired, when he'd heard that I was making preparations with Simon to put us in a good position to sell.

It is pointless, and neither of us is prepared to back down until I hear his wife in the background, a sleepy, angry interruption, and Larry apologises softly then comes back on the phone, loud and angry and clear.

'I'm not going to waste my time with this conversation. But hear me loud and clear, Jasmine: I. Will. Not. Drop. The. Gardening. Leave. Clause. Right now, if I could make it *two years* long I would. I don't care what you do for the year – take a holiday, go on a fucking retreat, try *finishing something you've started* for once in your life – I don't care, just don't fucking call my number again, and especially not at this hour. It's one year. One fucking year and then you can get back to starting and selling and never finishing, same as you always do, okay?'

He hangs up, leaving me shaking, reeling with anger.

I pace the kitchen, mumbling about finishing things that I've started, angrily compiling a list of as many things as

I can think of. He has hit a nerve. It was sudden and surprising and it has hurt me more than anything else he has said, more than the act of firing me. It is in fact, the most hurtful thing anyone has ever said to me and I am shaking. I continue to debate the point with him in my mind, but it is useless as I am me and I am him, and me as me will always win. I look at the mess of a garden, which sends me into a spiral of anger. I go outside and kick a roll of grass, my foot punctures the roll, and then I stamp on it, sending it tumbling off the pile and down on to the ground, opening and unravelling. The grass splits at the hole where I've kicked it. Embarrassed by my actions, and surprised, I look up and see your curtains flutter. I go back inside and slam the door.

I spend a long time in the shower, crying with frustration, the hot water stinging my skin and leaving it red and raw. I finish with one clear vow in my mind. I will not lower myself to becoming your company, particularly at night. I believe this has been my lowest point and I will not fall to this level again. I will rise above this, I will rise above you. It is not just the Larry conversation that has upset me. What got me to that point in the first place was you. It was you who caused me to charge home and pick up the phone and call him. Because it was your words that made me look at myself, at my situation, and made me want to get out of it.

I hear your voice over and over: *it was nice not to be alone out here for once.* You have brought me into your world, without my permission, without my say-so, you have included me in your crisis, in your state of mind, you have likened me to you. And by doing that you have made me feel ashamed, because I have always believed your words are poison, that they are the worst thing about you, that they are dangerous.

But when I let my guard down, your words gave me warmth. *It was nice not to be alone out here for once.* When you said those words, they comforted me. I did not feel alone then either.

I will not let you do that to me again.

11

For the first time in a very long time when I wake up my room is flooded with yellow light and a sense of calm. It is unusual, different to the blue-grey light that barely lit the room over the past few months. It is the first of February and though spring has not yet sprung, it gives cause to believe it just might win the battle. There is a sense of it in the air, or perhaps it is because for the first time in a very long time I have woken up late. I don't like lie-ins, they make me feel lazy; even after a late night I find a long walk by the bay is the only cure for me, but after the physical exertion of my late-night gardening I am exhausted. As soon as I move, I feel the stiffness in my limbs.

My radio tells me that I have slept for eight hours and once again the country has been battered by storms, 'storm factory' being the new term we're growing used to hearing, along with 'polar vortex' – no doubt new names for babies in 2015. They warn that there's another fortnight of mayhem on the way, thanks to unsettled weather from the Atlantic. The calmness outside is deceiving. Three cities are underwater, five-metre swells are forecast, and the talk on most stations turns to global warming and the melting polar ice that is fuelling the storms. January rainfall was

70 per cent above the norm and the outlook for February is more of the same. But not today. I look out the window and feel revived by the clear blue sky, the wispy occasional clouds. Even though I am still sore from my late-night workout in the garden, and embarrassed about you seeing it, I bury all that at the back of my mind.

I survey my hard work and am disappointed – no, devastated by what I see. At first I think somebody has come by and deliberately ransacked my newly laid turf, but on closer inspection I realise that I am in fact the culprit. Only with the benefit of my bedroom bird's-eye view I can see that it encapsulates perfectly my state of mind last night as I was doing it. It resembles a badly sewn, unfinished patchwork quilt, and I am horrified by what I see. It's as though my diary has been left open for everybody to read my deepest, darkest thoughts, and now I need to slam it closed before I am revealed to the world. I can't wait until Monday for the landscaper to return and fix my mess. There's no way I can endure two days with my fragile mental state displayed in the front garden for all to see.

Online research – something I should have made time for last night instead of letting adrenaline and anger rule me – is the answer. It educates me in how exactly to go about fixing the problem. One hour later I have returned from the garden centre and I'm ready and armed. Never do something that can't be undone, that's what I always tell myself, and I repeat it now as I assess the task ahead of me. Messy, time-consuming, challenging and frustrating, but possible. The landscaper had already prepared the soil for me perfectly; it had taken him longer than he'd said, but he had done it. Even though I had foolishly trodden all over the grass last night, as I realise today that I shouldn't have, I carefully roll each piece of turf up again before lifting it to its correct place. I lay the first row along the straight edge where the soil meets the stones, slowly unrolling it to minimise damage. The one I had kicked my heel through still lies on the driveway like a corpse at a crime scene. I place the next roll as close to the last as I can and ensure good contact with the soil by tapping down firmly with the back of the rake. All this I now know I should have done last night, but I also know that I would not have had the patience for it. Last night was about moving, being busy, doing something – not about doing it right.

As I rectify my mistakes on this oddly calm day, I feel a stillness coming over me. I forget about everything that has riled me up so much over the past few days and weeks, and devote all my concentration to the job in hand. Distraction. My mind quietens as I continue the process for a few hours, covering the area in a brickwork pattern. I'm about to turn my attention to the sides, trimming the edges with a straight-edged board and a half-moon cutting tool, both of which I have bought for the purpose, when a car drives past the house. I don't recognise the driver as one of my neighbours, but this happens a lot on weekends when people take drives along the coast and then explore the surrounding residential streets. I am used to seeing cars passing by, the back seats filled to the brim with kids, their faces pressed up against the glass for a gawk and older couples having a browse on their slow Sunday drives. We have the perfect cul de sac for window-shopping: it is pretty, welcoming, the kind of place people like to imagine themselves living in.

The driver has to do a three-point turn as it's only a short road. I watch him checking the numbers on the houses, which is not an easy task as everybody has chosen to display them differently in different places. You have a black plaque with pretty pink flowers to display your number, Dr Jameson has a goose in flight and next door has a garden gnome with one hand holding up a 2, the other hand is holding up his trousers, which have dropped to display enormous red-and-white heart boxer shorts. Mine is the least exciting of all: a black letter box attached to the wall with 3 on it.

He parks outside my house and gets out. I am positive he can't be looking for me, so I continue my gardening, but I'm unable to concentrate knowing he is looking around. Then I'm conscious of the fact his eyes have settled on me. I hear footsteps as he comes closer.

'Excuse me, I'm looking for Jasmine Butler.'

I look up, wipe sweat from my grimy forehead. He's tall, brown-skinned, with chiselled high cheekbones. His eyes are a striking green, which jar with his skin tone, and his Afro rises and then descends down over his eyes in tiny tight corkscrew curls. He is wearing a black suit, white shirt, green tie, shiny black shoes. He makes me remind myself to breathe.

From the way I'm looking at him dumbly, he thinks I haven't heard him.

'Are you Jasmine Butler?'

He is remarkably familiar but I haven't seen him before, I would remember that. And then I realise it's his voice I recognise. The telephone salesman.

'Or perhaps you're Penelope Paddington,' he says, and as he purses his lips together to hide his smile, two enormous dimples appear on his cheeks.

I smile, knowing I'm caught out. 'I'm Jasmine,' I say, my voice coming out in a croak. I clear it.

'My name is Monday O'Hara. I called you a few times on the phone during the last couple of weeks.'

'You didn't leave your name or contact details,' I say, wondering if I heard his name correctly.

'True. It's a private matter. I wanted to talk to you myself, and not . . . your housekeeper.'

I continue to look at him. So far he hasn't given me enough to get off the grass for, or even welcome him into my home.

'I work for Diversified Search International. I've been hired by DavidGordonWhite to find suitable candidates for a new position, and I think you more than meet the requirements they are looking for.'

I feel myself floating as he continues.

'I called your office quite a few times but couldn't reach you. I didn't leave any messages there, don't worry. I didn't want to raise a red flag so I told them it was a personal matter. But they were stronger gatekeepers than I assumed they'd be; you may or may not be happy to hear that.'

I struggle with how to respond to that. It was clear when we spoke on the phone that he doesn't know I've been fired. I am unsure as to why nobody told him that, perhaps because technically I haven't been fired, I am still contractually tied to them even though they won't let me past the front door.

'You're a difficult woman to find,' he says, with a smile, which is a beautiful thing to behold. Two definite dimples and a tiny chip in his front tooth: even his imperfection is perfectly perfect. In my humble opinion.

My house is a mess. I haven't got around to cleaning the muck I trampled into the floor during my rampage last night and my dirty knickers are in a pile on the kitchen floor in front of the washing machine, waiting for my towels to finish their cycle. I cannot bring him into the house.

'I'm sorry to bother you on a Saturday, but I find

105

out-of-work hours are the best time to deal with people. I'm very conscious of the need to keep your office from finding out about our contact.'

I'm still thinking about the state of the house, a long pause that he mistakes for mistrust, so he apologises and digs in his pockets and retrieves a business card. He hands it to me. He has to lean his long arms across the grass to reach me; he knows not to step on the grass and I like that. I examine the card. *Monday O'Hara. Headhunter. Diversified Search International.* The whole thing makes me smile.

'We don't have to talk now, I just wanted to make contact first and—'

'No, no, now is perfect. Well, not *right now* . . .' I run my hand through my scraped-back dirty hair and find a crusty leaf in it. 'Would you mind if I took twenty minutes to quickly change? We could meet at the Marine Hotel around the corner?'

'Perfect.' There's a flash of that gorgeous smile, but then it's all locked away in a very square jaw and he nods, business-like, at me and makes his way back to his car. I have to work hard not to dance into my house.

I sit in on an oversized couch in the Marine Hotel lobby, feeling refreshed and looking more human, while Monday heads off in search of a waiter. I feel nervously excited about what's to come. At long last, something that feels like a step forward. He has no idea that I've been fired, and I still haven't told him, or even let on that I'm no longer working there, and if it does slip out, he doesn't need to know that it wasn't my decision to leave. I know exactly why I'm keeping it to myself: because I want to play. I want to play along, feel like the desired woman with two companies fighting over her, instead of the loser, fired from her job and with nothing on the horizon. Or maybe, just maybe, in an embarrassing bout of ego and weakness, I don't want the handsome man to see me as the fired failure that I currently feel like.

A woman and a little girl, her daughter, around four years old, sit at the table in front of me. The little girl picks up her spoon and lightly taps on the glass.

'I'd like to make toast,' she says, and her mother howls with laughter.

'*A* toast, Lily.'

'Oh,' she giggles. 'I'd like to make *a* toast.' She clinks the glass again, stretches her neck and puts on a posh, serious face.

Her mother cracks up laughing again.

The little girl is funny, but it is her mother's reaction that makes me join in the laughter. She is laughing so hard, she's crying and patting at the corners of her eyes to stop it.

'So what's your toast about?'

'The toast would like to thank,' Lily says in a deep, posh voice, 'the butter and the jam.'

Her mother rolls over on the couch, laughing.

'And the egg, for making it into soldiers.'

Lily sees me listening and stops, embarrassed.

'Don't let me stop you,' I call. 'You're doing a great job.'

'Oh,' her mother sits up and wipes her eyes, trying to catch her breath. 'You crack me up, Lily.'

Lily makes a few more speeches, which have me laughing to myself. I sit still as can be while they are busy together, but I will not be still and alone for long. My headhunter returns. This man has hunted me, it feels animalistic. I feel myself blush and I try to put a stop to the ridiculous antics in my head. I fix all my attention on Monday, all thoughts of the little girl gone from my mind.

'I ordered you a green tea,' he says, checking.

'Perfect. Thanks. So, your name is Monday. I've never heard that before.'

He leans over, placing his elbows on his knees. This brings him quite close, but to sit back would be rude so I get lost in his face and then try to remember that I shouldn't be, that I should be concentrating on the words coming through his chipped white tooth and out of his sumptuous mouth and why I am here. Because he has found me, sought me out, and thinks I'm a highly qualified, wonderful person. Or something like that.

I can tell he is completely at ease with my question, and has no doubt been asked it a thousand times.

'My mother is nuts,' he says with an air of finality, and I laugh.

'I was hoping for more than that.'

'Me too,' he replies, and we smile. 'She used to be a cellist with the National Symphony Orchestra. Now she gives lessons in a caravan in Connemara, in the garden of a house that she refuses to live in because she's convinced she saw the ghost of her dad. She named me Monday because I was born on a Monday. My middle name is Leo because I was born in late July. O'Hara is her surname, not my father's.' He smiles and his eyes move from mine to my hair. 'Her hair is as red as yours, though I didn't inherit that. Just her freckles.'

It's true, he has a beautiful smattering of freckles across his nose and the tips of his cheeks. I picture a red-haired woman with freckles and pale skin in a field in Galway with a cello between her thighs. It's a bit racy.

My turn. 'My granddad brought my mum a bunch of winter jasmine from his garden when she was in hospital after I was born. So she named me Jasmine.'

He seems surprised. 'People rarely reciprocate my name story.'

'If you have a name story, you have to tell it,' I say.

'I don't usually have a choice,' he says. 'A mere introduction requires explanation. It's the same for my sister, Thursday.'

'You do not have a sister called Thursday!'

'No.' He laughs, enjoying my reaction.

'Well, I *do* have a sister. My granddad brought a bunch of heather to my mum after she was born. So she called her Heather.'

'That's a bit predictable,' he teases, curling his lip.

'I suppose. My brother Weed lucked out.'

He narrows his eyes suspiciously, then laughs.

'Where's your dad from?'

'Spanish sailor.'

'You don't look Spanish.'

'I'm joking. *The Snapper*? Anyway. No, it's my mother's equivalent – a travelling salesman, apparently. Never met him, no idea who he is, she's never told anyone. Though my friends and I used to guess it was every black man that we saw when I was growing up, which there obviously weren't many of in Galway. It used to be a game. Guess who Monday's dad is. There was a busker on Quay Street who played the saxophone; my friends used to joke that it was him. When I was twelve I asked him.' He laughs. 'It wasn't him, but he said he'd meet my mum if I wanted.'

It's sad but we both laugh, and then he suddenly snaps out of it and into business mode. 'So. The job.' He lifts a leather folder on the table and unzips it. 'I have been hired by DavidGordonWhite – are you familiar with them? If not, here you go.'

He places a business folder down before me. Very

corporate, very serious, very expensive-looking: a photo of a man and a woman in pinstripe suits in front of a glass building, both of them looking into the sky over the camera as if a meteor is headed at them but they are not in the least bothered. My heart sings. They want me. They need me. They think that I am highly qualified and wonderful. They think that I am necessary, that I am an asset. They want to pay me to distract me from the world and real worldly issues. I am beaming and I can't help it.

'They're a tax advisory company,' I say.

'Top ten in the world. Correct. You are aware that corporations such as these have corporate social responsibility programmes?'

'PR exercises,' I say.

'You might not want to mention that in the interview.' He grins, then the professional face is back. 'If it were just a PR exercise then it wouldn't qualify as a charity, which is what they have in mind: the DavidGordonWhite Foundation, a charity campaigning for climate justice – human rights and climate change. They want you to work for them . . .' He pauses, obviously waiting to see whether I will ask a question or if he should continue. I am so disappointed I don't know what to say. It's not a proper job; they want me to work for a *charity*. 'I'll keep talking about everything, you stop me if you have any questions, okay?'

I nod. I am annoyed. At DavidGordonWhite. At him, for fooling me with his handsomeness and flattery, making me think I was being offered a proper job. I feel my cheeks flush. He talks and talks and talks about the job. Nothing in what he says piques my interest.

Eventually he stops and looks at me. 'Shall I continue?'

I want to say no. I want to say more than that, I'm

feeling hot-headed, but I mustn't take out my personal frustrations on this man, handsome as he is.

'I'm confused as to why I'm in the running for this,' I tell him. 'I have never worked with or for a charity. I create start-ups, I make them into brilliant successes, and then I sell them on for as much money as possible.'

Even I know that that is an awful way to describe what I do. In fact it sounds like something Larry has barked at me in the past, when in reality I am incredibly passionate about what I do. There is more involved than what I have said, but I want to make it sound as far away from a charity as possible. He has got it wrong. How did my name pop up in the system when he typed in 'charity', apart from the fact I'm starting to feel like a charity case.

He seems a little surprised by my outburst but takes a mature moment to choose his next words, fixing me with his caring, green-eyed, I-understand-where-you're-coming-from look. 'You would be responsible for the general control and management of the charity. It is a business like any other and it's starting from scratch.' He can see the uncertainty on my face and he is trying to sell it to me.

He goes on to talk about what I've done in all of my businesses, as though I don't know myself, but it is clever, it is an ego boost and he has researched me well. He openly admires me, praises my decisions and good work, and I am feeling mightily flattered and as though there is no one cleverer than me. I am being reeled in. He tells me that while he was asking around for the best candidate my name came up on a few different occasions. His handsomeness helps, because I want to please him, because I want him to think that I am talented and clever and all of those things; he is the perfect hire for a headhunter, able to fill people with self-belief, convince them that there is something out

111

there greater for them than what they are currently doing. He almost has me. I mean, *he* has me, but the job . . . not so much. My gut isn't jumping up and down the way it usually does when I have an idea for a new project, or come across someone else's idea that I can improve on.

He looks at me, hopefully.

My green tea arrives. As the waiter places it before me I have time to think. This job is not for me, but there is nothing else on offer. I'm torn between expressing interest and being honest. And I like him, which should be an aside, and it really is, but at the same time it's inescapable. Being fired has knocked the confidence out of me, has made me question the how, what and why of every decision I make. Do I wait for the right thing, or do I grab the first thing, just in case?

He studies me, intensely, those hazel green eyes gazing deep into mine, and I feel as if I'm falling into them, being sucked in. Then I feel like an idiot because all he is doing is looking at me and I'm the one reacting. I break our stare, though he continues to watch me. I'm convinced he knows, that he is seeing deep into my soul. I can't do it, I can't lie to him, this one person who is offering sunshine in the middle of the longest of my winters.

'Actually, Monday, I'm sorry . . .' I rub my face, ashamed. 'There seems to be a misunderstanding. I no longer work at the Idea Factory. I lost my job over two months ago. A disagreement between me and the co-founder.' I feel my eyes spark as I talk. 'So, I don't have a job at the moment.' I don't know what else to say. Feeling my cheeks flush, I take a sip of the green tea just to give me something to do. It burns my tongue and all the way down my throat and it's all I can do not to react, but at least it's headed off the tears that were about to come.

'Okay,' he says, quietly, his posture relaxing and changing to a different mode. 'Well, that's good, right? They don't have to steal you away from another job. You are actively looking, I assume?'

I try to look bright-eyed and wonder whether to explain the gardening leave. I can't do it. I can't watch the only opportunity I've had for a new job fall by the wayside by admitting my dirty little secret: that I'm on Larry's payroll for another ten months, preventing me from working. Nor can I *not* tell him, a headhunter. He makes my mind up for me by filling in the silence.

'I'm going to leave this with you . . .' He slides the folder across the coffee table. 'It's information about the position. You can read up on it then give me a call. We can meet again, discuss any questions you might have.'

I look at the folder, suddenly desolate, forlorn. What had begun as an ego boost, the highest of all highs, has left me feeling flat. It is not a job that I want, but I know that I need one. I take the folder and hug it to my chest. He downs his espresso and I try to drink up my scalding tea so that we can go.

'We can meet again before the interview,' he says, showing me to the door and holding it open for me.

I smile. 'Who says there'll be an interview?'

'I'm sure there'll be one,' he says confidently, pleasantly. 'It's my job to know that you'd be right for the position, and I happen to be very good at my job.' He gives me a big smile to ease the sales pitch, make it seem less phoney. It should have come across as a cheesy sales pitch, but it doesn't. Something tells me he is great at his job. His voice takes on a gentle note as he adds, 'And it would be good for you, Jasmine.'

We're outside. The day has turned, the wind has picked

up again; in the space of an hour the trees have started to whip from one side to the other, violently, as if we're on some tropical island – only we're not, it's Ireland and it's February. Everything is skeletal and grey, people walk by with screwed-up faces, purple-lipped, tight blue hands glowing in the dull light or thrust into their pockets.

I watch him walk to his car.

It didn't bother me when he pretended he knew me and flattered me, but it bothers me when he pretends he knows me and speaks the truth. Because although we've only known each other one hour, he's probably right. As things stand, a job – any job – would be good for me. It might be the only thing that can stop me slipping into whatever it is I've been slipping into.

12

The storm that swept in that evening reached hurricane level, with winds in some parts of the country touching 170 kilometres per hour. According to the news there are two hundred and sixty thousand people without electricity. There are reports of accidents on the motorway, trucks blowing over, falling trees crushing cars, images of destruction on people's houses, roofs being lifted off buildings, windows shattered from flying debris. The east coast was relatively unaffected. I see branches littering the road, leaves, wheelie bins lying down and surrendering, and children's toys where they shouldn't be, but compared to those whose homes are flooded we are incredibly lucky. However it has been a wild night for our street, and for so many reasons.

While trying to read my folder and discover how human rights and climate change are related, I am interrupted by you. It is different to the usual interruptions. You don't drive home with your music blaring: you are already at home, in fact you are completely sober. This isn't entirely unheard of, you are not all guns blazing every night, and it is not always on the same level. Since your wife left you, you have been quieter; there has been no one to scream at, and even though some nights you have forgotten this and shouted as if she was there, you have quickly remembered that there is no one to hear you and settled down to sleep in your car or at the garden table. While all the other garden furniture in the neighbourhood has been flying around in the terrible storms – the Malones lost a favourite gnome when it fell over and smashed its face in – yours has remained entrenched in your bog marsh of a front garden. It lists to one side, the right-hand legs having sunk deeper into the grass than those on the left, and I have watched you at night doing the thing that seems to help you focus on whatever it is your mind is pondering: again and again you place your lighter on the higher end of the sloped table and then watch it roll down into your open palm at the lower end. I don't know if you even realise you are doing it; the expression on your face suggests your mind is somewhere else entirely.

Most nights you've either remembered your own key or driven off elsewhere when you couldn't find it, but I have had to let you into your house with the spare key three times in total. Each time you stumbled into the house and closed the door in my face, and I knew that you would not remember it the following day. It is ironic, to me at least, that the very thing that I hate you for is something that you probably have no recollection of, and the very things that feed that hatred you forget every single time you wake up.

At three a.m. this morning it is not your car that disturbs me from my reading, it is your son, Fionn. The wind is so loud that I can't make out the words, but the shouting is being whipped around in the air and occasionally tossed in my direction: random words that don't add up to enough to reveal the subject of the argument. I look out of my bedroom window and see you and Fionn in the garden, the pair of you screaming, arms waving. I can see your face, but I can't see Fionn's. Neither of you is wearing a coat, which tells me you weren't planning on this discussion under the stars. Fionn is a whippet of a thing, a tall, skinny fifteen-year-old who keeps being blown over every time there's a gust of wind; or so it seems, until I realise it has nothing to do with the wind: he is falling-down drunk. You are solid, you are tall, you are broad, you have your trainers firmly planted on the ground; your body is wide and you look as though not long ago you were fit although you've become softer around the edges. I can see the hint of love handles, and your gut has swelled a bit since your wife moved out, or maybe it's just that the wind is blowing your shirt tight against your waist and revealing a body I wouldn't ordinarily see. You try to grab Fionn's arms when they flail close to you, but each time you reach out to him, he swings his arms wildly, fists clenched, trying to hit you.

You manage to grab him by the waist and pull him towards the house, but he bends over and squirms out of your grasp. He punches out, fist connecting with some part of your body and you fall back as if hurt. But it isn't that which makes me move, it is the two younger children standing at the open door, looking so petrified in their pyjamas, one squeezing a teddy bear to his chest, which has me out of bed and pulling on my tracksuit before I can give it a second thought. When I undo the lock on the front door I'm almost knocked over by the force with which it flies open, so strong is the wind. Everything in the hallway – the notepad on the phone table, hats, coats – seems to take off, scurrying to the far corners of the house like mice when the light is switched on. I have to battle to pull the door closed behind me; using two hands, I tug with all my might. The wind is icy, wild, angry. It rages, and across the

117

road the two of you flail wildly at one another as if tapping into Mother Nature's anger.

I see it happen, the thing you will never forgive yourself for, and though I am not your biggest fan, I know that it wasn't intentional. You don't mean to hit your son, but that is what you do. While trying to reach for him and protect yourself from his fists, you somehow make contact with his face. I happen to be looking at your face in that moment, and before I know what it is you've done, your expression tells me. Someone who had not seen your face might not have understood that it was accidental, but I did. Your eyes are suddenly haunted, scared – appalled. The revulsion is so strong, you look as if you're going to be sick. You're desperate to reach out to him and protect him, but he is screaming and pushing you away, holding his bloodied nose, shouting at you, accusing you, calling you names a father would never want to be called by his son. The children at the door are crying now and you are trying to keep them calm, and all the while the storm rages; the clumpy garden chairs, which had previously seemed embedded into the ground, suddenly blow over as if to join in the family drama. One chair topples backward, another is lifted and skids across the ground as if it is weightless, landing dangerously near the window. My intention is to protect the little ones, to bring them inside and distract them. I have no plan to intervene in father–son fisticuffs, I know that would not end well for me, but as I make my way towards you both, your son announces that he never wants to set foot in your house again and sets off down the road, alone, with no coat, drunk, against a one-hundred-and-something-kilometre wind, with a bloodied face – and that changes things.

And that is how your son ends up sleeping in the spare

bedroom of my home on the stormiest night the country has seen. He doesn't want to talk, and that is okay, I'm not in the mood either. I clean his face, thankful that your thump hasn't broken his nose. I give him fresh towels, a pint of water and a headache tablet, an extra large NYPD T-shirt that somebody gave me as a gift years ago, and I leave him alone. Then I sit up all night, drinking green tea and listening to him making trips from the bedroom to the bathroom, where he throws up relentlessly.

Shortly before four a.m. I wake to the sound of a bird. This confuses me; I'm sure the bird is in some kind of distress, has been stolen from its nest in the middle of the night. But no; as I listen, I realise it is simply singing. It seems like another lifetime when I heard birdsong at four a.m. It is bright by seven, the air is still, no wind, no rain, it is pleasant, Mother Nature looking as though butter wouldn't melt, while around the country people deal with the devastation and destruction she heaped on them during the night.

With a cup of coffee in hand I survey my front garden, glad that I had laid most of the turf when I did. The remaining rolls of grass lie destroyed, broken and ripped apart, caught under the wheel of my car.

The moment you see me, your door opens and you cross the road, as though you've been waiting for me to open the door all night.

'Is he okay?' you ask, concern etched across your face. I genuinely feel sorry for you.

'He's still asleep. He was up all night being sick.'

You nod as you digest that, a faraway look on your face. 'Good. Good.'

'Good?'

'Means he'll be less eager to do it again.'

119

I survey the broken grass scattered around the ground. 'All your hard work,' you say.

I shrug, as if it's no big deal, embarrassed still that you witnessed my hard work, which could also have been described as a complete meltdown. My garden is flat but slopes to a lower level, which runs to the side and back of my house. The second level is paved in the same stone as the driveway, but the slope is an ugly mess, devoid of grass. I hadn't managed to do that part. Another job not finished. I think of Larry and I get hot and angry inside.

'You could make a rockery with those,' you say, indicating the broken stones in the skip. 'My grandparents had a hill in their garden. They turned the entire thing into a rockery. Planted in between it. I could get Fionn to help. They're probably heavy.'

My head runs through a dozen sarcastic, ungrateful things to say to that, frankly, ludicrous idea, but I bite my tongue.

You are looking past me into the house, hoping for an invitation.

'You should let him sleep it off,' I say.

'I know. I would, but his mum is coming soon.'

'Oh. When?'

You look at your watch. 'Fifteen minutes. He's got a rugby match.'

'Not a great day for a hangover.' That's one more thing Belvedere won't be too happy about. 'What happened?' I don't want to know, but at the same time I do.

'I was supposed to pick him up from rugby yesterday. He wasn't there when I arrived. Went out with his friends. Came home last night, high as a kite. Well, not high, drunk. I think.' You frown again then, looking into my house. 'Started having a go at me.'

'Look, we've all been there,' I say, remembering the times

I'd overdone it as a teenager. Why I offer you solace is beyond me. You, the man who's rolled home having had too much to drink more times than he's had a cooked breakfast, but you seem to appreciate the gesture. 'Look,' I clear my throat, 'I still have that letter—'

Suddenly Amy's car pulls up in front of your house. You stiffen.

'He's in the spare bedroom, upstairs on the left.'

'Thanks.' You head into the house.

I watch her go into your house and the door closes and all is silent. Moments later, you come down the stairs, closely followed by Fionn, who looks shocking. A brown-black bruise on his nose, dried blood caked around it. Despite my best efforts to clean him up, it must have bled again during the night. He looks white and drawn, exhausted and hungover. As soon as the light from the open door hits him, he winces. His clothes are crumpled and I'm sure I'll find the NYPD T-shirt hasn't been slept in. He shuffles along behind you and your wife appears at the front door of your house with her hands on her hips.

I don't want to see any more. I don't want to be drawn in to give my side of the story, I want to stay out of your life, but somehow I keep being pulled in. Once indoors, I listen nervously for the doorbell, afraid you'll call over to continue the battle here, but then I see an image on the television which makes me freeze.

It's the little girl. From the hotel yesterday. The four-year-old wispy blonde with her pixie face, blue eyes, button nose, who wanted to make a toast. The television is muted so I could listen out for Fionn, so I don't know what they're saying, but it can't be good. Her photo is followed by an image of her mother. Big smiles from both of them, the little girl – Lily, I recall – is sitting on her mother's knee, her mother's arms wrapped around her daughter; they look at the camera as though somebody has said something funny. Behind them is a Christmas tree from a few weeks ago. And then there is an image of a car and a truck on the motorway, the car crushed, the truck overturned, and I have to sit down. I turn up the volume and listen to the facts – both dead, the driver of the truck critical – and I am wracked with grief.

When the doorbell rings I ignore it, still listening to the news. It rings again. And again. Still crying, and angry about the intrusion, I charge to the door and pull it open. I am confronted with three startled faces.

'I'm sorry,' Amy, your wife, says. 'I've called at a bad time.' The anger I sense from her immediately dissipates.

'No . . . I just . . . I just saw some bad news.'

They look over my shoulder. I've left the door to the living room open and the television is still switched to the news. 'Oh, I know. Isn't it awful? They only live around the corner – Steven Warren's wife.' She looks at you. 'Did you hear? Rebecca died. And the little girl . . .'

'Lily,' I say, her name catching in my throat.

'I hadn't heard,' you say.

We're all lost in our silent thoughts for a moment. Fionn, thinking this is his cue to speak, blurts out in a croaky voice, 'Eh, thanks for last night.'

'You're welcome,' I tell him, unsure what exactly Amy believes went down.

Relieved to be out of the firing line, Fionn wanders back across the road to the house, dragging his feet, his crumpled trousers dropping low beneath his boxers. You and your wife are still looking past me at the television. Amy is actually watching it, you are trying to figure something else out entirely.

'I saw them yesterday afternoon – Rebecca and Lily,' I say their names as if I know them, which feels like a lie, but it's the truth.

'It happened yesterday afternoon. You must have been one of the last to see them,' Amy says, and that statement does something to me. It's not an accusation, I know that, it's not really anything, she is merely thinking aloud, but it gives me a sense of responsibility. I'm not sure what to do with that. It's as if I have some form of ownership over them, over the last moment of their lives. Should I share it with people, so that the right people have the moment with them that I had? Put it back to the way it should have been. I am over-analysing this, I know, while you are standing there, looking at me, but I suppose that is what shock does. And I am tired, having not slept very much for fear Fionn would collapse, hit his head, choke on his own vomit, or up and leave in the middle of the night and then I'd be in trouble for losing a minor.

'Matt, you know them too.' Amy turns to you.

'I don't really—'

'You do, you used to play badminton with him.'

Of all the things I could have heard, this makes me raise an eyebrow at you.

'A long time ago.'

'He always asks for you.' She turns to me. 'Matt will go round there with you,' she offers.

'Pardon?'

'He'll go with you. To pay his respects. Won't you? Do you some good,' she says, and not in a nice way. 'Anyway, sorry to disturb you, I only wanted to say thank you, for taking care of Fionn.'

She backs away. You remain at the door, looking to me for your next instruction, doing as you've been told by the wife who just left you, as if hoping that obeying her will put you in her good books. Or maybe I'm wrong. Then it occurs to me that you're trying to tell me something. You're messaging something to me. I look deeper into your eyes. Try to figure it out. You want me to defend you. To tell her what I saw. I call out to her.

'Amy – about last night. The knock was an accident. Matt didn't mean to—'

I stop because I can tell from the way she glares at you, the way her face looks at you with such hate and disgust, that I've put my foot in it. She had no idea that you'd hit him.

Amy starts bundling the children into the car and you run over to say your goodbyes. The engine has started up, she is ready to go, seat belts are on, doors are closed. You have to pull at the handle, forcing her to unlock the door so you can open it and stick your head in the car to kiss the two children in the back. You give Fionn an awkward pat on the shoulder but he doesn't look at you. You close the door, give the roof two taps and you wave them off. Nobody is waving back at you; in fact nobody even turns to see you. I feel for you and I don't know why I do because I witnessed everything that your wife experienced, from the outside at least: the late nights, the drunken behaviour . . . I don't understand why she didn't leave you sooner, and yet I watch you standing alone outside your house, hands shoved into your jeans pockets, watching your family driving away, leaving you alone in the big house that surely they should be staying in and not you, and my heart goes out to you.

'Come on,' I call.

You look up.

'Let's go to Steven's house.'

I suspect it's the last thing you want to do, but you need distraction. I know it's the last thing I want to do, but I could use some distraction too.

You grab your coat, I grab mine, and we meet in the middle.

'Sorry about what I said there,' I say. 'I shouldn't have. I was only trying to—'

'It's fine, she would have found out anyway. Better it came from me first.'

In fact it didn't, but I think what you mean is that it came from your *side* and I'm unsure as to how I've found myself on your side when every night I watched you banging on the doors, locked out, I was willing her not to let you in.

'Where are Amy and the kids staying?' I ask, as we walk down the road.

'Her parents' place.'

'Is she coming back?'

'I don't know. She won't talk to me. Those sentences you heard were the most she's said in days.'

'She wrote you the letter.'

'I know.'

'You should read it.'

'That's what she says.'

'Why don't you read it?'

You don't answer.

'Here.' I hand you the letter. You look at it in surprise for a moment, then take it and stuff it in your pocket. I don't believe you will read it, but at least I have given it to you. My part is done. I feel a little relief, but I'm not content my job is done. You haven't even opened it.

'Are you going to read it?'

'Jesus, what is it with you and this letter?'

'If I was given a letter by my wife who'd just left me, I'd want to know what it says.'

'Are you a lesbian?'

I roll my eyes. 'No.'

You chuckle.

'I've noticed you're not working,' you say. 'Time off or—'

'I'm on gardening leave,' I cut you off, before I hear whatever offensive term you're about to use.

'Right.' You smile. 'You know that doesn't actually mean you have to do your garden.'

'Of course I know that. What about you? I read that you lost your job.' I say it bluntly, harshly, and you look at me and study me in that confused, intrigued, insulted way that you do when I snap at you, which is often when I remember that I don't like you.

'I didn't lose my job,' you say. 'I'm on leave – gardening leave, too, as a matter of fact. Only, unlike you, I've decide to sit in mine.'

'Moonbathing,' I say.

You laugh. 'Yeah.'

Heather and I always called it that when we were younger: lying out under the moon. The thought of Heather reminds me of my views on you and I clam up. I know you notice the change in me, the way I go from hot to cold with you within seconds.

'It's only temporary though, the leave. Pending an investigation into my conduct,' you put on the formal voice.

I read between the lines. 'You're suspended.'

'They're calling it gardening leave.'

'For how long?'

'One month. You?'

'A year.'

126

You suck in air. 'What did you do to get that?'

'It's not a prison sentence. I didn't *do* anything. It's so I don't work for the competition.'

You study me in the long silence it takes me to gather my composure. 'So what are you going to do?'

'I have a few ideas.' I say. 'It's good to have the year to think about them.' I do not believe one word of what I have just said. 'What about you?'

'I'll go back to it when I get the all-clear. I have a radio show.'

I look at you to see if you're joking, but you're not. I'd have thought you would assume everyone knows who you are, that you wear your name on your chest like a badge of honour – though I'm unsure as to where the honour would lie – but you're not joking. You have not assumed that I know who you are. I like this about you, and it makes me dislike you more. You can't win.

'I'm aware of your show.' I say this in such a disapproving voice that you chuckle in that chesty, wheezy cigarette laugh.

'I knew it!'

'You knew what?'

'That's the reason you are the way you are with me. Uptight. Edgy. Always on the defensive.'

If my friends were to describe me, these are not the words they would use. I am taken aback to hear myself described as such. I don't like it that someone would think that of me, and for some reason I don't want you to think that of me, though that is exactly how I have portrayed myself. I had forgotten that you wouldn't know this isn't how I always am; you wouldn't understand the effort I have to make, deviating from the real me in order to be positively rude to you. My friends would say I'm a free spirit; I always

127

do my own thing, never dance to the beat of anybody else's drum, never have. They might say I'm headstrong, stubborn, at the worst, but they would only know the free-and-easy side of me, whereas you bring out the worst in me.

'You're not a fan.'

'You better believe I'm not a fan,' I say, hot-headed again.

'Which one insulted you?' You pop a nicotine gum into your mouth.

'What do you mean?' My heart pounds. After all these years, we are actually here, at the point where I can explain. Here we are. My mind works overtime to find the words to explain how you have hurt me.

'Which show? Which issue? What did I say that you didn't agree with? You know, I have an instinct for listeners who hate the show. As soon as I walk into a room, I can tell whether someone's a fan or not. My sixth sense. It's the way they look at me.'

Your arrogance disturbs me. Trust you to take a negative – people hating you – and turn it into a positive. 'Maybe it's you and not the show,' I say.

'You see, that's the kind of thing I'm talking about.' You smile and click your fingers. '*That* kind of underhand comment. It's not me, Jasmine. It's the show. I lead the discussion. It doesn't represent my personal views. I invite guests on air for the debate.'

'You stir it up.'

'I have to. That's what gets them calling in. Gets the debate going.'

'And you think these debates are necessary?' I say. I've stopped walking and we're standing face to face outside Steven's house, where the lawn has disappeared beneath a mass of flowers and gifts, teddy bears, candles and hand-written cards. 'It's not as if your show does anything to educate people about the facts. All you do is invite a bunch of lunatics on to vent their oppressive, racist, uneducated opinions.'

You look at me seriously. 'Every person, every voice on there is real. They represent what real people in this country are thinking. I think people need to hear that. It's no good spending all your time with your politically correct friends, thinking the world is a wonderful open and understanding place, only to turn up at the voting booths and suddenly discover it's not. Our show gives everyone a voice. As a result of our show, some of these issues have been discussed in the Dáil: bullying, same-sex marriage, we've closed down dangerous nursing homes, crèches . . .' you start to list things off on your fingers.

'You seriously think you're doing the country a service?' I ask, flabbergasted. 'Surely that only applies if it's a decent debate. Not when it's idiots who are half drunk, or high, or who've escaped a lunatic asylum. Allowing those people to air their opinions is a good thing? They should be silenced, if anything.'

'Good idea, Kim Jong-un. Free speech bad,' you say, clearly annoyed.

'Perhaps you should invite him on your show – give the man a chance to share his fine opinions. Anyway, from what the newspapers are saying, it sounds as if your show isn't coming back on air,' I say, chin high in the air and walking up the pathway to the front door, hoping that will silence him, that I can get the last word in. My final bitchy, defensive, edgy, uptight comment.

'Oh, it is. Bob and me are like that.' You hold up your crossed fingers. 'Bob's head of radio, he's been with me since the start. He's only doing this to follow procedure. Wouldn't look right if he didn't. When a show gets as many

129

complaints as we did, you have to go through the motions.'

'You must be so proud,' I say, pressing the doorbell.

'I really must have pissed you off something good,' you say, your breath close to my ear. When I look at you, your eyes are twinkling mischievously. It occurs to me that you like it that I dislike you, and in a sick way, I do too. Disliking you has given me something to focus on. Disliking you has become my full-time job.

Suddenly the door opens and a woman with red eyes, a red nose, crumpled tissues in hand answers. She recognises you straight away, seems delighted and honoured to find you at her door, and quickly ushers you inside. This baffles me – don't people hear what I hear? You are gentlemanly enough to let me enter first.

Inside, the kitchen is filled with people standing around engaging in long silences that are occasionally broken up by small talk, reminiscing and nervous laughter. The table is overflowing with food: lasagne, cakes and sandwiches that neighbours have dropped by. We are shown through to the living room, where a man sits alone in an armchair staring out the window. The walls are filled with professional studio photographs of the young family: black-and-white portraits of Steven, Rebecca and Lily. Mummy and Daddy in black polo necks against a white backdrop, little Lily in a pretty white dress, glowing under studio lights like an angel, showing a big smile with tiny teeth. One of Lily holding a lollipop, one of Lily twirling, one of Lily laughing, one of Lily sticking her tongue out while Mummy and Daddy look on, big smiles on their faces.

I recognise Steven from the photos and as someone I see regularly around the area, in the supermarket, butcher's, jogging along the bay . . .

'Matt,' he says, standing up and offering you a hug.

'I'm so sorry, Steven,' you say, and you both hold the hug for a long time. Close badminton buddies. I look around and then stare at the floor awkwardly while I wait.

'This is my neighbour, Jasmine. She lives around the corner, on my street.'

'I'm very sorry for your loss,' I say, offering my hand, which he takes.

'Thank you,' he says solemnly. 'You're a friend of Rebecca's?'

'I . . . No . . . Actually . . .' I feel silly. I'm not sure where to start. Perhaps this was a mistake. I'm not sure. The responsibility I felt earlier has waned and now I feel like an intruder. The woman who answered the door is in the room too and all eyes are on me. 'I saw them both yesterday afternoon at three p.m. In the Marine Hotel.'

He looks confused. He turns to the woman. She looks confused.

They both look at me. They don't believe me.

'I'm not sure they were there . . .' he says, frowning.

'Lily was having a hot chocolate. "Hot choc stop," she called it.'

He smiles, covers his mouth and chin with his hand and sits on the arm of the chair.

'She was in great spirits. Rebecca couldn't stop laughing. I could hear her as soon as I walked into the lobby. Lily was trying to make a toast.'

He looks at the woman, who I now understand to be his sister; I can see the likeness. 'Because of the party last week, Beth,' he says, and she nods happily, her eyes filling. Steven looks back at me, his face open, gentle, eager for more to come from my mouth. You are watching me too and that is slightly off-putting, I don't know why you make me so nervous, but I try to ignore that you're there and speak only to Steven. The more I look at him, the more I see the resemblance to Lily in his blonde lashes and his elfin face. So I stand there, a complete stranger in his home, and I tell him about her toast, about her many toasts, about the conversation she and her mother were having, about the conversation I had with her. I tell him every single thing that I can remember. I stress the laughter, the happiness, the utter joy of their last hour together before they got in the car and began the journey to visit Rebecca's parents on that stormy day. I tell it because I would want to know.

Steven absorbs it all, almost as though he's in a trance yet taking in every word I'm saying, studying me as I say it, probably trying to figure out if I'm for real, hoping that I am, then eventually believing that I am. He watches my eyes, my lips, and when he thinks I'm not looking runs his eyes over me. And then when I'm finished there is silence and it probably seems to him that they have been killed again, as they go from being present to suddenly gone. His face crumples and he breaks down. I freeze, not knowing what to do, wanting to comfort him but knowing it's not my place. His sister steps in instead. You pat him on the shoulder and leave the room. I follow, feeling like a spare part, feeling awkward; my every move is mechanical, I'm convinced I've made a mistake in coming here and sharing what I shared, but I'm not sure. I want you to reassure me, but at the same time I don't want reassurance to come from you.

Once outside, you discard the nicotine gum and light a cigarette. My face burns crimson as we walk and you don't say anything the entire way home. When we stop outside my house, you look at me and maybe you sense my inner turmoil, or maybe you see my discomfort, or perhaps my face is a picture of the despair that I feel, because your eyes linger for a moment, your handsome face studying mine, soft, caring, still curious and studious as it always is, trying to figure things out, as if I'm a puzzle, but a humorous one.

You stub out your cigarette. 'I'd have wanted to know too,' you say. 'That was nice.' You reach out and squeeze my shoulder.

I realise I've been holding my breath the entire way and finally release it. The relief I feel surprises me; *you* have done that to me, you count to me, but this jars with what I have always felt about you.

'Jasmine!' A familiar voice breaks into my thoughts and I spin around to see Heather sitting on my front porch. She stands up and makes her way over to us.

My head swirls as I realise that you are about to come face to face with the person I have tried to protect against you all of my adult life.

13

One Sunday a month Heather's circle of support meets. We have had these meetings ever since she was a teenager; in fact, Mum was the person who set all this up and even while she was undergoing treatment she continued to attend, no matter how sick she was. Even when I was a teenager and had better things to be doing with my time, she insisted that I come along. Although I didn't appreciate it at the time, I am now glad that I did, because when Mum passed away I knew exactly how things were run and what direction they needed to go in. Person-centred planning is a group of people who meet together regularly to help somebody achieve what they would like to do in their lives. Heather is in charge of who she wants to invite and what she wants to talk about. We talk about Heather's PATH – Planning Alternative Tomorrows with Hope – we talk about her dreams, how she could achieve these dreams, what is going on in her life and what are the next steps she needs to take. We talk about making her dreams a reality.

The meeting used to be weekly in the days when she was making plans for school, secondary school and what she wanted to study in college – which ended up being a residential college to learn how to live independently, how to get about on public transport, how to shop for food and essentials, cooking skills and preparation for the workplace. It was important to keep the meetings regular while she planned the direction she wanted her life to go in, but when the time came it was Heather herself who decided to switch to monthly meetings.

People who have attended in the past have included teachers, her support assistant – who Heather interviewed herself – someone from her college, the careers officer, her employers, and always me. Dad has come along a handful of times, but he isn't good in these situations. He misunderstands the purpose. It is about planning, yes, and it is about doing. But it is also about listening to Heather and hearing how she feels about her place in the world and where she wants to be. Dad doesn't have the patience to listen to these things. If it's a job she wants, he'll get it for her; if it's an activity she wants to do, he'll sort it out for her. But what I've learned from this process is that it helps me get inside Heather's head. I want to hear the explanations for how and why and when. Like the time she announced that she wanted to leave her job packing bags at the local supermarket, even though it was a job she had spent a long time planning for. Dad was present at the meeting and wanted to rush through it all, gung-ho about getting her out of there because he hated her doing that job anyway. He completely missed the fact that the reason she wanted to leave the job was because somebody at the supermarket was being mean to her. The lady at the till was moving too fast, constantly snapping at her heels, making her feel like she wasn't doing a good job, taking over the packing to hurry up the process when she felt Heather wasn't moving fast enough. These are exactly the sort of things we need to hear from Heather at the meetings.

The meeting was planned for two p.m., yet here she is at one o'clock, making her way over to me and you, face to face with the man who embodies everything I have tried so hard to protect her from since I was a child. Words cannot describe how I feel in this moment, but I'll try. I have gone from feeling warm and consoled by your words once again, consolation I was deliberately seeking from you – and that in itself makes me feel conflicted – to wanting to protect my sister from you. No wonder you can't figure me out.

I fix all my attention on Heather, step towards her so she doesn't come any closer to you, positioning myself so we're two against one, with my arm wrapped around her shoulders protectively. I can't look at your face; I don't want to see how you might sneer or judge or analyse, or try to calculate another part of me through seeing her. I only look at her, beam at her with pride, oozing love for her from every pore, hoping you'll pick up on it, remember your show, feel awful about it, reassess yourself, your job and your whole life. I give it that much energy. I'm sure Heather will sense how disgusting you are, how deplorable and unfair and nasty and judgemental you are. Regardless of what you say about it being purely to get the debate flowing, those words still pass through your lips, you are the source, the root, the creator. Heather possesses this talent to read people and there is never a better moment than now to see this skill in action. I want you to hold out your hand to her, I want her to deny you as she did with Ted Clifford. I want to see you wriggle and squirm with that surprised face you give me when I snap at you, when I turn from hot to cold.

'Hello,' I hear you say.

'Hello,' Heather responds.

She looks at me, then nudges me, wanting to be introduced.

'This is my sister Heather,' I say. 'The most amazing person in the world.'

She giggles.

'Heather, this is Matt. A neighbour,' I say flatly.

You give me that intrigued, curious, studious look again. You know my hot and cold, my in between.

You wave at her. This bothers me, because it is correct behaviour for somebody in the Orange Wave Circle. Then Heather reaches out her hand. I turn to her in surprise, but she is looking at you with a polite smile on her face. I want to stop this exchange, this handshake with the devil, but I'm not sure that I can explain why I'm doing that to Heather, especially after the ruckus at Dad's house – who I still haven't heard from.

'A pleasure to meet you, Heather,' you say, shaking her hand. 'That's a cool bag you have.'

She is wearing the shoulder bag that I got her for her birthday five years ago. She wears it every day and keeps it looking brand new, making sure she cleans it, snips it of any tears. It's a retro-style DJ bag, which is for storing vinyl records, along with the portable record player. Seeing as she prefers to listen to her vinyl records, I thought it would be a nice gift for her to be able to bring it from place to place. And she does, almost everywhere. The picture on the outside is of a vinyl record, so even on days when she's not transporting her collection, she uses it to carry her purse, lunch and umbrella to and from work. Always those three things; I plead in vain with her to carry her mobile.

'Thank you. Jasmine got it for me. It fits fifty records and my portable record player.'

'You have a portable record player?'

'A black Audio Technica AT-LP60 fully automatic belt-driven record player,' she says, unzipping her bag to show him.

'Hey, that's very cool,' you say, stepping forward to look in but not stepping too close. 'And I see you've got some vinyl records there too.'

You are genuinely surprised, genuinely interested in her, genuinely want to see what she has in her DJ bag.

'Yep. Stevie Wonder, Michael Jackson . . .' she flips through her collection and I watch your face.

'Grandmaster Flash!' you laugh. 'Can I . . .?' You reach towards her bag and I prepare for her to deny you.

'Yes,' she says happily.

You slide it out of its compartment and study it. 'I can't believe you have Grandmaster Flash.'

'And the Furious Five,' she corrects you. 'The Message featuring Melle Mel and Duke Bootee, recorded at Sweet Mountain Studios, produced by Sylvia Robinson, Jiggs Chase and Ed Fletcher. Seven minutes eleven seconds in length,' she continues.

You look at me, astonished, then back at her. I can't help but glow with pride.

'That's amazing, Heather! You know everything about these records?'

And Heather goes on to tell you about her Stevie Wonder record: when it was recorded, each song on the album – she even names the session singers, the musicians. You are mightily impressed, amused, entertained, and you tell her so. Then you tell her that you're a DJ. That you work on radio. Heather is interested at first, until she hears that mostly what you do is talk. She tells you that she doesn't like listening to talking, she likes music. You ask her if she has ever been to a recording studio to see how musicians record their songs and she says no, then you tell her that you could bring her if she likes. Heather is unbelievably excited, but I can't speak, I am too stunned by the exchange. This is not how I thought this would go. Never. I start to back away, lead Heather to the house, say goodbye in some kind of vague way, while you two, already firm buddies, promise to keep in touch through me. *Through me.* Once we get inside, Heather is all talk about what you have promised her and I start to feel angry, trying to figure out ways to hurt you if you do not do what you have promised. And when that gets too violent in my head, I try to come up with ways to make Heather forget what you have said, preparing for the very strong probability that it will not happen, owing to the very strong probability that I will not let it happen.

Present at the meeting that day, aside from me and Heather, are her support assistant Jamie, whose only concession to winter wardrobe is to wear thick sport socks with her sandals; Julie, her employer from the restaurant; and Leilah, who is present for the first time. What I like about Leilah is that she doesn't even try to apologise on Dad's behalf; in fact she doesn't even mention him, and I respect that. The good thing about Leilah is that she has never gotten involved. This is largely because there has never been anything to get involved in, but her presence is a lovely gesture and I'm guessing that in order to understand what happened at her home last week, she needs to understand Heather more.

While the others are waiting in the living area, I make a pot of tea and mugs of coffee. Heather is beside me.

'Heather . . .' I begin, trying to keep the lightness in my voice. 'Why did you shake that man's hand outside?'

'Matt?' she asks.

'Yes. There's nothing wrong, don't look so worried, but you don't know him and I'm just wondering . . . share with me.'

She thinks about it. 'Because I saw you talking to him. And you looked very happy. And I thought, he is a nice man to make my sister happy.'

Heather never fails to surprise me.

I concentrate on organising the tray while trying to come to terms with the exchange between you and Heather. What I need to do right now is to shake you off. These meetings are important to Heather and they are equally important to me.

'So, take it away, Ms Butler,' I say like a cheesy TV host. Heather giggles.

'Jasmine,' she says, embarrassed, then composes herself. 'I would like to do a new activity.' She looks at me in a certain way and I know that this will concern Jonathan, the name I keep hearing. My heart starts to beat manically. Jonathan has been her friend for some time. He too has Down syndrome, and I know that she has a crush on him, which scares me because I know that he feels the same way about her. I can see it when he looks at her. I can feel it when they're in the same room as each other. It's beautiful and it terrifies me.

'Jonathan has a job as a teaching assistant in a Taekwondo class,' she explains to the others. I know this already because I went with her one week to watch him teaching under sevens and I wasn't allowed to utter one word to her for fear she would miss one of his moves. 'I would like to learn Taekwondo.'

Jamie and Leilah are wonderful at being genuinely interested in this and they ask her plenty of questions. While they do that, I worry. Heather is thirty-four years old and

140

certainly not agile, just as I am no longer as agile as I once was, and so this class concerns me. However I appear to be the only one with misgivings, and so I find myself agreeing that she will try a class next Saturday morning instead of her pottery and painting class, which she has grown tired of after two years.

'I have an idea,' Leilah offers. 'In case you don't like the Taekwondo, or if it doesn't work out for any reason, you could take part in one of my yoga classes. Maybe I could teach you and Jonathan together?'

Heather beams at this suggestion and so do I. I like this idea: time alone with Jonathan in Leilah's company makes me comfortable, and Heather starts to plan yoga and Taekwondo into her already busy week. I make notes in my diary, noticing how her activities fill my blank pages.

'Next,' I call, and she laughs again.

'Jonathan and I would like to go on a holiday together,' she says, and there is a stunned silence that even Jamie doesn't quite know how to fill. They all look at me. I want to say no. No, no, no – but I can't.

'Wow. Well. That's. I see. Well.' I take a sip of tea. 'Where would you like to go?'

'Daddy's apartment in Spain.'

Leilah widens her eyes at me.

'Did Dad say you could?'

'I didn't ask him. He couldn't come here today,' Heather says.

'Well, I mean, I'm not sure if it's free. Is it, Leilah? Is it free?'

'I don't know,' Leilah says slowly, not liking that I've put her on the spot for such an important issue, and not realising I want her to say no, or else realising it and not wanting to lie.

'She hasn't even told you the date,' Jamie says, not hiding her unhappiness with how this is going.

'Springtime,' Heather says. 'Jonathan says summer is too hot.'

'Jonathan is absolutely right,' I say, my mind racing. I know now how Dad felt when I told him I was going on my first holiday with my boyfriend. Then I remember how I felt even broaching the subject with him, and I look at Heather and I finally relax. 'Heather. You and Jonathan have never been away together before, and Spain is quite far *for a first trip*.' I emphasise these words so she won't think I'm shutting her down straight away. 'Why don't you go away for a night or two first, somewhere lovely in Ireland that you've never been before? You can get a train or a bus and be close to home but not too close?'

She looks uncertain. She and Jonathan have already saved their fare and set their hearts on Spain. Talking her back from such a big move takes a lot of gentle persuasion, but Heather listens, she listens to us all, she always does, she's a clever woman, taking in everybody's opinion.

Over the past few weeks I had come up with a plan to take Heather to Fota Island which lies in Cork harbour and is home to Ireland's only wildlife park. I suggest this venue now, because I can't think of anything else on the spot. She is immediately convinced. Spain is forgotten. Jonathan loves animals, he loves trains, this is perfect. I can't help but feel sad, that the place I was excited to take her to will be an experience she shares with someone else.

'So,' I take a deep breath. 'The bedrooms.'

I can tell Heather is embarrassed about this part so I take control.

'Options are: two bedrooms *or* one bedroom with two single beds. Or . . .' I can't bring myself to say it. Jonathan and Heather are two people with desires and passions just like everyone else, but I feel like an overprotective parent whose child has announced she likes boys. I take a breath and force myself to say it: 'Or one double bed in one room – but Jonathan might be a diagonal man, who knows?' I add playfully. 'He might take up the entire bed and you might roll out on to the floor in the middle of the night.'

Heather laughs.

'Or maybe he snores,' Jamie says. 'Like this—' She makes a loud piggy sound and we all laugh.

'Or maybe his feet smell really bad,' Leilah says, pinching her nose.

'Jonathan does not smell,' Heather says, pouting, her hands on her hips.

'Oooh, Jonathan is *so* perfect,' I tease.

'Jasmine!' Heather squeals, and we all laugh.

The laughter quietens and the room descends into silence, waiting for her decision.

'Separate bedrooms,' she says quietly, and we hurriedly move on. While Jamie is talking about the logistics of getting there, I wink at Heather and she smiles shyly.

This is not the first time Heather has been away: she has travelled before with groups of friends, but always with her support assistant or another adult that I know in attendance. This is her first time alone, with a man, and I have to fight the nervous ball of tension in my stomach, the lump in my throat and the tears that are welling.

We move on to discussing her next issue, which is that, while she is very grateful for the three jobs that she has during the week, her main love is music and none of her activities seem to cover this. She would love to work in a radio station or a recording studio, and she tells everybody in the group about the conversation she has had with Matt

Marshall. Everybody remarks on what a wonderful coincidence it is that she has met him on the very day she wished to discuss this.

'Jasmine, perhaps we could invite Matt Marshall to the next meeting to discuss the possibilities?' Jamie suggests.

Heather is giddy with excitement at the prospect.

I always like these meetings to be positive, so I summon up all the cheeriness I can. 'Perhaps we can plan it for the next time. Maybe. Perhaps. After I talk to him and see if there's anything he can do. If he has time – though he is having a personal moment out of work at the moment. So . . . yes. Maybe,' I finally say.

Leilah eyes me warily. I'm grateful when we move on to the next subject.

It is with a heavy heart that I close the door on everybody after the meeting is finished and go upstairs to my bedroom. I am not jealous of my sister, I never have been. I have always wanted a better life for her, even though I know that she is happy with the life she has. Today, however, it has occurred to me for the first time that she has always known the direction she has wanted to take in her life, she has always had a team to help her, advise her, guide her. She has always had it sussed. It is me who hasn't. It is me who suddenly has absolutely no idea what I am doing, it is me who has no PATH whatsoever. The realisation hits me like a ton of bricks and I can't seem to catch my breath. I couldn't tell anybody my dreams if they asked me right now, nor my hopes and desires. If I was asked to put a plan into action, I wouldn't know where to start.

I feel utterly lost.

Spring

The season between winter and summer, comprising in the Northern Hemisphere the months March, April and May.

The ability of something to return to its original shape when it is pressed down, stretched or twisted.

14

All my life I have followed and respected signs. When driving through an estate where there are signs for children at play, I respect that and slow down. When I see a sign for a reindeer as I'm driving through Phoenix Park, I know to be on my guard in case one appears from behind a tree and dashes across the road. I always stop at stop signs, I yield when I'm supposed to yield. I trust signs. I believe they are accurate – apart from when some vandal has quite obviously twisted a sign to point in the wrong direction. I believe that signs are on my side. This is where I get confused by people who say they believe in signs, as if it is an enlightening and remarkable thing, because what's not to believe about something that points you to something and instructs you to do something? What is not to believe about a physical thing? It's like saying I believe in milk. Of course you do, it's milk. I think most people who say that they believe in signs actually mean that they believe in symbols.

Symbols are something visible that represent something invisible. A symbol is used abstractly. A dove is a bird but it is also a symbol of peace. A handshake is an action but it is also a symbol of amity. Symbols represent something by association. Symbols often force us to figure out what the invisible thing is; for it's not always obvious. While jogging along Dublin Bay towards my house on 1 March, the first day of spring, I see the most beautiful rainbow, which from afar appears to land directly on top of my house, going through my roof and into my home, or landing in my back garden. This is not a sign. It's not instructing me to do anything. It is a symbol. As were the snowdrops which fought to rise above the ground in January and February, standing shoulder to shoulder, pretty and timid-looking, as if butter wouldn't melt, as if in doing what they had done, achieving what they had achieved against the elements was no mean feat. They'd made it look easy.

Monday O'Hara is another example. Him coming into my life, headhunting me for a job, seeking me out and thinking I am worthwhile. This represents something invis-ible too. I think of him often, not just because of how handsome he is but for what he represents. We have spoken on the phone twice since our meeting and I never want to hang up. Either he is very dedicated to his job, giving me so much of his time, or he doesn't want to hang up either. The month he gave me to think about the job is up. I'm looking forward to seeing him again.

The rainbow over my house, the snowdrops, the carpet of purple crocuses in the Malones' side garden, and Monday O'Hara are all symbols for me. They are all visible things representing something invisible: Hope.

I begin the day by decluttering. Before long the house is in such a mess that I realise I need a skip – which I have, but it is currently on my driveway, filled with expensive paving that attracts a string of untrustworthy types who keep knocking on my door to ask if I'd like help getting rid of it. So in order to fill the skip with my indoor junk I must first empty it of stones, but having removed the stones

I must place them somewhere. It is then I recall your rockery suggestion. Even though it annoys me to take your advice – and worse still, for you to see me taking your advice, given that the skip is in front of my house, directly in line of your view – I know it has to be done. It's too late to ask the landscaper for help. When he showed up after the storm, expecting to find the pile of turf destroyed by the rain and wind and instead discovering my not-so-perfectly laid front lawn, I told him I would do the rest of the garden on my own. Finish what I started, as it were. Not that I would give Larry the satisfaction of knowing that his comment had prodded me into doing something for myself.

Abandoning the ransacked house that I have made even more cluttered in my effort to declutter, I shift my focus to the garden. I am going to do this garden properly, this has my full attention. I draw up a list and set off to the garden centre to buy what I need to buy. I am focused. I am in the zone, the gardening zone. I receive two text messages from friends, suggesting we go for a coffee but just as I'm about to say yes to the first one – something I've taken to doing automatically, jumping at the chance of midweek, midday company – I realise that I am actually busy. I have a lot of work to do before the storm clouds start gathering again. The second text is easy to send: I am busy. Very busy. And that feels good.

Today is the ideal day to work because the ground is dry. Having realised that my 'Indian Natural Sandstone' paving stones are not going to give me the rugged look that I envisage for my rockery, I have made arrangements for the ideal natural stone to be delivered. Right on time, the helpful young man from the garden centre who has been educating me on each trip pulls up in his car, towing the rocks behind him on a trailer. He studies my sandstone.

'Shame to waste it,' he says.

We stand staring at the slabs with our hands on our hips.

'You could make stepping stones,' he says eventually. 'Like they've done next door.'

We both look into the Malones' perfect garden and see their heart-shaped stepping stones leading to a fairy house. Eddie wasn't exactly careful with the jackhammer, so my stones are irregular shapes. It's more natural that way and I rather like it. The garden centre man goes on his way, leaving me to amuse myself moving sandstone slabs around on my new grass. I improvise, using the end of my rake to decide how deep to position the slabs. Then I measure my stride and lay the stones so that there's a stone underfoot for each step. I take my half-moon edger alongside the paver, step down on it to cut completely through the turf's roots. I make an outline of the stone and then strip out the sod. I dig down to a depth equal to the stone's thickness, then I repeat this process for the ten stones I have leading away from my house towards where the rockery will be. I mix stone dust with water in my new wheelbarrow until it is the consistency of cake batter. I add two inches of mix to each hole to prevent moving or sinking, and then I wiggle the stone into its slot and pound it with a rubber mallet. I use a leveller to set each stone evenly. All this takes me some time.

By six p.m. it is dark and I am sweating, hungry, sore, tired – and more satisfied than I can ever remember feeling. I have completely lost track of time, though at some stages I was conscious of Mr Malone pruning his roses and trimming the overgrowth while telling me in a jolly voice that he should have done this in January and February but couldn't, not with Elsa so sick.

As I collapse into bed that night, relaxing into freshly

changed sheets with the smell of 'summer breeze' tumble-drier sheets, I realise that an entire day has gone by without me giving a minute's thought to my current problems. My mind was well and truly on the task at hand. Maybe it's the genes I inherited from my granddad, or maybe it's the fact that I'm Irish, have sprung from the land and this compulsion to dig, and the digging itself, breathes life back into me. I may have walked into my garden all tensed up, but as soon as I started to work, the tension disappeared all by itself.

When I was seven years old, Mum bought me my first bike, a Purple Heather, with a white-and-purple wicker basket in the front, and a bell that I used to love playing with even when I was sitting on the grass with the bike lying down around me. I loved the sound of it, I felt like it was the voice of my bike. I would ask it a question and *briiing* it would answer. I spent every day cycling out on the street, circling, going up and down the kerbs, fast, slow, braking, almost as if I was an ice skater swirling around with an audience watching me, judges holding up numbers and everyone cheering. I'd stay out for as long as possible in the evenings, eat my dinner so quickly it would be painfully stuck in my chest before racing back out to the bike. At night I cried, leaving it. I would park it outside in the garden and watch it, alone, as it waited for me and our next adventure. Now I feel like that child again, staring out the window at my darkened garden, knowing exactly what will go where, imagining each feature, how I can mould it and nurture it, all the possibilities.

I am having the most delicious dream about Monday O'Hara. He is listing, in complete awe, all the things I have achieved in my garden – which is no longer my garden but Powerscourt Gardens in Wicklow. I shrug off his compliments, telling him I'm a snowdrop and that's what snowdrops do, no big deal, we're tough, we push up above the soil, like fists being raised in victory. Things are beginning to get juicy between us when the sound of 'Paradise City' intrudes on my dream, blaring from a Tannoy system strapped to the roof of the groundskeeper's van as he tries to clear the gardens for closing time – which leads Monday to realise that I'm a phoney, that the gardens I've shown him aren't mine after all, that I'm a liar. Then the groundskeeper rolls down his blackened window and it's you. You are looking at me and smiling, a smile that grows and turns into a laugh that gets louder and louder as the music blares. I awake suddenly to hear 'Paradise City' still playing. I squeeze my eyes shut, hoping to get back into the dream with Monday, to pick up where we left off before the groundskeeper ruins it, but when I do fall asleep I find myself in a different dream, with Kevin sitting on the grass, making daisy chains. Everyone around is dressed in black and he is speaking and acting as if he is ten again, even though he looks like the man I met in Starbucks, and when he goes to put the daisy chain on my hand I discover it is actually made of roses and the thorns slice my skin.

I wake up to voices outside. I stumble out of bed, disorientated, and look out the window. You are sitting at the table in your front garden with Dr Jameson. The table is now so worn the wood is chipping and peeling off. It needs to be treated – why this should occur to me as more important than the sight of Dr Jameson sitting outside with you at 3.10 a.m. confuses me. Dr Jameson is facing my house; you are at the head of the table as always. There is a collection of cans on the table and you knock one back, face parallel to the sky as you squeeze the can of every last drop. When you've finished, you scrunch up the can and throw it at a tree. You miss and immediately pick up a full can and fire it angrily at the tree. You hit the target and beer foams out from the burst tin.

Dr Jameson pauses to watch where it has landed, then carries on talking. I'm confused. Perhaps he has lost his key to your house and the two of you are too polite to bother me for my set. I find this highly unlikely. You burp, so loudly that it seems to bounce off the end wall of the cul de sac and echo. I can't hear Dr Jameson's words, though I want to, and I fall asleep listening to the soothing rise and fall of his gentle tone.

This time I dream about a conversation with Granddad Adalbert. Though I am an adult, I feel like a child again. We're in his back garden and he is showing me how to sow seeds. Under his watchful eye, I sprinkle sunflower seeds, cover them up with soil and then water them. He is talking to me as though I am still a child. He is showing me how he prunes his winter-flowering jasmine, which he tells me can be pruned when the flowers have withered completely. He shows me how he prunes any dead or damaged wood needed to extend the framework or coverage of the plant, and then he shortens all the side growths from the main framework to two inches from the main stems. This will encourage plenty of new shoots that will flower next winter. 'Plenty of new growth, Jasmine,' he says, busily feeding and mulching.

'This is not a sign, Granddad,' I tell him in a baby voice that I am putting on, because I don't want to hurt his feelings by reminding him that I am an adult now. It might make him realise that he has been dead for so long, and that could make him sad. 'This does not tell me which direction to take,' I say, but he has his back to me as he continues working.

'Is that so?' he says, talking as if I'm babbling and not making any sense.

'Yes, Granddad. The jasmine is pruned back, but it is ready now, ready to grow, and that is not a sign, that is a symbol.'

He turns around then, and even though I know I am in a dream, I'm sure it's him, that it's really really him. He smiles, his face crinkles, his eyes almost close as his apple cheeks lift in that hearty smile.

'That's my Jasmine,' he says.

I wake up with a tear rolling down my cheek.

15

It's Saturday and as soon as I open my eyes to the golden light in my bedroom I want to leap out of bed, throw a tracksuit on and race outside to the garden, like the boy in *The Snowman* who can barely contain himself, he's so eager to see his new friend. Of course in my case it's not a snowman but a pile of rocks that I need to place on my sloping garden.

While I'm outside looking at the stones, Amy arrives with the children. They get out of the car and slowly, unhappily trudge away from her. You open the front door, and before you can get down the driveway to greet her she takes off. You are left watching her drive away. Not a good sign. The children hug you – not Fionn, he just carries on dragging his feet all the way up the driveway and into the house.

Finally there's silence, and I like that, only it doesn't last long. Mr Malone is back in his garden and I can hear him brushing his paving stones.

'You shouldn't power-hose,' he says, noticing me watching him. He's on his knees, scrubbing the stones by hand. 'It ruins the look of the stone. I've got to have the place looking tidy for Elsa. She'll be home tomorrow.'

'That's great to hear, Jimmy.'

'Not the same,' he says, clambering to his feet and walking to meet me in the middle where his shrubbery and grass ends and where my car and paving begin.

'Without her?'

'With her, without her. She's not the same. The stroke, it . . .' He nods to himself, as if finishing the sentence in his own head and then agreeing with it. 'She's not the same. Still, Marjorie will be happy to see her. I'll tidy around in there as well, but I don't know if she'll notice a great deal.'

My spell of duty feeding Marjorie ended as soon as Dr Jameson returned from his holiday, but I'd noticed that Jimmy hadn't been coping too well without his wife around. The kitchen sink was piled with dirty dishes and a foul odour emanated from the fridge. It wasn't much and it wasn't invasive, but I'd cleaned the dishes and thrown out the mouldy vegetables and the milk that had gone off in the otherwise empty fridge. He was so used to being looked after domestically that he hadn't noticed, or at least he hadn't commented. Still, once Dr Jameson returned to his hands-on neighbourly role, I doubted his duties would include dishwashing. Though his duties with you last night, if that's what they were, had extended to 3.30 a.m. What you both talked about till then – you blind-drunk, singing and shouting, and Dr Jameson in his North Face jacket and his suntan – is a mystery to me.

I leave a respectful silence, though I know he hadn't expected an answer. Then I ask, 'Jimmy, when is the best time to plant a tree?'

He snaps out of his maudlin mood, perking up instantly at the question. 'Best time to plant a tree, eh?'

I nod, and immediately regret asking. I'm probably in for a long-winded answer.

'Yesterday,' he says, then chuckles, the sadness still in his eyes. 'Like everything else. Failing that, *now*.' Then he goes back to cleaning his stones.

Your door opens and Fionn steps out, dressed all in black, hoodie covering most of his face, but the teenage spots and freckles belie his eerie choice of clothing. He comes straight to me.

'Dad told me to help you,' he says.

'Oh.' I'm not sure how to respond. 'I'm, erm, I don't need help. I'm okay, really. But thanks.' I like the peace of working alone. I don't want to have to make small talk or explain what it is I want done. I'd rather just get on with it by myself.

He's staring at the rocks longingly.

'They look heavy.'

They do indeed look heavy. I remind myself I don't need help, I never ask for help. I'd rather do things myself.

'I don't want to go back in there,' he says, so quietly that when I look at him staring at the rocks it's as if he hasn't spoken and I question whether I really heard it. How can I tell him no after that? And I wonder whose idea it was to come out here and help me. I doubt it was yours.

'Let's start with this one,' I say. 'I want to put it over here.'

Having Fionn there makes me move more quickly, make decisions faster than I otherwise would have. At first I struggle to come up with things to say to him – cool things, witty things, young things – but as time wears on and his monosyllabic answers continue, I realise he no more wants to chat than I do. And so we labour on in silence, starting from the bottom of the slope and working our way up, the only communication a word here or there about moving a stone to the right, to the left – that kind of thing. As the hours pass, he starts offering suggestions as to where to place things.

157

Eventually we stand back, sweating and panting, and examine the rocks. Happy with their position, we set about thoroughly embedding each rock so it's securely in place, at least half of the rock buried below the ground. We mix planting compost and sharp sand to make sure the rocks stay in place. On the next level we move the smaller rocks, leaving plenty of pockets for plants. At each stage we stand back and take a good look from different viewpoints.

Fionn is quiet.

'It will look better with the plants and flowers in,' I say self-consciously, protective over my patch.

'Yeah,' he says in a tone I can't read. His voice is a monotone, expressionless, seeming to care and not care at the same time.

'I'm thinking of putting a water fountain in,' I say. I have looked into this and am excited to have found a video demonstrating how to build a water fountain in eight hours. I'm further excited to see that I can use my Indian sandstone for the actual fountain.

We're both silent as we survey the garden for a place.

'You could put it there,' he says.

'I was thinking more over here.'

He's quiet for a moment, then: 'Where's the nearest electrical socket?'

I shrug.

'You'll need that for the pump. Look – you have lights.' He goes on a wander around the garden, seeking out the source of electricity for my garden lights. 'Here. It would be better to put it near here.'

'Yeah,' I say, my voice as even as his – not meaning to, but it's addictive. It's so much easier not to make an effort, I can understand why he does it. 'I'm going to put a pipe up through the middle of the stones like this, see.' I layer the sandstones on top of one another to show him. 'The water will come up through the middle.'

'Like, explode?'

'No, like . . . gurgle.'

He nods once, unimpressed. 'Are you going to do that now?'

'Tomorrow.'

He looks disappointed, though it's hard to be certain, given the general drift between nonchalance and misery. I don't invite him back tomorrow. I haven't minded his company, but I prefer to do this alone, particularly as I don't know what I'm doing. I want to find my way by myself, not have to discuss and explain it. Not that there would be much discussion with Fionn.

'Are you going to use them all?'

'Half of them.'

'Can I have the other half?'

'For what?'

He shrugs, but it's clear he has something in mind.

I look at him, waiting for more.

'To smash them.'

'Oh.'

'Can I borrow this?' He indicates my rubber mallet.

It's the most hopeful I've ever seen him look.

'Okay,' I say uncertainly.

He places the paving stones in the wheelbarrow and wheels it across the road to your table. Then he comes back for more. It's as he is doing this that you come outside to see what he's doing. You actually ask him what he's doing, but he ignores you and returns to my garden for more stones. You watch him for a moment then follow him.

'Hi,' you say, walking up the path to me, hands deep in your pockets. You survey the rockery. 'Looks good.'

'Thanks. Dammit,' I say suddenly, seeing my cousin Kevin turn the corner into the street, casually strolling, looking left and right as he searches for my house. 'I'm not here,' I say, dropping everything and darting towards the house.

'What?'

'I'm not here,' I repeat, pointing at Kevin, then pulling the front door to. I leave it open a crack, I want to hear what he has to say.

Kevin strolls up the driveway. 'Hello,' he says to you and Fionn, who is placing paving stones in the wheelbarrow very carefully, despite his apparent intention to smash them.

'Hi there,' you say. You sound more DJ-like when I can't see you, as if you have a 'phone voice' reserved for strangers. I side step to the window and peek up over the windowsill to watch. Kevin looks priestly, poker-straight back, brown cords, a raincoat. Everything is precise, neat, earthy tones. I can picture him in sandals in the summertime.

'Jasmine's not in,' you say.

'Oh.' Kevin looks up at the house and I duck. 'That's a shame. Are you sure? It looks like . . . well, the door is open.'

For a moment I'm afraid that he's going to come looking for me, like when we were kids and I absolutely did not want Kevin to come find me. That game when whoever finds you has to join you and hide with you, and you both wait for the rest of them to find you. Kevin always had a knack of finding me first, pushing his body up against mine, cramming into the tight space with me so that I could feel his breath on my neck, and feel his heart beating on my skin. Even as a child he made me uncomfortable.

You are quiet. I'm surprised you can't come up with a lie – not that I have any proof of you being a liar, but I think so little of you at times that this is something I'd assumed you'd be a natural at. It is Fionn who comes to my rescue.

'She left it open for us. We're her gardeners,' he says, and the lack of emotion, the lack of caring, makes him entirely believable. You look at him with what seems to be admiration.

'Oh dear. Okay, I'll try her mobile again then,' Kevin says, starting to back away. 'In case I don't get her, will you tell her Kevin called by? Kevin,' he repeats.

'Kevin, right,' you say, clearly uncomfortable to be in this position.

'Sure, Kieran,' Fionn says, taking off down the path with the wheelbarrow.

'It's Kevin,' he says good-naturedly but a little concerned.

'Got it,' you say, and Kevin slowly wanders back wherever he came from, continuously looking over his shoulder at the house to make sure I don't jump out. Even when he has disappeared from sight, I don't feel safe.

'He's gone,' you say, and you knock on the door.

I open the door slowly, and slip in beside you, hoping you will screen me from view in case he returns.

'Thanks.'

'Boyfriend?'

'God, no. Wants to be.'

'And you don't.'

'No.'

'Seems like a nice guy.'

I need to hit this little candid chat on the head straight away. I do not want to talk about my lovelife or lack thereof with you.

'He's my cousin,' I blurt out, hoping to end the conversation about Kevin.

Your eyes widen. 'Jesus.'

'He was adopted.'

'Oh.'

'Still,' I say in my defence. It is and always will be disgusting to me.

Silence.

'I've a cousin: Eileen,' you say suddenly. 'Had the biggest pair of tits, even as kids. All I remember when I think of her are . . .' You hold your spread hands out over your pecs and clasp great big jugs of air. 'I always had a crush on her. Crumb Tits, we always called her, because everything used to fall right there, you know. Like a shelf?'

We are both looking at Fionn as you talk, not at each other. Our backs are to the wall of my house, facing out.

'She's had a few kids now. They're more down here these days . . .' You drop your hands so those imaginary boobs fall around your waistline. 'But if she told me she was adopted tomorrow . . . I would, you know?'

'Matt,' I sigh.

I look at you and see you have that mischievous look on your face. I shake my head. Whether your story is true or not, you are deliberately winding me up. I don't bite.

'Your sister, she—'

'Has Down syndrome,' I pre-empt you, crossing my arms, ready for the fight. Always ready: *What did you say about my sister?* The cause of most of my adolescent fights. Some things never change.

You seem taken aback by me and I loosen my posture a little.

'I was going to say, your sister is a big fan of music.'

I narrow my eyes at you suspiciously and conclude that you seem genuine. 'Oh.' Pause. 'Yes. She is.'

'She probably knows more than me.'

'That's a no-brainer.'

You smile. 'I've organised something for her next week. A tour of the station. Do you think she'd be interested? I thought she might be – I've done it for people before, but never anyone like her who I think would really appreciate it, get the full benefit. What do you reckon?'

I stare at you in shock, manage a quick nod.

'Good. I hope it's okay to ask, but I just want to know what's the correct way to go about it? Do I drive her there, or do you want to drive her? Or will she make her own way?'

I continue to stare at you in surprise. I don't recognise you. That you've organised a tour for her and that you are thoughtful enough to worry about the logistics is beyond my comprehension. 'You've organised a tour for her?'

You look confused. 'I said I would. Is that okay? Should I cancel?'

'No, no,' I say quickly. 'She'll be so happy.' I struggle to find the next words. 'She gets the bus by herself,' I say, defensive again. 'She's perfectly capable of that, you know.'

'Good.' Your eyes examine me; I hate this.

'But I could bring her,' I say. 'If that's okay.'

'Of course.' You smile. 'You're a protective big sister.'

'Little,' I say.

You frown.

'She's older than me.'

A penny seems to drop. You have that look of realisation. But it's sarcastic. 'That would make sense. She's more mature.'

A smile tickles at the corners of my mouth but I refuse to let it happen. I look away to Fionn. You follow my stare.

We watch Fionn picking up the mallet.

'Are you seriously okay with him doing that?' you ask.

'Are *you* okay with it?'

'They're not my stones.'

'A piece could fly into his eye,' I say.

Silence.

'Could slice his arm. Hit an artery.'

You take off after him across the road.

I don't know what you say to your son but you haven't handled it well. Before you even finish your sentence, Fionn is smashing up pieces of my expensive Indian sandstone on your garden table. You jump back so that the pieces don't hit you. It's as if you're not there to him.

For twenty minutes he smashes everything up into tiny pieces, his cheeks flushed from the exertion, his face screwed up in anger. Your daughter, the blondie who dances every-where instead of walking, is watching him from inside the jeep, the closest you will allow her to go, and you are at the front door, arms folded, standing upright, watching with less embarrassment and more concern as he batters my expensive stones. When he's finished, he surveys his work, his arms loose and gangly and free of tension. Then he looks up and around, suddenly aware of his surround-ings and the people watching him, as if he's coming out of a coma. He tenses up again, the hood goes back up, the turtle disappearing into its shell. He drops the mallet into the wheelbarrow and he pushes it across the road to me.

'Thanks,' he grunts, before shuffling off again, head down as he passes his family and pushes past you, in through the front door. From across the road I hear a door slam upstairs in the house.

It makes me think I should call my dad.

I should. But I don't. A few months into this gardening leave I realised I'd slammed my door closed a long time ago, I don't know when it happened – when I slammed the door and when exactly I realised it – but it is obvious to me now, and I'm not quite ready to come out of my room yet.

16

I awake in the middle of the night to the same low voices being carried in the gentle wind over to my house, as though the breeze is a messenger, carrying the words especially to me. As soon as I wake, I know that I am wide awake and will be for the long haul. This despite the fact I'm exhausted, completely and absolutely spent; the gardening yesterday was so backbreaking and intense that I feel the effects of it each time I move, but it is a satisfying ache. Not the headache I used to get from spending too long talking on my mobile phone, the hot-eared, hot-cheeked pain and ache in my eyes from staring at a computer screen all day or the lower back problems and the right shoulder strain from bad posture at a desk, hunched over a computer. It does not equal any of these, nor does it equal the pain I experience after working out after a break from exercise. This feeling is so completely different and satisfying I am almost buzzing. Even though I'm exhausted, my mind is alive. It is invigorating, I am pumped and some of that is due to the fact my soul feels fed by the earth, but mostly it's down to the fact I can't figure out why Dr Jameson has once again joined you at your garden table, sitting out in the cold night air until one o'clock in the morning. What is so

165

important that it can't be discussed during daylight? Even more confusing, what on earth could you and he possibly have in common? You two are the least likely candidates on the street for an alliance, perhaps less likely than you and I – and that's saying something. I eventually reason that you are a fuck-up and Dr Jameson is someone who needs to clean everything up, fix things. You must be part of his neighbourhood watch effort; perhaps he considers you a potential menace to the people on this street with your streetlight, window and garage smashing.

I throw off the bedcovers and admit defeat. You have suckered me.

I cross the road in Ugg boots and a Puffa coat carrying a flask of tea and some mugs.

'Ah, there's the woman herself,' Dr Jameson announces, as though the pair of you have been talking about me.

You look at me, bleary-eyed, drunk as usual. 'See, I told you: she can't get enough of me,' you say drily, but it is half-hearted.

'Hello, Dr Jameson. Tea?'

'Please.' His tired eyes sparkle in the moonlight, his second night on the trot up past midnight.

I don't even bother to offer you one. You are nursing a glass of whisky and the bottle is half-empty on the table. I don't know how many you've had. Two or three perhaps, of this bottle anyway. There is a strong smell of whisky in the air, but that could be drifting from the open bottle and not your breath. You have a different energy about you tonight; you seem defeated, the fight all gone out of you. Though it doesn't stop you from nipping at my heels, it is done with less vigour than usual.

'Nice jim-jams,' you say.

'They're not jim-jams.' I take care to check the chair for

broken pieces of stone, which are still scattered all around the place despite Fionn sweeping up after himself yesterday evening, obviously against his will from the angry sound of the bristles hitting the concrete. 'They're lounging pants,' I reply and you snort.

I sit opposite you at the other head of the table and wrap my hands around the mug of tea to keep me warm.

'Now the mad hatter's tea party is complete,' you say. 'Is it cry o'clock yet?'

That stings but I don't rise to the bait.

'I'm afraid our friend is a wind-up merchant,' Dr Jameson says, conspiratorially, jovially. 'I wouldn't take much notice.'

'That's what I get paid for,' you say.

'Not any more.' I peek at you over my mug. Perhaps I'm looking for a fight, I'm not sure. I was aiming to match your tone, but it doesn't work when I do it. You give me a stony look that surprises me and I know that I've hit a nerve. And I like it.

I smile. Payback. 'What's happened, Matt? Bob not going to fix you up? Thought you were like that –' I cross my fingers the way you had done.

'Bob had a heart attack,' you say darkly. 'He's in hospital on a life-support machine. We don't think he's going to make it.'

I feel horrendous. My smile quickly fades. 'Oh. God. Matt. I'm so sorry.' I stutter my way through an apology, feeling just awful.

'Bob was fired,' Dr Jameson says. 'Matt, please.'

You chuckle, but it doesn't sound happy and I'm raging that you reduced me to feeling like that, for making me apologise to you.

'Dr J, this woman is up and down more than a stripper on a pole.'

'Now now,' Dr Jameson cautions.

I can't debate this fact – the up-and-down bit, not the stripper bit. It's true of me with him.

'So your buddy got fired,' I say, slugging back my tea, feeling back on top again. 'That doesn't look so good for the routine investigation into your conduct, does it?'

'No, it doesn't, does it.' You stare at me.

'Unless they're going to hire a new friend of yours to take his place. Someone else who's willing to overlook your extreme error in judgement. Again.'

You give me a dangerous look and knock back your whisky. I should read the signs but I don't, or I do but carry on regardless. I thought you were a man on the verge before but you were perfectly solid in comparison to this. I want to reach out my finger and push you. It feels like therapy for me.

'Uh-oh,' I say sarcastically, reading his look. 'They've hired someone who doesn't like you. Shocking. Wonder where they found him.'

'Her, actually,' Dr Jameson says. 'Olivia Fry. An English woman. From a very successful radio station in the UK I believe.'

'An awful radio station,' you say, rubbing your face, the stress obvious.

'Not a fan?' I say.

'No.' You look at me darkly again.

I take another sip.

'Try not to look so sad about it, Jasmine.'

I throw my hands up. 'You know what, Matt, I can understand in a weird way, how you think that what you do is for the greater good—'

You try to interrupt.

'Wait, wait,' I raise my voice.

168

'Sshh,' Dr Jameson says. 'The Murphys.'

I lower my voice to a hush but keep the power. 'But New Year's Eve? The woman in your studio? What the hell?'

There's a long silence. Dr Jameson looks from me to you and back again. I can tell he's curious to see if you'll give the honest answer.

'I was wasted,' you finally say, but it is not a defence, it's acknowledgement. I look at Dr Jameson in surprise. 'I mistakenly took my anxiety pills with some alcohol before the show.'

'And you shouldn't do that.' Dr Jameson shakes his head violently, already knowing this story. 'Those pills are strong, Matt. You shouldn't have been drinking at all. You can't mix them. Frankly, you shouldn't be on those pills.'

'I've mixed them before and it would have been fine, except I still had sleeping pills in my system from that morning,' you explain. Dr Jameson holds his hands to his head in horror.

'So you admit that your show on New Year's Eve was wrong,' I say, more surprised by the admission of wrong-doing than the concoction of drugs you'd taken.

You look at me, eyebrow raised, unimpressed by my goading you. When I see you're not going to repeat it, I look at Dr Jameson.

'So, how was your holiday?'

'Oh, well,' he gathers himself. 'It was rather nice to see the children and—'

'It rained for two weeks, they were stuck inside and they made Dr J do all the baby-sitting.'

'It wasn't all doom and gloom.'

'Dr J, you tell me to face facts, it's time you did the same. They used you.'

Dr Jameson looks defeated.

What rings in my ears is you saying *you tell me to face facts*. A little glimpse into your relationship with the good doctor; facing facts is not what I thought you'd be doing at this hour, outside in your garden.

'I'm sorry to hear that,' I say to Dr Jameson.

'It's . . . you know, it's . . . I was hoping to stay with them for Christmas, you see, but no. That won't be happening now.'

'Dr J's spent Christmas Day on his own for the past fifteen years.'

'A little less than that,' he says. 'I was hoping this year would be different. But,' he perks up, 'no matter.'

We sit in silence, each of us lost in our own thoughts.

'You've done a nice job on your garden,' Dr Jameson says.

'Thanks.' I look at it proudly.

'She's on gardening leave,' you say, then laugh and cough 'fired' into your whisky glass.

I feel the anger building. 'Fionn helped me with the rockery. He wanted to get away from his dad,' I say.

Dr Jameson is amused by our banter. I'm not.

'He's fifteen. No one wants to be with their dad when they're fifteen,' you say.

I concur.

'And there's nothing to do here,' you continue. 'The three of them just want to sit around all day playing on their iPads.'

'Then *do something* with them,' I say. 'Think of something. He likes being out and about, do a project with him.' I look at the table. 'Sand and varnish this thing. That'll keep him busy. Do it together. You might even communicate.' I gasp sarcastically at the idea.

Silence again.

'Gardening leave, Jasmine,' Dr Jameson says. 'For how long?'

'One year.'

'What was your business?'

'I was co-founder of a company called the Idea Factory. We came up with and implemented ideas and strategies for other companies.'

'Consultancy?' you ask.

'No.' I shake my head.

'Advertising then.'

'No no,' I object.

'Well, it's not very clear what exactly—'

'It's not talking out loud for people to hear, Matt, that's what it's not,' I snap.

'Hoo hoo hoo,' you sing-laugh, knowing you've touched a nerve and I've reacted perfectly, played right into your hands. 'I've offended her, Dr J, somehow, sometime,' you explain.

'Why stop at one time? Why can't everything you say offend me?' I know that that's no longer true and I feel bad. I think of the times when your words comforted me.

I look across at my garden, the only thing that can take my mind off everything these days, the only thing that will lift me out of this conversation and stop me from saying something I might regret. You have been good-spirited up till now, but I know that if I keep on pushing your buttons you might crack, and likewise with me.

'What will you do?' Dr Jameson asks, and it feels as if I've had to come back from somewhere far away to answer him.

'I'm thinking of building a water fountain,' I say.

'I didn't mean—'

'She knew what you meant.' You watch me thoughtfully.

'That couple who live beside me, Dr J,' I say, without realising I'm now using your nickname for him until you react.

'The Lennons,' he reminds me.

'I saw them calling door-to-door yesterday. What were they doing?'

'A secret swinging society,' you say. 'Right under our very noses.'

I ignore you.

'I think she fancies me,' you say to Dr J.

'You are so childish.'

'You are so easy to wind up, it's almost a waste not to.'

'Not normally. Only with you.'

'The Lennons were saying goodbye,' Dr Jameson says as though our childish spat isn't happening. 'They've decided to let their house and go on a cruise for a few months. After what happened with Elsa Malone, they'd rather live while they have the chance.'

'Who'll be renting?'

'Your cousin,' you say.

'Really? I heard it was your wife,' I shoot back.

'A corporate man. Lone man. Companies pay an absolute fortune for their managing directors now, don't they? He moves in next week sometime. I saw him having a look around. Young fellow.'

You make a bizarre tooting sound that I realise is directed at me. A schoolboy jeer. 'You never know, Jasmine.' You wink at me.

'Please.'

'Time is getting on. You're not getting any younger. Tick tick tick, you'll need to start making those kids soon.'

Anger burns within me again. You have the knack, I'll give it to you, for relentlessly prodding at people's weaknesses. 'I don't want children,' I say, disgusted by you and knowing I shouldn't respond, but I can't give you the benefit of feeling like you're winning. 'I've never wanted children.'

'Really,' you say, interested.

'That's an awful shame,' Dr Jameson says, and I want to get up and walk away from these two men who suddenly feel what I do or don't do with my body is any of their business. 'I see older women regret that decision. You should think about it, consider it deeply,' he says, looking at me as if I'd just shot those words out of my mouth without giving the matter any thought.

I've always known that I didn't want children. Ever since I was a child, I've known.

'There's no point in me regretting something now that I might not regret later,' I say, as I always say to people like Dr Jameson who come out with exactly the same thing he said. 'So I'll stick with my decision, since it feels right.'

You are still looking at me, but I avoid your eye.

'Did the Lennons say goodbye to you?' I ask you.

You shake your head.

'Why didn't they say goodbye to us?' I ask nobody in particular. 'You and I were standing in my garden when they called to every single door. They walked straight past us.'

You snort, swirl your whisky around in the glass. You've barely drunk anything since I sat down, which is good because your children are in the house, for their one night of the week with Daddy and you're outside, drunk.

'Why would they say goodbye to you? You're hardly the neighbour of the century. Two months of digging to help get over some kind of psychotic break . . .'

I can feel myself rising and I know I shouldn't. It's exactly

173

what you want, to stir things up so that everyone around you explodes – apart from you. Hurt people hurt people. But I can't help it, I'm hurt too. 'So what does a fired DJ do then? Are there other stations lining up at your door?'

'I haven't been fired.'

'Not yet. But you will be.'

'They've extended my gardening leave for an as yet undecided amount of time,' you say, with a mischievous twinkle in your eye. 'So it looks as if we're stuck here together. You and me.'

Something twigs in my head. Snaps, more like. I have realised something and I feel the heat of the anger burn through me.

'You'll still be able to go to the station next week though?' I ask.

'No,' you say slowly, lifting your eyes from the whisky to meet mine. 'They're planning to restructure the station. I will not be setting foot in that place until they tell me what's happening with my job.'

'But you promised my sister you'd bring her on a tour.'

You study me to see if I'm serious, then when I don't smile or laugh or respond you bang your glass down on the table, which makes both Dr Jameson and I jump.

'You honestly think I give a fuck about your sister right now?'

The anger explodes inside me, runs around my veins like a poison. Everywhere. Hate. Anger. Repulsion. Rage.

'No, I don't actually.'

I feel Dr Jameson look at me, sensing something in my voice that I feel but that you don't hear.

'I've got three kids in there. And a wife that I'd very much like to come home to me. They are what I'm concerned about right now.'

'Are you? Interesting. Because it's now two-fifteen in the morning and you're drinking whisky in your garden when you should be inside with them. But responsibility isn't something that sits that well with you, is it?'

I should probably stop, but I can't. All I've heard all week is Heather's excitement about visiting the radio station. Every single day. Non-stop. She's been researching it. She can reel off the station's entire schedule, who works on what show and at what time, she's been looking into the producers' and researchers' names. Every day she's called me to tell me. The last phone call she made was to tell me she might stop working in the solicitor's office that she has always loved so much to try to work in the radio station, if Mr Marshall would help her. It was as if she could sense my disapproval of the entire thing. But it wasn't that I disapproved; I was reticent, hesitant to fully go with the flow because I was afraid that something like this would happen. That just made her try to sell it to me even more, trying to make me see how much she cared, showing her excitement so that I couldn't step in and cancel it. My rage is bubbling very close to my skin, I can feel it about to erupt.

'Your wife has left you, you've lost your job, your kids can't stand you—'

'Shut up,' you mutter, shaking your head and looking down at the table.

I decide to keep going because I want to hurt you. I want to hurt you like you hurt me all those years ago. 'Your kids can't bear to be around you—'

'SHUT UP!' you shout suddenly. You pick up the glass and hurl it at me. I can see the hatred in your eyes, but your aim is atrocious and I don't even need to dodge the missile. It flies past me and lands on the ground somewhere

175

behind me. I don't know what you're going to do next. Take aim with something larger, like the chair you smashed through the window, or maybe your fist, like you did with your son – only this time it wouldn't be accidental.

'Now now,' Dr Jameson says, in a loud whisper. He is standing up, as we all are now, and holding his arms out to keep us apart, like a boxing ref, only the length of the table keeps a distance between us anyway.

'You crazy bitch – how dare you say those things,' you hiss.

'And you're a drunk,' I say, swallowing the last word as the courage leaves me and the sadness and terror creeps in. 'Sorry, Dr J, but he promised my sister. He should keep his promise.'

I turn then and leave them, my body shaking from head to toe with rage and fright. I don't bother to collect the flask of tea and mugs, wondering as I walk away from him if at any moment a flask or mug will fly through the air and smash against the back of my head.

17

As an assignment for school whilst studying Greek mythology, we were asked to write our own versions of the Achilles story. We were then asked to read them out loud, and as one by one my classmates read their stories, actual stories of people through history, leaders brought down by their weaknesses, I realised I'd misinterpreted the brief – but not misunderstood it. I wrote about a witch who hated children because of their cruel hearts, for the hurtful things they would say about her favourite cat. She plotted to catch them, kill them and eat them, but the problem was she was afraid of lollipops and it seemed that every time she came near a child, they would have a lollipop in their mouth which served as a sweet protective forcefield around them. Word of her fear spread and soon all children carried lollipops with them, holding them out at her, sticky and sweet, waving them in her face so that she was so repulsed she had to run away and hide from children for ever.

I got a C+, which was annoying, but more embarrassing was the way the children laughed as I was reading it, some thinking it was a deliberate joke to annoy the teacher, most just thinking it was stupid. The reason the teacher gave me a C+ was not because I had misinterpreted the assignment but because he thought I'd failed to grasp the meaning of the story. Lollipops could not be the witch's Achilles Heel, he told me, they were something she feared but did not bring about her downfall. He never gave me the opportunity to respond – this didn't happen in school, you were either understood or not – but it was he who was wrong, not me, because it wasn't the lollipop that was the witch's weakness, it was her cat. In her effort to protect her cat she ended up being cast off from the community and alone for ever.

I wrote that story when I was ten years old. I knew then what I only face up to now, in this moment, which is that Heather is my weakness. Any row, misunderstanding, failed relationship, or possible relationship that was never given a chance can without exception be traced back to a reaction, a comment, remark, or something relating to Heather. I couldn't associate myself with a person who betrayed arrogance or ignorance, whether innocent or not, toward my sister. One sideways look at Heather and they were immediately ruled out. I never engaged in a discussion of their thought processes or core beliefs, I didn't have the patience or the time for that. Boyfriends. Dad. Friends. I cut them all out. I don't know if it's how I've always been or if it's because Mum is gone and I'm behaving in a way that I think she would want me to. I have a memory, a feeling that she was as protective of Heather as I am, yet I have no actual memories or examples to corroborate that. For the first time, it occurs to me that my actions have been dictated by something that has absolutely no substance, it's totally unjustified. This rocks me.

Feeling horrendous after the spiteful things I have said to you tonight, I nevertheless force myself to block it all out. Sleep comes easily, because my mind does not like the alternative of facing up to what I said. My last thought as

I fall asleep is to wonder if the witch's cat would feel happier if the witch was less protective of her. After all, what use is the witch's discontent to her?

I park around the corner from my aunt Jennifer's house. My plan is to drive here, park and then my plan is all out of ideas. I debate whether to go inside or not. Do I know what I'm doing with Heather, with *everything*, or do I not? Big question, when I'd once felt so sure. From inside the car I stare at the house, my mind racing and empty at the same time. My plan is to get out of the car and then my plan is all out of ideas.

There is never any need to ring Aunt Jennifer in advance of a visit. Her house is one of those homes that's always busy with her four children coming and going, plus their spouses and children, all equally unannounced, and now that she fosters children there are often people there that I don't necessarily know. It has always been that kind of a house, and I had always felt welcome there – just as well, because I had nowhere else to go when Mum was sick. It was always the deal that if and when Mum died I would move in, but then the Kevin incident occurred, which tainted my view of the house, tainted my relationship with Kevin and over time tainted my relationship with Jennifer.

I can see how it was a great stress for her at the time, losing her son and the niece she was promising her sister would be safe with her. She hadn't exactly lost us, we were right there, but when Kevin moved away I still couldn't bring myself to settle in the house and I decided to live on campus in Limerick University, a fresh break from everyone, a fresh start for me. I saw Heather every second weekend. I settled in with friends and we created a family of our own, and I allowed myself to be mollycoddled by friends' families for festive weeks. Heather was happy in the accommodation Mum had set up for her before she passed away, and on family occasions she would stay at Jennifer's and Dad would come over to eat and catch up with Heather like it was the base for their relationship. It all worked fine for everybody, including me, and while it was all happening I created a mother for Heather in my mind that I don't know necessarily existed by giving her ideals that I don't know she actually held.

I slowly walk towards the door. My plan is to walk to the door and then my plan is all out of ideas.

'Jasmine,' Jennifer says, surprised to open the door and find me there.

She has red hair, dyed, and it's been in a pixie cut for as long as I can remember. She wears earthy tones, wishy-washy greens and tans in crushed velvets, long hippy dresses with leggings underneath, shoes that always have thick soles like hovercrafts, big chunky necklaces. Her lips are always the same colour as her hair, though hers is more mahogany than my fire-engine red.

'Isn't this a lovely surprise? Come in, come in. Oh, I wish I'd known you were coming, I would have told Fiona to stay. She's gone to Mass with Enda. I know, don't look at me like that, nobody in this house has been to Mass since Michael's wedding, but Enda is making his communion this year and they're encouraged to go so that he doesn't walk in looking like a tourist. Apparently the kids can play at ten a.m. Mass. If they keep thinking like that, the Catholic Church won't have a free pew.'

She ushers me in to the kitchen, which should feel the same as before, should make me feel some sort of connection to the past, but it has been completely altered.

'My sixtieth birthday present,' she says, noticing as I take in the new extension. 'They wanted to send me on a cruise. I wanted a new kitchen. What has my life come to?' she says jovially.

I like that it is different; it immediately puts me in a new place, away from the memories of years gone by. Or at least it helps me see them in a different light, from a different angle, less of an active participant in it and more of an observer as I try to figure out was it over there, or over there, and is this where the bean bags would have been.

'I can't stay long,' I say as she settles down, a pot of herbal tea between us. 'I'm meeting Heather in an hour. We're going to build a water fountain in my garden.'

'How wonderful!' Her face lights up and I can see the surprise.

My plan is to tell her what's on my mind and then my plan is all out of ideas.

'I've come to see you because . . . I've been doing a lot of thinking recently. I've had a lot of time on my hands, as you know.'

'Good thing for you.' No sympathy. I like that.

'I've been thinking about Mum. Well, I've been thinking about a lot of things,' I realise out loud. 'But I've specifically been thinking about how she was with Heather.'

I register her surprise, but she keeps it in check. I'm sure she was expecting me to talk about Kevin.

'There are some blanks.'

'I'll help you if I can,' she says.

'Well, it's vague. How was she with Heather? I mean, I know she was protective, of course, she was. I know she wanted Heather to be independent, set up a good life for herself, but I don't know how she *felt*. What was she afraid of? Did she ever talk to you about Heather? Did she confide in you? Like what did she want to keep Heather away

181

from? Heather is really spreading her wings now – she always has,' I acknowledge. 'She has a boyfriend.'

'Jonathan.' She smiles. 'We hear about him a lot. Had him over for tea.'

'You did?'

'Then afterwards he did a Taekwondo display. Had Billy up, doing some moves. Billy kicked over my china Russian dolls.'

I laugh and then cover my mouth. The Russian dolls made of china always made us laugh.

'It's okay,' she laughs. 'It was worth it to see Billy raise his leg that high.'

We hold an amused silence and then it alters.

'You know, Jasmine, you're doing a great job. Heather is happy. She's safe. She is incredibly busy – my goodness, she needs a PA to help her manage her diary! I can't keep track of her.'

'Yes, I know. But . . . sometimes I would love Mum's guidance.'

She thinks hard. 'A woman once said something about Heather. Something awful. Not deliberately, just naïve.'

'They're the worst ones,' I say, but my ears have pricked up. This is what I need to hear.

'Well, your mum thought about it long and hard, and invited her to our Tuesday-night bridge.'

'She did?'

'Absolutely. Invited her at seven p.m., even though it didn't start until eight. Pretended she'd made a mistake and made her sit in the living room while she got the two of you ready for bed.'

I frown. 'That was her comeback? Making a woman give up an hour of her evening unnecessarily?'

Jennifer smiles and I know I've missed the point. 'She

wanted her to see Heather at home, the way she was all the time, her natural self, with the three of you going about your evening routine just like any other family at that time of the day. She made sure that woman saw and heard absolutely everything – the normality of it all, I suppose. And do you know who that woman was?'

I shake my head.

'Carol Murphy.'

'But Carol and Mum were best friends.'

'Exactly. They became friends after that.'

I struggle to digest that information. Carol was Mum's firmest friend. They were thick as thieves for as long as I can remember. I can't process this information, that Carol had once held those sort of views about Heather. I know it's possible, but I struggle with it and my fondness for Carol is suddenly tarnished. In an instant. In the way my feelings about a person always shift when I become aware that they don't know better, know enough, know exactly the right thing to say or do regarding Heather.

As if sensing this turmoil, Jennifer goes on: 'Your mother never wrote anyone off, Jasmine – because that was the very thing she was afraid of people doing to Heather.'

And that's what I was looking for. My plan is to take this information and put it into practice in my life in some way. And then my plan is all out of ideas.

I downloaded instructions on how to make a water fountain. I'd watched the video a few times on YouTube, an aristocratic sort of man in a padded vest and bottle-green wellington boots with a large bulbous nose explaining the process to me outside his manor as though I were a child. When it comes to gardening I like to be spoken to like that, because my knowledge of it is on a par with a child's.

He says it will be finished in eight hours and he proves it by completing the task in this time – edited down to eight minutes, naturally. I reckon it will take me a week, despite Heather coming over to help. Or probably because Heather is coming over to help. I certainly hope it will take that amount of time, as I have made no other plans.

'Ooh, Jasmine,' Heather says as soon as she sees what I've done with the garden. 'I can't believe it's the same garden.'

'I know. Do you like it?'

'I love it.'

She looks at me in silence, which makes me feel self-conscious.

'What?' I look away, busy myself with our tools.

'I'm surprised that Jasmine did this,' she says, as if I'm not there but she's looking directly at me. Her tone surprises me. 'Busy, busy Jasmine.'

'You're one to talk!' I try to keep my voice light. 'You've a busier schedule than me.'

She moves a hair from in front of my eyes to behind my ear. She has to stand on tiptoe to do this. 'I am proud of you, Jasmine.'

Tears prick behind my eyes and I'm embarrassed. I don't recall her ever having said that before, and I don't know why it moves me so much, so suddenly, so deeply.

'Yeah, well, I am on gardening leave, after all. So,' I clap my hands. 'Before we start, I got you something.'

I give her the gardening clothes I'd ordered online. Green wellington boots with pink flowers, overalls, a warm hat and pink gardening gloves.

We are busy digging a hole big enough to fit the basin of the bowl in when your door opens. I try not to look up and succeed in doing this, my heart drumming at the thought

184

of another confrontation with you, but when I hear footsteps approach, the dragging and shuffling sound tells me that it's Fionn and I'm no longer afraid to look up. His Beats by Dre are around his neck, and his hands are shoved deep into his pockets. It's like a Mary Poppins bag illusion. His hands are far too large to be squeezed into pockets of that size; the effort of jamming them in has pushed his shoulders up past his ears. He doesn't say anything, just stands there and waits to be addressed.

'Hi, Fionn,' I say, straightening up my already aching back.

He grumbles something inaudible.

'This is my sister Heather.'

The test of a good person right there. And then I remind myself that I need to stop setting so much store on that one moment: the introduction. But Fionn passes the test, grumbling the same inaudible response to Heather and looking neither of us in the eye.

Heather waves.

'My dad was wondering if you need help.' He surveys the tools and the hole. 'Are you doing the water fountain?'

'Yes, we are.' I feel awful, but as wrong as I was to say the things that I said to you last night, I'm not going to spend the day minding your son again. Besides, I've planned to spend the day with Heather. But I can't do it. I can't reject him. You are probably still in bed, hungover. I picture your dark, stuffy bedroom, you as a lump beneath the covers, blackout curtains keeping out the daylight, while your children are downstairs, still in their pyjamas at noon, throwing cereal around the kitchen, stamping on it, mushing it into the carpet. Setting things on fire.

Just as I'm handing Fionn the shovel I hear a burst of children's laughter and you and the two blonde children

185

come around the corner from the back garden behind your house. You are saying something, very jovial, chirpy, playful. There's a spring in your step, you're in good form for someone who was throwing whisky glasses at my head in the very same garden less than twelve hours ago.

You whistle. A call.

I know it's for Fionn. Fionn knows it's for Fionn, but he doesn't turn around. Nor do I look up.

'Fionn, come on, buddy,' you say good-naturedly.

'I'm helping.' Fionn's voice comes out whiney, and then breaks.

'No you're not,' you say happily, setting some things out on the table.

I want to see what they are but I don't want to look at you.

'Hello, Heather,' you say cheerily.

'Hello, Matt.' Heather waves back and I'm stunned by their exchange.

You ignore me. I'm afraid to look you in the eye.

Fionn sighs, drops the shovel and, without a word to Heather or me, he trudges back across the road, hands disappearing in the magical pockets again, the weight of his long arms pushing his trousers down to reveal the top of his boxer shorts.

In a cheery voice you start to explain to the children what you're going to do. I want to listen, but Heather is talking and I can't tell her to stop. Then you turn music on in your car. The kids are excited and the girl who dances everywhere dances around and the other focuses hard on his task. I try to glimpse what you're doing without being obvious; I try to position myself so that I'm facing you but look as though I'm engrossed in my work. You're all gathered around the garden table. You are all sanding, and I

186

almost stop what I'm doing to stare in shock. You have taken my advice.

Heather is still talking.

I finally tune into what she's saying. She wants to go over to you and talk about the tour of the radio station. She's been doing some research, there are certain studios that she would like to see. I tell her that it's not appropriate, that it's Sunday and you're having family time.

'I'll be polite, Jasmine,' she says, her eyes pleading, and that breaks my heart because I was never in any doubt that she would be polite and I don't want her to think that it's her I'm worried about. Finally I stop working.

There is another thing about my sister. She gets things into her head and she must absolutely do them. Absolutely. If she can't, she cannot fathom it and it rocks her world. Maybe there's something to be said for having challenges in life; it makes you work harder to face things, it won't let you take no for an answer. You do more than most people would ordinarily do to rise to the challenge and ensure that your fear or whatever it is that threatens to hold you back cannot win. When I had finished my home-work and could watch TV, Heather had speech therapy. When I was able to go out and play with my friends on the road, Heather had extra reading classes. Learning to cycle was a prolonged effort, while I just took off. She always worked harder for everything. This is why the meet-ings are important, because if she suggests something that isn't ideal, then at least as a group we can talk about it before it takes over her mind. She did discuss visiting the radio station at the group, everybody agreed that a trip would be a great idea – everybody but me, and I didn't voice my opinion. By failing to speak I let her down.

I once met a mother who, describing her son's character

traits, said, 'Typical Down syndrome.' I wanted to slap her. You cannot define a person by any one thing at any time; we are all unique. This part of Heather's personality has absolutely nothing to do with having Down syndrome. If so, then Dad and I have Down syndrome too because there's no stopping any of us when we get the bit between our teeth.

I think about lying. It's on the tip of my tongue. I always feel that if I can somehow personally guarantee Heather's happiness then everything will be all right in the world. But my philosophy has always been to tell Heather the truth; I might sugar-coat things occasionally, but that's my worst offence. I've never told her a full-on lie. Realising that I'm about to break my code of ethics, I stop. A boyfriend of mine once told me that I was a people-pleaser, only I know that I wasn't, because I didn't please him – I didn't even try. He seemed to be the last person on my list who I tried to please. What I realise now is that I'm a Heather-pleaser. There are very few other people I try to please; everything revolves around her. I realise that this does not make me a caring person. In fact it makes me rather selfish, because it has meant that in the end everything revolves around me too.

For years I have told myself that Heather looks to me to fix everything. But does she? Or is it that I think she wants me to fix everything? I realise now that she has never asked me to sort things out, has never given any sign that she expects anything to be altered by me, it is I who have placed that pressure on myself. I am having an epiphany. In my garden. Standing knee-deep in a hole that I have dug.

My first thought when I was fired was *I can't tell Heather.* I thought it would upset her, that I had to protect her from knowing about the bad things in the world, that she would become scared about being fired herself. What was I thinking? What kind of education is that? Heather knows more than I the cruelty of the world. She hears abusive comments thrown at her, degrading things said about her by ordinary decent people who don't know any better, both to her face and behind her back on a daily basis. I merely accompany her on that. As I hear you and your kids sanding and laughing on the fresh, bright, sunny spring day with Pharrell's 'Happy' blaring from your iPhone, I have an epiphany. Everything in my life does not have to be altered in order to please me and Heather. I can't continue sheltering her from everything, but maybe I can simply be there to help her if and when she gets hurt.

'Okay,' I finally say, hearing my voice shake. What am I doing? I am sending her over there to have her heart broken by you. *I* am doing this. *I* am letting it happen. I am so shaky, I can't catch my breath and I sit on the garden bench and watch her cross the road.

The two blonde children stop sanding to watch her, warily.

'Hello,' Heather says happily.

You and Heather are talking. I can't hear what you're saying and it is killing me. I want to know. I need to know so that I can help control the conversation so that I can steer it away from hurting her. I feel helpless, but I feel like an executioner too. I have sent her over there to kill her faith in people, perhaps in me.

I watch you explaining something to her, your soft expression, your hands gesturing gently to shape the points. Then you stop talking and watch her. You wait to hear her reaction, but she is not saying anything. Your hands go to your hips. You watch her, uncertainly. You're not sure whether

189

to reach out to her; you do and then you don't make contact, know better not to. Then you look over at me. You are concerned. You don't know what to do with this young woman who is staring at you and not saying anything. You don't know what to say. You need my help.

It kills me to do this to Heather but I'm not going to give it to you.

You start to say something else but Heather turns away from you and comes back across the road. Heather looks like she has been slapped. A stung look to her face, glassy eyes, a pink nose. I stay where I am, watching her, as she comes towards me and then passes me by.

This is what happens, Matt Marshall, when you let people down. You will learn it all and you will remember it by simply seeing it on the face of my sister.

Heather stays in the house and listens to her music on her record player, silently dealing with her heartbreak at not being able to visit the radio station. She doesn't really want to talk about it and that's okay, because neither do I. I carry on digging the garden, and the deeper I dig into the ground, the deeper I dig into myself. When I have gone deep enough, and I am raw and exposed, it is time to close the wound. I lay two inches of gravel in the hole I've climbed out of and place the basin on top of the gravel. I measure the distance from the hole to the nearest electrical outlet, then I cut a piece of PVC conduit to the same length. I thread a string through a conduit and duct tape one end to the plug of the water pump that I'll add later. I pull the plug of the water pump through the PVC conduit and tape the plug to the end of it. This part takes me some time. I lay the PVC conduit in the trench and cover it with soil. I centre the water pump in the basin and lay a screen on top of the basin. Using my new utility scissors I cut a hole at the centre of the screen.

Next, I'm supposed to connect the water pump to the piping, but I can't. It is too complicated and frustrating and I'm mumbling and grumbling and cursing to myself when I hear a voice behind me.

'Hi, Garden Girl.'

It is not you. I know that straight away. I jump and drop the scissors into the basin.

'Shit. Monday. Hi. Sorry. You gave me a fright. I'm just. Feck. My scissors. I'll just . . . there. This thing,' I sigh, and wipe my sweaty face. 'I'm trying to build a water fountain.'

I'm on the ground, in a hole, and from down here Monday is even more majestic than usual. He is in a navy-blue suit and instead of wearing his tie, he is wearing an amused expression on his face, one which is fixed and directed solely at me. I steal a quick glance over at you. I catch you looking away quickly, as if I haven't caught you, and return to concentrating on varnishing the table with the kids in that cheery scout leader voice that you've managed to keep up for almost an hour now.

'I called you a few times but you were in your own world,' he says, smiling. He lowers himself to his haunches. 'What have you got here?'

'A great big mess.' I show him what I'm supposed to be doing.

'May I?'

'Please.'

He reaches out his hand and I take it, and allow him to pull me up out of the hole I dug. Not a sign. Not even a symbol. An actual thing that's happening. As soon as my skin touches his I don't know if it's just me but I feel it all over my body. He doesn't step back from the edge of the

191

hole and I'm pulled up close to his body, my nose touching the fabric of his shirt, able to see the flesh beneath the open buttons of his shirt. I would like to stay there for ever, feeling his hard body next to mine, but instead I clumsily move away, unable to look at him in case he sees how he's flustered me. He takes off his jacket, and I bring it inside for him, taking the opportunity to clean myself up, fix my hair, my eyeliner, defluster myself. When I return, he has rolled up his shirtsleeves and he's on his knees on the grass, brow furrowed in concentration as he works on connecting the water pump to the piping. I try to make small talk but he's busy concentrating and I feel like a pest, so I watch him for a while, then feel wrong for admiring him in all the wrong ways, then sneakily steal looks at you and your children varnishing the table. Apart from Fionn, who has deserted the task and is sitting in one of the chairs playing on an iPad, the other two are having fun. You are animated, engaged, communicative, funny. You are a good father, and I'm sorry for saying that you weren't. The cynical side of me wonders if this is all a show for me after what I said last night, but then I see the genuine looks and sounds of happiness and am ashamed of myself for thinking that once again it is all about me. I then have an argument with myself about feeling ashamed considering all that you have done in the past, how you have let Heather down and the fact you threw a glass at my head. The winner of that argument is me; you deserve me to mistrust you so.

Monday is looking at me and I snap out of my trance. He has obviously said something and is waiting for an answer. I wait for him to repeat it but instead I'm embarrassed to see him shift his gaze to follow mine. His eyes settle on you.

'His voice is familiar. Is that Matt Marshall?'

'Yes.'

Monday is neither impressed nor unimpressed, and I'm surprised by how I feel about that. I don't want him jumping up and down declaring that he is a fan and running across the road for an autograph, but I ready myself in a nervous kind of way for his dislike of you, as if I'm ready to defend you. It's a peculiar response, considering I'm supposed to despise you so much, particularly after the way you hurt Heather. If we were in a relationship I would have to leave you and move far far away. Which is what your wife did, come to think of it. Perhaps you have that effect on people.

'This is going to take me a few minutes longer,' Monday says, fixing me with a look that makes me smile.

'You don't have to do this.'

'I know. But it might give you a few more minutes' thinking time about the job. You've seemed to have needed a lot of that.'

I bite my lip. 'Sorry. You said I had a month to decide.'

'Tops. We can talk about it after I do this, if that's okay.'

I look at the wires in his hand. 'Do you know what you're doing?'

'I bought an old cottage in Skerries and did it up myself. New roof, new plumbing, new electrics. Took me a few years, but it's habitable now. Don't worry, I haven't blown anything up. Yet.'

I try to picture him in his little cottage in the sleepy town of Skerries, wearing an Aran sweater and buying his fresh fish daily from a fisherman, but I can't. All I can see is him, naked from the waist up, ripping up floorboards and stripping wallpaper with enormous power tools in his hands.

'Do you have time to talk after?' Registering my blank stare, he adds, 'We had arranged to talk today . . .'

The penny drops. 'Ah. I thought you meant over the

phone, which is why I'm . . . we never actually agreed a time, but today is fine.'

He seems embarrassed that he has shown up unexpected on a Sunday, or is there something more to his awkwardness? If so, it is quickly covered up. Or perhaps I'm imagining it, kidding myself that I can see that vulnerable side of him, that he's dropped by unannounced because he genuinely wants to see me. In the flash that passes between us I believe that is a possibility, but now it's business as usual – or not quite, as he is destroying a perfectly good suit as he bends over a hole in my garden.

Thirty minutes later, as I have prepared tea for me and coffee for him, Monday and Heather are sitting at the kitchen table. Heather is telling him about her jobs. She is always proud of her work and finds it the easiest thing to talk about around strangers. I like that she does this, she is good at conversation, though I worry about her security. I don't want her to tell random men about her weekly schedule in case they turn up where she is. I'm not worried about her telling Monday, obviously. Nor is she, because when she is finished, she asks him about his job.

'I'm a headhunter,' he says. 'My job is to identify suitable candidates who are employed elsewhere to fill business positions.'

'Isn't that like cheating?'

'Not really.' He smiles. 'I don't like cheating. I see myself more as a problem-solver. It's like a jigsaw puzzle. I put the right people in the right places. Because sometimes people aren't in the place that they should be.'

We catch each other's eyes when he says that. He doesn't speak slowly, as if she's incapable of understanding, or loudly as though she is deaf, though she does wear a hearing aid. His sentences are short and simple, to the point.

Heather then starts to tell him about me, about my jobs – a simplified version, the version I've told her over the years. I'm confused as to what she's doing, thinking she surely has misunderstood his job, but then I realise that she's trying to sell me to him, which touches me so much I stop moving and can't quite figure out what I'm doing. I'm completely transfixed, overwhelmed that Heather would do this for me, that she would *know* to do this for me. He is a person who gets people jobs and she is trying to get me a job. She lists my attributes and comes up with anecdotes to illustrate those attributes. It is something she has learned to do herself when attending a job interview and she has applied it to me.

She begins each sentence with 'Jasmine is . . .' The first sentence she completes with 'kind' and then gives an example of my kindness. She tells him I paid for her apartment.

'Jasmine is smart,' she says. 'One day we were in the supermarket car park and Jasmine found twenty euro by the ticket machine. Beside it was an appointment card for somebody's doctor appointment. So Jasmine posted the money and the appointment card to the doctor and told him that the person you have on this date at this time dropped their money in the car park on this date.' She beams. 'Isn't that smart?'

'That's definitely very smart.' He smiles.

I hope she's finished now; it's lovely but difficult to listen to praise. Instead she continues, 'Jasmine is generous,' and I shake my head and go back to what I was doing.

One peek at Monday shows me he's touched. He is looking at her intently, fixated on her. He must sense that I'm watching because he looks over at me, smiles gently, then I have to start moving again. He doesn't always

195

understand her, he asks her to repeat some things; despite years of therapy, her speech isn't so clear, but though I have understood everything, I stop myself from interrupting. She is not a child. She doesn't need a translator.

'Jasmine sounds like a great person,' he says, eyes on me again. 'And I agree. I think lots of people would be lucky to have her.' I'm not looking at him but I can see him from the corner of my eye, the angle of his face on mine, and every single move I make is sloppy, while my heart bangs and my stomach flutters. I fumble with the milk carton, spill milk on the counter when trying to pour it into the jug.

'She is,' Heather agrees.

'And you're a great sister to say that about her.'

The next thing she says sends me into an emotional spin and catapults me out of the room so fast that even Monday has the brains to leave, and text me later – from his personal mobile – that he would like me to call him when I have the time.

'I'm her big sister. When our mum died, she told me I'm the big sister and I have to look after Jasmine. I do all of these other things, but protecting Jasmine is my main job.'

18

First thing on Monday morning I'm woken by the sound of a lawnmower right outside my window. This hurts me on many levels. Firstly because it is just after eight a.m. and is generally an intrusive sound, and secondly because I had a bottle of red wine before going to bed. Perhaps I'm lying about the amount, it could have been more and it also could have been an entirely different spirit, but I'm feeling it today, the thud, thud, thud that penetrates my skull right to my brain cells, killing them as it does, and then drills back through to the back of my head where I feel it pulsating on the pillow. The thoughtless lawnmower user could be any of the four retired couples around us who work to their own schedule, avoiding any thought of others', particularly as they know that I no longer have a job. It could be anyone, but already I know it is you. I know that it is before even lifting my head up from the pillow, because it goes on far too long. Nobody in the world has that much grass; only an inexperienced gardener would take that long. When I look outside it is as though you have been waiting for me to appear. You glance up immediately and give me a big fine wave. I see the sarcasm dripping from every pore. Then you turn the lawnmower

197

off, as if you have succeeded in doing what you set out to do, and make your way across the road to my house.

I can't move. I am too dizzy, I really need to lie down again, but you are at the door, pressing the bell, too loud, for too long, as though you have a finger on a bruise on my skin and are pushing it in short bursts of Morse code torture. I collapse on the bed, hoping that if I ignore you, you will go away, but apparently like every other problem, you do not, you only get worse. In the end it is not you that moves me, it is the sight of the bottle of vodka beside my bed that catapults me – at the pace of a snail – out the door.

I pull the front door open and daylight burns holes in my eyes. I grimace, and cower, retreat back into the safety of the darkened, curtain-closed room. You follow me in.

'Yikes,' you say at the sight of me, sounding too much like Dr Jameson. 'Good morning.' You are overly cheerful and loud, sprightly. Annoyingly so. If I didn't know better, I would think you must have watched me drink myself into a drunken stupor, then deliberately got up early, the earliest I have known you to have risen, so you could make a racket outside my window. What's more you have forced yourself to be cheerful, the most cheerful I have ever known you to be.

My intention is to say 'hi', but it comes out as a deep croak.

'Wow,' you say. 'Rough night? All rock'n'roll over here at number three on a Sunday night.'

I grunt in response.

You walk around and start opening the curtains, and the window, which makes me shudder and reach for the cash-mere blanket on the couch where I have collapsed. I wrap it around me and look on warily as you make your way to the kitchen, which is all open-plan – my entire downstairs is completely open-plan – and then you start rooting around in the cupboards.

'The lemon bowl,' I say weakly.

You stop. 'What's that?'

'Your keys. In the lemon bowl.'

'I'm not looking for my keys, I'm not locked out.'

'Hallelujah.'

'Why the lemon bowl?'

'Glad you asked.' I smile. 'Because I think of you as a lemon.'

'Isn't it you that's the bitter twisted one?' you say, and my smile fades.

You continue to move around the kitchen. I hear cups, I hear paper rustle, I smell toast, I hear the kettle. I close my eyes and nod off.

When I wake you are holding a mug of tea and buttered toast towards me. My stomach heaves but I'm hungry.

'Have that, it'll help.'

'From the expert,' I say groggily, sitting up.

You sit in the armchair across from me, beside the window that is so bright I have to squint. You look almost angelic with the light cast on you, your right side seeming to blur at the edges as though you're a hologram. You give a weary sigh, nothing saintly about that. The sigh, I realise, is not because you're tired. You look rejuvenated somehow, flushed from the fresh early morning air, your clothes smelling of cut grass. You're weary because of me.

'Thanks,' I say, remembering my manners.

'About the other night . . .' you begin.

I grunt and wave my hand dismissively at you, and sip my tea. It is sweet, sweeter than how I usually take it, but I like it. It is good for now. It is not vodka and for that my body says thank you. I don't want to talk about the other night, about what happened between me and you.

'I'm sorry I threw the glass at you.'

For this you are deadly serious. Perhaps emotional even, and I can't take that.

I chew my toast slowly and swallow. 'We were both wrong,' I say, finally. I want to move on.

This isn't what you want to hear. You are hoping for an apology from me.

'Well, Jasmine, I was reacting to what *you* said.'

'Yes, and I accept your apology,' I say. Why is it I can't bring myself to apologise to you, when I know that I should?

'You said some shitty things,' you say.

'Have you come here looking for an apology?'

'No. To apologise.'

I think about it again. 'Like I said, we were both wrong.'

You stare at me intently while your mind works overtime. You make a decision not to fire yourself at me, for which I'm thankful even though I know I deserve it. I am being horrible. I offer you a little bit more.

'I was disappointed you let my sister down.'

'I'm sorry about that. I didn't think she would be so upset.'

'She doesn't break promises. She trusts people easily.' Unlike me; I don't trust people at all.

You nod, digest that. 'You know I didn't say it could *never* happen, just not in the immediate future.'

'What are the chances?'

'Right now it's looking slim,' you say, grimly.

I should be thinking of the repercussions of you losing your job, what it will mean for you and your family, not of Heather and her lack of a trip to the station. I have been described as sensitive because of my feelings about Heather, but when it comes to others it seems I am utterly desensitised.

'Because of what you said, I'm off the drink,' you say.

I stare at you in surprise. I am surprised more by the fact that I could have said something to influence you, but I'm not at all surprised by the admission you've given up drink. Because I don't believe you. I don't believe you mean it or that it will happen. It is as though you are a cheating husband and I am numb to your declarations of how you can change. We are, oddly, that comfortable with one another.

'I really am,' you say, reading my look perfectly. 'You were right – what you said about the kids.'

'Oh please, Matt,' I say, exasperated. I give up. 'I wasn't right about anything. I don't know you. I don't know your life.'

'Actually,' you stall, as if trying to decide whether to say it or not, 'you do. You see it every day. You see more than anyone.'

Silence.

'And you do know me.' You look at me thoughtfully. 'I think you think you know me more than you do, and you're wrong about some things, but that's just one more thing to prove to someone.'

'You don't have to prove anything to me,' I lie. I wish that I could mean what I say, but I don't. Every single word that comes out of your mouth I analyse for confirmation that you're the bad egg I'm convinced you are.

'Anyway, I want you to take this –' You hand me the crumpled envelope containing your wife's letter.

'You still haven't read it? Matt!'

'I can't,' you say simply. 'I don't want to know what's in it. I can't.'

'Is she speaking to you yet?'

You shake your head.

'Because she's said everything she wants to right there, and you're ignoring it! I don't understand you.'

'Read it to me, then.'

'No! Read it your bloody self.' I throw it on the coffee table.

'What if it says she's never coming back?'

'Then at least you'll know. Instead of this . . . waiting around.'

'I'm not waiting around. Not any more. I'm going to prove it to her.'

'Prove what?'

'Prove myself.'

'I think you have already. That's why she left,' I say this half-joking, thinking you'll smile, but you don't.

You sigh. You look at the letter and I think I've finally gotten through to you. You pick it up and stand. 'I'm putting it with the lemons.'

I smile and am glad you can't see me.

A car pulls up outside your house.

'Visitor,' I say, relieved that this conversation has ended and that you will go. My head is spinning and the toast is sitting on top of vodka and cranberry juice, surfing an indigestion wave.

You examine the car from the window, hands on hips, face in a scowl. You are handsome, still. Not that you're old – you're in your early forties – but despite your lifestyle, the late nights, alcohol and concoctions of anxiety pills, sleeping pills and whatever else you do, it hasn't affected you on the outside as much as it should have.

'I don't think it's for me,' you say, still examining the car. 'He's just sitting in the car.'

'Why didn't you ever work in TV?' I ask suddenly. Usually, successful DJs with an audience like yours and a fan base such as yours make the transition, and it occurs to me right now that you are quite handsome, to some people, and TV

being TV, handsomeness is as high up on the list as intel-
ligence – often higher.

'I did,' you say, turning around, surprised as I am that
I've asked you a question about yourself, about your life,
about your job. 'About five years ago I had a late-night
talk show, a discussion show like on the radio. Wednesday
nights, eleven thirty.'

You are looking at me as if I should know this, but I
shake my head.

'We sat around a table with a bunch of people someone
else booked, talking about things I wanted to talk about,
but not talking about them properly. I packed it in. You
can't say anything on TV. Far more freedom on radio.'

'Like orgasms to ring in the New Year.'

You sigh and sit down. 'Women aren't the only people
to talk about things, you know that.'

I'm confused.

'I have a friend. Let's call him Joey.'

'Or we can call him you?'

'No. Not me.' And I believe you. 'One day Joey tells me
that he and his wife are having fertility problems. They've
been married seven years and never had kids. Over a pint
one night he tells me that he's been faking it when they're
in bed. First I ever heard of it. Of a guy doing it, anyway.
No harm comes of it when a woman fakes, obviously, but
it's different when it's a guy and his wife wants kids – then
it becomes a problem. He can't tell her he's been faking.
He's really got himself backed into a corner, you know?
She's had herself checked out and everything seems okay
from her end . . .'

Really, the way you phrase it is inspiring.

'So she wanted him to get his thing checked. For fertility.
But he didn't want to because he knows he's fine. Or

presumes he is. So instead of admitting that he's been faking it most of the time, and that he'd rather do things in bed maybe a different way that would help him, you know, he tells her he doesn't want kids. Which he does, but he panicked and didn't know what else to say. Anyway, they broke up. All because he couldn't tell her.' You shake your head. 'Thought that was worth talking about on air.'

'Well, it is,' I say. Personally I wouldn't particularly want to hear five people shouting and arguing over each other on bad phone connections at midnight talking about it, but I can see his point.

'So Tony has this idea to ring in the New Year with the woman. I said, okay, whatever. I didn't really care. Thought it was funny. It tied in with the discussion. No big deal.'

'Who's Tony?'

'Producer. He arranged it. Brings this woman into the studio. She starts making sounds down the mic. No, it wasn't real,' you say to me. 'Contrary to tabloid reports. But she was a prostitute. That's the problem. Tony paid her.' You shake your head. 'Jesus. Tony's fucked as well. He'd been having girlfriend problems for a while. She took off, he's . . . well, he's not doing as well as me.'

'Sounds to me like a lot of this is Tony's fault.'

'No. It's my show. I should have known what I was doing. To be honest, I was so fucked that night, that whole week, I didn't know what was going on. I've done that plenty of times and gotten away with it, but this time . . .' You stand up and look out the window again. 'What's this guy doing? He's just gawking at my house.'

I finally stand up from the couch and look out the window. The car is directly outside your house, the man is peering in. 'You get many fans?'

'Yeah, this one girl was so mad about me she moved

into the house across the road from me. Redhead. Big tits. Couldn't get enough of me.'

I actually smile. 'Maybe he's waiting for you because he knows you're not at home.'

'And how would he know that? Unless he's been watching me. I'm going over to him.'

I can hear the anger in your voice and I know that this won't go well.

'Wait, Matt, he's getting out of the car.'

You come back to the window and we watch him. He has something in his hand, something black. A camera. He lifts it up and starts taking photos of your house.

'The little . . .'

It's a delayed reaction. The photographer has taken quite a few shots before you realise what's going on. We watch as he examines them on the camera's LCD screen, then he moves along the road to get another angle.

'Don't do anything stupid, Matt,' I warn. 'You'll only get yourself in more trouble,' I shout after you, but my advice goes not on deaf ears but on absent ears as you fire yourself out of my house. It's as though my words have given you an idea, because you do exactly what I cautioned against: you charge at the photographer. He turns and sees you, sees the aggression on your face and smiles with delight at the photo opportunity. But you don't stop charging. You reach for the camera, grab it, throw it down the road, then you manhandle the photographer into the car. I don't see it all exactly as it happens, because I'm watching from behind my hands. Besides, something tells me it's better that there are no witnesses.

As a result of your behaviour, one hour later I am still in my dressing gown and there are three more photographers camped outside your house, facing my house, while you pace up and down my living room, blocking my view of *Diagnosis Murder* and shouting down the phone to your agent. The news that you've been fired has been leaked to the press before the station informed you, and they've put you on six months' gardening leave so that you don't immediately sign up with a rival station – which is what you are ranting about doing.

I know exactly how you feel, but I also see that your wanting to work for another station is purely a way of getting back at your current employers and not because you genuinely want to get back to work. It occurs to me that perhaps taking six months out to think about what your next move should be is the best thing for you. This is an interesting concept, one I had not thought of before. While you feel you are imprisoned, I see opportunity for you. Perhaps I am moving forward.

I am unable to work in my garden because of the photo-graphers outside, though the water fountain is calling me to finish it, and my hangover desperately needs some fresh air. I'd hoped they would leave for a mid-morning snack, but instead one of them disappears and comes back with a carrier bag full of EuroSpar rolls and they all lean against the car and snack outside. I did attempt to go outside while they were taking this break, but as soon as I opened the door, ham, egg, coleslaw and brown paper bags went flying as they discarded their food and grabbed their cameras. Despite my protestations of being a private citizen, they kept snapping at me. Only when they finally realised their memory cards would run out of space and I'd still be on my knees gardening did they eventually stop. However I was feeling too self-conscious to keep working under their gaze, especially given that I don't know what I'm doing, so I retreated back into the house.

'Sorry,' you say when I slam the front door on them all and turn to you, red-faced. When the heavens open for the rest of the day and they all retreat into one car, huddled together with their enormous cameras on their laps, I shout 'Ha!' in their faces. 'I hope your cameras rust!'

You look up from your own silent fury to watch me with amusement.

Dr Jameson calls over, pretending to be annoyed but secretly loving the dilemma and excitement. He wants to discuss the paparazzi problem on our street and what we can do about it. I go upstairs to lie down.

Unusually, my friend Caroline rings and asks if she can call around. I'm surprised to hear from her for two reasons: she works in a bank, repossessing people's homes and possessions and is never available midweek, and even when she is free she is busy having sex with her new boyfriend who is eight years younger than her and whom she met after discovering her husband had had multiple affairs. I have been happy not to be seeing her, knowing that she is now in a better place. Literally.

She calls over, so excited she is fit to burst, and the only place we can talk is in my bedroom because you are pacing the floor and talking to your solicitor because the paparazzo whose camera you grabbed is threatening to press charges against you for criminal damage. These charges will not stick because he has already made money selling the photos he took. They've surfaced on the internet, on a variety of gossip and entertainment websites, and he's captured you charging at the camera, looking as if you're going to kill someone. He's shot you from a low angle, so you look like King Kong with two double chins and a bulging belly, intent on crushing everything in your path.

Dr Jameson and I huddle around the laptop screen to examine them.

'Jesus fucking Christ,' you say. 'I'm glad my kids aren't there.'

'My rockery looks nice,' I say, zooming in on my garden in the background. 'Wish I'd finished the water fountain though.' I pout.

I head upstairs before you can do a King Kong on me, and Dr Jameson goes back to watching *Homes Under the Hammer*.

'That flat looked better before the makeover,' he says as I leave the room.

'This house is a madhouse,' Caroline says, taking the cup of coffee I've brought her.

'Welcome to my new world,' I say wryly.

'So, where was I?'

'You were at the popping candy bit.'

'Oh yeah.' Her eyes light up and she resumes the account of her and her new boyfriend's bedroom shenanigans, which have long since left the bedroom. 'So anyway,' she takes a breath when she's finished, 'the reason I'm *really* here is because I've come up with an amazing business idea . . . and I want you to work with me on it,' she squeals. 'All I have is this mega idea and no clue where to take it. You've done this loads of times. Will you do it? Please?'

'Oh my goodness,' I say, wide-eyed, very excited but a little anxious too. Working with friends is a tricky thing and I haven't even heard the idea yet. I mentally plan my exit, expecting it to be crap. 'Tell me about it.'

She is more prepared than I thought. She takes out a folder labelled *GÚNA NUA* – Irish for 'new dress'. The idea is that you post a photo of your dress on a website – she's already bought the domain name – and you choose another dress to swap with. That dress then leaves your hands and a new dress arrives in its place. No money changes hands, everything comes with the promise of being dry-cleaned and in mint condition.

'There will be a selection of designer dresses, vintage, high street – whatever you like. It's like getting a free dress, and it's a way to get rid of the stuff you don't want in your wardrobe.'

'So how do you make money?'

'A sign-up fee. Membership. For fifty euro a year you can get as many free dresses as you want. Honestly, Jasmine, I know there's a market for this, I'm seeing people's situations every day and it's depressing. Dress-swapping is the way to go, I'm sure of it.'

It is not a flawless business idea by any means and I think fifty euro is too expensive, but any problem I can see, I can also see a solution. I'm bordering on interest.

'I know you really need this right now too, so *really* think about it,' she says, in an effort to convince me. In fact, this does the opposite.

It sounds as if she is doing me a favour, which is not the case: she needs me to help develop this further. So far it's a good but badly thought-out idea. She needs me to help make it a reality. I don't like her spin of it being a help to me. I feel prickly hot inside with frustration. She isn't sensing it though and she continues.

'Your garden leave is up in when, November? We can be quietly working on this until it's ready to launch and by then you'll be finished gardening leave. Which is perfect, because I don't think there'll be any more room down there for daffodils.' She means this to be complimentary, but it doesn't feel it.

'Daffodils don't grow in November,' I say, defensive of my garden.

She frowns. 'Okay,' she says slowly.

I leave a long silence.

She snaps the folder shut. 'If you think it's shit, say it's shit.' She brings it to her chest and hugs it.

'No, it's not the idea. It's, it's just that, I'm not *stuck* for work, Caroline, I appreciate you thinking of me and that this would be good for me, but I do have a job offer already.'

'What job?'

'I've been headhunted – by this gorgeous man, by the way,' I smile and try to be serious: 'It's to set up an organisation dealing with climate change and human rights.'

'Climate change? Why the sudden interest? Did your snowdrops come up late this year?' she laughs.

This is meant to be funny. My friends have all been teasing me lately about my dedication to my garden. I have refused coffee dates, I have talked about the process on nights out. It's the new thing: let's all tease Jasmine about the garden. I get it, I really do, but . . . The way Caroline looks at me makes me question if I should even be thinking about going for the job, but I don't care for her attitude, the implication that *I need her.*

'So you're taking this job?'

'I've been thinking about it.' I surprise myself with this honesty.

'Would you get to meet Bono?'

Finally her face softens and I laugh and rub my face tiredly.

'Jasmine,' she says gently, 'do you want to work with me? Yes or no? I won't take it personally.'

I bite my lip, unable to make a decision there and then. 'Tell me about the popping candy again.'

Understanding I need more time, she says, 'Okay but whoever it is you're planning this with, you'll have to tell them to shave everything down there because it gets a bit sticky.'

And as she talks, all I can think of is Monday. Not because of the popping-candy scenario, but because I don't want to let him down, this man I barely know who seems to have so much faith in me.

'Monday,' I say into the phone, feeling light-headed at the sound of his voice, and a little nervous about what I have to tell him.

'Jasmine. Perfect. I was just thinking of you. Which isn't unusual these days.'

It is a beautiful sentiment that is quite unusual, given our relationship, but he moves on quickly as though he hasn't dropped it in at all. He sounds like he's out; I can hear traffic, people, wind. Busy man in the city, headhunting people, while I'm here, in my garden, the place I've chosen to ring him because it's the only place where my mind can find peace and clarity these days. It's day three and the paparazzi are in the car, hiding from the chill, waiting for Matt to come home and misbehave again, placing the pressure on him to explode while the revelations of what actually happened on New Year's Eve in his studio come to light in the tabloids, a story that was perfectly corroborated by what he'd told me but which has taken on a life of its own in the press, with the prostitute in question selling her story and revelations of her 'relationship' with Tony coming to light. It's a seedy affair that any radio station would back away from.

'How's your water fountain coming along?' he asks.

'Almost finished. I'm making a deck for it. With hammer and nails in hand. If my old colleagues could see me now.'

'Those paparazzi better watch out.'

211

I pause and look around to see if he's there, though I know from the background on the phone that he's not.

At my silence he explains, 'I saw the photos online. Your garden looked nice.'

'Wish I'd finished the fountain though.'

I can hear the smile in his voice. 'The rate you're going, you will. So, the reason I was thinking of you is because I read today that the bluebell will struggle to maintain its range in the face of climate change. During periods of cold weather, spring flowers such as bluebells have already started the process of growth by preparing leaves and flowers in underground bulbs in summer and autumn.'

He sounds as if he's reading and I sit down on my new garden bench and smile as I listen.

'They are then able to grow in the cold of winter or early spring by using the resources stored in their bulb. With warmer springs induced by climate change, bluebells will lose their early start advantage and be out-competed by temperature-sensitive plants that start growing earlier than in the past.'

I'm not quite sure how to reply to that. 'That's a shame. But I don't have bluebells in my garden.' I look around, just to be sure.

'It would be a shame, though, wouldn't it, not to have a beautiful blue haze in the woodlands?'

It's a beautiful image but why he thinks that in particular would convince me to take the job is beyond me.

'Monday,' I say and I hear the seriousness in my voice. 'There's something I haven't told you.'

He stalls for a moment, sensing danger ahead. 'Yes?'

'I should have said it to you before, but erm . . .' I clear my throat. 'I'm on gardening leave. For one year. It's up in November.'

'November?' he asks, in a tone that I know is not a happy one. He is too professional to show his anger, though he must be angry. I have wasted his time, I see that now, playing some little game with him while he was trying to do his job.

'It would have been helpful to know this a few weeks ago, Jasmine.' The way he says my name makes me cringe. I'm so mortified I can't say anything. I feel like I've been caught with my pants down and the paparazzi are around me, snapping away. The one saving grace is that me and Monday are not face to face.

'I'm sorry I didn't tell you, I just . . .' I can't think of an excuse, but he leaves me hanging in silence, waiting for me to explain myself. This tells me he's annoyed and wants an explanation. 'I was embarrassed.'

It sounds like he's stopped walking. 'Why on earth would you be embarrassed?' he asks, genuinely surprised, the annoyance gone.

'Gee, I don't know. I got fired and I can't work for a year.'

'Jasmine, that's normal. That is nothing to be ashamed of. In fact, it's a compliment that they don't want you to work with anyone else.'

'I hadn't thought of it like that.'

'Well, you should. Between you and me, I wouldn't mind getting paid to not work for a year.' He laughs and I feel so much better already.

There's a long silence. I'm not sure where to go with this. If this job is no longer a possibility then we will have no reason to meet again, but I want to meet him again so badly. Do I mention this? Do I ask him out? Is this goodbye? He saves me by speaking.

'Do you want to go for the job, Jasmine?'

I envision the scenario where I say no. He hangs up, I never hear from him again, I return to my gardening leave, my future uncertain, my present boring and terrifying. I don't want to go back to how I have felt these past few months.

'Yes. I want a job,' I say, then realise my mistake. 'I mean, *this* job.'

'Good,' he says. 'I'll have to go back to them with this and see what they say, okay?'

'Yes, of course. Sure.' I straighten up, professional face back on. 'I am really very sorry.'

I hide my face in my hands and cringe for a good five minutes and then, as a way to hide from the conversation I've just had, I return to my garden. Eventually all thoughts disappear from my mind as I focus on hammering my deck together, spaced a few inches apart, to place over the basin of water.

It is as I am stacking the Indian sandstone slabs on top of each other and marking the centre with a pencil in order to drill a hole for the pipe, that I suddenly drop the tools on the grass and hurry inside. I go straight to my wall of photographs beside the kitchen table and scan it, knowing exactly what to look for. When I see it, my hands quickly cover my mouth and I can't believe how quickly I am overcome with emotion. That the image would mean so much to me and also that Monday would know that.

Beside where Monday had sat a few days ago is a photo of me, Heather, Dad and Mum – the only photo I have of the four of us together – taken on one of our regular trips to the Botanic Gardens. We're all wearing big smiles for the camera, me with my front tooth missing, as we lie in a field of bluebells.

19

The photograph makes me think, it makes me think for a long time about a whole lot of things. This I do while completing my water fountain, and also while hammering together a trellis and painting it red in honour of Granddad Adalbert Mary and attaching vine eyes and wires to my house wall so that my newly planted winter jasmine can climb. And then, when I think I can't think any more, and people are after me to make decisions about my life, I decide to lay more grass at the side of my house and sow a flower meadow. Eddie returns to dig and I'm no fool this time, he completes the small patch in one full day, I prepare the soil and the following week I sow a meadow seed mix including poppies, corn chamomile, ox-eye daisies and cornflowers. It is a small area, but I sow them beside the space I am keeping for the soon-to-be-delivered lean-to greenhouse which will stand against the free wall of my semi-detached house. To prevent birds from eating the seeds, one of my Sunday activities with Heather is to set up a series of strings with CDs threaded on them across the sown area. Even this we do with thought, choosing songs that we think will scare the birds away.

I plant, and I plant, and I plant. And as I plant, I think;

except I'm not aware that I'm thinking. In fact, sometimes I am sure that I'm not thinking and yet suddenly a thought will come to me. It will arrive so suddenly and unexpectedly that I stand up straight, my aching back stretched, and I look around to see who it was or what it was that gave me that sudden thought and did anyone see me having it. March moves to April and I'm still thinking. I do the weeding. I protect the new growth from the cold snaps and while the days are gradually getting warmer there are still some strong winds and heavy showers. I think about my flowers when I'm out at night with friends, especially if there's a particularly heavy rainstorm and people walk into the restaurant shaking off umbrellas and discarding sodden coats. The first thing I think about in the morning is my garden. I think about my garden when I'm lying in the arms of a man I met in a bar and listening to the wind howl outside his bedroom window and I want to be home with my garden, where things make sense. I keep on moving. I don't want my grass to grow too long and then appear yellow when it's cut. It can't be neglected. I regularly rake out 'thatch', not wanting dead grass and mess to accumulate, hoping for healthier grass, for moss and weeds not to establish in it. And all the time I do it, I think.

The daffodils that once rose proud and tall from the ground, the first of the colour in the grey early spring, are now withered. The flowers are going over and so, with sadness, I snap the heads off behind the swollen parts; leaving the stalk intact. If the spent flowers are left on, the plant's energy will be diverted into the production of seeds. By removing the dead heads the plant's energy is instead diverted into the formation of next year's flower bud within the bulb.

In the garden there is always movement, there is always

216

growth. No matter how stuck in time I feel, I go outside and things are changing all around me. There are suddenly flowers where there was once just the tiniest bud, and the open flower will stare at me, wide open and proud at what it has done while we all slept.

Monday has confirmed that the job is to begin in November and he is currently looking for other candidates to offer them too, so the interview is put off until 9 June. I can't wait; I long to get back to feeling like the old me again. I long for my year to be up, and though I have wished the year away on countless occasions I wonder what will I do when the time comes? In November it will be cold, dark, grey and stormy again. Of course that comes with its own beauty, but it will be time for me to make decisions about my life, hopefully begin the new job – if I get it. Suddenly I want the time to slow. I look at my transforming garden, the movement in the water fountain, the spring flowers that are raising their heads, and I realise that I can't stop what is waiting for me. So much of gardening is about preparing for what is about to come next, what season, what elements, and I must now start doing that in my life.

Despite my fears that I would never hear from him again, I did hear from Monday, in fact we met on a few occasions to talk, though invariably we ended up talking about everything else but the job. I feel so comfortable with him, so at ease; there's no need for pretence about my not working, the way there is around other people. Though I am enjoying my gardening, it does not take away from the moments when I still feel lonely and worthless; it doesn't for a moment make me feel more secure about my future, it merely stops me dwelling on it. Monday, on the other hand, takes away my loneliness. His eagerness to meet and talk for any amount of time takes away my worthlessness. Truth be told – and I know this sounds the complete opposite to what I've been expressing – I wish there was no job, I wish that Monday and I could continue to meet like this, talking about the ways of the world, the things we want or don't want, instead of the reality.

It is just an interview, it is not yet a job, so I'm not ready to make a decision about Caroline's proposal. We have met on a few occasions about Gúna Nua, and I have helped her idea along without fully committing to a long-term involvement. This will make it possible for me to slip away if I must, but businesswise it is not the ideal situation for either of us. I know that it is not enough for us to be friends. I thought the same thing about Larry, who subsequently fired me and landed me with a one-year 'prison' sentence. A prison sentence that feels, on glorious days in my garden, like a gift – though he wouldn't want to hear that. And so my present ticks along, sometimes nicely, other times with frustration, but my future is as uncertain as ever.

It has been over two months since the incident with Heather in Dad's home. Heather has gone about her usual wonderful way of forgiving or forgetting or being seemingly unaffected, and her relationship with Dad has carried on the same as ever. Mine has not. Not speaking to him has been somewhat helpful, but in other ways it's made things worse. It has meant I do not have to deal with him, and it has meant that I have become increasingly maddened by him as I continue the arguments in my head. But it also means that, in not seeing him, I have not seen my little sister Zara, and that is unacceptable. It is for her mostly that I pick up the phone. I arrange to meet them at the playground beside Howth pier. It is a bright day, though we need to wrap up against the chill of the sea wind. Our winter wardrobes have made way for lighter wear, spring coats are being aired or given their first outing, people lie out on the grass eating Beshoff's fish and chips, the vinegar mixing with the salty air and making my mouth water.

'Jasmine!' I hear Zara before I see her and she comes running towards me for an embrace. I pick her up and spin her around, immediately feeling bad about not seeing her. There is no excuse, my behaviour towards her has been unforgivable. Her growth since I've seen her is a sign of our silence. Ten weeks is a long time in her short life.

It should be awkward between Dad and me, but it's not because we immediately speak to each other through Zara. Dad begins it.

'Tell Jasmine about how we fed the seals some fish.'

She does.

'Tell Jasmine about how the fishermen let you hold the rod.'

She does.

Zara is the kind of child who seems to attract attention, always asked to be the magician's assistant, allowed into the cockpit to meet the pilot, shown around professional kitchens by chefs. She is one of those children who exudes interest in life, engages with people, and in return people want to please her, reward her, impress her. Finally, when Dad and I can't speak to each other through her any more, we have no choice but to stand side by side outside the playground and watch her fire herself around with her new best friends that she met two seconds ago.

He won't bring anything up, I know that. He would rather we stand like this, in awkwardness, than risk talking, in awkwardness. Even when forced into a discussion on something, on the rare times he can't escape it, his feelings on the issue would be limited. This is frustrating on the rare times I want to communicate about something important. I get this trait from him. When you have two people who don't talk about things, the situation can be more explosive than with those who do. Or rather, implosive, because the war is within.

'That incident with Ted Clifford wasn't right,' I say suddenly, unable to properly broach or phrase the subject.

'He has a position for account director going. Forty K a year. He wanted to talk to you directly,' he says, the anger in his voice. He didn't need to build up to it, it was there ready, for whenever I brought it up. 'You could have talked about it between yourselves. Not for everyone to hear at the table. A perfect opportunity. Do you know how many people would want that job?'

It's not at all what I meant. I was referring to his treatment of Heather, his reaction to Heather, not about the job, which was another issue – a less important one, but one that was bothering me enough that I was planning to tackle it next.

'I meant, with Heather.' I look at him for the first time and the expression on his face reveals it's a struggle for him to work out what I could be referring to. Eventually it comes to him.

'I spoke to Heather about that the very next day. All over, Jasmine.'

'And?'

'And now I know the Circles concept.'

'*Now* you know.'

'Yes. Now,' he says, glaring at me.

'She's thirty-four years old, we've been doing the Circles concept for quite some time.'

I should have said it louder, but I mumble it. I don't even know if he hears. I hope he does, but I'm not able for this:

to discuss, to confront. Or maybe I'm okay with confrontation but then all I want to do is back away like it never happened and I don't exist. The child in me quivers a bit at having my dad angry with me, however much the teenager in me rebels. 'You treat her like she's different. Like she's *special.*'

'I do not. I treat her the same as everyone else and that's what gets you mad. It's you that treats her differently,' he says. 'And you should think about that. And if you don't mind me saying so, you don't exactly practise what you preach. It's always been one rule for you and another for everyone else. This Circles concept – seems to be different for you than for everybody else, because everyone and anyone who comes near you is orange. No, Zara love, don't climb on that.' He cuts the conversation short and runs to her aid.

'Is that your granddad?' a child asks, and Zara laughs as though she's never heard such a ridiculous thing. 'This is my daddy!'

They end up on a see-saw together, Dad's gut barely able to squeeze behind the handles. As he goes down I see the bald patch in the back of his thinning hair. He does look like her granddad.

I'm quite stunned by what he has said to me. He said it so easily, without anger, which should make it easy to ignore, yet it isn't. It's the very calmness with which he said it that makes me listen, that makes me hear him loud and clear.

The Orange Wave Circle is the furthest circle away from the Purple Private Circle that represents the person concerned, in this case, me. It's the circle for distant acquaintances, for those you have no physical or emotional contact with at all.

Everyone and anyone who comes near you is orange.

That's not true, I want to shout at him. But I don't know if that's correct. Heather is the only person I have ever really kept close to me. Orange is certainly the circle I seem to have firmly planted him in. I came here to confront him about his own actions – no, I came to see Zara, but secondary to that was to make him see that his behaviour must change, I didn't expect the tide to change, for me to be staring down the barrel of my own finger.

Though perhaps my red circle is the largest of all. *Some people remain strangers forever.*

Confused, I drive back to my garden with my tail between my legs. I go back to thinking. I must snap the dead heads off and prepare for summer.

Summer

The seasons between spring and autumn,
comprising in the Northern Hemisphere the
warmest months of the year:
June, July and August.

The period of finest development, perfection,
or beauty previous to any decline:
the summer of life.

20

I love June, and June in a garden showered with love is the greatest reward a gardener could receive for their hard work. Every month and season has its beauty, but summer is when it is at its most vigorous, its brightest, its proudest, its most dramatic. If spring is hopeful, summer is proud, autumn is humble and winter is resilient. When I think of spring I see big and youthful bambi-like eyes looking up at me through long lashes, when I think of summer I see shoulders back, a chest heaved up and puffed out. When I think of autumn I think of a dipped head with a small smile lost in nostalgia, and for winter I imagine bruised knobbly knees and fists, growling, ready for the fight.

June brings constant watering, mulch renewal, weekly mowing, a half-dozen hanging baskets, pink peonies, cream roses, perennials of all different colours and an ample herb garden, which I have growing in a pot outside my kitchen. June brings frequent visits of you and your children to your garden where you have also begun to take a keen interest by beginning a kitchen garden at the side of your house to rival my garden, sowing runner beans and French beans, carrots, Brussels sprouts and courgettes. We race to see who can get outside the earliest each morning to tend to our gardens and when it is us first we smugly give the morning wave to the late arrivals. Now it is a competition to see whose bedroom curtains open first. There we both work, you in your garden, me in mine, while the Malones sit outside their front door, Mrs Malone in her chair, the stroke rendering her immobile and unable to speak and read, while Mr Malone reads to her, Patrick Kavanagh's poems in Mr Malone's soft Donegal lilt, drifting over the honeysuckle to me. You and I can go hours without speaking, without calling random thoughts or gardening questions across the road, but it feels as if we are working together. Maybe that is just me. And there is something nice about that. When I see you take a sip of refrigerated bottled water, it reminds me to take mine. When I straighten my back and announce I'm going to eat lunch, you agree that you will too. We don't eat together, but we stick to the same schedule. Sometimes I'll sit on my garden bench and eat my salad, and you'll sit at your table that you still haven't moved from the front lawn, and we'll be in each other's company but not really. We both wave good morning and good evening to the corporate man who is renting number six, who drives past us in his BMW but who has failed to notice us so far and drives on unaware of our neighbourly salutes. At first his nonchalance annoyed me. Now it both annoys me and makes me pity him, because I know exactly what is on his mind. He has no time for us, for our mundane neighbourly intrusion in his life. He is too busy. He has *things* on his mind. Real things. Distractions.

And I am coming closer to possibly becoming that person again as June brings my job interview. As soon as Monday informed me of the date I started willing it to come quickly, but now it's almost here and I want the week to slow down. June ninth, June ninth, I'm so nervous about it, I try not to think about it, though Monday won't let me off the hook, calling over to run through questions with me over a dinner I've cooked. I'm not nervous about it because I don't feel competent, I'm nervous because I feel I am competent and as the weeks have gone by I have grown to realise I want this job more than ever and I worry I won't get it. If I don't get this job, it's the beginning of unemployment becoming an issue, because it is out of my control while I'm on gardening leave. I don't want to *officially* feel bored, worthless, uncertain and panicking about my future. In a way, this is the calm before the storm, and if *this* is calm . . .

'Okay, so tell me again from the start, Ms Butler.'

'Monday,' I groan, as we sit at the kitchen table and he goes through the interview for the tenth time. 'Do you do this with all your headhuntees?'

'No.' He looks away, feathers ruffled.

'So why am I getting special treatment?'

Say it, say it, I will him to say the something I want to hear so badly.

'I want you to get the job.'

'Why?' I leave a long silence.

'All the other candidates have jobs,' he finally says. 'You deserve it.'

I sigh. Not the answer I was hoping for. 'Thanks. Who are they, anyway? Are they better than me?'

'You know I can't tell you that,' he says, smiling. 'Besides, you knowing wouldn't make a difference.'

'It might. I could sabotage their chances on the day of the interview. Slash their tyres, put pink hair dye in their shampoo, that kind of thing.'

He laughs, looks at me in the way that makes my insides melt, as though I both interest and baffle him at the same time.

'By the way,' he says, while I clear away the dishes. 'There's been a change of plan. The interview has been moved to the tenth.'

I stop scraping leftover food into the bin and look at him. My throat tightens, my stomach clenches. He notices the silence, looks up at me. 'And you just thought you'd mention that now.'

'It's only a day later, Jasmine – don't look so scared,' he says, smiling, rubbing his hand along his jaw as he studies me.

'I'm not scared, I'm . . .' I debate whether to tell him or not. I don't know why I wouldn't tell him, but not telling him reveals to me that I'm not – in this moment – fully committing to this interview and that scares me. I need this interview. I need this job. I need to get back on track.

June tenth is the day Heather goes on her four-day holiday to Fota Island with Jonathan. All that I intend doing while she's gone is to sit around at home waiting, waiting for the phone to ring, waiting for a neighbour to bang on my door and tell me something has happened, the way they do it in the movies, waiting for a guard to take his hat off and dip his head respectfully. If I go to the job interview that day I won't be able to fully concentrate on wondering what Heather is doing. Some would say the distraction would be good for me, but no, it will mean switching my phone off for at least an hour, it will mean not being able to listen to my senses, the possible sudden strike of fear that could alert me to the fact that something is wrong, leaving me unable to jump in my car and drive to Cork at a moment's notice. I want to get a job, but Heather should be my main priority. This debacle won't do.

'Jasmine,' Monday says, joining me in the kitchen. 'Is there something wrong?'

'No,' I lie, and he knows I'm lying.

After he leaves, I stay at the kitchen table and bite all of my nails down to the quick.

Monday calls me on Thursday ninth when I am in Heather's apartment packing with her, to make sure everything is okay for her trip the following day. He is suspicious and he is right to be, I am vague, and though I am committed to going to the interview in my head, when I say the words aloud even I don't believe them. I need the job. I need to get my life back on track. But Heather. My heart is completely torn and I am overwhelmed with worry.

'See you tomorrow, Jasmine,' Monday says.

'See you tomorrow,' I finally say and I almost choke on the final word.

The following day I am seeing Heather off at Heuston train station as if she's a soldier going off to war, and at eleven a.m. when I should be sitting in a boardroom selling myself and getting my life back on track, I am instead sitting in the carriage connected to Heather and Jonathan's, watching them play Snap, as we travel to Cork. Monday calls me four times and I ignore each one. He couldn't understand right now, but I know I am doing the right thing.

A man sits in the seat diagonally to me and blocks my view of Heather. I always thought that the garden, that nature, was honest, truthful, open. You work hard on it and you receive the rewards, but even in a garden there is deception and trickery. It seems to be natural, we do it to survive. The Stapelia asterias plant knows how to attract beneficial insects by looking and smelling like rotting flesh. It emits a putrid stench to go with its less than pretty appearance. I take its lead. I clear my nose of mucus and try to clear my throat, noisily. The young man is rightly grossed out by me and moves to another seat. I can see Heather again. It's natural to deceive.

Monday calls my phone for the fifth time. The passion flower vine developed little yellow spots that resemble Heliconious butterfly eggs, which convinces female butterflies to look elsewhere so their offspring won't have to compete with other caterpillars when they hatch. I think of my friend who, when in a nightclub and asked to dance by a man she's not interested in, mentions the baby she doesn't have and watches him turn on his heel quickly. I ignore Monday's call. It's natural to deceive.

There is a car to greet Heather and Jonathan at the train station; we organised this with the hotel and I see the driver standing with a sign with their names on it before they see it. Heather and Jonathan walk by him, searching in the wrong direction, and I want to call out to them but bite my tongue at the last minute. It's just as well because they turn around, as if hearing my thoughts, and see him as they make their way back.

The male orchid dupe wasp is so attracted to the tongue orchid that it ejaculates right on to the flower's petals. Flowers that can trick insects into ejaculating have the highest rates of pollination. I think of my friend who got pregnant so that her boyfriend would marry her, and then got pregnant again to keep them together when they were falling apart, and I remember that it is natural to deceive. I get into a taxi and follow their car to the hotel.

Heather and Jonathan check in and they take two single rooms, as discussed. I hadn't realised I was holding my breath until the air suddenly whooshes out of my mouth and I feel my body release tension. I check into the room I booked while on the train. I have asked to be on the same floor as Heather and Jonathan. All I have is my work briefcase and it seems strange not to have luggage when checking in, but I have survived a spontaneous dirty weekend on disposable spa thongs and I know I can do the same here.

I don't spend any time in my room. I go straight back down to the lobby to wait and hope I haven't missed them. They hold hands as they explore the grounds outside, I try to keep as much of a distance as possible, but it's not enough for me to see Heather from afar, I need to see her face. I need to be able to read her to make sure she is really okay. I get a bit braver and hide behind nearby trees. They find a playground beside a group of holiday homes that is alive and swarming with children. Heather sits on a swing and Jonathan pushes her. I sit on the grass and lift my face to the sun and close my eyes, and listen and smile at the sound of her laughter. I'm glad that I'm here, I've done the right thing.

They spend ninety minutes in the playground and then they go swimming. I watch her yellow swim hat bobbing up and down in the water, as Jonathan pretends to be a shark, as they play volleyball, badly, as she shrieks as he splashes her. He is caring and thoughtful and takes care of her every step of the way, almost treating her as though she is fragile, or perhaps precious, as though it is his honour to assist her. He opens doors, he pulls out chairs, he is a little clumsy but he accomplishes everything. Heather is so independent and yet she allows him to do this, seems happy for him to do this. She has spent so many years not wanting to be a person that needs unnecessary assistance, seeing her like this surprises me.

They change for dinner, Heather wearing a new dress we shopped for together, and lipstick. She doesn't usually wear make-up, and lipstick is a big deal. It is red and it doesn't match her pink dress, but she'd insisted on it. She looks mature as they walk together and I notice her hair is flecked with grey at the roots and wonder when that happened. When they are safely in the lift I follow the path they took and breathe in the perfume she is wearing. Faced with the impossible decision of which one to wear, she'd asked me which one Mum wore, and bought that. Mum's scent fills my lungs as I follow Heather's trail.

They eat downstairs in the main dining room. I choose to sit in the bar where I can still have a view of them. Heather orders the goat's cheese starter and I'm confused because I know she doesn't like it. I think she has misread it. I order the same to see what it's like, if she ever talks about it in the future, I'll know exactly what she's talking about. They order a glass of wine each, which concerns me as Heather doesn't drink. She takes a sip and makes a face. They both laugh and she pushes the glass far away from her. I order the same and drink it all. I'm contented, sitting here and watching her, feeling a part of it despite not completely being a part of it.

She eats the apple and beetroot from her starter but leaves the goat's cheese. I hear her explain to the waiter that she misread it and thought it was normal cheese, she doesn't want him to think it was the chef's fault. She's nervous; I can tell by the way she keeps fixing her hair behind her ear, even though it never comes loose. I want to tell her that it's okay, I'm here, and for a moment I consider letting her in on my secret, but then quickly decide against it. She needs to think she is doing all this alone. They eat three courses, Jonathan finishes off his entire steak and sides, Heather eats battered fish and chips. They taste each other's desserts. Jonathan spoons his chocolate fondue into her mouth, only he must be nervous too because his hand jerks and she ends up with chocolate on her nose. He turns puce and looks as though he wants to cry, but Heather starts laughing and he relaxes. He dips his napkin into his glass of water and leans over to tenderly clean the chocolate from her face. Heather does not take her eyes off him for one moment and it occurs to me that I could have sat right beside them and they would never have noticed me at all.

The Lithops plant is commonly called the Living Stone. These plants thrive in deserts, hidden away in rocky beds so that when their yellow flowers burst into bloom it's as if they've sprung out of nowhere. Surprise! I want to do that now, but no. I'll stay right here where they can't see me. It's natural to deceive.

That night when I turn on my phone there are four more missed calls from Monday and the text messages range from angry to concerned.

Caladium steudneriifolium pretends to be ill; the pattern of its leaves mimics the damage done by moth larvae when they hatch and eat through the plant, and this prevents moths from laying their eggs there. I tell Monday I have been terribly ill. It's natural to deceive.

Heather calls me when she and I are back in our rooms and tells me everything that has happened to her today. It is everything that I have seen already and I feel happy that she has shared it all with me, not leaving anything out.

I drink a bottle of wine from the minibar and I listen out for the opening and closing of bedroom doors in the corridor. Each time I hear a door I think is in their direction, I peep out and duck back in again. They stay in their rooms all night.

The following day they take a trip to Fota Island. They

spend a long time looking at and photographing the Lar gibbons, who sing loudly and swing wildly, much to Heather's delight. They take photographs of each other and then Jonathan asks a teenage boy to take a photograph of the both of them. I don't like the look of the teenager, he is not someone I would have personally trusted with my phone, and Jonathan doing this annoys me. I move closer, just in case. The teenager's gang of friends are already sniggering at Jonathan and Heather's happy faces pushed together for the photo. I move closer and closer, ready to pounce on him when he runs off with Jonathan's phone. The boy takes the photo and hands it back to them. I freeze, then step in behind a tree so I'm not seen. Jonathan and Heather examine the photos and then surprise me by heading back in my direction, and as they do my phone beeps. It is a message from Heather; the photograph of her and Jonathan. This makes me feel sad inside, disappointed at myself for being here. It is as though somebody has taken a pin and popped my balloon. Why didn't I trust that Heather would keep me informed and therefore involved every step of the way? I had wanted to share this place with her, had been put out by my own suggestion that they come here and yet, she is sharing it with me. Feeling unnerved, I hang back a little further.

Heather and Jonathan spend four hours in the park. It is hot and humid and busy with school tours and families. Wishing I had a change of clothes more suited to this weather than the black suit I'd put on for my interview, I stay in the shade, but I never lose them. They stop for ice cream and talk for an hour, then they return to the hotel. They sit in the bar, both drinking 7UP and they continue their conversation. I don't think I have ever spoken to anybody for so long at one sitting, but the words flow from each of them and their attention is completely focused on one another. It is beautiful, but again I feel a tinge of sadness, which makes me feel ridiculous. I am not here to feel sorry for myself. They eat in the bar and go to bed early, tired from their long day outside.

I have one message from Monday. *Call me. Please.*

My finger hovers over the call button but instead my phone rings and I talk to Heather for forty-five minutes about the day she had. She tells me absolutely everything that I have already witnessed and the jubilation I felt yesterday at being here and knowing she is sharing everything with me has disappeared. I feel like a traitor. I should have trusted that she would be capable. I shouldn't be here.

It is day three. They will be leaving tomorrow and they are sitting outside the hotel talking. What began as a beautiful day has quickly turned. While everyone moves inside to shelter from the cool breeze, Heather and Jonathan, oblivious to the cold, continue to talk. Sometimes they don't talk and sit comfortable in each other's company, and I can't stop watching them, absolutely fascinated by what is going on with them.

Something inside me shifts. Although it has already dawned on me that I shouldn't be here, I realise that I should leave *now*. Because if Heather ever finds out, I know it would jeopardise my relationship with her. This trip is important to her and my being here is disrespectful to her. I know this and yet it only hits me now. I have betrayed her by coming here, and I feel ill and upset with myself for that. I betrayed Monday for this – another betrayal. I have to leave.

I hurry to my room to collect the few belongings I brought with me. I check out. As I scurry through the lobby, suddenly eager to flee the scene, I run smack-bang into Heather and Jonathan.

'Jasmine!' she says, shock written all over her face. At first she is happy to see me and then I watch how she processes it, joy turning to confusion. Bafflement, then wonder. She is too polite to be angry with me, even if she has figured it out.

I'm so stunned by the sight of them, and feel so caught out, that I don't know what to say. Guilt is written all over my face. They both know it and look to each other, seeming as appalled as I feel.

'I wanted to make sure that you're okay,' my voice wobbles. 'I was . . . so worried.' My voice cracks and I whisper. 'I'm sorry.'

Heather looks at me in shock. 'Did you follow me, Jasmine?'

'I'm going now, I promise. I'm sorry.' My lips brush her forehead quickly as I leave, clumsily bumping into people in the halls as I make my way to the door.

The look that Heather gives me, and the way that I feel, is not natural.

For the next few hours I sit on the train, face in my hands, repeating the mantra. I have let Monday down, I have let Heather down, I have let myself down.

The taxi pulls up outside my house and I climb out, exhausted and desperately in need of a change of clothes. I look at my garden, hoping to feel the familiar sense of relief or rejuvenation that I've come to expect from it. But I don't. Something isn't right. It has lost its vibrancy.

Reality has taught me a lesson, the universe has gotten me back. I have neglected my garden in a heatwave for three days without any instruction to anyone to help. The flowers are thirsty. Worse, slugs have eaten their way through my garden. My cream roses are drooping, my pink peonies are ravaged. I have managed to keep it in all day, but the sight of my precious garden brings me to tears.

I have let Monday down, I have let Heather down, I have let myself down.

I missed an important opportunity in my life, in order to be there for Heather. But Heather didn't need me. I repeat this to myself. Heather didn't need me. Perhaps it is me that clings to her, looking for help, for escape from my own world. Instead of living my own life for myself, I have taken on the role of guiding her and in a way mothering her. Whether this was a result of caring for her, or the reason I chose to do it, I'm not sure. I don't think it matters either way, but I know now that it's a fact.

Feeling out of control this year, I have turned to my garden to maintain control, thinking it would bend to my will. It has shown me that it will not. Nothing can bend to our will. I neglected my garden and I allowed the slugs to take over.

That is exactly what I have done with myself.

21

Apart from betrayal, June also brings a christening, godmother duties and a one-night-stand with my ex-boyfriend Laurence, the boyfriend who lasted longest, the one everybody thought I'd marry, including me, but the one who left me in the end. Sleeping with him again after two years of Laurence-celibacy was a mistake, it was an enjoyable mistake, but it won't be happening again. I don't know what I was thinking, but after a day spent drinking in the sun, the old familiar feelings came back, or the memory of them did, their echo, and so I confused them as easily as I had the male from the female toilets and the glass of water from the straight vodka. Just another oopsie on that long summer's day. And maybe I was longing for a moment of security, to go back to the feeling of being loved, of feeling in love. Only it didn't work out that way, of course it didn't. Recreations never work. The 'here's one I made earlier' can rarely be replicated. Don't try this at home, kids.

And so I end up outside your house at two in the morning, drunk, throwing pebbles at your window, with a bottle of rosé and two glasses in my hands.

You open the curtains and look out, your face sleepy

and confused, your hair standing high on your head. You see me, then disappear from view and I sit at the table and wait for you. Moments later you open the door, tracksuit on, and sleepily make your way to me. When you register my state, the groggy inquisitive look on your face quickly changes to amusement, the expression that makes your blue eyes sparkle mischievously, though smaller and surrounded by the crinkles that squeeze them when you smile.

'Well, well, well, what have we got here?' you say, coming towards me with an enormous grin. You give my hair an annoying big-brother ruffle before joining me at the garden table. 'You look fancy tonight.'

'Just thought I'd call an urgent neighbourhood meeting,' I slur, then push a glass towards you and lean over to fill it. I almost fall off my chair as I do so.

'Not for me.' You place your hand over the top of the glass.

'Still not drinking?' I ask, disappointed.

'Have I made you get out of bed in the middle of the night lately to get me into my house?'

I think about it. 'No.'

'Not for four weeks.'

I top my own glass up some more. 'Party pooper.'

'Alcoholic.'

'Potato, potato,' I say. I slug back some wine.

'That's supportive,' you say good-naturedly.

'You're not an alcoholic. You're a pisshead – there's a difference.'

'Wow. That's controversial. Explain that please.'

'You're an eejit, that's all. Selfish. Choose late nights over early nights. You're not addicted, you don't actually have a drink problem, you have a life problem. I mean, do you go to meetings?'

'No. Well, kind of. I sit with Dr J.'

'A retired GP doesn't count.'

'Dr J is an alcoholic. Hasn't had a drink in over twenty years. There's a lot about him that you don't know,' he says, seeing my shocked expression. 'His wife said she wouldn't have children until he cleaned himself up. He didn't stop until he was over fifty. Too late. She stayed with him though.'

'Well, she's dead now.' I drain my glass.

You frown. 'Yes, Sherlock. She's dead now.'

'So she got away in the end.' I have no idea why I'm saying the things I'm saying. Probably for the sake of being annoying, which I clearly am. It's fun to be you, I can see why you do it.

You get up and leave the table and disappear into the house. I think you've gone for good, but you return with a bag of cheese nachos.

'Are the kids in there?'

'Kris and Kylie asked if they could stay another night. They're enjoying the plot.'

'Kris and Kylie. So that's their names. They even sound like twins.'

'They are.'

'Oh.'

You have quite an impressive plot of vegetables growing at the side of the house. Though it's dark, I eye the area. You laugh.

'You're jealous.'

'Why would I be? When I have that.' We look at my garden. It's the best on the street, if I do say so myself. 'Don't try to compete with me, Marshall,' I warn.

'I wouldn't dare,' you say, mock-serious. 'Fionn still isn't getting into the spirit of things.'

'He might not ever,' I say thoughtfully, my finger running around the rim of the glass. 'No matter what you do.'

'Well, that's positive, thanks.'

'I'm not here to be positive. I'm here to be realistic. If you want cheery tips, talk to okey-dokey Dr J.'

'I do.'

'I'm surprised about him, you know. He's lucky he didn't kill someone at the practice.'

'He was a functioning alcoholic. The worst kind.'

'Lucky for you, you weren't.'

You take both insults: that you're an alcoholic and that you couldn't function.

'I know. He's made me see that.'

We go quiet and you munch on the nachos. I slug my wine. I realise I've been doing the usual thing of attacking you.

'Every boyfriend I've ever been with has left me. Did you know that?'

'No, I didn't.' You have that amused expression again. 'But I can't say I'm surprised,' you add, sarcastically, but gently.

'Because I'm very difficult to live with,' I say, to your surprise.

'Why are you difficult to live with?'

'Because I want everything done my way. I don't like mistakes.'

'Jesus, you wouldn't want to live with me.'

'You're quite right. I don't.'

Silence.

'Where's this coming from tonight?'

'I slept with my ex.'

You look at your watch. It's two a.m.

'I left when he was asleep.'

241

'He was probably pretending to be asleep.'

'I hadn't thought of that.'

'I used to pull that trick all the time.'

'Well, it worked. She left.'

You don't like that joke so much, probably because it didn't come out as a joke.

'So is that what he told you? That you're difficult to live with?'

'Not in so many words. I came up with it all by myself. It's something I've realised since . . .' I look over at my garden, beautiful and blooming, drawing the magical source of knowledge into myself. The more I dig into the soil, the more I dig into myself.

'Then how do you know it's true? Maybe you're not difficult to live with at all, maybe you're just a busy, successful, beautiful woman who won't settle for anything but the best – and why should you?'

That moves me, almost to tears.

'Maybe,' he says.

My tears instantly dry.

'Or maybe you're crap in bed and impossible to live with.'

You start laughing and I throw a nacho at you.

'He told me tonight that he was lonely in my company. That's why he left me.'

Silence.

'Lonely in your company,' you say slowly, thoughtfully.

'Lonely in my company,' I repeat, refilling my glass.

Imagine how I felt – imagine how he'd felt, being with somebody who made him feel lonely. It's quite an awful thing to feel lonely in the company of someone you love. It is quite something to say it, it is unbearable to be the one to hear it, to be the one to have it said of you.

'He said this before or after you slept with him?' you ask, leaning forward, elbows on the table, interested, studying me.

'Before. But I know what you're thinking. It wasn't a line.'

'It was a line,' you say, annoyed. 'Come on, Jasmine, it was a line. I bet you two were on your own somewhere, bet it was the end of the night, he takes you aside, talks to Jasmine, still single and jobless, bound to be in a vulnerable state, her friends popping sprogs all around her. Even though she says she doesn't want them, it's still going to get her thinking. And then he pulls the line out of his pocket. He looks at you, all red hair and big tits . . .'

I snort, trying not to smile.

'Smudged eyeliner . . .'

I wipe under my eyes.

'It's a line. It's bound to go one of two ways: either you get angry and throw your drink on him, or you feel guilty and he gets laid. Nine times out of ten, it works.'

'To quote Dr J: "*Codswallop!*" You did not try that ten times,' I say, dubious.

'Twice. Got a drink in my face once, got my happy ending once. And the drink in question was a Sambuca, which really stung my skin, with the coffee bean still on fire.'

I laugh.

'Finally. She smiles,' you say softly.

I light up a cigarette.

'You don't smoke.'

'Only when I drink.'

'Wild thing.'

I roll my eyes.

'So what about your boyfriend? You going to tell him about what you did tonight?'

'What boyfriend?'

'The good-looking guy who calls around all the time. The one who's not your cousin.' You hold your hands up and laugh. 'Sorry, I couldn't help it.'

'He's not my boyfriend. That's Monday. He's a head-hunter. He was trying to get me to go for a job.'

'Monday?'

'He was born on a Monday.'

'Right. And Monday is headhunting you.'

I don't like the amused look on your face.

'Was. Or do you think that was a line too?' I'm being sarcastic, I don't expect you to give it serious consideration.

'What was the job?'

'Working with the DavidGordonWhite Foundation.'

'The tax consultants?'

'They have a new foundation dedicated to climate justice.'

You look at me pointedly. 'You do start-ups.'

'It's new. I'd have to start it up.'

'And you're telling me he's not trying to get you into bed?'

'I wish he would,' I reply, and you laugh. I drop the cigarette on the ground and pivot on it with my strappy heel. For a moment I'd contemplated extinguishing it on the varnished table, but the thought of the children's hard work stopped me. 'Anyway it's too late. I missed the inter-view.'

'Why? Get scared?' You're not teasing this time.

'No.' But I was scared, though it wasn't over the job.

I think about telling you the truth. It would mean having to explain my fears about Heather going away on her own, and I don't want to reinforce your stereotypical view of Down syndrome, even if my own thinking was wrong. She has been home for one week and while we have spoken

244

on the phone – of course she's talking to me, Heather couldn't be any other way – things are not the same. She is distant. I've lost a piece of her, the invisible piece that held her and me together.

'Did you miss the interview because you were drunk?' you ask, concerned.

'No,' I snap.

'Okay, okay. It just seems to be a recurring theme these days, so I thought I should mention it, seeing as you so *kindly* brought my drinking to my attention.' You hold your hands up, defensively.

'I'm fine,' I say, more calmly. 'I'm just . . . so . . .' I make a fart noise with my mouth and then sigh, unable to sum up my feelings any more than that.

'Yeah. I understand.'

And despite my inability to explain, I think that you do understand exactly. We sit in a comfortable silence which makes me think of how Jonathan and Heather were together, the jealousy I felt, not realising I have that comfort right here with you.

'That man who comes over to your house with the little girl. Is that your dad?'

I nod.

'He seems like a good dad.'

I think you're going to start picking at me again, but as you run your hand down the smooth varnished wood I know that you're thinking about yourself and your current predicament.

'He is now,' I say. I want to add *to someone else*, but I don't.

You look up at me. Study me in that way that you do, which I hate, because it's as though you're seeing, or trying to see right through to my soul.

'Interesting.'

'Interesting,' I sigh. 'What's interesting about that?'

'It explains the things you said to me, that's all.'

'I told you you were a terrible dad because you were a terrible dad.'

'But you noticed it. It bothered you.'

I don't respond. I drink instead.

'Is he trying to make up for it now?'

'No, he's interfering in my life – different thing altogether.' On your questioning look, I explain: 'He's trying to get me a job. At his old company. Pull in a few favours, that kind of thing.'

'That sounds helpful.'

'It's not helpful. It's nepotism.'

'Is it a good job?'

'Actually, yes, it is. Account director, manage a team of eight. Forty thousand,' I repeat dad's mantra in a bad impression of him.

'It's a good job.'

'Yes, it's a great job. That's what I said.'

'Not something that he'd give to anyone.'

'Of course not.'

'You'd have to do an interview.'

'Of course. It's not his company any more. He's only putting my name forward.'

'So he believes in you. Thinks you're capable. I'm sure he's a proud man. He wouldn't want to be embarrassed by an underperforming daughter.'

I prickle at that and wonder if you're referring to Heather. I ready myself, but realise you're not. I don't know what to say to you.

'I'd take it as a compliment.'

'Whatever.'

'You and Fionn have a lot in common,' you say, and I know you're criticising my childish response, but I go for the jugular.

'Because we've both got crap dads?'

You sigh. 'If I told you I knew someone with a great idea for a start-up, and they were looking for someone to work with, would you be interested?'

'Is her name Caroline?' I say, and hear the dread in my voice.

'I mean hypothetically.'

'Yes. I would meet them.'

'But your dad knows someone who's looking for someone and you won't entertain it.'

I don't know how to answer, so in the spirit of Fionn, I shrug.

'I wouldn't rule it out if I were you.'

'I don't need his help.'

'Yes, you do.'

I'm silent.

'You've a headhunter hunting you for a job you would have taken by now if you were in any way interested, and a friend who wants you to help her set up a website about dresses. I was in your house, I heard,' you explain, seeing my reaction. 'Of course you need help.'

I'm silent.

'I know you don't like other people's opinions. You think they're wrong. That they're not open-minded. Don't look at me like that, you've told me this. Sometimes – just sometimes – I think you look at things entirely the wrong way. I don't know what you think you're defending your-self against, but it's all the wrong things.'

You let that hang for a while. I preferred it when I hated you and we didn't speak. But seeing as you've picked

247

through me and my issues, I feel we've reached the point where I can tackle yours. 'What's with the Guns N' Roses song?'

You look at me blankly. 'What do you mean?'

'"Paradise City"?' I smile. 'It's blaring out most nights when you come home.'

You stare at me blankly. 'Nothing. The CD player in the jeep is jammed. It's the only song that plays.'

I'm disappointed. Where I thought I found meaning in you, it turns out I am wrong. Where I thought I had a glimpse of something, I am mistaken.

'I better get back to bed, the kids will be up early in the morning. We're picking our peas tomorrow and planting tomatoes.'

I make a faux impressed face. I'm actually jealous. My peas failed.

'You okay here?'

'Yeah.'

'Just for the record, Jasmine: I would have said the opposite about you.'

'What do you mean?'

'If it wasn't for you, I would have been alone too many times. I've never felt lonely in your company, not for a second.'

My breath catches in my throat. I watch you disappear inside the house. I suddenly feel stone-cold sober. Although I'm dizzy, I have clarity of thought. I'm sitting at the head of the table, at the seat you usually sit in. Your drinking table. How the tables turn in life.

22

The following morning I'm woken by the sun streaming in on my face and the doorbell is ringing. My head is hot, as though I've been lying on the tarmac with a magnifying glass held over my face, God's childish joke on me. I didn't bother closing the curtains when I fell into bed. Everything comes back to me in an instant, as though I'm being hit over the head with a stone-filled sock. The christening, Laurence. I don't even care that I dragged you out of bed last night, it is Laurence that beats everything, hands down. The doorbell continues to ring.

'She's not here, Dad!' I hear a little girl's voice shout beneath my window. Kylie. Or maybe Kris, whose voice hasn't broken yet.

'She's there. Keep trying,' I hear you shout across the road.

I grunt as I open my eyes and try to adjust to the white light. My mouth is like sandpaper and I look to my bedside locker for water and instead see an empty bottle of vodka. My stomach heaves. This is becoming all too familiar and I know, I just know, that this is the last time this will happen. I can't take any more. Wanting to be out of my system is now all out of my system. I want to come back now. My alarm clock tells me it is noon and I believe it, the midday sun on my hot cheeks.

I trip going down the stairs and catch myself on the banister. My heart is pounding from the shock, but it gives me the wake-up call I need. I pull open the door and two blondes and Monday stare at me, two looking my dishevelled state up and down with distaste, the other with an amused expression. I immediately close the door in their faces and I hear him laugh.

'Come on, kids, why don't we give her a second to get ready.'

I open the door a little for him to enter and then run upstairs to take a shower and humanise myself. I come back downstairs feeling refreshed but tender. Everything is achey – my head, my body . . .

'Rough night?' Monday asks, mildly entertained by my state. 'Or are you still ill?' The last sentence comes out angry, and it makes me wince.

I can barely look at him, I feel so guilty about not showing up for the interview, but mostly for not having the nerve to inform him I wouldn't be. He has made coffee, he's dressed casually, and somehow he seems more vulnerable out of his business suit. This doesn't feel like a business call, he can't hide behind the work persona that he usually disappears behind. Suddenly I feel guilty in the pit of my stomach about Laurence, as though I've betrayed Monday, even though there was never anything between us. He is a headhunter and I am unemployed and there was never anything more, or even a hint, but the deception I feel tells me that there was something. It was silent and hidden but it was there. And of course it took sleeping with someone else to realise that.

'Monday,' I take his hand, which takes him by surprise. 'I

am so sorry about last week. Please don't think that it was a decision that I took lightly, because it wasn't. I want to explain everything to you now and I hope you'll understand.'

'So you weren't sick then,' he says flatly.

'No.' I bite my lip.

'I don't think we'll have much time to talk,' he says, looking at his watch and my heart falls.

'If you can, please stay, I'll explain everything—'

'No, I'm not leaving,' he says, leaning against the kitchen counter, folding his arms and looking at me.

I'm confused but I can barely hold his look without smiling. He softens me so much, turns me to mush. He finally smiles and shakes his head, as though doing so is against his better judgement.

'You're a mess, you know that?' he says it gently, as though it's a compliment and I take it as such.

'I know. I'm sorry.'

He watches my lips and swallows hard and I wonder when on earth it's going to happen, I mean, I think it's really going to happen, maybe I should say something, make the first move to kiss him, but the doorbell rings and he jumps, startled, as though we've been caught.

I sigh and open the door and in you walk with your blonde children, my dad, Zara, Leilah, who is looking very apologetic, and behind her is Kevin, closely followed by Heather and her assistant Jamie. Heather is looking very proud of herself. You look like you're finding this hilarious. Monday is suddenly looking at me with concern. He steps away from the counter and drops his folded arms.

'Are you okay?'

My body has started to tremble from head to toe. I'm not sure if alcohol withdrawal has something to do with it, but the sense of terror that has engulfed me over what is to come is certainly playing a part. The earlier heart-pound of passion is gone, now it is dread, anxiety, nerves. My brain is telling my body to *run*. Now! Fight or flight, and flight has well and truly kicked in. I know what this is, I know what they've done. I can tell from the proud look on Heather's face that she feels she is doing this for my own benefit, that I will be happy about this.

Kevin gives me a warm hug, which makes me freeze with my hands elevated in the air, away from his body, unable to touch him.

You chuckle, my life your Saturday entertainment on this match-free summer weekend.

Finally Kevin pulls away. 'Heather asked me to invite Jennifer, but she wasn't home so I thought I'd come along myself.'

I open my mouth but no words come out.

'You're the gardener?' Kevin says to you, remembering you from the day he called by.

You look at me, amused by the entire situation.

'Matt is my neighbour. His son was helping me out with some work around the garden a while back.'

Kevin fixes you with a steely stare.

'Come on, don't tell me it's the first time you've been cock-blocked,' you say, grinning like a Cheshire cat.

Everybody moves to the living room and sits, some taking the kitchen chairs with them as there isn't enough seating. You're looking around with a big smile on your face, all eager beaver. The kids sit together at the kitchen table, with their colouring books and Play-Doh. I pace the kitchen pretending I'm making tea and coffee, but I'm making escape plans, excuses, get-out clauses. Monday has hung back, though I am so much in my head I am not present any more.

'Are you okay?' he asks.

I stop pacing. 'I want to die,' I say firmly. 'I want to fucking die now.'

He drops his hand and looks over at the gathering, biting his lip with his front chipped tooth. He looks as though he's trying to figure out a way to get me out of here. I cling to hope.

Jamie makes her way over to the kitchen. I can hear the soles of her feet sticking and unsticking to her sandals as she walks. I think I prefer it when she wears her sport socks.

'I brought some biscuits,' she says putting a packet of Jaffa Cakes on the counter. I hate Jaffa Cakes.

'Jamie, what the hell is going on? What is this?'

'Heather wanted to do this for you,' she says. 'It's her circle of support for you.'

'For fuck's sake,' I snap, a bit too loudly, and I hear you chuckle in the living room.

'I'll have coffee, two sugars, splash of milk, dear,' you call.

Caroline walks in, wearing black sunglasses large enough to cover half her face. 'Oh my God, I'm so hungover. These christenings are killing me. Oh my God!' She slaps me playfully on the arm and hisses, 'I heard you slept with Laurence last night!'

I cringe. I know Monday is right over my shoulder and he has heard. I feel his eyes searing into my back. I feel sick. I look at him and he looks away, busying himself. He brings a tray of cups into the living room and sits down.

'Oh,' she says sensing the atmosphere. 'I'm sorry, I didn't know you two were—'

'Doesn't matter.' I rub my face tiredly. 'You knew about this meeting though?'

She nods, takes a pack of headache pills from her bag and knocks two back with a bottle of water. 'Wasn't allowed to tell you. Heather wanted to surprise you.'

I am panicking inside. I want to run, I really do, but one look at Heather – who is sitting at the head of the circle wearing her best blouse and trousers, looking so proud, beaming, confident and bright-eyed about what she has pulled together – and I know I can't back out on her now. I must endure.

I sit down in the single armchair that has been left free for me, all eyes on me. Yours are twinkling with merriment, so happy to see me looking uncomfortable and vulnerable, vulture that you are. Monday's eyes are hard and cold and he stares at the leg of the coffee table, whatever previous concern he had for me now dead and buried. Caroline's eyes are bloodshot and she refuses the passing plate of Jaffa Cakes as though it's a ticking bomb.

Kevin is staring at me intently, leaning forward with his elbows on his knees, trying to channel his good happy positive pervy thoughts in my direction. This is unsettling. His hairy toes in his flip-flops poking out from beneath his skin-tight brown cords are unsettling. He is unsettling, period. Leilah is afraid to look at me, I know it; she's chewing on her lip and looking around the room and wondering why she didn't marry a man with a less complicated family. Dad is on one side of her, texting slowly with big thick fingers. Monday is squeezed on the other side of her.

'Have you two met?' I ask, and they both nod simultaneously, Monday still not looking me in the eye.

Jamie begins. 'Thank you all for coming here today. Heather has taken the time to contact you all individually, she has put a great deal of planning and thought into this, and you're all welcome. Over to you, Heather.'

I tuck my legs up on the couch and hug them, protecting my body. I try to tell myself that I'm doing this for Heather, this is an exercise for her, she has organised this and, as patronising as it sounds, it's true, and it helps me. But as soon as I hear her voice I want to cry, I'm so proud of her.

'Thank you all for coming. For over fifteen years, my sister Jasmine has been coming to my circle of support and it has helped me so much, now I want to give her the same experience. You are Jasmine's circle of support, her circle of friends.' She looks around proudly.

I look at the people who have shown up and I feel pathetic. You wink at me and stuff a biscuit into your mouth and I want to physically harm you. I *will* physically harm you.

'We want to show you that we love you and support you and we are here for you,' Heather says, and starts clapping.

The others join in, some enthusiastically, Caroline gently because the noise is hurting her ears. You wolf-whistle. Dad looks at you like he wants to punch you. It is as if Monday is not here, but I know he is, I feel his energy every time he's in a room, my eyes are drawn to him each time I'm near him, my body is drawn to him each time, every single part of me wants me to move towards him.

'My little sister Jasmine was always busy. Busy busy busy. When she's not busy, she minds me. But now she is not busy and she doesn't need to mind me any more. She needs to mind herself.'

Tears spring to my eyes. I cover myself with arms, legs, hands, everything twisted and folded and saying 'Closed'.

They all stare at me. I. Want. To. Die. Right now.

I clear my throat, stop hiding behind my legs and instead place them on the ground. I cross them.

'Thank you all for coming. I'm sure you all know this is a surprise so I'm not really prepared for this, but thank you, Heather, for organising it. I know you have my best interests in your heart.' I'm going to keep it basic. Give them something but nothing, not let anybody in, but look like I'm playing along. Take all constructive criticism with a smile. Thank them. Move on. That's the game plan. 'Losing my job in November was really tough. I did *love* that job and it's been very difficult the past six months, not being able to get up in the morning and feel . . . useful.' I clear my throat. 'But now I'm realising – or *have* realised – that it isn't as bad as I thought.'

Would telling them that I'm enjoying aspects of it, in a way I never thought I could, give too much away? I look at your eager face, then at Kevin so engaged, at Monday who instantly averts his pan-faced gaze to the coffee-table leg, and decide they don't need to know about my gardening therapy. Telling them that it's helping me would be tantamount to admitting that I needed help, and I don't want to go there.

'So. The plan is,' I direct this at Heather, seeing as it is her concerns which have led to this meeting and therefore her no longer being concerned could quickly draw this meeting to a close. 'To carry out my gardening leave for the remaining six months and then, get a job, so thank you all for your help in the past and your support now, and for coming here today.'

I end it chirpily and perkily and positively, no cause for consternation or alarm. Jasmine is A-okay.

'Wow.' You break the silence. 'That was moving, Jasmine. That was deep. I really feel like I have a sense of you now,' you say, voice dripping with sarcasm. You pop a Pringle into your mouth. I can smell the sour cream and onion from here and my stomach churns.

'Well, what do you plan to do after *your* gardening leave, Matt? Share with us.'

'Hey, this isn't *my* circle of friends,' you reply, that smirk on your face.

'Nor mine, evidently,' I snap back.

'Let's keep this positive,' Kevin says in his priestly voice, hands raised. He lowers them slowly, as if hypnotising us into calming, or like it's a dance routine from a nineties boyband.

'I'm calm,' you say, picking up another Pringle.

You should have gained weight with all the snacking and picking you've been doing since quitting smoking, but you haven't. You seem trimmer, fitter, fresher than before, which is because of the no alcohol.

'I think it's fair to say that, aside from Peter and Heather, I seem to have known Jasmine the longest amount of time.' Kevin looks at me and smiles. I shudder. 'So I feel that I understand and know her the best.'

'Really,' you say, turning on him. 'So you can tell us which of the three jobs is best suited to her then.'

You have landed both Kevin and I in the shit. Neither of us have a clue, for different reasons of course.

'*Three* jobs?' Caroline says, annoyed.

Monday's head snaps up to look at me with a frown, trying to figure me out, this great big liar who has appeared before him. Discussing the two other jobs with him was pointless as the only one I was considering was the one he was offering. But this point that you have so kindly raised makes me look like a three-timer.

It is ironic that it is you that knows me best out of all these people and that is the most loaded question to ask, because the three people who offered me those jobs are here and for the most part they know nothing about each other. They are all looking at me and waiting for an answer. You miss stirring it up on air and so you're using my life for your own amusement.

I realise I'm staring at you in loathing in a long silence.

'What are the three options?' Kevin asks, looking at me with a gentle, soft, understanding smile as if he's helping me out. 'Hmm?'

I don't like the way he's looking at me. Suddenly I break the tension with, 'Monday, I don't know if you've met my cousin?'

Monday snaps to attention at his name being called, I can't imagine how this must feel for everybody who has been called here but I'm awkward so they must feel worse.

'Have you met my cousin?'

'Well, we're not really—' Kevin interrupts.

'He's my *cousin*,' I say. 'Kevin, this is Monday.'

They shake hands across the coffee table and you smirk, knowing exactly what I'm doing.

Silence.

'So the reason I mention Monday is because he's with Diversified Search International and he headhunted me for a job at DavidGordonWhite.'

Dad leans forward and gets a look at Monday as if suddenly he counts now.

'But that job is gone so, Monday, if you feel like you want to leave here now, nobody will be insulted,' I say, smiling nervously. I want him to go, I don't want the man I adore to hear how messed up I am in this circle of terror, and after what he heard Caroline say I can feel him seething. Let him go.

'Why isn't the job an option any more?' Dad asks.

I look at Monday. It's now his opportunity for retribution but he doesn't say anything.

'Um. I didn't make it to the interview,' I answer instead. Dad effs and blinds.

'Peter,' Leilah elbows him and Heather's eyes widen and look at me with surprise.

'Well, why didn't you make it to the interview?' Dad asks, exasperated.

'She was ill,' Monday finally says, though I don't feel like he's defending me. His voice is still flat and devoid of . . . Monday. 'I think we should hear about the other jobs,' he adds. 'I wasn't aware there were other options for you.'

The way he says *other options* makes me wonder if he's not talking about the job, if he's talking about Laurence. There is so much that I want to explain to him when this is all finished – only to him, though. I don't care what anybody else thinks. As for you, you are the only person who knows everything already.

'Sick, my arse,' Dad mumbles and he gets another elbow from Leilah.

'You were sick, Jasmine?' Heather asks, so concerned. 'Were you sick in Cork?'

'Hold on, you were in Cork?' Jamie asks, sitting forward. 'I thought we agreed that Heather should go alone. Didn't we say that?' She looks at Leilah, who had also been at the meeting.

Leilah looks at me, clearly feeling conflicted, not wanting to step on anybody's toes. I can see the battle going on in her head.

'Well?' Dad asks her.

'Yes,' she says, as if the word has been coughed up by a slap on the back. 'But I'm sure Jasmine went for a reason.'

Jamie addresses the circle. 'Heather had her first holiday away with her boyfriend, Jonathan. At Heather's circle of

259

support we all agreed that she was more than capable of going alone, and any actions contrary to this would be seen as unhelpful to Heather—'

'Okay, Jamie, thank you,' I snap. I rub my face tiredly.

'So why did you go?' Jamie asks, her voice less strident now.

'She was worried about her,' Kevin speaks up on my behalf. 'Obviously.'

'When did you go, Heather?' Monday asks gently.

'Friday till Monday.' She smiles.

He nods, absorbing this. 'Did you have a good time?'

'The best!' She grins.

Monday is looking at me with newfound softness. Everyone but Dad is. Dad's shaking his head at me and concentrating on his phone in an effort to stop himself from blurting something out. This is not good. I feel a burning behind my eyes. I cannot cry.

'I was just . . . she's never been . . . it was the first time that she . . . you know, with a . . .' I sigh, all eyes on me. I hear the wobble in my voice. I finally look at Heather. 'I wasn't ready to let you go.' Before I can do anything to stop it, a tear falls and I wipe it away before it reaches my chin, like it never happened.

Heather's cheeks turn pink and she speaks shyly. 'I'm not going anywhere, Jasmine. I'm not leaving you. You missed your job interview for me?'

On that, another tear falls. And another. I wipe them all away quickly, eyes down, not wanting to see them watching me.

'Can I please be excused?' I say, sounding like a child.

Nobody answers. Nobody feels like they have the authority to tell me yes or no.

'Hi, Monday. I knew about you,' Caroline suddenly says,

snapping out of her hangover, stepping in to save me. 'I'm Caroline, I'm Jasmine's friend.'

'Hi.'

'I have a website idea that she's helping me with.'

That immediately makes me grind my teeth, but I hold my tongue.

'What's wrong, Jasmine?' Kevin asks, studying me.

'Nothing,' I say. But it's clipped and my nothing sounds like a something. 'Well, it's just that I'm not exactly "helping" with it. I am developing it with you, which is what I do, development, implement . . . "helping" sounds . . . you know . . .'

Her neck almost snaps in the way her head fires around to look at me.

She looks at me in that way she does when she's offended. The single blink, the tight shiny forehead – though that is also due to the Botox – and I would usually retreat because she's my friend, though in business I would persevere, which immediately tells me we're doomed.

'And then there's Dad,' I say, quickly moving on.

'Hold on a minute,' Kevin says. 'I think we should continue here.'

'Kevin, this is not a therapy session.' I smile tightly. 'It's just a little chat. And I think we're getting close to the end now.'

'I think for you to get the best out of this you should—'

I interrupt Kevin. 'This isn't the time to—'

'I'm happy to thrash it out.' Caroline shrugs as if she hasn't a care in the world, but her language, not to mention body language, says differently. I do not wish to *thrash* anything out with her.

Everyone is looking at me and her. You sit forward in

your chair, elbows on your thighs. All you're missing is a bowl of popcorn. You pump the air lightly with your fist and quietly chant, 'Fight, fight, fight!' then chuckle.

'We're not going to fight,' I snap at you. 'Okay,' I clear my throat, smile at Heather to centre myself. 'I feel that I could be of more use to you than you are currently allowing me to be.'

That wasn't even bad, yet she has screwed her face up so much I think she's going to spring back at me like a jack in the box.

'How so?' she squeaks in a shrill tone.

'You've come to me to help bring the idea further, but you won't actually take on any of my suggestions.'

'You have experience in setting up companies. I wouldn't have the first clue.'

'Yes, but it's not just about giving you my contact list, Caroline. In setting companies up I have a hand in developing strategies, implementing them. If I can't develop this with you then I have no real personal interest in it. It has to represent me too,' I say gently, but firmly.

We all sit in silence while Caroline stares at me in a delayed kind of stunned state.

'What's the other job option?' Kevin asks then, and I'm grateful to him for moving things along.

'Her dad,' you say, and everyone looks at you first and then at Dad.

Probably already bored by the gathering, he gets straight to the point. 'Accounts director, print company. Team of six. Forty K. If the job's still there.'

'It is,' Leilah says to me, which annoys Dad.

'She could do it in her sleep,' he says to the room, looking at the mobile phone in his hand as though he's reading it, but he isn't. 'If she shows up to the interview.'

262

Monday doesn't join in with Dad on that jibe, which is what he was hoping. His smile disappears.

'I don't exactly want a job I can do in my sleep,' I say, with a smile.

'Of course you don't, you want to be different.'

The comment surprises me. You love it, but not in the same way as the previous comments. You turn your studious gaze to him. Kevin of course is deeply offended on my behalf.

'Now, Peter. I think that you owe Jasmine an apology for that comment.'

'What are you talking about?' he snaps.

Heather looks deeply uncomfortable now.

'You've always been the same, ever since we were kids,' Kevin says, the anger rising in him. 'Any time Jasmine hasn't wanted to do what you want, you push her away.'

This is true. I look at Dad.

'Jasmine has *never* done what I've wanted her to do. Has never done what *anyone* but *herself* has wanted her to do. How do you think she's found herself in this mess in the first place?'

'Isn't it a good thing for her to want to go her own way?' Kevin asks. 'Shouldn't you want her to be independent? Her mother died when she was very young. She was sick for years before that. I don't remember you being there all that much, apart from when you stepped in to tell her what to do and when you thought she'd got it wrong.'

And in that moment all my conversations with Kevin flood back to me. All the worries, the fears, frustrations of my teenage years come flooding back. The late-night talks with Kevin on the swing before he kissed me, at parties, walking to school. He always listened. Everything that bothered me about my life would be shared with him. I

263

seemed to have forgotten about all that, but evidently he hadn't.

'With all due respect,' Dad says without the slightest hint of respect, 'this is nothing to do with you. Frankly, I don't even know why you're here.'

Kevin continues calmly, as though he's wanted to say this for years, as if it's himself he's talking about. 'Her mother brought her up to make her own decisions. Take care of herself. Find her own way. She was going to have to, because her mum wasn't going to be there. She set up her own businesses—'

'And sold every bloody one of them.'

'Didn't you sell yours?'

'I retired. And trying to sell her last business is what got her fired.'

Dad is red in the face now. Leilah puts her hand on his arm and says something in a low voice, but he ignores her, or doesn't hear her, because he continues the back and forth with Kevin. I zone out.

Larry treated his business like his daughter. He'd refused to let go. My mother raised me knowing she had to let go.

I come up with ideas and sell them.

I don't want babies. Mum didn't want to leave Heather, now I can't let Heather go.

'*You never finish anything you start,*' I hear Larry saying to me.

I feel dizzy. Too much is circulating in my mind. Conversations I've had with people are coming back to me, my personal beliefs are staring at me oddly, amused, almost singing, 'We knew this all along, didn't you?'

Raise babies to let them go.

Kevin told me I was going to die.

Build companies to sell them.

Hold on to Heather because Mum couldn't.

'And what business is this of yours?' Dad raises his voice and Heather's hands go to her ears. 'You've a problem with everyone in this family. Always have had. Except her, of course. Always in cahoots or whatever the hell you two were—'

'Because neither of us felt like we belonged in this insane, controlling—'

'Oh, shut up and go back to Australia. Save it for your therapist—'

'Excuse me, I will not, and this is the very reason that she and I—'

'Are you okay, Jasmine?'

It's you. You're looking at me and for the first time you're not smiling. You're not laughing any more. Your words sound very far away.

I mumble something.

'You're pale,' you say, and you're about to stand but instead I get to my feet. But I do it too quickly. I'm dehydrated from the night before and emotionally drained from this spectacle and Monday reaches out to stop me from keeling over. I steady myself on the back of his chair and keep my eye on the front door. This time I'm not asking for permission.

'Excuse me,' I whisper.

The floor moves beneath me as I make my way to the one target that stays in place while the walls move around me, getting narrower, coming towards me. I need to get out before they squash me completely. I make it to the door, to sunlight, fresh air, the smell of grass and my flowers and hear the trickle of my fountain. I sit on the bench and tuck my legs close to my body and I breathe deeply in and out.

I don't know how long I'm outside but they get the point eventually. The door opens and Caroline walks out, straight past me to her car and, without a word, drives away. She's followed by Dad, Leilah and Zara. I put my head down. I smell Monday's aftershave and he hovers near me but eventually walks away. Then you step outside. I know it's you; I don't know how, but the atmosphere has the feel of you in it, and then the kids join you and I know for sure.

'Well, that was a tough one,' you say.

I don't respond, just put my head back down. I feel your hand on my shoulder. It's a gentle but firm squeeze and I appreciate it. You walk away and halfway down the drive you say, 'Oh, and thanks for dropping Amy's letter in to me last night. You're right. Maybe it's time I read it now. It's been six months and she's still not talking to me. Can't do any more harm, I suppose. I hope.'

As you walk away I hear Jamie calming Heather in the house. I hurry inside to her. Kevin is hovering around, unsure what to do.

'You go, Kevin, I'll give you a call.'

He still doesn't move.

'Kevin,' I sigh. 'Thank you for today. I appreciate you trying to help. I'd forgotten . . . all of that stuff, but clearly you haven't. You were always there for me.'

He nods, gives me a sad smile.

I put my hand to his cheek and kiss him gently on the other.

'Stop fighting everyone,' I whisper.

He swallows hard and thinks about that. He nods simply and leaves.

I bring Heather to the couch and wrap my arms around her, plaster a smile on my face.

'What are these tears for?' I laugh. 'Silly billy, there's no need to be sad,' I wipe her cheeks.

'I wanted to help, Jasmine.'

'And you did.' I hold her head to my chest and rock her back and forth.

In order to fly one must first clear the shit off one's wings. First step is to identify the shit. Done.

When I was a child, maybe eight years old, I used to love messing with waiters' heads. Since learning about the silent language in restaurants, I wanted to speak it. I liked that there was a code that I could communicate to someone, to an adult, that put us on an even playing field. In our regular haunt there was a particular waiter I tormented. I would put my knife and fork together, then when I saw him coming over to collect the plates, I would quickly separate them again. I loved to watch him suddenly dart away, a few feet from our table, like an aborted missile. I'd do this several times in one sitting, not so much that he'd realise I was doing it deliberately. I did this too with the menu. Closed meant order decision had been made, open meant it hadn't. I would close mine, along with my family's, and then as soon as he was heading over with pen and pad in hand I would open it again, screw my face up and pretend to be still deciding.

I don't know what it means that I've thought of this now. I don't know what insight into me it gives, other than the fact that I liked, from an early age, sending mixed signals.

23

It was as I was walking back home after seeing Heather to the bus stop, at her insistence that I didn't drive because I was, in her opinion, 'upset', that what you had said registered with me. Finally, with a moment to think to myself, I hear you thanking me for dropping the letter by last night. Alarm bells start ringing and I stop midstride. There is indeed something terrifying about being told you've done something that you haven't done. First I think you are mistaken, I know you are mistaken. I have tried to give you your wife's letter on many occasions and you have given it back or asked me to read it. It is in the lemon bowl, because you are a lemon, we both agreed on this fact. But. *But.* You said *last night*. You thanked me for giving you the letter *last night*.

So then I think it still wasn't me because I was in a heap last night, drinking to find the genie in the bottom of my vodka bottle. Perhaps your wife has delivered another letter to you and you think that I gave it to you, but you didn't mention that to me when we met last night at the table in your garden, which leaves me to believe it was delivered to you *after* our meeting. And I would know if your wife was responsible because I was awake until six a.m.,

268

drinking, and I would have heard her, I would have seen her – hell, I would have run across the road and invited her in to bake cookies.

'Good day, Jasmine,' Dr Jameson says, all jolly-like. 'Say, I was thinking of having a little soiree on Midsummer's Day. A barbecue at my place to celebrate this fine summer we're having. What do you say? I've had no response from the chap in number six, I'm about to try him again.'

He looks at me and there's a long pause.

My mind is racing, ticking, going through events.

'Are you okay, Jasmine?'

Suddenly I dart, break out into a run which becomes a sprint, leap across Mr Malone's sprinklers and into my house. Once inside, chest panting, I stand still and look around for clues. The living room is still a crime scene from the earlier circle of disaster, the kitchen is a kiddy version of a crime scene with crayon marks from their colouring session and dry Play-Doh stuck to the table and on the chairs and floor. The lemon bowl. The lemon bowl is empty. Not of lemons and your house keys, but of the letter. Clue number one.

I race upstairs and take in my bedroom properly for the first time. My bed has been hastily made but appears normal. My bedside locker holds the empty bottle of vodka and . . . the open letter Amy wrote for you. I dive across the bed and grab it. I'd read it sometime between two a.m. and six a.m. Probably closer to six a.m. The hours that I don't remember. I had been searching for guidance, for myself. I had been hoping for inspiration, some words of encouragement and love. Even someone else's, and when I'd opened Amy's penned letter for you I found:

Matt,

Get your act together.

Amy

It had enraged me. I remember that. I had cried with disappointment at Amy, at the world. And? I can't remember what I'd done next. I thought I'd fallen asleep, but why was the letter which you say you are now in possession of here and not in your house?

I narrow my eyes, look around the room. There must be some clues. Under my dressing table I see a balled-up piece of paper. I see an entire bin of overflowing balled-up pieces of paper. And suddenly I'm afraid to look any closer. But I have to.

I get down on my hands and knees, and groaning, I uncurl the ball of paper.

Dear Matt,

I can't talk to you face to face about leaving you. I didn't think you would listen . . .

'Oh no,' I groan. 'Jasmine, you idiot.' I search through every single piece of paper, reading various versions of the same opening line, some completely different, all horrifically inappropriate drunkenly scrawled versions of what I think Amy should have said to you, what I think would motivate you, and cringingly my feelings of hatred towards you. I have absolutely no idea which version has made it across the road, but I'm glad at least that none of the ones I have frantically speed-read have made it out of this bedroom.

What I want to do is throw myself down on my bed dramatically and howl. What I should do is run across the road, admit everything that I've done in my drunken stupidity. You will understand. But I can't and I don't. I thought my day could not sink any lower; it turns out it could and it has. I need to get the letter back from you, undo this silliness, get a job, stop acting like a crazy person.

The doorbell rings and it gives me such a fright I hear its shrill ring in my head and pounding in my heart long afterwards. I feel like I've been caught red-handed. Frozen like a deer in headlights, I stand still in my bedroom, rigid, unsure of what to do. You have read the letter. I am caught.

I look out the window and see the top of your head. I brace myself and go downstairs. I will admit everything. I will do the right thing. I pull the door open and give you a nervous smile. You have your hands on your hips with a screwed-up frown on your face. It drops for a moment.

'Are you drunk again?' you ask.

'No.'

Silence.

'Are you?'

'No.'

Convinced, you resume your screwed-up face. 'Have you seen the people going into Dr J's house?'

I'm confused. What has this got to do with the letter? I'm trying to find the link.

'If you're drunk, just say so,' you say.

'I'm not.'

'I won't care. It will only make it easier for me to communicate with you. I can phrase things differently. Talk slower.'

'I'm not fucking drunk,' I snap.

'Fine. Well? Have you seen people going in and out?'

271

'Why, is he having a party and you're not invited?' I say, feeling more relaxed now that I'm not caught – yet.

'He's having something, all right. Half-hourly. Since noon.'

'Jesus, you really need to get a job,' I say, realising you sound like me now.

'A woman arrived at three. Stayed for thirty minutes. Then she left and a man arrived at three thirty, then he left just before four, and a couple arrived at four thirty. Then—'

'Yes, I believe I get the half-hourly thing.'

We both fold our arms and watch Dr Jameson's house. Next door, Mr Malone is reading *The Field* by John B. Keane to Mrs Malone, who is sitting in a deckchair with a blanket across her knees. He is doing a good job of acting it out. Every day he reads for fifteen minutes, goes back to the gardening, and then returns, picks up where he left off. He has a good reading voice. Mrs Malone always stares into the distance with a faraway look, but Mr Malone carries on, talking in his good-natured tone, commenting on the weather and the garden and his own musings, as though they're both having an animated conversation. It was Jackie Collins last week; he likes to mix it up a bit. It's beautiful how he's coping, but it makes me sad.

A car rounds the corner into the cul de sac and my heart hammers and my stomach flutters before I even see him. But I know that it's him. Or I sense that it's him. Or I hope that it is him. Every time someone comes near me or the house, I hope that it is him. Monday steps out of the car.

'Well, if this morning didn't put him off you, nothing will,' you say and I smile.

Monday gets out of the car, and taking long strides with his long legs, spins the car keys around on his finger.

I hope that you get the hint as I glare at you to leave,

but you don't. Or you do, but you don't leave. You have a point to prove.

'Hi,' Monday says, approaching us.

'Forget something?' you say smartly, but without venom, it's playful.

Monday smiles and looks me directly in the eyes, the softness back in him, tenderness, and my stomach does somersaults. 'Actually, yes.'

'We're watching Dr J's house,' you say and explain the half-hourly situation that has you so worried. Monday stands beside me and watches too, bare arm against mine, and I forget why on earth we're staring at the house and instead concentrate on the electricity that is rushing through my body at this very slight touch. Monday watches the house and I fight the urge to take every part of him in but lose, stealing glances when I can, those green-flecked hazel eyes watching Dr Jameson's house. Then, just when I think I'm safe to stare a little longer, suddenly he turns and those eyes are on mine. He gives me a cheeky look as though he knows he's caught me, then makes a face at you, teasing your intensity in this house-watch.

'Over there. There!' you say, coming to life suddenly, breaking our moment, and you move away from the wall. 'See?'

'Hmm,' Monday says, moving down the driveway to take a closer look at the suspicious-looking woman making her way down the road. 'That's not good.'

'Told you,' you say, relieved someone's on your side. 'They've been all different kinds of people,' you say. 'Odd-looking, most of them.'

'Maybe he's interviewing housekeepers,' I say.

'Would you want her to clean your house?' you ask.

'She'd clean out your house,' Monday says, and I have

to smile as you both team up and become the Turner and Hooch of the neighbourhood. You are Hooch, by the way.

'She might not be here for Dr J,' I say, watching her. She's wearing an Adidas tracksuit, fresh-looking trainers. She's either drunk or on drugs. I'm guessing drugs; she has a heroin look about her. 'Could be a fan of yours,' I say.

She studies the houses, looking at the numbers, then turns in Dr Jameson's house. Monday takes off down the driveway, getting a closer look. You follow. I tag along because what else am I going to do? We cross the road and decide to sit at your table where we can have a better view of Dr Jameson's house and listen out for trouble inside. At least, that's what you both decide after a quick discussion of whether to break in or not. You both plan a story of what you'll say if you have to call in. An extraction plan, which you both get rather excited about.

'Have you read that letter yet?' I ask you, casually.

'What letter?'

'The one I gave you.'

'No. Not yet.'

'I was thinking. I want to read it to you after all. You know, if that's what you'd like.'

You look at me thoughtfully, suspiciously. So does Monday.

'It's probably better that you're not alone. Who knows how you'll react. You're doing so well, I don't want you to go straight to the pub, that's all. You should have some- body there, if it's not me, then somebody.' I know that you wouldn't ask anybody else, but it makes you less suspicious, which is what happens and you seem genuinely grateful.

'Thanks, Jasmine.'

'Why don't you give it to me now?'

'Now?'

'Yeah,' I shrug casually. 'Get it out of the way.' I look at Monday to explain. 'His wife left him. She left a note. He won't read it. Which is correct,' I look back at you. '*I should read it. You should give it to me.*'

Monday hides a smile at me behind his fingers. He has long beautiful fingers. Pianist's fingers.

'Well, not now,' you say, panicking a little that I'm pushing the moment.

'Why not?'

'I'm keeping an eye on Dr J.'

'I'll read it while you watch.' No I won't. I will burn it as soon as you hand it over to me. I'll cleverly switch it with the real thing. I would rather save myself than worry about him reading her awful letter.

'The kids. I don't want them to hear.'

I'm about to say that the kids aren't anywhere near to hear, but they spoil my plan. The two blondes appear from the garden of number six wearing frowns.

'What's wrong?' you ask, going over to them.

'What have you done?' Monday asks me, amused expression on his face.

'Nothing,' I reply, blank-faced.

He laughs and shakes his head, tuts as though I'm a naughty girl. I like it and I can't help but laugh back. He knows me and I like this. It's been a while since someone has known me that way. Apart from you, of course, who kicked down my do not disturb sign when I wasn't paying attention.

'He wouldn't buy any,' Kris says.

'He's the only one on the street,' Kylie says.

'What didn't he buy?' I ask.

'Our perfume. We made it from petals and water.'

'And grass.'

275

'And a dead spider.'

'Nice,' I say.

'You bought two bottles,' you say to me. 'You owe me a fiver.'

It's then that I realise they have set up a stall in the driveway, consisting of a fold-up table and chair covered by a red checked paper tablecloth. There are bottles of a brown substance with things floating in it and a sign advertises one bottle for fifty cent. Why I owe you a fiver is a mystery, but seeing as I have forged a letter to you from your wife who has left you, I let you off.

'What did he say?' you ask them, angrily.

'Who?' Monday mouths to me.

'Number six. Corporate man. Renter,' I reply, then turn back to the kids, fully engaged.

'Nothing really. He was on the phone. Then he said no thanks and closed the door.'

'The cheeky little shit,' you say, and the kids giggle.

'That man is starting to wind me up now,' you vent, and I can see your hands close into tight fists.

'Me too. I've waved at him every single morning since he's moved in and he hasn't even bothered to look at me,' I say.

Monday laughs. 'You two seriously need to get jobs. You're letting everything mess with you too much.'

'Then get her a job, Monday,' you say, that mischievous glint in your eye.

'That's the idea, Matt,' he replies, meeting your gaze.

'Maybe you should bring her out for dinner. For the job,' you say, and I know what you're implying, as does Monday, but he remains cool.

'If that will work,' he says, but a little less confidently.

I don't want you to make him leave by continuing with this. I turn to you to continue my case. 'And all he had to do was fork out some money for the kids who've been working so hard on their perfume. Did he even ask to smell it?'

'No,' Kris huffs.

'Well, that's just mean,' I say.

This incenses you even more, which I knew it would, because that was my intention.

'I'm going over there,' you say.

'Good for you,' I say.

'What are you going to say?' Monday asks, face full of a smile, as he crosses one leg over the other, ends of his jeans frayed, and a hole in one thigh revealing bare skin.

'Just that he should consider being more neighbourly if he's going to live in a neighbourhood. They're only seven,' you say.

'I think you mind more than they do,' Monday says.

'And he won't get back to Dr J about the Midsummer's Day barbecue,' I add. 'And Dr J only ever means well.'

Monday smiles and frowns at me at the same time, trying to figure me out.

That's enough to convince you to go over.

I'm thrilled. You've left your front door open. While you're arguing with Corporate Man I can slip inside, find the letter I wrote and destroy it. It is a perfect plan.

'You – come with me,' you suddenly say.

'Me?'

'Yes. You.'

'Yeah, Jasmine,' Monday adds, leaning on the table, chin on his hand, looking at me lazily, mischievously, knowing that he is ruining whatever it is I am planning. He is playing with me, which I wouldn't mind if it was in another way. I could think of many ways Monday could toy with me, but not like this.

'You don't need my help,' I tell you, ignoring Monday. 'They're your kids. You can speak for them without me.'

'Go on, Jasmine,' Monday says.

I know that my chance to destroy the letter has slipped away. I throw Monday a look of sincere disgust that makes him laugh, and even though it's annoying it makes me like him even more because he is prepared to contest me. He will not tiptoe around me, try to please me. He will test me, he will give as good as I give. Monday wants to play.

'I'll keep an eye on Dr J's house.' He winks at me.

'What are you going to say?' I ask nervously, standing at number six's door.

'We are going to say exactly what I said we'll say. About neighbourly behaviour.'

'Right.' I swallow. Neither of us are exactly the perfect candidates to be preaching such things.

We can hear him talking on the phone inside. You press the doorbell again, long and hard. It's not a work call. He's laughing, sounds casual. It's not even important. He mentions rugby. Some nicknames. Liggo and Spidey, and the guys. I want to vomit in my mouth. He talks about a match. You're getting angrier by the minute and I'm not far behind you. I see him peek out the window at us, then continue talking.

'It's one of the neighbours again,' he says, his words drifting out the open window.

You storm off, toward the open window and when it looks like you're about to climb in, Corporate Man is saved when we hear Monday call out.

'Hey!'

We look up and see Monday taking off down the road after the woman who has left Dr Jameson's house.

You and me run after him.

'Get your hands off me!' she's yelling at Monday, who's ducking and diving to avoid her flying hands and punches.

'Ouch! Jesus!' he yells as she catches him a few times. 'Relax!' he shouts and she calms down and stops hitting him. She takes a step away from him, eyes him warily, her jaw working overtime like she's a cow munching on grass.

'It looks like you've got something under your jumper that might belong to my friend,' Monday says.

'No, I don't.'

'I think you do.' He's smiling, those hazel-green eyes alight.

'I'm pregnant.'

'Who's the daddy? Apple? Dell?' Monday says and I finally get a chance to see her stomach and bite my lip to try not to laugh. There is a rectangular-shaped lump beneath her jumper.

'Hold on a minute,' you suddenly say, under your breath. 'Maybe we shouldn't look.'

'Why not?' I ask.

'Because maybe' – you turn your back on the woman, who looks like she's considering making a run for it, and you speak from the side of your mouth – 'maybe she got it from Dr J. Know what I mean?'

'You think she got a laptop-shaped container of drugs from Dr J?' I ask, and Monday coughs to hide his laugh as you glare at him.

Dr Jameson appears, cup of tea on a saucer in his hand. 'Yoo-hooo!'

'Ah. The drug lord himself,' Monday says conspiratorially, and I have to laugh.

The woman starts to waddle away quickly. Monday catches her, holds on to her arm while she shouts abuse at him and accuses him of sexually harassing and abusing her.

279

Dr Jameson makes his way over to them, the cup of tea and saucer still in his hand.

'Mags! I just went to make you a cup of tea. You're leaving so soon?'

There's tugging and messing going on between Monday and Mags, and suddenly something crashes down between her legs.

'I think her waters broke,' I say, as we all look down and see Dr Jameson's laptop on the ground.

You, me and Dr Jameson are sitting at the table in your front garden watching Monday fixing the laptop, which has minor damage, and listening to Dr Jameson explaining the advertisement he has placed in the local newspaper. When I hear him explain, it is heartbreaking; he has placed an advert in the paper looking for companionship for Christmas Day.

'Carol died when she was sixty-one – too young. Too young. We never had children; as you know, I couldn't get my act together until it was too late. I'll never forgive myself for that.' His eyes are watery and his jaw works hard to control the emotion. Monday stops working on the laptop and focuses on him. 'I'm eighty-one. That's twenty years without her. Seventeen Christmases on my own. I used to go to my sister, but she passed away, God rest her soul. I didn't want to go another Christmas Day on my own. I heard of a lad in my golf club who put an ad in the paper for a housekeeper – she and him are practically inseparable now. Not in that way, of course, but at least he has someone. Every day. Now, I don't want someone every day, not neces-sarily, but I did think that perhaps for the one day when I can't tolerate the loneliness, perhaps I could find compan-ionship, somebody else who feels the same way as I do.

There must be people who don't want to be alone on Christmas Day.'

It is unimaginably sad and there is not one of us at the table who has a smart remark to make, or even tries to talk him out of it. The man is lonely, he wants company: let him find it.

I can see that this strikes a chord with you. Of course it does. Your wife has left you, taken your children with her, and if you don't manage to win her over in some way, you face your first Christmas alone. Perhaps you won't be physically alone, not like Dr Jameson; someone, a friend, will invite you over, but even amongst the company of friends you will probably feel more lonely than ever. I can see you mulling this over. Perhaps it will be you and Dr Jameson together, sitting at opposite ends of his polished mahogany dining table, making strained conversation, or better yet, with dinner plates on your lap, watching Christmas specials on TV.

Amy's timing couldn't be better. She arrives to collect the kids. As usual, she doesn't get out of the car to talk to you, she remains inside, sunglasses on, looking ahead, waiting for the children to leap into the car. Fionn is beside her; he doesn't acknowledge you either. You try to talk to her, she won't open the door. Your continued knocking and pleading face leads her to lower the window ever so slightly. It is sad to watch. I don't know what you're saying to her, but it is not fluid. It is a disjointed attempt at you making conversation. Polite conversation with a woman you love. The kids come running down the driveway excitedly with bags in their hands. They give you a quick hug and as they're climbing into the car they announce that they caught a heroin addict. Your face looks pained. The window shoots up. Amy speeds off.

I try to coax you into getting the letter so that I can have it in my possession, but it doesn't work. You are most certainly too raw for that now. I formulate a plan. Operation Lemon Bowl will come to fruition as soon as your lights go out tonight.

24

I watch your house all night. I watch you like a hawk, more than I ever have before, which is saying something. I see you in your sitting room, lights on full as you watch the television. Some Sunday sports event, I can tell by the way you rise in your armchair in anticipation, then collapse back with disappointment. Each time you get up to move around the house I'm afraid you're going to get the letter, but you don't, you honour your word and I respect that about you, even though what I have done and what I'm about to do doesn't command that respect. But you don't know that.

Though I'm wired from the very idea of what I'm about to do, last night's late hour and drinking is making it hard for me to keep my eyes open, to be alert. The headache pill makes me even sleepier and the five cups of coffee make me feel wired but an exhausted kind of sick at the same time. Finally, close to midnight, the living-room lights go off and I watch you head upstairs. I'm ready for action, but then the bedroom light goes on, stays on, as does the TV and I know I'm in for another long night. I nod off. At three a.m. I wake up, dressed, and look out to check your house. The lights are all out.

Action time.

The entire street is quiet, everyone is sound asleep, including Corporate Man, especially Corporate Man with his busy, important Monday morning ahead of him. I steal across the road and go straight to your front door with the original, now vodka-and-Coke-stained, letter and your keys from the lemon bowl. I have thought about the possibility of an alarm system, but in the entire eight months of watching you come and go, I have seen no evidence of one and surely a code would have come with the set of keys. I quietly push the key into the lock and it turns easily. I'm in. I take my shoes off and stand in the hallway, my eyes adjusting to the darkness while my heart hammers in my chest. I have not just entered a house willy-nilly, I have a plan, I have had all night to make a plan. And I have a torch.

I begin at the table in the hallway. There are envelopes on the counter, opened and unopened bills, and a postcard from Aunt Nellie who is having a ball in Malta. I check the drawer, no envelope.

I move to the kitchen, which is surprisingly in a tidy state. A few cups and plates in the sink that you've left until morning, but nothing offensive. Your fruit bowl has three black bananas and an under-ripe avocado. No letter. I take my time searching through the kitchen drawers. Everyone has a rubbish drawer in the kitchen and I find it: place mats, takeaway menus, batteries, bills, new and old, a TV licence, old birthday cards, pictures by the kids. No letter. There is a whiteboard with nothing on it, probably unused since Amy left the house. No notes, no reminders, shopping lists, no communication needed for a busy household because you are all alone. I suddenly feel for you, living alone in this empty family house that was once so full of life. I think of the man Amy left and I have no sympathy for him, he deserved it, but you, I feel for you. It spurs me on to find the letter.

I move to the TV room. It smells of coffee and vinegar, which matches the takeaway bags I saw you carry home from the car at eight p.m. before I was about to break in the first time. That was a good lesson. It taught me to wait, to be patient. I shine the torch on the shelving unit in the alcove. Books, DVDs – you like crime thrillers. I even see *Turner and Hooch*. There are framed photos on the shelves, family photos, babies, holidays, fishing trips, beach trips, first days of school. I wonder why Amy hasn't taken them with her and I see it as a sign that she's coming back, until my torch falls upon the naked walls adorned with hooks and realise that all *this* is what she left behind, including you. I am surprised to see a Psychology degree in your name and a framed photo of you in your graduation robes holding the scroll, but then I think of how you look at me sometimes, the way you try to read me as if seeing my soul and how you like to analyse me, everyone, and it makes sense. Your face grins up at me from underneath your graduation cap, as if you've just said something rude. You had a cheeky face, even then.

I think I hear a movement upstairs and I freeze, turn the torch off, hold my breath in the still dark silence and listen. The house is silent. I turn the torch back on and continue to root through the pigeonholes of the home-office desk in the corner overlooking the back patio. Old photos, car insurance, vouchers, random keys, no letter. I have been avoiding going upstairs for obvious reasons. It is my last resort, my worst-case scenario, but for a family home it is surprisingly clutter-free, no little piles of paperwork or collected mail. Perhaps upstairs is where I must go. I try to think of where you would keep such a thing. Not in a filing cabinet, that is too clinical, too impersonal. You have been keen to read it, which means you have been keeping it close at hand, somewhere you can regularly check on it, touch it, return to look at it. If it is not in your coat pocket that is hanging on the banister, then I must go upstairs.

It is not in your coat pocket.

I take a deep breath and then think I hear another noise at the back of the house, in the kitchen, and hold my breath, afraid someone will hear me exhale. I'm starting to panic, I need to exhale and my pulse in my ears is so loud it is stopping me from listening out and hearing what's in the room next to me so I slowly exhale, a long shaky breath. This is ridiculous, I know it is. I should be at home in bed, not sneaking around your house. Watching it all these nights has somehow made me feel entitled; maybe I am a stalker, maybe this is what all stalkers feel, that their actions are entirely normal. But then I think of having to explain to you about writing the letter and I can't and so I take a determined step on to the stairs. It creaks immediately and I freeze. I backtrack. There must be somewhere downstairs that I can find the letter instead of creeping into your bedroom while you sleep, which is an entirely new level of creepiness. And then I have a thought, an early memory, of something you said about how you've given up drink.

'I have a photo of my father on the fridge. That helps me every time I go to open it to take a drink.'

'That's sweet.'

'It's not really. He was a raving alcoholic. The photo is there to remind me I don't want to be like him.'

I redirect the torch down the hallway and move quickly and surely into the kitchen. I think the fridge is my answer. It was filled with drawings and gymnastic certificates but I didn't check it for the letter. I lift the torch to shine it on the fridge door and I see the envelope, the real envelope with the fake letter and I grin with happiness but then BAM! Something hard whacks me across the side of the head, I feel it mostly in my ear, it slaps my face and I'm knocked to the ground, fall like a sack of potatoes, my legs dead beneath me, screaming in agony to the ground. I hear feet on the stairs and all I can think is that a burglar has attacked me. I have disturbed a burglar and now you are coming downstairs into danger and confusion and I must alert you, but first I must get the letter from the fridge and switch it with the original and that I could do if it were not for the ache I'm feeling in my head and the stickiness on my face.

'I told you to wait!' I hear you hiss, and I'm confused. You're in on this too? The burglary of your own house? I think of insurance fraud and how I have stumbled into dangerous territory, and if you are in on it – which you must be, since you're hissing at your accomplice who clubbed me, who seems to have entered the house from the back kitchen door – then I am in great danger. I should run. But first I should switch the letter on the fridge door. I lift my head up from the floor and I feel everything move beneath me. Though the room is still dark, the moonlight is casting the windowpane's reflection on the tiled floor. It lights up the fridge and I have a surreal moment where I believe the moon, the universe is on my side, lighting the way for me, guiding me. But I can't move.

I groan.

'Who is it?' you ask.

'I don't know, I just hit him.'

'Let's turn the lights on.'

'We should call the police first.'

'No. We can take care of this ourselves, teach this guy a thing or two.'

287

'I do not condone—'

'Come on, Dr J, what's the point of a neighbourhood watch if we can't—'

'*Watch*, not tie up and *torture*.'

'What did you hit him with? Jesus, a frying pan? I told you to grab a golf club.'

'He came at me quicker than I planned.'

'Hold on, he's trying to get away. He's sliding . . .'

The light suddenly goes on. I am at the foot of the fridge, mere inches away from the letter. If I stretch my arm up, which I am doing, I can almost, *almost*, reach it.

'Jasmine!' you exclaim.

'Oh dear Lord, oh dear Lord,' Dr Jameson says.

The light is so bright I can't see a thing and my head, *Jesus* my head.

'You hit Jasmine?'

'Well, I didn't know it was her, did I?! Good gracious.'

'It's okay, sweetheart,' you say and you both try to lift me up and carry me away from the fridge, which makes me groan, and not just from the agony. I can see the letter get further and further away from me as you take me from the kitchen to the couch. I was so close.

'What is she saying?' Dr Jameson asks, moving his flopping oversized ear to my mouth.

'She's saying something about the fridge,' you say, placing my head down on a pillow, concern etched all over your face.

'The fridge, not a bad idea, Jasmine. I'll get ice.' Dr Jameson hurries away.

'Will she need stitches?'

Stitches?

You examine me and I can see your strawberry-blond nose hairs. One wiry grey pokes out and I want to pull it. 'What frying pan did you use?' you ask Dr Jameson.

'Non-stick, Tefal aluminium,' he says, returning with provisions for my head. 'I've got the entire set. Five SuperValu coupons and you only have to add fifteen euro. I do a mean French toast on it,' he says, face pushed up close to mine as he concentrates. His breath smells like barley sugar.

'Jasmine, what on earth were you doing?' you ask incredulously.

I clear my throat. 'I used my keys, I thought you had an intruder. Must have been Dr J,' I say weakly, closing my eyes as he dabs at my head. 'Ouch.'

'Sorry, dear. It wasn't me because I contacted Matt as soon as I saw your torch,' Dr Jameson says.

'Jasmine,' you say in a low warning voice. 'Cough it up.'

I sigh.

'I gave you the wrong letter. From Amy. The one I gave you was one that I had written. For someone else. I got them confused. Mixed up the envelopes.'

I open one eye to see if you're swallowing it.

Your arms are folded across your chest, you're looking down on me, assessing me. You're wearing a faded Barcelona '92 Olympics T-shirt and stripy baggy boxers. You seem unconvinced by my story, but not completely. It could still work. You suddenly back out and head to the kitchen.

'Don't open it,' I yell, and the shouting makes my head worse.

'Hold on, don't move,' Dr Jameson says, 'I'm almost there.'

You bring the envelope in. I don't like the look on your face. It's that naughty mischievous look. You're tapping the envelope against your open palm, slowly, rhythmically, while you pace the floor before me. You are going to play with me.

'So. Jasmine. You broke into my house—'

'I had a key.'

'—to retrieve a letter that you say that you wrote for someone else. Why wouldn't you just tell me that?'

'Because I was afraid that you would open it. It's very personal and I don't trust you.'

You hold a finger up. 'Plausible. Well done. I *would* have read it.'

Dr Jameson instructs me to hold the bag of frozen peas to my head and as I sit up to face you, he sits down beside me.

'That's plausible to me too,' he says. He has messy bed-head hair, unbrushed eyebrows and is wearing smart leather shoes with a shell suit that I've never seen before, obviously the first things he grabbed when getting out of bed.

'What am I, on trial here?'

'Yes,' you say, narrowing your eyes at me as you pace. You are so dramatic.

'Are you sure my head hasn't fallen off?' I ask Dr Jameson.

'Is your neck sore?'

I move it. 'Yes.'

He moves closer and starts prodding at my neck. 'Is it sore here?'

'Yes.'

'Is it sore here?'

'Yes.'

'Is it sore here?'

'Yes.'

You stop pacing and look at me. 'Who is your letter addressed to?'

I stall. Assess the situation. I know you will check it.

'Matt,' I say.

You laugh. 'Matt.'

'Yes.'

'That's a coincidence.'

'Hence the mix-up.'

You hold it out to me and I quickly reach out. It's just beyond my grasp, millimetres away from my fingertips when you whip it back and tear it open.

'No!' I groan and cover my face with a pillow.

'Read it out loud,' Dr Jameson says, and I throw the pillow at him and reach for another to hide behind.

'*Dear Matt,*' you say, the mischievous cheeky face on, a reading voice that drips with sarcasm, but as you read ahead silently to yourself to see what's coming, the sarcasm drops. You pause. You look up at me, then resume reading with your normal voice.

'*We all have stand-out moments in our lives, periods which influenced small or profound changes in us. I can think of four life-changing moments for me: the year I was born, the year I learned I would die, the year my mother died and now I have a new one – the year I met you.*'

I cover my face. It's all coming back to me now.

'*I have heard your voice every day, listened to the un-savoury words that formulate your tasteless thoughts and made a judgement on you. I did not like you. But you are proof that you can think you know someone yet never re-ally know them at all.*

'*What I have learned is that you are more, more than what you pretend to be, more than what you believe your-self to be. You are less an awful lot of the time, but being less has driven people away. I think sometimes you like doing that and I understand that too. Hurt people hurt people.*'

You clear your throat and I peek at you through a gap in my hands, thinking you might cry.

291

'*But when you think no one is listening or when you think no one is paying you any attention, you are so much more. It's a pity that you don't believe that yourself, or show the people you love.*'

For the next part your voice warbles and I peek at you. You are genuinely moved and I am glad, but I am horrendously embarrassed. I watch you read.

'*The year I met you, I met myself. You should do the same, because I think you'll find a good man.*'

You stop reading and there is a long hush in the room.

'Well, well,' Dr Jameson says, eyes twinkling.

You clear your throat. 'Well, I'm sure whoever this Matt is, that he'll be very appreciative of what you've said to him.'

'Thanks,' I whisper. 'I hope so.'

I stand up to take the letter from your hand and as I do, you refuse to let go of the letter. I think you are playing with me, but when my eyes meet yours, I realise you are serious. Your hand brushes mine instead. You nod in thanks, a sincere, touched thanks.

I return it with a smile.

25

We are in the middle of our second heatwave this summer. We are also in the midst of a water shortage; the council have cancelled water for a few hours every day and if anyone is seen using a hose to clean their car, garden, dog or self they are liable to be hanged on the spot. Or something.

Sick days records are at an all-time high this week, greens are packed with half-naked bodies, the scent of suncream and barbecue are in the air and overflowing buses from the city centre to the seaside sway from side to side as they carry their merry load.

Caroline and I are staring across the garden table at each other in a long impatient silence, both clearly wanting to say something but biting our tongues. It is a beautiful Saturday and we are sitting out under the sun umbrella in her back garden, the first time I have seen her since Heather staged the intervention into my non-moving life. What has led to this staring stand-off is yet another of my propositions which she has once again batted away. I have suggested she change the name of her idea to 'Frock Swap', in order to give it more of an international appeal. I know that she knows it makes sense but she's finding it hard to let go of her clever logo and the fact that this new name isn't her idea. I understand this but what I was afraid was happening is actually happening. She has recognised my success in this area, which was why she came to me in the first place, and there is nothing wrong with that, only she is chasing success and success alone. What she has failed to take into account is the reason why my projects have worked: because I have injected my sensibilities, my passion, my ideas and my heart, and not blindly followed other people's orders. I know that this will never work with us. I now understand how it is that I work; how I want to work and how I have to work.

And though this makes for uncomfortable conversation, it would be one I could have maturely if it were someone I have no personal ties to, but not Caroline, my friend of ten years, whose garden I'm sitting in, whose head I've held over the toilet bowl, whose swollen breasts I've held cabbage leaves to, whose tears I've dried when her marriage ended, and whose daughters' home-made fairy cakes I am now eating. It has taken us this long to come together after the circle of support meeting in my house and I know it is because neither of us want conflict or confrontation, but at the same time neither of us is prepared to settle.

'Caroline,' I say gently, and I take her hand in mine. She shifts uncomfortably in her seat. 'I fear that we must consciously uncouple from working together on this.'

And on that she throws her head back and laughs, and I know that we're okay.

The sun still shines and I venture out to Bloom, Ireland's largest gardening, food and family event, that takes place in Phoenix Park over the bank holiday weekend and attracts thousands. There are cookery and craft demonstrations, free gardening advice from the experts, Irish produce, live entertainment, gardening workshops. My own little slice of heaven, and I was invited by Monday, who left the ticket in my postbox along with a dried bluebell pushed between the pages of the invitation. The only communication we've had since then was a phone conversation where he allowed me to stay on just long enough to accept the invitation and then tell me rather mysteriously that I'll know where to find him. I think the bluebell is a clue. In fact it is. Worried that he would end up sleeping overnight in Phoenix Park while I wander off following the wrong clues, he texts me, 'The bluebell is a clue,' which is rather pathetically sweet of him.

There are kids' zones, cooking zones, main stages and smaller stages with chefs doing cooking exhibitions, audiences crowded around, tasting, Irish dancers, DIY displays, bubble displays and fashion shows. The park is buzzing with event after event, something for everyone. Around me, award-winning garden designers have created entire new worlds in their small plots of land. There is a sharp and sleek Scandic garden, a Japanese garden, a Chinese garden, a *Wizard of Oz* garden, some fun, some quirky, some breathtaking, all of them taking me into another world.

Though my heart is bursting to see him, I take my time wandering around, not wanting to miss a clue, and also enjoying the atmosphere. This time last year I would not have thought about being here, I wouldn't have considered this event to be for someone like me, unless I was there to work, unless I was pitching something to someone and with my eye on the prize. And if I had been here under those circumstances I would have missed the beauty of the place. It is almost a cliché to hear people talking about 'slowing down', but it is true. I have slowed down and through slowing, I see so much more.

It is when I see a recreated Irish landscape with Connemara drystone walls and a caravan – the idea being to capture the 'staycation', holidaying in Ireland in summertime – that I sense I'm close. There is a field of bluebells, the purple haze like a carpet, leading the eye all the way past the drystone walls, the bog marshes and the lake . . . and there he is. Monday stands at the door of a sixties caravan, which sits in the long grass as though it has been there, abandoned for years. The door is open, there is a floral window blind flapping in the breeze.

I stop by the rusted gate.

'*Fáilte*, Jasmine,' he says, a coy smile on his face, and I sense nervousness too.

I laugh.

'Come on in,' he motions, and as I push the gate open it gives the perfect creak, as though it's not real. I make my way through the tall purple flowers which line the pathway, mixed with fluffy cream-coloured blossoms that perfume the air with their fragrance: loosestrife and meadowsweet. It's a hot day and for the occasion I'm wearing a floral summer dress, though the poppies are more pop art than country garden. The fragrance of the meadowsweet gives way to pungent garlic as the wild garlic reaches my nose.

When I get closer, he sees the enormous lump caused by Dr Jameson's frying pan, and he holds my face in his hands, concern, and anger all over his face.

'What happened?'

'An accident.'

'Who did this?' Dark, concerned, angry face.

'Dr J. It's a long story . . .'

'What?'

'An accident. To do with the letter . . .' I bite my lip.

He smiles and shakes his head. 'Honestly, I've never met

anyone like you three . . .' He kisses my bruise tenderly. 'I've never met anyone like you, full stop.' He takes my hand, his thumb rubbing against my palm, which makes me shiver, and he leads me to the caravan. I peer inside and see the table has been set for lunch.

'Do you do this for all the people you headhunt?'

'Depends on the commission.'

'I can imagine what you give them when you get actual commission,' I tease. 'Really wish I'd got that job now.'

He fixes me with a look that makes my heart race and I try to calm my flustered innards as we sit in the tiny caravan, our knees touching under the fold-out table.

'So instead of always going to your house, I thought I'd bring you to my home and show you a slice of where I come from.'

'Monday, this is beautiful. And incredibly sweet.'

He blushes but forges onward, 'And in the spirit of being home, I brought you what I grew up eating.' He opens the containers. 'Blackberries, wild strawberries. We used to pick them and my grandmother made jam. Apple pie.' He reveals the delights, Tupperware box by Tupperware box. 'Wild garlic pesto with hot brown bread.'

My mouth waters. 'Did you cook all of this?'

He's embarrassed again. 'Yeah, but they're Maimeó's recipes. Foolproof. My mam can't cook to save her life, so for lunch I had . . .' he makes a grand gesture with a Superman lunchbox, 'salad-cream sandwiches.'

'Wow.'

'I know. She was hopeless. Still is. Maimeó raised me, really. Tough woman, moved over from the Aran Islands when my mam got pregnant with me, even though she was an Aran islander at heart and being away almost killed her. She brought me there every chance she could.'

'Is she still alive?'

'No.'

'I'm sorry.'

He doesn't say anything, just starts sharing out the food.

'Your home is a lot more peaceful than mine was the last time you were there. I'm sorry about the meeting . . .' I need to address it.

'Don't be sorry. I'm sorry it was sprung on you. That lady who works with your sister, Jamie, told me it would be a surprise for you. I thought maybe you'd like it.'

'You didn't think that I'd like that, surely.'

'I don't know you very well, Jasmine. But I want to.' No blushing this time, just hazel emerald eyes. 'How's your ex?'

'Oh God. Monday. I'm so sorry about that. Really—'

'You don't need to apologise. We weren't . . . there was nothing . . .' But I can see that it hurt him.

'And I'm sorry about the interview.' I cover my face in my hands. 'I haven't started very well at all, have I? If all I have to say to you is sorry.'

'I understand about the interview,' he says. 'I can understand how you'd want to follow Heather. You should have just told me, you know? I was calling and calling. I could have tried to change the date.'

'I know.' I wince. 'I couldn't think what to say to you.'

'The truth is always fine with me.' He shrugs easily.

'Okay. Yes. Sorry.'

'Stop saying sorry.'

I nod. 'Don't suppose you'd want to headhunt me for anything else?' I try weakly. 'I can be quite reliable—'

'I have a wonderful prospect for you,' he says, spooning clotted cream on to strawberry-jam-covered scones.

'Yeah?' I light up.

He stops what he's doing and fixes me with one of his looks. 'How about a six foot, black-haired, green-eyed, freckle-faced black man from Connemara? One in a million. Actually, one in four point seven million.'

My heart soars. 'I'll take it,' I say, and he leans in to kiss me and it is as long and luscious as I have daydreamed and imagined it would be.

'Your elbow is in the jam,' I whisper, mid-kiss.

'I know,' he whispers back.

'And you're not six foot.'

'Ssh,' he whispers again, kissing me. 'Don't tell anyone.'

We laugh as we pull apart.

'So now it's my turn to apologise,' he says, playing with my fingers. I'm no small lady but my hands look like doll's hands in his. 'I'm sorry it took me so long to—'

'Make a move?' I offer.

'Yes,' he finally looks me in the eye. 'I'm really quite shy,' he says, and I believe him. For someone who is so confident when it comes to work, he is endearingly awkward at this kind of thing. 'I used the job as an excuse to keep seeing you while I tried to summon up the courage, and every single time I prattled on about the job I was trying to figure out if you were going to say no, or laugh in my face. Obviously headhunting someone doesn't usually bring me to their house for dinner.'

'Or to help with their water fountain.'

He laughs. 'Or that. Or help them spy on their neighbour.'

'You weren't too shy to organise this,' I say.

'I'm more of a grand gestures kind of man,' he says, and we laugh. 'The ex-boyfriend thing gave me the kick up the arse I needed.'

I cringe again.

'Is he . . . keen to get you back?'

'Yes,' I say, gravely serious.

'Oh.'

'He called me at one a.m. a few nights ago singing All Saints' "Bootie Call". He sings like an altar boy.'

'Oh,' he says in a lighter tone, less concerned.

'So obviously you have a lot to contend with,' I add.

'Maybe a sing-off,' he suggests. 'You know, as soon as I saw your red head covered in muck and garden leaves I knew I wanted you. I just couldn't figure out what to do about it. The job bought me time. So none of it was a waste of my time, if that's what you're worried about.'

We kiss again and I could quite literally move into this little caravan and stay with him for ever, despite neither of us being able to stand up straight without bowing our heads, but we hear voices right outside the window as another group survey the garden.

'Hey, I bought you something.' He rubs his nose, scratches his temple, all of a sudden in a fluster and he is mumbling incoherently, and I find it so endearing I just sit at the table and watch with a great big smile on my face, doing nothing to help him out at all. 'It's for your garden,' he says, embarrassed, 'But if you think it's stupid, I'll take it back, no problem. It's not expensive, I saw it and thought of you, or thought you might like it, I mean, I don't really know anyone else who lives in their garden as much as you, apart from my mam of course who literally lives in her . . . anyway, I'll take it back if you don't like it.'

'Monday, that's a beautiful way to present something,' I say sarcastically, putting my hand on my heart.

'Get used to it,' he says gently, then reaches under the table and presents me with a gift for the garden. He covers his face with his hands so he can't see my reaction. 'Do you like it?' he asks in a muffled voice.

300

I kiss his hands. He lets them fall to his lap and his uncertain face breaks into a relieved smile.

'It's beautiful.'

'I wouldn't say it's *beautiful.*'

'It's perfect. Thank you.'

We kiss in the middle of a caravan in Connemara in the Phoenix Park with a battered garden signpost that says, *Miracles only grow where you plant them.*

26

Monday and I are lying in my bed. It is August. It is ten p.m. and my curtains are open. The sky is still bright. I can hear children from surrounding streets still out playing. My garden is still plump with life. There are still sounds of life and activity around us, the smell of barbecue in the air. I am in a wonderful bubble of bliss, lying naked with Monday, bathing in after-sex glory and contentment. I'm looking out at the sky, marvelling at the red sky.

'Red sky at night,' I start to say, and then your face suddenly appears in the window. 'Ahhhhhhhhh! Arrrrrrgggghhh!'

I almost give Monday a heart attack, jumping up and pulling the sheets around me, getting tangled in the process.

'Jesus bloody Christ,' Monday screams when he sees you.

You start laughing, a depraved lunatic sound, and I can see from your wired eyes that you're drunk.

'Nice trellising,' you shout, knocking on the window and I'm beginning to regret constructing the climbing frame on the wall of my house that leads to my bedroom window, from which parkdirektor riggers, a hardy perennial deciduous red rose, is growing up the front of the house.

Monday groans.

'I think he's drunk,' I say.

'You think?'

I look at him.

'Go,' he says tiredly. 'Go do whatever it is that you two do at ten p.m. on a Thursday night.'

I open the front door in my robe, and find you sitting at the table in your garden. You're wearing a tuxedo.

I whistle.

You swear at me.

Seeing your front door wide open, I drop your house keys into my pocket and I sit down.

'I see he finally gave you a job,' you say, and then snort and laugh that disgusting filthy chesty laugh again. You're back on the cigarettes tonight too.

'You forgot to cut your grass today,' I say.

'Keep your opinions to yourself, Delia Smith.'

'She's a chef.'

'Fuck off.'

You're angry tonight, Matt, back where we started. You finish the bottle of beer then throw it across the road. It breaks on my side of the path. Monday peers out the window, sees that I'm okay and disappears again.

'What happened tonight?'

'I went to the radio awards. I wasn't nominated. I was disgusted. I told them so. Said a few other things about a few other people who haven't been there for me like they should have been. Said it on stage into the microphone so everyone could hear what I had to say nice and loud. The organisers didn't like my behaviour. So they fucked me out of there.'

Two steps forward, one step back. It's the same with both of us. It's natural, I suppose. Nobody and nothing is perfect. I don't judge, not aloud anyway. You rant about work, about not working, about all the people in the world who work. It is difficult to keep up with, you start and stop, abandon ideas before they're fully developed. Your thought process is indicative of where you find yourself now. In a way, I agree with you. Some of what you say is how I felt at times during the past year, how I still sometimes feel as I struggle to find my place every day. Society is built around industry, you say, only children and retired people relax into not working and the percentage of retired people who die of heart attacks soon after retirement is a worry to you. You think you will die of boredom and make a note to visit Dr J about that.

You are struggling to find a job, in fact it's proving impossible. Your gardening leave is up, you are officially unemployed. Once hot property, you are now far from a desired commodity. You have been blacklisted. Nobody seems to want to hire a loose cannon like you with the potential for such notoriety, and those who do show interest want you for the wrong reasons, want you to amp up your dark side, turn you into a cartoon version of yourself. But this will not get Amy back, and that is a side of you even you are not comfortable with. You have had endless meetings with your agent, who doesn't return your calls as much as he once did, who is spending more time with a new TV personality rising star who has whiter teeth, and thicker hair, better skin and politically correct banter. Housewives love him, truck drivers can tolerate him. You threw a glass of water over him tonight and when no one was looking he took you outside, pretending he wanted to have a mature discussion, and instead boxed you across the chin, adjusted his Tom Ford tuxedo and went back inside with his plastic smile to present an award. Your words. You hope he'll die of a venereal disease. You attempt to list them all.

Then you move on to the DJ who won your award, the award you've won every year for six years straight, a man who talks about birds and gardening on air. I also know that you're trying to hurt me because of my new interests, but I don't bite. I know your tricks now. When you are hurting you try to hurt other people. It won't work with me.

Then you start on Corporate Man, who recently asked you and Amy to keep your voices down when the two of you were having a heavy-duty argument on the street one night and as a result has now become your main target of hate. You speculate that he loves to have meetings about meetings, loves the sound of his own voice and makes long-winded speeches about his love for butt-plugs and other such things that you make up on the spot.

I go into your house and come back with a roll of toilet paper.

'I have an idea,' I say, interrupting your Corporate Man rant.

'I'm not crying,' you say angrily, seeing the toilet roll. 'And I already took a shit. On your roses.'

'Come on, Matt.'

You follow me across the road. You finally smile when you see what I'm doing and you join in, eagerly. We spend ten minutes quietly draping toilet roll all over Corporate Man's garden, laughing so hard we almost pee ourselves, and have to stop for breaks, clamping our hands over each other's mouths so we don't make too much noise and wake him. We weave it around the branches of his chestnut tree and leave pieces hanging down like it's a weeping willow. We decorate the flower beds with it, we try to tie a great big bow around his BMW. We wrap it around the pillar on his front porch and then we break little bits up like confetti and sprinkle the grass. When we're finished, we high-five each other and turn around to find Monday and Dr J watching us. Monday is barefoot, wearing jeans and a T-shirt, looking hot and slightly amused but trying not to. Dr Jameson is wearing his emergency go-to outfit – shell suit and shiny shoes – and looking genuinely concerned for our welfare.

'He's drunk, but I don't know what your excuse is,' Monday says, arms folded across his chest. 'Seriously, you two really need to get jobs.'

'I hope to start on Monday, Monday,' you say, then chuckle at your wit. You look down at his bare feet. 'Ah, so you're into this too.'

'Into what?'

'Jasmine's little trick. I saw her do it once. In the middle of the night. Crying. In winter, like the crazy bitch she is.'

Monday laughs.

'I knew it!' I exclaim. 'I knew you were watching me. But I wasn't crying that night.'

'No, that was the night you made it look like your house had vomited grass on your garden.'

I can't help it, I have to laugh, but we are too loud and so Monday and Dr J guide us away from Corporate Man's house so he won't wake up and see how we've decorated his garden.

Ignoring Dr Jameson's advice to keep your shoes on, you walk ahead of us, kicking off your leather shoes and throwing your stinky socks in my direction. You decide to be rooted to the earth, grounding yourself, but doing an unusual hippy kind of dance which makes us all laugh whether we like it or not. It is quite amusing until you step on the piece of broken bottle that you fired across the road.

Dr Jameson goes running to help.

Autumn

*The season between summer and winter,
comprising in the Northern Hemisphere
usually the months of September,
October and November.*

A period of maturity.

27

Monday, you and I sit in a row on a couch, eating Stroopwafels, in Dr J's immaculately kept living room that smells like basil and lemons due to the row of basil plants lining the windowsill and the lemon tree in the corner catching the sun. The dog lies in the sun lazily looking at us with bored eyes. This is not the first time we have all been here, in fact it is the third Saturday in a row that we have been present in his interviews for companionship for Christmas Day.

We haven't been so cruel as to not invite him ourselves. You were the first to ask him, albeit because you are trying to earn brownie points from Amy who is still holding out on you, waiting for a sign that you are making an effort, that you are a changed man, that you have indeed got your act together. This note she wrote, incidentally, instead of disheartening you as I thought it would do, actually gave you hope. Apparently it is a note that she'd written a few times before in stages of your life together, one being when you tried to propose to her three times but chickened out. You see her note as an intervention, a kind of a circle of support for your marriage. You read between the sparse lines that there's a hidden clue meaning she will in fact come back to you, but it is August and there is still no great communication between you. You thought she would think of the Dr Jameson invitation as proof of how you have changed, instead she saw your kindness as thoughtlessness, the failure to put your family first as per usual, always thinking about your own needs, a sign that you didn't want to be with her for Christmas Day. She had a fine list of things to say, I heard her shouting it at you one night, another night when Corporate Man knew better than to complain. I'm sure Dr Jameson heard too, which made your offer all the easier, and awkward, to turn down. For his closest friend and neighbour on the street not to be able to invite him to dinner on Christmas Day must have been a further blow to him and I see that he looks older all of a sudden, more tired, though he is trying to appear as though he is enjoying it all.

'At least she's talking to him,' Monday had said as we'd both lain awake in bed listening to you argue outside at the garden table, thinking in our new early relationship smugness that we could never possibly speak to each other like that.

But it was bad timing when you'd broached the subject, your antics at the radio awards had hit the news again and you had scuppered any chance for a big job that you'd been hoping for on the few rival stations that would consider you. You are too much of a risk. Instead of what you'd been hoping for, you'd been offered a job on a lesser known local radio station, transmitting in Dublin only, but at least it's your own show, *The Matt Marshall Show* noon to three p.m. talking about issues of the day. You will have to be on your best behaviour. You started two weeks ago, and you have kindly arranged for Heather to work in your office one day every week, something we discussed when you attended Heather's circle of support. The new show means you have taken an enormous pay cut and don't have the same team around you that you once had, so you've gone back to basics and Amy is going back to work, but I think despite being pushed into it, the change will be good for both of you. I would know.

I have tuned right out of what the young woman before me is saying. To say she is a New Age hippy would be rude and dismissive, but she is currently living in a tree trying to stop developers demolishing it because it's the habitat of a rare breed of snail. I admire her strong beliefs: the snails need people like her to protect them from people like me, but in doing so she's preventing the developers from getting on with a badly needed new children's hospital. I wish people would fight as hard for the children as they would the snails. I don't think Dr Jameson is as empathetic about the snails as she hopes he'd be: they ate the lettuce on his garden plot. This is not why I can't concentrate, it is Monday next to me, so close I can feel the heat through his T-shirt which is soft and thin and almost see-through. I glance down and to the left and spy nipple. He catches me and gives me a look that I know well now, full of longing, and I think what a waste to waste it. He rubs the palm of my hand with his thumb, just once, then back again and that's enough. I want him. He looks at me, as if he wants me now, here. I almost would if I didn't think you'd commentate throughout the entire event.

It's September and it's muggy outside, heavy, as though we're about to have a thunderstorm; headache-inducing weather, the kind that drives animals – and you – crazy. I hope it rains because my garden needs watering. Across the road, Mr Malone sits alone in the garden chair, a cup of tea in his hands that's been there for the past hour. If he didn't occasionally blink I would think that he's dead, but he's like that most days since Mrs Malone died, a second stroke taking her life three weeks ago. I picture her weeding in the garden, on her hands and knees in her tweed skirt, then I picture her how she was after the stroke, sitting in the garden with Mr Malone reading to her, and now I see nothing, just him alone and it makes my eyes fill.

Monday looks at me again, concerned, and gives my hand a squeeze and my desire for him is increased even more. He hasn't officially moved in with me, but he may as well, he stays with me most nights, even has his own section of the wardrobe and his toothbrush and shaving tools sitting beside mine. On the nights he doesn't stay with me – when we tell each other we should slow down, see our friends, spend nights apart – it's torture, I look at these things and wish he was with me. He has a dog, Madra, a blond Labrador who acts like he owns the place, who has taken over my favourite armchair, which is fine with me now that I lie with Monday on the couch, and he even stays with me the nights Monday doesn't, which kind of defeats the purpose of the exercise. Sometimes you still need me at night, but nothing like before. Some nights I look out the window and hope to hear the sound of your jeep racing down the street with Guns N' Roses blaring, but nothing like before.

I asked Dr Jameson to join me for Christmas Day, though if he could take my place while I stay home he would be most welcome, as Christmas Day is to be spent with Monday's eccentric mother in Connemara and Stephen's Day in Dublin with my family. We had a meeting this week to discuss how Heather would like to cook the Christmas dinner as it will be the first time Jonathan will join us. We are both going to attend a cooking course together to learn how to make the perfect Christmas dinner. Neither Monday nor I are particularly looking forward to any part of Christmas. If I could have Heather all to myself, that of course would be a dream, but I can't. Dr Jameson has reminded us that family hassle is better than being alone. Seeing what he is going through just for a bit of company on a day so many people claim to want to be alone, I tend to agree.

'Okay,' you clap your hands once, loudly, while she is mid-sentence, unable to take any more of her chatter. Monday and I jump, we were so much in our own worlds. 'I think that's enough of that,' you say, and Monday laughs.

The lady looks at you, horrified and insulted, and I soften the blow by being polite as I show her to the door.

'Well, what do you think?' I ask, when I return.

Dr Jameson looks at me. 'I think . . . she smelled of moss.'

Monday laughs again. He does that a lot and doesn't think we notice, like we're a bunch of weirdos on TV and he's observing us and comes along for the ride. He forgets that we can actually see him.

'Well, there's one more to go,' I say, trying to perk everyone up. Dr Jameson seems more down today than ever.

'No. That's enough,' he says softly, to himself. 'That's enough.' He stands and makes his way to the phone in the kitchen. The house isn't open-plan like yours or mine, it is in its original seventies state, with the original tiles and what looks like the original wallpaper.

'Don't cancel,' I say, as he picks up the receiver and searches a little notepad for the number.

'What's her name?' he asks, searching through the names and numbers. 'Rita? No, Renagh. Or is it Elaine? I can't remember.' He flicks through the pages. 'There's been so many.'

'It's almost three, Dr J, she'll be here soon. She'll have already left, you can't cancel.'

'Car's here,' Monday says from the other room.

Dr Jameson sighs wearily and closes the notepad. I can tell he's given up and it breaks my heart. He takes his glasses off and lets them hang on the chain around his neck. We all go to the living-room window as we have done for all of his visitors and we watch. A small yellow Mini Cooper is parked outside. An elderly lady in a pale lilac cashmere hat and cardigan stares ahead. She's big and cuddly and looks like a teddy bear.

'Olive,' he says suddenly, the weariness gone from his voice and a lightness in its place. 'That's her name.'

I look at him, trying to hide my smile.

Olive looks at the house, then she starts up the engine.

'She's leaving,' Monday says.

'No she's not,' you say after a few seconds when she hasn't moved.

'She's just sitting there,' I say.

'Looks like she's getting cold feet. If we leave her for a moment, she'll probably get scared and drive away,' you say. 'That will sort it for you.'

Dr Jameson watches her for a moment, then without a word he leaves us. We watch him walk down his garden path and approach the car.

'He's going to tell her to fuck off,' you say. 'Watch.'

I sigh. Your humour is deliberately inappropriate and though I am used to you and your nuances, I still find you tiring.

Dr Jameson goes round to Olive's window and raps on it lightly. He gives her a sweet welcoming, encouraging smile, a soft look I've never seen him give anyone before. She looks at him, her hands wrapped around the steering wheel so tightly that her knuckles are white. I watch her grip loosen as she studies him, then the engine is killed.

'I think we should leave these two alone,' I say, and you and Monday look at me, confused. 'Come on.' As I drag the pair of you down the driveway, Dr Jameson offers no objection to us leaving. He waves us off cheerfully as he guides her into the house. It makes me smile to see that you're a little hurt by this.

Later that day I slide into a chair beside my dad in our local community hall to watch Heather receive her orange belt in Taekwondo. The orange belt signifies that the sun is beginning to rise and, as with the morning's dawn, only the beauty of the sunrise is seen rather than the immense power. This means the beginner student sees the beauty of the art of Taekwondo but has not yet experienced the power of the technique. I feel like I deserve a belt too.

Zara is sitting on Leilah's knee on the other side of Dad, so for once we don't have her acting as the bridge between us.

Heather sees me, lights up with excitement and waves. She never seems nervous about life's challenges, she sees them as an adventure, most of the time she creates them herself, which couldn't be more inspiring.

'Dad,' I say. 'About the job . . .'

'It's fine.'

'Well, I wanted to thank you.'

'I didn't do anything. It's gone. Someone else got it.'

'I heard. But thanks. For thinking that I'd be able to do it.'

He looks at me like I'm daft. 'Of course you'd be able

to do it. And you'd probably do a better job than the fella they hired. But you didn't bloody bother going to the interview. Sound familiar?'

I smile to myself. That's the biggest compliment he's ever given me.

Heather starts her display.

'Come to think of it, I found this—' he reaches into his back pocket and pulls out a photo, slightly creased at the corners from where it's been shoved into his pocket and moulded into shape by his arse. 'I was looking at some old photos of Zara and came across this. Thought you'd like it.'

It's a photograph of me and Granddad Adalbert Mary. I'm planting seeds, concentrating hard, neither of us looking at the camera, in his back garden. I must be four years old. On the back in my mum's handwriting it says, *Dad and Jasmine, planting sunflowers 4 June 1984.*

'Thank you,' I whisper, a lump in my throat, and Dad looks away, uncomfortable with my sudden emotion. Leilah tosses a tissue across to me, looking pleased, and I watch as Heather begins her display.

When I go home I frame the photo and add it to my kitchen wall of memories. A captured time when Mum was alive, when Granddad Adalbert Mary hadn't been planted in the ground and when I hadn't known I was going to die.

28

My garden in November is not necessarily dull. There isn't an abundance of flowers but I have a variety of herbaceous shrubs with colourful bark to make it more interesting. My winter jasmine, winter-flowering heather, evergreen shrubs and an elegant feathery grass that billows in the slightest breeze adds movement, bright-red berries bring colour and Mr Malone's honeysuckle is fragrant and colourful. The autumn gales have started to blow and there is high rainfall, so I spend most days raking up fallen leaves which I then use to make leaf mould. I clean my garden equipment and I store it all away for the winter, feeling my chest tighten as I do so, and I tie in my climbers to protect them from the winds. My November project is to plant bare-rooted roses and my research into how to go about this has amused Monday no end. It is a serious subject.

'They're only roses,' Monday said, but they're not only anything. And I told him exactly why this was so, and he listened, because he always listens, and when I was finished he kissed me and told me, for the first time, that is exactly why he is in love with me. And now roses remind me of his love for me.

But roses, like you and I, have their issues. Roses planted

in soil that has grown roses for a number of years are prone to a disease known as rose sickness. If you plant new roses in this situation you must take out as much of the old soil as possible and replace it with fresh soil from another part of the garden which hasn't grown roses before. This makes me think of Mr Malone, trying to grow in exactly the same place as his wife has died. It makes me think of anyone who is trying to grow where something, even a part of themselves, has died. We all experience that sickness. It is better to move, uproot ourselves and start afresh; then we will flourish.

I awake one November morning to the sound of dragging coming from outside – a familiar sound, like a screeching of nails on blackboard – and I leap out of bed. It brings me back, magically transports me to another time in my life. I move away from Monday's arm, which earlier in the night was protective but now feels heavy and dead across my chest, and I slip out of bed. I look out of the window and I see you, pulling the garden table across the drive.

My heart skips a beat, my stomach does an unusual flip, not of excitement but of sorrow and loss, unable and unprepared to move on, to accept change or say goodbye. Instant grief. I can't watch you do this. I throw on a tracksuit and hurry outside. I must help you do this. I grab one end of the table and you look up at me. You smile.

Corporate Man speeds by. We both take a hand off the table to wave. He doesn't register us. We laugh and continue. We don't speak, yet we work together well, manoeuvring the heavy table around the side of the house and into the back garden. It almost feels like a removal, as though we're carrying the coffin of a dear friend. We do it together and I feel a lump in my throat.

We place the table down in the back garden, on the patio area outside the kitchen and we replace the chairs that you have already carried around.

'Amy's coming back,' you say.

'That's terrific news,' I finally say, surprised I've managed to push sound past the lump in my throat.

'Yeah, it is,' you say, but you don't look so happy. 'I can't mess this up.'

'You won't.'

'Don't let me.'

'I won't,' I say, touched by the responsibility you have entrusted me with.

You nod and we make our way around to the front garden. Fionn is sitting inside the car messing with the stereo, changing stations to find a song he wants.

'You fixed it.'

'It wasn't broken,' you say, confused.

'But you said . . . Never mind.'

The penny drops as you realise your earlier lie has been caught out. 'The Guns N' Roses song.' You sigh. 'My dad used to hit my mum and me. The day we finally got rid of him, the day I finally faced up to him, me and Mum turned "Paradise City" as high as it could go and we danced around the kitchen together. I've never seen her so happy.'

Your freedom song. I knew it meant something, I wanted it to mean something on those cold dark nights when you came catapulting down the road like you'd been away the longest time and couldn't wait to get home to your family, but then always felt locked out even when you weren't. 'Thanks for telling me.'

'Well, it beats "Love is a Battlefield",' you say. My mouth falls open. 'What? You don't think I can't hear you blaring that thing every day. When your windows are open I can hear you, you know, and sometimes even see you with your hairbrush.' You imitate me, doing a woeful eighties dance.

'I do not sing into a hairbrush,' I protest.

You're smiling at me nervously and I realise this is just your attempt to move on from what you revealed to me, in the only way you know how.

'It's a deodorant bottle, I'll have you know, and I'm an excellent lip-syncher.'

'I'm sure you are,' you laugh.

I look across at my house and I see Monday watching us from my bedroom window. He moves away when we catch him.

'That's going well,' you say.

I nod. 'Today's the day,' I say, and on his confused expression I explain: 'My year's up.'

You look taken aback, surprised. 'Well. Fancy that.'

'I thought maybe you knew, with the table.'

'No. Just felt right.' We both stare at the place the table used to be. The grass is flattened where the table legs used to stand. The soil shows through. You will have to re-seed.

'Have you found anything yet?' you ask.

'No.'

'You will.'

'Yeah.'

'You've lost your confidence, but you'll get it back,' you say, reassuringly. And I know they're not empty words because, of all people, you know.

'Thanks.'

'Well. It's been an interesting year.' You hold out your hand. I stare at it, take it, shake it once, then step closer for a hug.

We embrace, on the grass in the front garden, where the table used to be.

'You never did tell me what I did wrong,' you say gently, into my neck. 'To make you so unhappy. But I think I know.'

I freeze, uncertain how to reply. It has been a long time since I've thought of you being that man, that man that I hated for so long. Neither of us move from the embrace, I think it's easier for both of us not to have to look at each other. You speak into my neck, I can feel your hot breath on my skin.

'It was your sister, wasn't it?'

My heart pounds and I'm sure you can feel it. It gives me away.

'I'm sorry.'

The apology shocks me at first, and then nothing. And I realise that's not really what I needed. You spent the year showing me you are sorry, that you never meant it in the first place. It doesn't matter any more. You're forgiven. I pull away from the embrace, kiss you on the forehead, then cross the road back to my house.

Madra is digging furiously in the garden, he and I clash on issues such as this. Monday is dressed and is standing at the open door. He waves at you, you wave back.

'Madra!' I shout. 'No! Honey, how could you let him . . .? Oh, my flowers!'

He's digging at the foot of the sign you bought for me, the one which says, *Miracles only grow where you plant them* and I fall to my knees to fix the mess, but as I do, my eye falls upon a box in the soil. A metal box, like a rusted treasure box.

'What the . . .? Monday, look!'

I look up at Monday, expecting surprise, but he knows already. He's smiling at me. He lowers himself to his knees and I think he's going to help me tidy my flowers but instead he says, 'Open it.'

And I do. And oh, do I do.

This year has been the metamorphosis of me. Not on the outside. On the outside I look the same, a little older perhaps. On the inside I have changed. I feel it. And it is like magic. My garden is the mirror of me. My garden that once looked barren and sterile is now full and blooming and ripe. It thrives and it prospers. Perhaps you could say the same of me. I lost something that I thought defined me and I felt like a shell of a person. Instead of trying to get it back, I had to figure out why I couldn't be whole all by myself.

The world is fascinated by instant transformations, human makeovers or a magician's sleight of hand hidden with a flourish. Quick as a snap, from there to here, blink and we've missed it. My shift wasn't instant, and often the slow pace of change can be painful, lonely and confusing, but without us realising it happening, it happens. We look back and think 'Who was that person?' when during it all we think, 'Who am I becoming?' And at what exact point was it that we crossed over that line, when one version of us became the next? But it is thanks to the slowness that we remember the journey, we reserve the sense of where we were, where we are going and why. Destination completely unknown, we can value the crossing.

This wasn't just my journey, this wasn't just about me falling down and a man rescuing me, though I did trip and you fell and love did happen for me and was mended and repaired for you. This is about you and me, our fall and rise with the seasons, and about what happened when one door closed for both of us. I don't know if I would be this woman now if it weren't for you, and you may not even think you did anything. Most people in life don't have to actively do *anything* to change us, they simply need to *be*. I reacted to you. You affected me. You helped me. You were the oddest friendship, the kindest loaned ear. You told me once during one of those long, dark, cold winter nights at the garden table, though you were embarrassed to say it and probably too drunk to remember it now, that you were locked out in the cold and I let you in time and time again. I had a simple reply at the time, but didn't realise the true meaning of my words – you gave me your key.

I think you did the same for me.

I helped you help me, you helped me to help you, that's the way it must be or the very idea of help would be obsolete. I always thought that being helped was a loss of control, but you must allow someone to help you, you must *want* someone to help you, and only then can the act begin.

The transformation from chrysalis can take weeks, months or even years – mine took one year. And although I have become this person, I'm still in the midst of a larger transformation, one that I won't recognise until I look back at me now and say 'Who was *that* girl?' We are constantly evolving; I suppose I have always known that, but because I always knew that, I feared stopping, and it is ironic that it was only when I finally stopped that I moved the most. I know now that we never truly stop, our journey is never complete, because we will continue to flourish – just as when the caterpillar thought the world was over, it became a butterfly.

Acknowledgements

Enormous thanks to the following whose support I value and honour:

Marianne Gunn O'Connor, Vicki Satlow and Pat Lynch. The clever HarperCollins team especially Lynne Drew, Louise Swannell, Liz Dawson, Martha Ashby and Kate Elton. Thank you to the very short Charlie Redmayne, without you I would be *nothing*. Good enough? I wish a fond farewell to Moira Reilly who has been with me since the beginning of this crazy journey, but it's not goodbye forever – see you at the bar… Booksellers all around the world and the readers, I cannot thank you enough for the life you have given me, allowing me to immerse myself in my passion every single day of my life. My gorgeous family who I adore, my friends who answer 'The Beacon' at the shortest notice, and most important of all, David, Robin and Sonny, you mad, crazy, beautiful things – I love you all.

Right, now I'm off to write the next one. X